FUTURISTICA

Volume 2

Metasagas Press

Published by Metasagas Press
411 Walnut St. #6797
Green Cove Springs, FL 32043

Cover art and design by Kanaxa Design

Interior layout and design by Chester W. Hoster

Edited by Chester W. Hoster and Katy Stauber

First published in 2017. Printed in the United States.

ISBN: 1-939120-08-X
ISBN-13: 978-1-939120-08-3

FUTURISTICA
Volume 2

Colleen Anderson — Ray Blank — Aaron Canton

Zach Chapman — Olha Chyhyrynska

George Cotronis — Ingrid Garcia — Abby Goldsmith

G. Scott Huggins — Amy Power Jansen

Fadzlishah Johanabas — George Allen Miller

Julie Novakova — Kate O'Connor — Sandra M. Odell

Mike Reeves-McMillan — Alexandra Renwick

Anthea Sharp — EJ Shumak — Katie Stevens

Metasagas Press

This book is dedicated to Duncan, Noah, Peter, Rory, Teyasia, and Zara.

Table of Contents

Iron Goddess of Compassion — Olha Chyhyrynska   1

Queenpin of the Wastes — Zach Chapman   24

Étude for an Extraordinary Mind — Julie Novakova   45

Lost in Translation — Sandra M. Odell   65

Somewhat Damaged — George Cotronis   79

A Song for the Barren — G. Scott Huggins   96

Across an Aeon — Abby Goldsmith   121

The Irrepressibly Original Daisy Wigmar — Katie Stevens   138

A Splendid Wedding — Anthea Sharp   167

Ours to Guard and Protect — Amy Power Jansen   182

Then Our Skins, Then Our Bones — Alexandra Renwick   197

Yamaduta's Deathsong — Fadzlishah Johanabas   215

Love in the Vapors — Colleen Anderson   237

The Thirty-Eight — George Allen Miller   250

Girl, from the Inside — Katy O'Connor   265

Have Space Bike, Will Travel — Ingrid Garcia   287

Someone to Listen, Inc. — Ray Blank   306

Time of the Hunter — EJ Shumak   333

Taking Pro — Mike Reeves-McMillan   353

News from the Extreme Chess Olympiad — Aaron Canton   364

Iron Goddess of Compassion
by Olha Chyhyrynska
translated by Anatoly Belilovsky

In my dream, rockets screech and fall, their warheads explode, part of my sleeping brain screams, *Grad! Down on the ground!* while another whispers, *Serves you right for sleeping on the job.* The next concussion is close, really close, even the floor shakes beneath me, and Zhang is yelling, swearing a blue streak, but it's all in Russian so my dream logic tells me not to worry, and then at the end of a string of well-chosen epithets Zhang says, "Who dropped wet scrap in furnace, she full of xuě." It's the Chinese word for "snow" that alerts me that things have gotten out of control and I dive, trying to fall flat on my face, and finally come wide awake. I'm lucky I don't react as fast to dream emergencies as I did in real life—instead of sprawling on the floor of the control room amid total confusion I manage to catch myself before my forehead hits the control panel.

The explosion was real. Fire licks the ceiling of the doghouse, sparks dash themselves against the safety glass a meter from my face, and in three seconds the flames abate and the white-hot drops of molten iron fade and extinguish, and all is well again. Scrap mixed with snow and ice got dumped into the furnace, blew up on contact with molten steel. This happens all the time. All in a day's work, except that it's the middle of the night.

"Why xuě? What for xuě in scrap?" Zhang yells at Pasha, the shift foreman.

"Snow," I say, but Pasha understands.

"Because Siberia," Pasha says. "Because it's winter. Xuě is everywhere. These old tank turrets are full of it."

It's standard procedure to preheat and dry the scrap before dumping it in the furnace. It should have been done. It should have been done the dozen other times this has happened. No harm done, this time. Unlike the time the electrode tore off its mount and fell into the melt—now *that* was a show to remember.

"Sì jiǎo dì yù," Zhang says and sits down in his chair.

Hell of four corners.

"Want me to translate that?" I ask.

He shrugs. "Ad v kvadrate," he mutters.

Hell Squared.

I like his translation better.

Working night shift with Zhang is a crashing bore, for the most part. He hardly ever lets me do any translating. Zhang's wife is Russian, and he thinks he speaks the language. Which he does, sort of; he certainly has no trouble understanding it. Most of the time, when the furnace roar sounds like the purr of a titanic pussycat and Zhang yells at the workers in idiosyncratic but comprehensible Russian, I fall asleep the moment I sit down.

I do not dream at all when the furnace is quiet.

"Sasha, tea?"

Zhang says it in Chinese so I wake up immediately. My sleep brain has developed a knack for waking me when Zhang needs help. When he runs out of Russian he peppers his speech with Mandarin, or worse, switches to English and handwaving, thinking it makes him easier to understand.

"With pleasure," I reply.

He reaches into his jacket pocket and pulls out a pack of Marlboros. He makes a face.

"You got my jacket," he says. "Again."

Zhang and I could be twins, except for our faces: same height, same weight, same shoulder width. Same lack of five o'clock shadow, on the rare occasion we get to five o'clock without getting a layer of dirt on every exposed surface. We even finish each other's sentences. My voice is lower: too many pack-years of unfiltered smoke.

"I thought you quit," Zhang says, reading my thoughts again.

"You've had it the whole shift," I say. "Did you see me go looking?"

I pat my pockets, reach in and pull out a vacuum pack of green tea in shiny foil. He takes it from my hand and turns to the teapot.

Zhang avoids the free teabags we get at work. As a matter of principle, he only drinks Tieguanyin tea, and only from a teapot. I'm not too crazy about Tieguanyin, preferring like most Russians the highly fermented black teas. When Zhang heard about that, he told me I know nothing of tea because the best white and green tea never reaches us, only the rejects, hardly better than garbage. What they sell in Russian stores under the name Tieguanyin is like a bald man attempting to pass for a Buddhist monk. Having tried the tea he brought from home, I have to admit he's right.

"Why you always sleep?"

I stretch, kneading my numb wrists. "You don't need me to translate. What else do I have to do?"

"I do need you. I always tell you to correct me if I say wrong."

"You know what Ni said when I asked him to take Russian electricians into the crane's main distribution board and show them what's wrong? He said that he's not paid to train them!"

"But that's Ni!" Zhang says in a mildly insulted tone. "Working with him is like plucking an iron rooster. This is me. Do you want me to pay you?"

"For translation, yes. You think Bering Tunnel is going to wait for its vault rings while we concentrate on your language lessons?"

"Of course not. Just correct me—"

"Zhang, you make so many little mistakes, if I start correcting each of them we'll never get anything done."

"What kind of little mistakes?"

"Well, first of all, pronunciation. Your consonants are hopeless. I don't blame you, Mandarin doesn't have many closed syllables, or any multiple consonants in a row, or for that matter soft and hard consonants. And because you tend to tack on a vowel at the end of a word, and because Russian feminine words usually end in -a, you automatically say *she* for everything. Like, you just called the metal *she*. But it is *he* in Russian."

"But you call steel *she*, and it ends in -l."

"Soft -l, palatalized, is usually feminine. Steel, furnace, casting machine are *she*. Metal, scrap, carbon are *he*. Lance, iron, blade are *it*. The pronunciation difference is like how you say *wan*, ten thousand, compared to *wang*, king."

"What about names? Why Pasha if he is a man?" Zhang asks.

"You just have to memorize it. Pasha for Pavel, always male. Masha for Maria, always female."

"And Sasha can be—"

"Exactly."

"Ah," Zhang says. "What a difficult language. So much to memorize."

"It's true. In Chinese, gender never rears its ugly head, not in nouns, not in verbs, not in prepositions. But the tones, and the ideographs! Do you know what we call something incomprehensible? Chinese Scroll!"

As we drink our tea, white-hot electrodes rise like infernal lights. A fiery maw gapes, and an assistant steelmaker, driving a device made from a converted Hyundai frontloader, starts to clean the threshold. Slag pours across the threshold in a solid stream. Zhang watches it, head tilted.

A steelmaker approaches the furnace, his sample probe like a lance in his hands.

"Why not automatic?" Zhang says in Chinese, too startled to think in Russian.

"Why are you checking the temps by hand again?" I ask.

"Day shift burned the autosensor again," Pasha says. "Forgot to replace the headpiece."

Zhang understands without my help; his brow wrinkles. "Sun Wukong rules under the heaven, though his limbs be hairy," he mutters under his breath. "Don't translate that."

"Why not? It's very much worth translating," I say. Turning to Pasha, I continue in Russian: "Comrade Zhang expresses his dissatisfaction with the lack of competence on the part of Russian personnel."

"All these boys they hired," Pasha says and shrugs. "What can they do? Monkeys have better hands."

"You are sure he doesn't speak Chinese?" Zhang asks anxiously.

I stifle a chuckle. Pasha caught the denotation of Zhang's proverb about the Monkey King after I only translated the connotation. "Calm down, of course he doesn't. And don't worry so much about insulting him, he's too smart to take offense easily."

Comrade Zhang sighs with relief. He had been warned how difficult Russians are to work with—how different their traditions are and how important it is to treat those traditions with respect. Chinese and Japanese workers balk at these customs; they struggle to respect Russian indifference and irresponsibility, both so at odds with the Far Eastern way of life. That is, they can feign indifference and behave irresponsibly, but respect such things—never. But the instructions say, Russians are quick to take offense, and God forbid you should call them ham-handed monkeys if they, for example, burn out the automatic temperature probe.

"Temperature fifteen hundred and seventy degrees. More heat?" the steelmaker says.

"Just little," Zhang says and shows with his fingers. "Sample done, we pour."

The lab hasn't sent us a sample test result yet but Zhang and Pasha have an understanding: as soon as they have a result, the ladle will pass to the vacuum degasifier.

"Tea?" I ask.

Pasha thanks Zhang, "Xièxie!" He places a plastic cup under the spout of the teapot. Zhang squints at me: Am I sure Pasha does not speak Chinese?

The fiery maw closes, and the electrodes descend.

"I'll go to jīngliànlú and liánzhùjī, see how they are doing there," I say, noting to myself that, while speaking Russian, I called the Ladle Refining Furnace and the Continuous Casting Machine by more or less Chinese names. Tower of Babel, well and truly.

Zip my jacket to the neck, cinch my balaclava over my face, cover it all with a helmet. The temperature in the plant was twenty-eight degrees below zero earlier today, probably more like forty below now. It's called "hot shop," but it's only hot close to the melt; walk three meters away and you freeze your arse off. If you work near the preheating ladles, your face burns while your butt gets frostbite.

Steelworkers pass, sweat shining on their unlined faces where they aren't covered with soot and coal dust. Children, nearly. Can't skimp on equipment, but people are a different matter. All the hardware is the ultimate—well, penultimate—in modern technology, and management decided it's easier to train youngsters straight out of vocational school than retrain old farts. On the other hand, you still need experienced people, so each shift has at least one senior steelmaker, over thirty with at least a decade on the job. Such as Pasha.

It's clear as daylight I'd be useless at the ladle or at the CCM, and if they needed me they could call me in over the phone. But everyone understands I need to stretch my legs. It's eight minutes to six, and it's the next-to-last tap of the shift. I get back right as the melt is being released, and Zhang and I marvel, for the sixth time this night, as the bottom of the furnace drops away like a gigantic arse sitting down, and a tight stream of liquid metal pours into a red-hot fireproof bowl.

"What number ladle?" Zhang asks.

"Fourteen."

"Footing must replace yesterday, why no replace?" he yells at Nikita, the apprentice steelmaker.

"Why is he screaming?" Nikita asks, uncomprehending.

"He is screaming because we can lose the ladle!"

"It's not his ladle," the young steelmaker says and shrugs. His expression makes my hands itch with the desire to grab his shovel and whack him over the head with it. Zhang clearly feels the same, but only walks away to the railing, pulls off his balaclava, and lights a cigarette before reaching for the lance. This isn't where the autoprobe got burned; it was never used here in the first place.

The stream of fire drops to a trickle, the damper closes, cutting off the still-hot icicles of steel, Zhang puts down the lance and pulls off the headpiece. I still can't believe a headpiece made of compressed cardboard survives immersion in molten metal. I understand the physics of the process, but I'm awestruck every time.

"Not enough slag," Zhang says, frowning, and throws the useless carton into the melt and the cigarette butt after it. I don't ask why that's bad as I did a month ago. I can trace the logic of the statement. Worn footing and not enough slag mean that the melt will cool faster than intended. This means in turn that it might overcool in the vacuum extractor degasifier and need to be reheated, and every extra minute the furnace is engaged means greater chance for the ladle to burn through.

"If we lose this ladle, too, what then?" Zhang says.

"Roll it into the parking lot, fill it with topsoil, and grow tea like Master Wei," I answer.

Zhang smiles. He never smiles just to be polite, only when a joke comes off. Can't work without jokes, not in our business, where equipment and people work till they wear out.

Zhang and I climb the bridge over the pit, waiting for the ladle to pass Position One. Directly above us is the prominent Pironelli logo. I often think of utterly irrelevant things: that "sparks" are called "fire flowers" in Chinese; and that, when Mao Xie or Mo Ye threw herself into the furnace, she actually added carbon to the mix, and a sack of coal would have solved Gan the blacksmith's metallurgic problem just as well. Right now I am thinking of the future that science fiction promised us, of the world united in friendship and in scientific curiosity. Now I see the practical embodiment of this ideal, steel for the Greater Silk Road smelted in a plant built by an Italian company in Siberian Republic, with workers from all over the world but under the management of the Chinese branch of Pironelli, closest geographically to Kurgan. So here we are with mainly Chinese and Vietnamese staff, some Japanese, Korean, Chilean, Filipino, and occasionally the west wind blows in a few Austrians, Croats and Brits.

We recycle what's left of the Soviet military.

We melt old tanks, BMPs and BRDMs and portable pontoon bridges and rails and rolling stock and old rebar from crumbling bunkers. We cast tunnel vault rings and rails and more rebar for concrete foundations for a railroad to run high speed electric trains feeding off low cost solar panels. On the map, dotted lines show planned extensions: the Sunda causeway via Singapore to Australia, the Bering tunnel via Alaska to Vancouver.

We Soviet children—yes, I am that old—were taught our country will always be in the vanguard of progress, assisted by fraternal Socialist allies. Being part of something great is a potent drug; my generation went through a nasty withdrawal when the Union ended along with our childhood. I don't recommend any of the substitute drugs we got into, not even the one I'm on right now, capitalism. Not even with the K2Pult, the Himalayan Orbital Mass Driver, on the drawing board somewhere in Beijing, its projected budget a significant but not impossible fraction of China's GDP.

And just like the stories hoped, there is a multinational crew building that enormous structure, but the old Soviet writers never imagined that the force that brought the workers together would be money and that the dreams that went through their heads would revolve about going home to bed at the end of a long shift, not to space or to other planets.

At the end of the day it's not matters sublime but base materialism and mutual profit that both bind and separate us. Even at the management level, no one is thinking about the global trade and transport network right now. Pironelli's priority for the moment is to be done, as soon as possible, with what they call "hot testing" or "test-launch," and the interest of Kurgan International Tube is to manufacture the most product on Pironelli's time and on Pironelli's equipment, before "hot testing" is finished and Kurgan assumes responsibility. The international Pironelli staff is completely freaked out by this approach. Under the guise of testing, the plant is running in full-capacity production mode and the entire personnel of KIT from director to the last steelmaker's apprentice does their job according to the time-honored Russian tradition: not my property, not my problem. What can I say? Weren't you all warned about Russia being a riddle wrapped in a mystery inside something incomprehensible? Well, there you are.

And suddenly as if by evil eye—mine, perhaps—there is an automatic signal that the ladle car is stuck before Position One. Trying to reroute it from the control panel via bypass gets us nowhere, and Zhang, swearing, goes over to look for an obstruction.

One of the reasons my services as an interpreter are so highly valued—considering my knowledge of Chinese and Japanese is medi-ocre at best—is that I never refuse. If I have to climb a crane on the heel of a foreign specialist, up I go. If I have to enter the collector, I'm there. Last time a tuyere slipped, I shoved it back into place—took less time and effort than screaming at the workers would have. Now I crawl under the ladle car with Zhang. As usual, at least a half dozen people are loitering by the pit—electricians, mechanics, part of the ladle furnace brigade—and not one of them even attempts to figure out the problem, while even my nonprofessional eye can see the long furrow on the rail.

"Shield stuck against the rail," Pasha says and knocks against the steel plate that protects the wheels of the steel carrier against splatter-ing melt. Zhang lifts his head and swears in Chinese. Pasha screams at the gathered multitudes, "What is this, a circus? You, ox-fucking mechanics, what are you doing standing around clacking your beaks? Can't you see the shield is stuck? Bring the torch, now!"

The multitudes fade away. The senior mechanic arrives, swearing up and down at his charges—that's the signal to start work. Half of them know what needs to be done, anyway—the mechanics at least.

"We're never getting out of this shithole," Pasha says and sighs, looking up where reflections of fire dance on the ceiling. "Never."

I know what he means, but this is none of my business. I am an interpreter, not a crisis manager. And it's not like Zhang and Pasha even need an interpreter; curses have become the universal language that science fiction writers dreamed of for so long. Yes, Sir Arthur C., some dreams come true, though not quite the way we imagined.

A winch lowers the acetylene torch. One of the mechanics crawls under the ladle car, but Pasha curses him roundly and cuts off an edge of the shield himself. I understand why he does it: he is ashamed on behalf of the dozen or more young, fit, and far from stupid men who watched the steel carrier rattle in place for fifteen minutes without doing anything constructive about it. Pathological lack of initiative. Everyone complains how difficult it is to work with Russians. Everyone knows that Russian traditions must be respected, but no one knows how to get any work done while doing so.

Having cut off part of the shield, Pasha returns the torch, we climb out of the pit, and Zhang gives the signal to start the ladle car. The car rolls smoothly to Position One, the crane operator reaches for the lever to pick up the ladle, and the ladle picks that very moment to burn through.

During the war I discovered that under fire I lose all fear, entirely. It's odd; I vacillate and waste time in online hack-and-slashes, but in a real battle I act rationally, and quickly. Quicker than anybody else, except for that last time death stared me in the face, when a Russian boy moved quicker. The boy who died all the way while I only died partially.

This time Zhang and I act faster. We pull Pasha beneath the protective cover literally from under the stream of fire. A thought flashes in my head, with luck, the score is even.

Twenty-six long and unpleasant seconds follow.

The awning isn't there to protect people. It covers the electric cables that power the ladle car. Vietnamese workers built it, completely to spec, of reinforced concrete covered by fireproof brick, and it held under the river of molten steel, but it was not deep enough for the humans underneath it to be entirely safe and comfortable. We push our backs into the concrete wall behind us while melted steel drips down in front of our noses, turning solid the second it hits the floor but still red-hot at a good seven hundred degrees. The wall behind us grows hot as well, two hundred or so degrees, and everything flammable around us catches fire, even the dust suspended in the air. We do not inhale fire—we are not even all that badly burned—but for a time we disappear from the world at large behind a wall of flame.

And then the world bursts in behind a hissing stream of fire extinguisher foam.

We jump out from under the steel-encrusted cover and spend the next minute getting our breath back while the ladle brigade puts out the fire on the car. The melt no longer gushes from the hole, it trickles and cools in sags like candle wax.

We are very, very lucky that the ladle burned through near the top and only a small part of its load poured out.

The ladle car looks like it survived a nuclear attack. I don't remember taking off my helmet, but suddenly it's in my hand, dented where my fingers clutched it.

Of course we all wear fire-resistant jackets, but hot as the wall was, it feels like I had my jacket ironed while still wearing it on my back.

They drag the three of us to the infirmary, cut our clothes off, and slather our backs in panthenol before we even realize how much we hurt. We each get a shot of anesthetic, and we lay on the infirmary beds facedown under sheets, waiting for ambulances.

Some time later the moment comes when awkwardness is possible.

"I don't know how I didn't piss myself," Zhang says, rolling a bit under his sheet to scratch his itching back.

"What's wrong with that?" Pasha says after I translate.

"I need to go now but they took all my clothes," Zhang says.

"There's an empty Coke bottle in the trash bin," I say. Zhang raises his eyebrows. "I'll keep my eyes closed," I add.

"Ah," says Zhang and pulls the sheet over himself before getting up. I close my eyes, as promised.

Pasha can think of nothing better to do as Zhang's urine trickles into the bottle than to start apologizing.

"Why?" I interrupt him.

He grows silent, sweat rolls down his brow, and he averts his eyes. And quite belatedly it dawns on me why he had never bothered me with stupid questions.

He thought I was maimed. Accidentally castrated or one born not quite complete. But a guy. Everyone in Russian crew thought so. Tall, broad, crop-haired, with voice low and rusty, with flat breast and big hands, I passed for a guy easily enough. If anyone had doubt in my masculinity, I "proved" it with a slipping tuyere. Who expects a woman to hold 60 kilos of metal for five seconds or so?

I never wanted to deceive them. Just got used to my gender neutrality. Just wanted to keep my sexless comfort along with my identity. Just preferred to forget that in Russia one cannot be sexless, it's a matter of policy, even now, when they do not imprison gays anymore.

Back *then*, the boy who had been quicker was called Sasha. That's a convenient name. Especially if sex isn't marked on the passport. Which it is not, if the passport is of the European standard.

"Did that happen... in the Ukraine?" he asks. And, tired, I cut him off, forever, "In Ukraine, Pasha. In Ukraine. It's a country, not a desert."

I hear Zhang chuckle behind me, and turn to find him standing there, smiling. He is not just smiling at his relief of the full bladder; he is smiling at the perfect punchline. Grammar is never apolitical; who knows this better than Zhang?

∞

Everything is complicated, Zhang. Everything is more complicated than you think.

We're very much alike, Russians and us. We're probably more alike than people from Guangzhou are to Northerners. Almost the same people. Some think we *are* the same people. Russians think so, mostly. But when they came… You may not believe this, but in three months they earned the hatred of all, including those who had greeted them with flowers.

What you see now is eight years later, after the war and after the defeat. I will say something that might insult a son of the Celestial Realm such as yourself, but all imperial ideologies are egocentric. All. Look at Americans. Each individually is a remarkable person, each wants only good for others, but how much trouble begins when they are asked to see things from someone else's viewpoint? Take an American; take from him his wealth, his power, and the magnanimity that comes of never knowing weakness or want. What is left? Exactly. That's what came to us. Russians didn't want to bring us evil… I mean the tank drivers themselves, not the cadaver in the Kremlin. They really, sincerely, thought we had been ruled by neo-Nazis, that we'd been forbidden to speak Russian, that we'd be happy to forget twenty-five years of independence and rush back into their embrace. It began with arrests of all those in any way involved with our government, except, of course, for those who'd run away. Who hadn't run away? Small fry, of course. Odious personages, most of them, corrupt and mendacious, but hardly guilty of the charges against them, oppressing the Russian minority. In the old days we wouldn't have bothered defending them, but the very lawlessness inflamed us. We protested. Things went downhill from there, monuments leveled, memorial plaques removed, holiday parades banned. We pushed back, threw empty bottles at patrols, wrote "Moskali go home" on walls… "Moskali" is pejorative for Muscovites. I wonder how to write that in ideographs—"Mosike" is Mandarin for Moscow; Li—is that with "li" for strength or "li" for profit? Or "li" for plum? Never had to write "Moskali Go Home" in Chinese.

Anyway, it started small, then someone blew up an urn, killed a sentry. Scapegoats were needed. Scapegoats were found, six students caught leafleting. Six boys and girls, shot summarily. Tortured to confession and executed.

You are from Nanjing, originally, you must understand. There comes a time when things can no longer be tolerated. Somehow, at that moment, many people started looking to me. Where did we find weapons? Not everyone turned them in when ordered. Buried in gardens or orchards. Some bought guns from the occupants themselves who were not averse to a little trafficking on the side when the upper ranks weren't looking. And the rest we captured.

How do you manage guerrilla warfare in the urbanized, deforested Eastern Ukraine? You'll laugh. Our biggest trump was our shared Soviet past. Same weapons, same vehicles, similar uniforms, standard ammo. We freed some POWs, wore clothes taken from defeated enemies. IFF codes were not just easy to get, but very easy. Once we camped in a small town, across the square from a Russian unit. They didn't know who we were until we destroyed their armored vehicles. Attacked warehouses, blew up rail lines and trains carrying reinforcements, preferably those with supplies and ammo rather than personnel. I don't like killing people, it's true, not as a matter of kindness but because building new tanks and guns and armored cars is more expensive than herding in new soldiers. You may find it laughable, coming as you do from China, but by European standards Russia was a very populous country. Then, too, there was the PR factor. We didn't have a snowball's chance of success, Zhang. We knew we could not defeat Russia. The most we could accomplish was to sabotage their plan for "peaceful reunification of historically Russian lands." To show the world that there was a war on. Last six months, a year at the most.

It was awful to watch the deaths of boys who joined us in those early days, when success came on the heels of success. They started dying... desperately. As if they sought the bullets that killed them.

We each took a nom de guerre, to save our families from retaliations. Just to the north of us was a squad led by a man who styled himself Porthos, after the strongest Musketeer. An ex-Soviet military man, that's all I knew about him. To the south, Owl, a funny-looking fellow with huge glasses. They died in autumn, and in the winter came our turn.

We held a council, and decided to lay down our arms. Surrender. The mission was accomplished, the world seethed with disapproval of the Russian actions, UN and NATO rattled sabers at Russia, and it looked like they'd be forced to withdraw from the left bank of the Dnipro. We chose captivity over death.

All but one of us. He wanted to fight on to the last. He was my friend. None of us could make the tough decision, I least of all. No one expected him to bring us a surprise on the day of our surrender, a suicide vest he'd built the night before.

A piddling little vest. It's time-consuming work, to make necklace after necklace of hex nuts and washers and wind them around the plastique core. He ran out of time. And plastique. And washers and nuts.

He had only brought enough for me and Sasha, the Russian boy who, at the same time as I, saw the trigger in my friend's hand. Sasha was quicker. He was the first to knock my friend down and jump on top of him. I ended up on top of both of them. My friend kept hold of the trigger.

Don't think I did this out of bravery. It's just that, as the squad commander, I had the bleakest future to look forward to if I lived. A death sentence, or a very long prison term. And no place to come back to. My children were in Europe with my ex-husband, emigrated long before the war; my parents did not survive the occupation. Simply put, I leapt on top of him, in certainty that the lethal outcome was the best thing that could happen to me.

Sasha was the real hero. Half my age, strong, handsome. He had a reason to live, and a chance to survive. His bones extruded from my body for months. My friend's bones, too. And the nails he had stuck in the bomb.

These aren't torture scars, as you had thought. These are the scars of my survival. Not a bit of skin left intact, neck to knee. Field surgery is save what you can, amputate the rest. Radical mastectomy, the hard way. The doctor said, if I had been a man, I would have died. Women are tougher.

There was a Russian writer named Shklovsky who managed to blow himself up with homemade explosives, also near the Dnipro. He wrote that when the bomb fragments extrude, they squeak and scrape against the underclothes. It's true.

Now that I think about it, my kamikaze friend probably saved my life. Had I surrendered whole, I would have ended up in Solonoye, the special camp for "disarmed terrorists." I'd have died of quiet strangulation there. But lying near death at the hospital gave them hope that I'd die unassisted. And you know what happened next: the famous "Ten-hour War."

Fifteen years ago, before the war, books about a nuclear war with the U.S. were very popular in Russia. Russia lost all these wars, but lost them heroically. A submarine would strike at America with MIRVs, and a nuclear holocaust would ensue. In reality, apparently there had been an idiot like that, but he was shot by his own crew. No one wanted to incinerate their families with American assistance. No one.

His Majesty the Tsar of All Russias, including ours, shot himself in the Kremlin, and the Provisional Governing Committee sued for peace. Russia fell apart... Siberian Republic, National Republic of Cossacks, Ingria, and what remained of Russian Federation, the central part. For that, they blamed us, of course. And Americans, but then it's convenient to blame Americans for everything. After that they released all the surviving members of the resistance from prisons and camps. I never saw the inside of either, spent the entire time in a hospital. They just transferred me to a different hospital, one of ours. Then Ukraine, being the victim of aggression, joined all the unions and pacts, speculating all the while on our reputations as heroes of the war. Our president sat out the war in Poland, came back scattering medals everywhere, called me in to get mine. I refused. Some of our boys became upwardly mobile as a result. I don't disapprove of them, we all lost much in the war, some wanted back a little bit of lost happiness. I didn't. In truth, I didn't really want to live. Got up in the mornings, forced myself to go somewhere and do something… It wasn't because of the injuries, I was never a beauty, and once you pass forty you stop worrying about your appearance. I lost friends, I lost my family, I lost the man I began to love… missing my tits seemed stupid after all that. If I had lost my hands, I might have decided not to live. Or maybe not. Modern prosthetics are fantastic.

Later the resistance fighters were declared military veterans, eligible for pensions and medical insurance including reconstructive surgery. And I thought, I lived as a woman for forty years, how about trying to live as an androgyne? And never went for reconstruction. In truth, I had grown sick of surgeries, and that might have played a role. I had had more than enough of cutting and stitching. And there's the story of a frontiersman who lost a horse and found a herd. If there hadn't been advantages to my situation I would not have remained in it.

Yes, I acquired my tattoos in China. Shanghai.

I changed my name. I changed it to Sasha, short for Alexander or Alexandra, take your pick. Passport office personnel were so busy, they didn't argue. Sasha didn't even faze them. Someone else in our neighborhood called himself Darth Vader.

So I went to work for Pironelli, and asked for the Eastern Division. That's all. This is my story.

There was nothing to keep me from going to any part of former Russia. I do not hate Russians, and though the war has thinned their ranks, I still have Russian friends. They didn't die, of course, they're all my age, well past the cutoff for conscription. None fought. Those who questioned the propaganda reels about how we crucified Russian boys on gates and fences are still my friends, and those who believed the lies... why mourn the lost affection of idiots? Some, though they didn't believe the propaganda, still turned away from me. How could you shoot at a Russian soldier?

We have a joke in Ukraine: "I'll go shoot some *Moskali*." — "What happens if *they* shoot *you*?" — "Shoot *me*? Whatever have I done to deserve it?"

You want the real reason? I hope that here there is something to save. These boys... could I succeed in pounding into their heads that slapdash, slipshod work is a bug and not a Russian national feature? That humans must be treated like humans and ladle footings must be replaced on time? That neither people nor ladles should be used until they break?

Why are you laughing, Zhang? You think I can't? But you like Pasha. Where Pasha is, is hope.

Why don't I ask you out loud what you think, instead of arguing with this Zhang I built in effigy in my mind?

Because I know what you'll say. You'll say that empires are built by people who do their jobs today while thinking about tomorrow, and fall under the weight of people who want to have their empire and eat it, too. That you like Pasha, too, but as the shift foreman he is responsible for the incident, and will likely be fired. Never mind the choice he had, or rather didn't, to go on as he did, or stop the process. He'd have been fired then, too.

We need to talk, Zhang. We need to find a way to save his face. Pasha's face. The face he'll likely turn away from me when he finds out I'm not only a neuter, but also the ex-commander of the Guliaipole guerrillas to boot.

Will I regret it?

Yes.

∞

"You could have killed me," Pasha says to me in the manager's office.

How odd. None of the Russians at the other end of a rifle from me has ever said, *I could have killed you.* I'm used to that.

"Pasha, strife is antagonistic to virtue. We didn't kill each other. That's cause enough to celebrate."

"But you haven't stopped fighting, have you? You brought your war here, to the plant?"

My eyebrows leap, startled.

"Pasha, what are you on about?"

"You know."

I do know. Pasha is the senior worker on the shift, the burn-through was his responsibility. It was his duty to see to the replacement of the footings. True, there was no other ladle. True, if he refused to work with a defective ladle it would have meant a stoppage of production, and he would have been assessed a staggering fine. Or they would have fired him, a father of two children. Hobson's choice: stop production and be fined; go on, cause a disaster, and then be fined and fired.

We made a deal. I take part of the blame myself. Pretend I hadn't translated Zhang's warning of worn footings, that I left Pasha in ignorance. Of course everyone on the shop floor knows Zhang and Pasha understand each other just fine without me, but the head office doesn't so they won't question the report. I lose my job; Pasha gets fined but keeps his. I get fired from the Kurgan division and quietly transferred to the Sichuan plant.

The deal was between me, Zhang, and Signor Caruzzo, head of the Kurgan office of Pironelli. Pasha wasn't in on it.

What I had not expected is that Pasha would believe it, too.

"You should have said something about the footings. You should have told me."

I rub my hand over my face to hide my look of astonishment. Of course, the Russian national trait is the ability to believe. They did believe that we were the Nazis and at the same time Russians, brothers and sisters oppressed by Nazis. They opened fire on us believing they were defending us. Why shouldn't he believe I should have done his job?

"You are right," I say. "You are never getting out of this shithole. Never."

His fist strikes me in the solar plexus; I slide down the wall to the floor.

"I don't hit women, usually," he says. "But you are not a woman. I don't know what the fuck you are."

We are alone in the corridor, and I do not call for help. In truth, the whole thing is overwhelmingly funny, and I laugh even as I'm writhing in pain.

Pasha leaves. I don't find it regrettable, Zhang.

Not a bit.

I find it very, very funny.

About the Author
Olha Chyhyrynska

I was born in Dnipropetrovsk, Ukraine, which is was a part of the Soviet Union then. Our generation was taught that we are going to live to see the Bright Future of Communism. It could have been the reason behind my interest in SF: I was supposed to live in it. And I could never have enough of this reading (Iron Curtain and so on), so I started to write SF myself. I grew up and studied Japanese in our university and never stopped writing. Now I am an SF and fantasy writer and a screenwriter.

About the Translator
Anatoly Belilovsky

Anatoly Belilovsky is a Russian-American author and translator of speculative fiction. He was born in a city that went through six or seven owners in the last century, all of whom used it to do a lot more than drive to church on Sundays; he is old enough to remember tanks rolling through it on their way to Czechoslovakia in 1968. After being traded to the U.S. for a shipload of grain and a defector to be named later (see the Jackson-Vanik amendment), he learned English from Star Trek reruns and went on to become a pediatrician in an area of New York where English is only the fourth most commonly used language. His work appeared or will appear in *F&SF*, *Year's Best SF #32*, *Grimdark*, *UFO I*, *Ideomancer*, *Nature*, *Stupefying Stories*, *Daily SF*, *Podcastle*, *StarShipSofa*, *Genius Loci*, *Cast of Wonders*, and *Toasted Cake*, among others.

Translator Website: http://loldoc.net/

Queenpin of the Wastes
by Zach Chapman

A frill-necked lizard skittered across crescent dunes, never pausing long on the baked sand. Lee crushed the reptile under the heel of her boot. All that damn sand kept the impact from making the satisfying *crunch* sound she'd wanted. Lee relished the minute noises. The purring wind. The light footfalls. The cracking bone. Sighing, she bent down, scraped up the lizard's carcass and tossed it to her red and white speckled hound. The lithe beast swallowed it in a single dry chomp. "Good, maybe now you'll stop limping around."

"Sorry?" Merk asked, startling her from behind. He was one of seven men who had been hovering at her heels for the past two hours, asking questions, cracking jokes, being jackasses.

"Talking to the dog. They'll be here soon?"

"Sure, sure. Very soon. Here, practically. You ready?"

"Do I need to be?" Lee asked. "You said they ain't got nothin' too dangerous on 'em that could hit us from afar."

"Oh, sure sure. I did. Lark messaged me, been patrolling the west. Like I said, nothing to fear. Small party, just five… You know. Hey, need anything?"

"Merk, just hand me the Sig and for the love of god stop crowding me."

"Oh sure sure. The five-five-six or five-one-five?"

"I don't give a shit," Lee replied. "Whatever punches out a bigger hole."

He handed her a gun. It made an audible *smack* as the grip slapped against her glove. The familiar feel of polymer on leather gave her a natural grin. "Theo got the rovers ready for the ambush?"

"Yes, do you want to ride shotty or drive?" Merk asked.

"Shotgun is fine."

"Huh? You want a shotty?" Simmons asked, unrolling the window as the car pulled up.

"Shut up." She hopped in the grey, battle-scarred vehicle. Her hound automatically boarded the back, and Merk followed. He squeezed in between the shedding beast and Tucker, an incompetent man in blue face paint who often complained of never being allowed to use the clan's high-powered rifles. Out of her clan, Tucker was easily the worst with snipes.

The others piled in another scanty car and together they rode across the windswept dunes, stirring up motes of tan clouds that rose impossibly high and blurred the waning sun. This would be the second encounter of the day, and the first had gone so well—yielding food, ammo, equipment, even a bit of gas. Scavenging was a mighty fine way to pass the time between the grander escapades. She forced her smile away; it wouldn't do for the others to see her grinning like a maniac. As they came upon the five, Lee twirled her finger and pointed ahead. "Message Theo. Tell him to go around, past 'em. Don't want them scrambling away once we attack."

From the rearview, she saw him nod. She checked her ammo, tapped the mag, snapped her goggles on. "You boys ready?"

Shedding their nebbishness, they all whooped in agreement.

Lee hid her compact Sig rifle in between her knees, rolled down the window and leaned out; her hair snapped in the dry wind. "Ay! You there! Need any help, friends?"

The travelers seemed to slump as Simmons pulled the car up near them. Two wearing yellow bandanas hesitated, waved wearily, and started for the car. A third attempted to run, yelling, "Trap!"

"Hey. They popped," Lee said, bringing the rifle up out of the window and sighting in on the running man. She pulled the trigger and a lead slug hamstrung the fleeing man, sending him rolling back down the dune. Tucker, Simmons and Merk were already out of the car, yelling, firing warning shots, corralling their prey. Ahead, Theo and his boys kicked up sand, steadying their guns on the five from a cautionary distance. You never could be too careful in the Dead Wastes.

∞

"We don't want to hurt ya. We just want to talk. Cool, right?" Lee said to her five bound prisoners. The one with the gunshot leg struggled against his restraints. Brown hair and eyes, no tattoos, hardly a sunburn, he looked like a real low-level guy.

The two yellow bandanas nodded eagerly. The others said nothing. Lee continued, "We're looking for recruits. People with guts. And good personalities."

"Go to hell. You're wasting our time," said the wounded one. Theo smashed the butt of his rifle across the guy's face.

"Okay, scratch him off the list," Lee said, moving closer to the others as if to examine them.

"I-I recognize you." The wounded one reached out with his bound hands, pointing, grinning. "She's a cripple. You can tell by the way she walks. You boys really taking orders from a cripple *girl*? You're pathetic."

"You're a cripple," Theo said and smacked the man's other leg with his rifle.

The yellow bandanas looked at each other. One of them said, "Really, we aren't with him. Only hooked up two days ago. Don't really know him." The second jerked a thumb at the others and shrugged.

"That's good," Lee said, not taking her eyes off the one she'd shot. "Merk, can you deal with these two?"

Merk dragged them by their restrained hands away from the group, took out a large gleaming knife, and sliced off their bonds. Simmons and Tucker jogged over to watch then sat cross-legged on the sand. Merk tossed his big knife at the foot of one, pulled out another, much smaller, blade and kicked it over to the other. "Only got room enough for one banana bandana wearer in Lee's gang. Let's see what ya got."

"Seriously?" One gaped as he picked up his knife. "You practically gave that guy the Buster Sword. How is that fair? What am I supposed to—"

"Tough cookies, señor," Simmons said.

∞

It was over quickly. The bandana with the bigger knife won. The other's limp body disappeared, leaving the knife, and a few minor pieces of equipment including his yellow bandana. Simmons slapped the new recruit on the back, "Not bad. What's your name? Banana? I like Banana. We'll go with that. See how long you last."

A gunshot blasted through the desert. Then another. Merk looked over his shoulder toward Lee. Two of the prisoners fell to the sand. Their bodies disappeared a second later.

"Guess you're the only one to make the cut, Banana. Lee's pretty picky. Just don't be a dick, you'll be fine," Tucker said and slid down the dune to off their final prisoner.

Ignoring his bleeding leg, the prisoner chanted insults with his eyes closed, calling Lee a cripple and worse. "You'll get what's coming to ya. I've seen you before," he said, then continued raving as loud as he could.

"I bet we've perma-deathed him before. Can we just do it again?" Theo asked.

"No." Lee said. "He's already such a low level, it's what he wants. He'll just start a new character tonight and go on trolling. Fresh slate. No. Screw this asshole. Let's b—" Lee paused for fifteen seconds, her eyes completely blank. Her hound looked up at her confused. Their prisoner went on shouting. Then the vacancy disappeared. "Sorry. Damn it, Dad's almost home. Bury this ass hat. I want him to have to wait until this avatar dies naturally, or he contacts Dead Waste's support. Or pays for another character slot."

"You're wicked," Simmons said.

"Oh go on worshiping her," the prisoner said. "Go on with this cripple. Look at the way she walks, she's probably some dude in a wheelchair in his parent's basement. Fat. Pimply."

"No, she's sent a pic. She has purple hair IRL," Simmons said.

"Don't argue with him. Just bury his ass. And Christ, stop saying abbreviations. Simmons, I might see you on later tonight, probably tomorrow though," she said as she started the forty-second log off process that kept cheaters from disconnecting in PvP areas.

"TTYL."

"Shut up."

∞

Her eyes still closed, Lee focused on wiggling her toes. Nothing. Feet? No. Legs? Nothing. Nope. Still crippled in the real world. Just minutes ago, she could walk and run and kick and jump in Dead Wastes, albeit with odd ticks she'd formed from never having walked in the real world. Now she was restricted to the chair. She flipped her hearing aids on. Although she could not hear Dad shut the door over the painfully loud screech of feedback, she could smell the instant he came home. Grass, gasoline and cigarettes. Sighing, Lee fiddled with her aids until she got the settings right, just in time to dully hear her father's jovial voice. "Hey girlie, I'm home. And I bought some vanilla almond ice cream. You eat dinner yet?"

"Just a sec," she called from her dim room as she scraped the VR nodes off her temples and tossed them on top of a white tower rig decorated in vinyl Dead Wastes stickers. She wheeled out of her room and joined her father for dinner.

Lee studied his hands as they ate. Cracked, callused yellow, scabbed brown, dirt under the fingernails—her hands would never be like that. Well, that wasn't entirely true. She *did* have calluses from gripping her wheels. And the inevitable chipped fingernail polish that revealed all the cheap colors underneath. Her Dead Wastes character had perpetually dirty hands *just* like her father's. And flawless fingernail polish. A perfect VR anachronism.

Her Dead Wastes character didn't quite have Lee's shade of purple hair and the sidecut ran a bit too high. It didn't have her broad shoulders either.

Despite his grimy hands, her father squeezed his rare burger, dribbling ketchup across his sweat-stained shirt and took large bites between mentioning how he found a new potential bonsai tree from an old stump in a client's yard. The client had wanted it dug out, so he kept it. He'd pick up a pot for it tomorrow after work and stick it with the other sad attempts at bonsai trees on their tiny apartment porch.

After the buzz of his second beer, Lee's father spoke of buying her cochlear implants that she knew they couldn't afford. She preferred a helper dog, anyways. A big, red, speckled thing with pointed ears and sharp teeth, like her hound from Dead Wastes. Yes. Something she could take to school. But they couldn't afford that either. After his third beer, after the television was on, he complained of hippies, Luddites and politicians. Of their protests and lobbying and bullshitting against the research that could lead to her standing up out of her wheelchair.

He was lovable but predictable. Lee wheeled to her room and logged back on, but all of her friends were offline.

∞

Lee felt the vibrations of Rod flicking the back of her chair but said nothing. Since class started, he'd been at it with his damn stylus while Coach Davis taught health from a tablet that might have been as old as her. She considered reaching back, snagging the pen out of Rod's hands, and breaking it. But that would piss Davis off and the coach and her father had been jock buddies growing up. Lee liked him despite the pathetic glances he gave her on occasion.

At five till, Davis turned and dismissed her from class with a nod. She was halfway to history when the first bell sounded and the rest of the school piled out of their classrooms. The hallways became a murmur of flesh and bony elbows and curses and laughs and shoves. She thought her hearing aids had been adjusted properly, but at that moment the feedback grew as loud as the angry hall. She reached up to make an adjustment and her hand was slapped. Hard. Stunned, she let her arm slump. Another slap came harder this time, knocking her head sideways and sending her right hearing aid off.

"Asshole!" she said as she turned. She was slapped, softer this time, with something sticky and hard. It clung to her ear, its rough edges scratching her painfully. Had someone wadded up paper and stuffed it in her ear? She quickly gained her bearings but the assailant had disappeared amongst the sea of passing torsos, as lost as her hearing aid.

"Bastard."

Her ear felt hot. It was tape—a nasty ball of the stuff. It tugged at her ear and hair as she pulled until it was free. In anger, she tried to fling it, but the stupid tape clung to her fingers. She snatched it with her other hand and—what was this? Something small and black. A miniature hard drive lay wrapped in the curls of clear tape.

∞

Lee twirled the tiny drive between her index and thumb, completely immune to her chemistry teacher's murmuring lecture—only in part due to her missing aid. A strand of her purple hair stuck to the drive, caught in the tacky residue that the peeled off tape had left behind. Twice she had fought off the temptation of sticking it in her personal tablet to see what mysteries it might hold. Could be viruses, malware, Trojans, phishing programs. Or maybe just jokes, memes about wheelchairs and hearing aids. After much consternation throughout chemistry class, the bell rang, signaling the end of the school day. She took it to the library, found a computer in a lone corner, held her breath, and plugged it in.

No blue screen of death. No instant malignant windows full of obscenities. Only the familiar chime of the school's computer reading a new device. Lee exhaled then opened the drive. It was empty but for a single file with a .txt extension.

She read the file: "TO THE QUEEN OF THE WASTE. KILL YOUR CHARACTER. OR LOSE MORE THAN A HEARING AID."

∞

Kiss the Scorpion, Locked Dodgers, Washers, Venom Hits, Nuka-Cola and a hundred other less exciting bottle-cap betting mini-games buzzed all around Lee's clan as they sat at a round table in Shutger's Hotel and Bar—an enormous PvP safe zone. Hound lay curled up at Lee's feet. She was staring at her palms, noticing the lack of detail. If this were all real, would her palms be as scarred and grass stained as her father's? She tried not to think of the black drive, sticky from the tape.

"Then Banana-boy stabbed him in the eye. Like four times. Like he hadn't just been playing with the guy for hours. Hardly lost a drop of HP. 'Nana's quick for a low-level kid," Simmons told a member of the clan who hadn't been logged on last night.

Banana nodded. Merk smacked the back of his head. "Shuddap. I gave you the bigger blade. You were supposed to win."

"I'd have won anyway," Banana said. "This is my third character."

"The mouth on him," Tucker said, his back turned to the table, tossing a washer at a board.

Lee faced Merk, nudged him and whispered, sending him a private message only he could hear, "Merk, you don't think I walk like a freak?"

The fuss of Shutger's became a low volume hum, similar to what she heard in the real world if she shut off her aids. Merk glanced at her, accepting their single channel conversation. His voice was clear over all others. "Freak? No. Princess? Sure. You strut about with royalty, my liege."

"Can you tell that I'm… you know, in a wheelchair? You're the only one I've officially told. The others suspect, I'm sure."

"They don't care. I don't care. No big deal. It's cool."

"What would you guys be up to if I stopped logging on? What direction would you take the clan?"

"Dunno," Merk said. "Continue humbling folks. Continue raids. Quests. Maybe grab a new member if any of us gets killed. That sorta thing. Why? You going on a trip? I went to Venice once. With my stepmom and dad. Sucked. They took away my VirtualPack. Made me look at bloody bricks and painted things for hours. I think I stood for eight hours straight. Sucked."

"I wouldn't know."

"About trips or…" He looked like he regretted the words as they came out.

"Either."

∞

At dinner, Lee told her father she lost her hearing aid. She could hear him. Mostly. But not when he turned the television on and tried to talk over it. He wasn't angry and hid his disappointment well. She didn't mention how she'd lost it, the tape, or the drive. She'd tossed the drive after reading the plain text file and was sure that would be the last of it. Just a stupid joke. And she'd been pranked many times. This time was just like the others. If it wasn't, well she had a miniature bottle of pepper spray in the armrest pocket of her chair.

After they ate, she logged back on Dead Wastes. With her crew, Lee cleared two raids, an instance, and finished the night with a round of sweeping low-level scrubs off the outer plains near Shutger's. Easy. It got her mind off the drive.

∞

The next morning during second period, Lee discovered her backpack, which hung behind her chair most of the time, had been slashed open. She'd lost her makeup bag, likely taken by the vandal. Stuffed in its place were a dozen plastic bags, twisted, balled up and wrapped one inside of the other. At the center of the Russian-doll mess lay another drive. She tasted acid in her mouth and she thought of her pepper spray defensively.

This time she couldn't wait for the library. She jammed the thing into her personal, school-issued tablet. Her tablet took a moment to read the drive. Finally, when the icon became visible, she swiped at it. But her command wasn't registered. Her tablet froze.

And there was that acid in her mouth again.

The screen went blue, catching the attention of several students sitting near her. She couldn't hear them shifting in their seats, but she felt their eyes on her. Then the tablet read: "Delete your character. Or. Bang bang."

Sound erupted from the miniature speakers on the tablet. Weapons being fired. It was so loud the little speakers cracked and hissed with distortion. In the quiet room, it was as if a bomb went off. Everyone stared as she frantically swiped the screen, trying to shut off the noise. She pounded at it. Nothing. Mrs. Anders was watching, hand on her hip, a half drawn diagram forgotten.

"Lee." Mrs. Anders looked down over her horn rimmed glasses. "Do I need to take that from you? Shut it off."

"I didn't… I'm not doing it. It just started making noise. I can't control it. The stupid thing won't turn off." She could feel heat in the tips of her ears, knew her face was crimson with embarrassment.

"Lee, what's gotten into you?"

"I'm sorry I can't—"

∞

Lee sat between the IT and vice principal's office, waiting. A troublemaker in a ratty grey hoody also awaited his fate, staring with red-rimmed eyes at her and what she held tightly in her arms. The tablet had not shut off. Or stopped rattling off gunshots. After the most embarrassing five minutes of her life, Mrs. Anders finally understood the noise was truly out of Lee's control. Together, while half of the class snickered, Lee and Mrs. Anders wrapped the tablet in Mrs. Anders' coat to quiet the damn thing and she was sent to the IT office to have a new one issued to her. The shot speakers vibrated in her hands and she wondered if they were making enough noise for other students to hear.

A student leaving the IT office held the door open for her. Lee mumbled her appreciation as she passed him. She didn't mention the drive or yesterday's harassment. What could IT do, suggest a crazy stalker app? Download an anti-bully program? The tablet was snatched away from her and frowned at by three men whose knowledge on technology likely did not surpass her own. They handed her a battered up replacement.

When Lee left IT, they were still scratching their heads. As she rolled out, she heard the vice principal scolding the hooded creep. Through the open door, their eyes locked. Miss Freedman, the vice principal, walked past the slouched figure in her office.

"James, keep sitting. I'm not done with you. Falling asleep in class.

Up all night playing that violent game!" Miss Freedman lowered her voice as she met Lee in the waiting room. "Lee, still having trouble getting to your classes on time? What's with the purple hair? You aren't in middle school anymore."

Lee rolled her eyes. "I'm not tardy any more than normal. Usually leave five minutes before the bell. My hair... it's to give them something to look at."

"That's good you're getting to class on time. I was worried about that. Your hair, yes. I'm sure it's a little distracting to the students."

"Not as much as my chair. I'll see ya later."

"Lee, wait! A hall monitor found a hearing aid in the hallway. I think it was stepped on. It looks like you're missing one? Is everything okay?"

∞

Miss Freedman had been right. Lee's aid had been stepped on. It worked, but hissed occasionally with feedback. Her dad mentioned the noise later that night, sighed and said they'd still need to get her a new one.

The next day in first period, another drive appeared in the center of her handicap accessible desk. She threw it away. At every class a drive awaited her, perfectly centered on her desk. She asked, but not one teacher had seen or remembered who had left the drives behind. She threw them all away.

Then it was the weekend and she was not troubled by the physical presence of psychotic stalkers or drives—that she knew of anyway. But *delete your character* permeated the back of her mind—a burnt-in image on a dying tablet. *Bang bang.*

She spent her time on Dead Wastes leading her clan in slaughtering scrubs and power-leveling Banana while her father smoked cigarettes and wired juniper branches, trying to mold them into perfect bonsai trees. More out of kindness than curiosity, she asked him how they were coming along. He said that in two months his best might sell for enough to cover the cost of new aids. Lee lied, telling him the feedback from her hearing aid didn't bother her.

∞

Sunday night he approached her, a level three scrub hot off the starter desert wearing a sun-bleached rancher hat and a sagging ruck-sack. She was just outside Shutger's safe zone. Minutes ago, the others had logged off to work on homework.

Lee was about to do the same when he whispered, "Howdy, girl."

It was a private message. Hound was growling, his speckled coat rising along his spine. His AI had learned her well.

"Piss off. Unless you wanna die. I'm about to log off."

"The Queenpin's still alive. That isn't a good thing for Miss Lee."

"You're—"

"Who? The one behind the drives?"

"The creep." She tried to look hard.

"Yes and no. Not really. It's not just me. There's dozens of us. One for every drive, at least."

"Liar," she said. He was trying to make her paranoid.

"Delete your character. You wouldn't want a wheelchair accident. Roll too close to the stairs at school and—"

She put three bullets in his head before another word came out. He was slow, his defense non-existent compared to her maxed gear. His body vanished before it hit the ground; Lee didn't bother looting the bag. Just as the digital sun set over Shutger's, Lee logged off. She'd have to tell the others tomorrow.

∞

In Davis's class, Rod picked at Lee's backpack. She attempted taking notes on her tablet, but Davis was boring and Rod was distracting. She felt him switch from drumming on her water bottle to tugging at her zippers. She was about to turn and say something when he fully unzipped the backpack's front pocket. A cascade of black plastic fell to the floor. He looked at her stunned, apologetically. Davis did not look up from his lesson.

"What is all this?" Rod said, loud enough for her to hear.

She rolled back and felt plastic crunch under her. Hundreds of black drives littered the floor, all different sizes and makes. Rod was out of his seat, trying to clandestinely clean up the mess. He scooped up two handful of drives and dumped them on her lap while mouthing apologies. Numb, she accepted them.

Class went on without her.

Lee regained her bearings as the bell rang. She waited for all of the students to leave before dumping the drives from her backpack into the trash. Davis looked at her quizzically, scratching his stubble and saying nothing. She bit back words—confessions of her stalker and not wanting to delete her character.

How had the creep snuck that many of drives in? When could he have done it? Before class? Maybe she'd have heard him but for her broken aid. But she should have felt him. Lee decided tonight, as her father made them BLTs or ordered Chinese delivery, she'd tell him.

∞

But Lee's father did not come home at five. Or six. Maybe he was digging up another juniper to add to his collection, though she found that unlikely since the sun was setting fast. Waiting irritated her, so she signed on.

Lark, Simmons and Banana joined up with her at Shutger's. Banana's health was critical; apparently, he almost got wasted in a PvE area. His gear was torn to hell and he was completely out of ammo. She laughed. "This the first VMO you ever play?"

"No!"

"Banana, we ought to frag your ass right here. You're worthless," Simmons said, tugging on his yellow bandana.

"I'm just a low level."

"Yeah, that's not all. Hey, Lee." Simmons turned to her. "You wanna go on a mini raid in Lark's car while we wait for Merk to get on."

"I s'pose." Laughing felt good yet underneath there was uneasiness. She wished she'd turned the lights on in her room before logging on. Once she logged off, the whole house would be dark. Once she got off, she'd have to tell her dad about the stalker. He might freak on her.

They loaded up, Lark drove. Out of all of them, he had the best driving stats. And it showed. Rough tundra became blacktop. Lee's aiming was smoother, her shots more deadly while Lark was behind the wheel. An even ride, ten full clips and a good crew. Despite herself, she smiled.

In half an hour they had gunned down an army of thug AIs and looted their corpses. The drops were crap so everything was given to Banana.

"Boys, I think my dad's home. I'll try to get back on… but later. After ten or so. Only if he falls asleep."

"Ah shit, really?" Simmons said. "I guess we're stuck babysitting the scrub."

"Don't leave me here with him. I'll kill him."

Lark looked too serious.

"C'mon guys. I'm not all that bad."

"Shut up." She started the process of logging off. She'd heard something. Her dad closing the door, maybe. It was hard to tell with her busted aid.

Then she was off. Too soon. The logout process hadn't cleared. She cursed. The power to her tower was cut off. Power failure? Maybe.

Unlikely. The thing had a billion failsafes she'd designed herself. She cursed again. Her character would be vulnerable for two minutes—the penalty for disconnecting before properly logging out. And her father, he was… she could smell no gasoline, no cigarettes, no freshly cut grass.

Lee became aware that half the cords to her tower were severed. Acid filled her mouth. Panic. She tried to focus on the shadows. But everything was too dark, too twisted. She slapped off the VR nodes as quietly as she could. The apartment was as silent as a crypt.

The creep was here. And she couldn't see. And she couldn't hear. And if she moved or breathed, would she make too much noise? Without thinking, she reset her aids. A blare of pain burst from her right ear. The damn hearing aid crackled with feedback. Panic held her for a moment. Then she yanked it out and threw it through her open door into the short hallway.

Faintly, with her left ear—the one with the good aid in it—she could hear the crackling of her aid in the hall. A thud. Then silence. A voice too muffled to understand. Shadows moved outside the door, writhing black silhouettes alive with danger. Now another voice, a *second* voice. How many voices? Hushed. Angered.

Shadows curled from in the hall and entered her room. She wheeled back. A shaking hand slid from the darkness and jammed on her brake. "Where you going? Don't you need help, friend?"

There were three of them. As her eyes adjusted, she recognized the one holding the frame of her chair. She'd seen him wearing a hoody outside the vice principal's office. James. Rod was standing behind him. The other boy looked familiar, maybe she'd passed him in the halls.

"See if she's died from the two minute penalty," James said as he rocked her chair, the brake still locked, ruining her rubber tread.

"Get off me!" Lee yelled.

"James, take it easy, man. It's not like she can hurt you." She recognized the voice but couldn't place it. The teenager had acne on his round face. She was sure she'd seen him somewhere at school. He pulled out a tablet and tapped on it for a minute, its light filling the room. "Dead Wastes tracker app shows she's logged out successfully. Just, easy man."

"Once her character is dead she will have to start over like the rest of us. I'll track her down every time and make sure she never survives past level five."

"Get out of my house. Now," Lee said.

James leaned heavily on her armrests, smiled, then cuffed her across the cheek. Rod laughed.

The familiar pimply one looked worried. "C'mon man. No need to get rough. We'll just make her delete the character and get the hell out of here."

"You know what I'm thinking?" James said. "I'm thinking that's not the only reason I came. Got some unsettled business, her and I. She's killed me three times. Death of her character ain't enough, I think."

"Not my fault you suck at the game," Lee said, trying to look hard. He hit her again for that. She could scream. Maybe a neighbor would hear. There was the pepper spray in her chair's armrest. She just needed a distraction. But James moved forward and gently grabbed her throat.

"James, what are you doing?" She finally fully recognized the voice. Merk. It was him. He'd played with her in game for months, must have known who she was, seen her in school. The bastard had never said hello and now he was a part of this. "We just need her to delete her character. After that I'll be head of the clan. You can make new characters and I can power-level you safely."

"Shut up. It was never about that for me. Her clan, your clan, that's your business. Mine's about getting even."

"Merk." She choked for dramatic affect. "How could you?"

"Shit, girl, it's no hard feelings. I told them to just SWAT you. My dad said he used to do it all the time."

James looked at him. "Shut up about swatting. I tried it. Jack-shit happened. Top chick gamers are in some flagged, protected database. Don't think you've got the stomach for what comes next. I'm going to make her roll over that tower until it's smashed to bits. That should keep her off Dead Wastes until next Christmas. Until her daddy buys her a new tower. Before then his poor ass will be mowing out a loan for her next hearing aid."

She glared at them. If she could only get him on her side...

Merk looked away. "Whatever. James, just make sure her character's gone, right?"

"She'll be offline until Dead Wastes 2 comes out."

Merk slipped out of the room. James snorted. "Weak. Rod, lug that tower over here."

"Cool," Rod said. "The closet-gamer jock commands his pot dealer with a bad back to do the heavy lifting."

Lee cleared her throat before James could speak. "Simmons. Lark. Even Banana, they know. Leave now and I'll tell them not to say a word about this *misunderstanding*. They'll follow my orders."

Rod stumbled away from the tower in a panic. James steadied him.

"Relax, Rod," James said. "Lee, do you expect me to believe you were texting them this whole time? I've been looking right at you, idiot, making sure you're not trying anything smart."

She fought hard not to shake as she shrugged her shoulders. "Yeah? What about my backup webcam? Did you check that too?"

She pointed at the dust-covered webcam perched above her monitor. She'd never used it. Merk would have known. Not these idiots. They turned and it was just enough time for her to draw the bottle of pepper spray.

"Idiots. That thing doesn't work," Lee said. "But this does."

As they turned back, she sprayed a line of the venomous liquid across their faces. *Double Kill.* They both dropped, shrieking loud enough to make her aid flair with feedback. The spray was so strong that just being in the room began to burn her lungs.

Down the hall the door slammed. "Lee, what's going on? Are you okay?"

Dad's home, Lee thought. *Perfect timing for him to take out the garbage.*

∞

Two nights later she was back on, her cut power cords had been reimbursed immediately. Lee was talking with her clan outside of Shutger's. Lark and Theo had pulled up their cars, and Simmons and Tucker were loading up guns, frags and plenty of ammo.

"You realize," Simmons said. "You're going to have to tell that story another one hundred times before you satisfy the gang? Nice trick with the webcam. Please tell me you said something like: Say cheese!"

"I'll remember it for next time I kick their asses. IRL."

"You are a badass, *in real life.* Damn. So those two idiots you and your dad slammed are in juvie? Shit," Simmons said, dumping a handful of magazines into the back seat. "*And* he brought home the paper work to get you a damn service dog. Cooler than cool. Your dad's a badass. Must be where you get it from. It'd be scary but cool to meet him some time. *IRL.*"

"He gets it from me. All he did was take out the garbage after I finished them off... So, you'd want to do that? Hang out outside of Dead Wastes?"

"We already spend a lot of time together online, so why not?"

Lee was silent for a while then nodded. "So you really think we'll find Merk?"

"His dumb ass is somewhere on this server. He can't hide in Shutger's forever."

"You're right. Merk can't hide *in real life* either. I know what his face looks like."

"If you're planning something, I'm in!"

"We'll see," Lee said. "For now we'll keep it in game. Suit up Banana, you look like a level three scrub. I'm putting a bounty on Merk's head. You could use the cash, am I right? I want him alive though. We bury his ass."

About the Author
Zach Chapman

Zach Chapman is an author, editor and gamer. He currently lives in Austin, Texas with his librarian wife Taylor, a cat, a rabbit and a lazy-eyed rescue dog named Dingo. You can find him on Twitter @chappyzach.

Author Website: http://chappyfiction.com/

Étude for an Extraordinary Mind
by Julie Novakova

PRELUDE

Doctor Stephenson leaned forward and smiled reassuringly. "Tell me, Mandy, what do you experience when you switch between your implants?"

The girl across the table remained silent.

"Your parents are worried about you."

No response.

She was usually difficult to get to talk and would just sit silently crouched in her chair like some frightened little animal, but there was something different about her now. Doctor Stephenson was suspicious of its cause.

"Am I talking to Mandy?" he asked, suddenly with a very stern expression.

"No," the girl said defiantly.

"I want to hear her opinion now."

"Why? It's my damned life too! Who ever cares about my opinion? Nobody!"

"I will hear you out, I promise. But I need to talk to Mandy first."

After a short pause, she spoke: "Fine."

The girl changed in front of his eyes. It wasn't dramatic, one might not even notice it at first sight, but he knew the signs. Her look changed. She lowered her shoulders and stooped a little. Her muscles spasmed briefly during the transformation. Her deep-brown eyes unfocused for a second. Stephenson thought she maybe paled somewhat, but it was harder to tell with her darker skin. She seemed a little nervous but also distant. For a moment, she touched the little surgery scar above her ear.

"Now, Mandy," he said softly, "you do remember my question. Please, tell me."

∞

MANDY

The grass leaves were moving rhythmically in the wind. Amanda Burnham sat on the lawn and watched them carefully. Their motion was not regular as it depended on the whims of the wind, but she could see repeated patterns there. They were really quite simple, could be reduced to a few basic curves. But the way they interfered and changed was unique. Every chime of the wind was itself unrepeatable although the larger patterns were few. Like music, she thought. Just a few basic tones but bring them together and you have a unique melody. But on an even larger scale, the patterns repeated once again. To capture them, you'd need a piece more complicated than ever composed.

She wasn't aware someone was talking until her mother entered her view and knelt beside her.

"Mandy, it's time to go to the hospital," she repeated. This time Amanda noticed but still didn't quite comprehend. What hospital? Why? She looked at the swaying leaves again. They almost grasped her full attention again when Mother interrupted.

"Mandy, please come."

Mother's face seemed different than usual. Her expression changed. But Mandy could not tell what it meant, however hard she tried.

What hospital, she wanted to say but remained silent. The words sort of stuck in her throat as so very often happened when she considered speaking. She stood up and followed mother to the car.

∞

Mrs. Burnham clutched her husband's hand firmly as they waited outside the operating room.

"I just hope we didn't make a mistake," she said hoarsely.

He squeezed her hand comfortingly. "It'll be all right, you'll see."

She drew a deep breath. "Yes. It will."

Meanwhile, the surgeons just a couple of yards from them were carefully guiding the robot operating on Amanda Burnham's brain.

They had waited for so long. According to the law, the surgery had to wait until their daughter reached fourteen. Since they found out about them when she was ten, implants helping people on the autism spectrum proved even more efficient than they had dared to hope. They enabled people to communicate better, learn to recognize other people's emotions, and express their feelings and thoughts.

But still they felt like fainting when the lead surgeon came out of the door. And then he smiled.

"It went okay, no complications whatsoever. The preliminary test suggests the implant is working normally. However, we'll know more in the next few days."

They hardly heard his last sentence. By that time, the Burnhams were hugging, almost in tears, thinking of their little girl. She was a teenager, but a little girl still. Not only in their eyes; she just never behaved like a teen. She never fitted in. She was always by herself.

That might change now.

They stood there in the dimly lit hospital corridor, silently, happily, without doubts.

∞

"It cannot be switched on all the time. Best to learn to switch it on in the morning and off before going to sleep. Also…"

Mrs. Burnham listened to the tutorial absentmindedly. She'd heard it maybe a hundred times. She couldn't wait to actually see it *work*. She clutched a sheet so hard that her knuckles were all white.

Mandy listened too. Her mother could not tell if the girl was happy, nervous or anything else and was impatient to find out. She might—in a moment!

"So, Amanda, would you please try it like I instructed you?" The doctor smiled.

She looked at her parents hesitantly.

"Turn it on. Please," Mrs. Burnham said, her voice just above a whisper.

Her daughter did. And a whole new world opened before her.

∞

MANDY & BECCA

It took weeks for Mandy to adapt to her implant. At first she was afraid of switching it on; everything seemed so different, and yet the same. It was scary and confusing. After she got used to it, Amanda started testing her enhanced personality in situations that previously repelled or scared her. They didn't seem so anymore. She became so self-confident! She was almost talkative compared to her older self. Her parents were delighted—and she, much to her surprise, found herself feeling that strange pride too.

If stimulating certain parts of her brain to form and facilitate new synapses could make her feel this confident and not isolated anymore, what else could it do for her?

One afternoon, nearly four months after the surgery, she practiced her violin and an idea suddenly occurred. That very night, she brought it forward to her parents.

"That's not going to happen! It's too dangerous, be sensible!" they kept saying. Mandy had expected this and stood her ground. She still remembered the day before the surgery, the faint leaves in the wind and a melody hidden behind them, one she tried to reach but failed. She needed a door into this kind of world and was determined not to let go until she succeeded.

Eventually, after endless weeks of persuasion, crying, quarrels and discussions with doctors, her parents gave in.

When Mandy turned off her implant that night, she instantly became terribly scared.

Did *she* really do this? She could remember herself reasoning with them, listing arguments, *yelling* at them. That just wasn't her. The memories gave her chills.

But she did get what she wanted, didn't she? Wasn't it *good*?

She couldn't sleep at all that night. In the morning, she felt extremely tired and nervous. The memories of her behavior had haunted her most of the night though she knew she didn't do anything bad and it probably didn't matter much.

Immediately after she turned her social implant back on, she became horrified by the fact she spent nearly a whole night just wondering about such stupidity. She really was different under the implant's influence, better. Without it, she could become absorbed in unimportant details and worried sick about them. All her doubts and concerns from the night seemed so pointless now.

During one of her regular sessions with a specialized therapist from the hospital, she considered telling him about her experience but decided not to. Hell, he'd think she was crazy. She had to switch the implant off during the sessions, but didn't tell him anyway. Sometimes she agreed with her "other self's" opinion. But often she just couldn't understand herself—her own memories about decisions, feelings or conversations didn't make sense to her without the implant. It was as if it turned on a whole new side of her personality.

After the session, she flipped the implant back on.

That's actually quite funny, imagining myself as a new person! I should get my own name…

It was just for fun, but she secretly named herself Becca. She always liked the name, unlike Mandy or Amanda. They were so dull.

I'm Becca, she repeated wordlessly and smiled.

∞

HENRIETTE

When she had her new musical implant switched on, Amanda Burnham could think of little else but music. It was everywhere and in everything. As she requested, the implant induced a special state of synesthesia in her brain so that she could perceive any sensation as a sound. The color of her mother's hair sounded like a waterfall with a hint of Vivaldi's "Summer". The grass outside the house reminded her of early Stravinsky. The leaves performed some a ballet resembling Tchaikovsky's "Swan Lake". However, when the wind was strong, the lawn was nothing but the most chaotic and visionary pieces by Shostakovich.

At first she was overwhelmed by it but she gradually learned to control her new forms of perception. It was a world she was unable to grasp ever before and one she always longed to reach, and it was so clear now. Playing pieces she had learned before on her violin and piano seemed trivially easy now. She started learning more complicated ones, but it still wasn't enough. There was so much exciting music all round and no one seemed to give it any attention. No artificial music she ever heard could approximate how beautiful the sound of autumn was or how startling a dusty bookshop's tones seemed.

She would show them all.

It took her only a week to finish her first composition, a short experimental piece for a solo violin, so far a not very ambitious étude. She didn't expect the thrill it caused in her parents and teachers, nor that it would lead them to find her a high-ranking private music teacher. She soon didn't need her at all. When the teacher left, she admitted that she'd never had a more talented pupil.

She felt an urge to distinguish herself from her more common, less musically talented selves. However, she couldn't explain it to her parents like that. Therefore she came up with a reason she knew they wouldn't resist.

"I want to use a pseudonym as a composer," she declared. "I'll go under the name Henriette. It sounds like sand by the lake we used to visit on holidays. I loved being by the lake but never told you."

She noticed with satisfaction that her words touched them more than anything else could.

Henriette could hear the faint eerie twinkle of their moved expressions.

∞

MANDY

Sometimes Becca or Henriette grew tired of themselves. Then she would become old Mandy again—unable to express herself and connect with others, but full of reliving and tasting memories from her time as them. It was strange. Everything she did with the implants on seemed a bit different with them off. She was often startled by her own courage or ideas.

However, some memories could hurt too.

Mother's warm smile when she talked with her as Becca.

The proud look on her father's face after she finished her first violin piece as Henriette.

She knew they had always loved her with all their heart. But now they loved her most when she was not quite herself—when she was improved, augmented, just better at everything.

Becca could sometimes be problematic—impatient, willful or disobedient. In the end, they'd always forgive her and hug her, talk with her, take her to the cinema...

When she was Henriette, they seemed a little reserved in her memories, almost scared, but they admired her like never before.

I'm right here, she wanted to say to them without the help of any implant. She would look at her parents, the words longing to come out. *This is me. Don't you like me this way?*

But she could never bring herself to actually say it.

∞

BECCA

There was something tragically beautiful about the town at night. Becca looked at it from up above, sitting on an old railway bridge, and she could see it from one edge to another. The street lamps. The lit windows. The slowly moving cars. The occasional pedestrian. All the suffocating middle-class surroundings of Sheffield.

"They're all so normal," she said, interrupting the silence. "So bloody normal. Living their tiny ordinary lives, nine to five, orderly families, small sins and lies. How can they cope?"

Gary smirked. "Hey, one would almost think you envy them!"

"Shut up."

She knocked off the ash from her cigarette. He was right, of course, but she would rather die than admit it.

It made her sick. Everyone else knew who they were. From birth to death, they had just one life and managed well. She was sometimes confused about who she really was. When she transferred to a normal high school, she started calling herself Becca publicly—a nickname, she'd explain to her parents. They seemed slightly worried but her communicativeness assured them again that everything was all right.

In truth, *nothing* was all right.

She closed her eyes and remembered her last performance. Almost blinded by the badly aimed lights, seeing the audience just as a vast darkness full of strange human-like shapes, but paying attention to none of it; playing was everything. She kept totally focused. She and the violin were one. She felt out of time and space, confined just to the world of music, until she stopped. A moment of transitional silence went past, followed by thrilled clapping. Everyone said she had a straight path to Carnegie Hall.

She was deeply satisfied with that but longed most for performing, practicing, and composing again. Her name was Henriette.

Then she was scared by that hall full of people and such anticipation after she became the old Mandy.

The day after that, with just her social implant switched on, she was envious of Henriette and disgusted by Mandy.

She realized nothing would be all right ever again.

"Damn," she said when her lighter stopped working. Becca turned to Gary. "Hey, do you have yours?"

She was grateful for his presence. They soon stuck together at school, both quite different from the others. He was still unsure about his sexuality, shared a home with a neurotic mother, and hoped that he'd never again see his father. He introduced her to Led Zeppelin and Pink Floyd. She grew a liking to them, which made her life even more complicated. Henriette tried to suppress the memories of their songs, she found them almost painful to reminisce. The memory of her dislike clashed uncomfortably with Becca's opinion. They even started dressing differently; Henriette felt best in long skirts and high-collar blouses, whereas Becca rebelliously chose to wear punk clothes. Mandy, anxious in the center of attention, would stick to jeans and hooded sweatshirts.

Hell, nothing was normal anymore, she sometimes even felt like competing with them. Her parents had noticed, of course. Nevertheless, she couldn't talk to them. It would be weird for Becca, impossible for Mandy and unimportant for Henriette.

Fortunately she had Gary.

She breathed in the smoke and savored it for a while. "It's weird, you know? Having this... split personality, sort of. I heard my parents discussing it with a doctor once. He told them not to worry, that some patients experience this for a while and then it just fades away... which means that *I* will just fade away."

"Even if that was true, why don't you let the other ones disappear?"

"I guess it doesn't work that way. I'm not the... *original* one. But that..." *That would be nice*, she was going to say but couldn't bring herself to actually say it. *They're me too. There is no they.*

"Anyway, I have to start seeing a new therapist. Not just that... a bloody *psychiatrist*! As if I were crazy! They want me to see him every week." She sighed. "Sometimes... it feels like being crazy. Maybe they'd better lock me up somewhere."

"That's what worries you?" Gary put an arm around her back and pressed her shoulder reassuringly. "You're not crazy."

I wish you were right. She smiled unhappily.

∞

MANDY

In the deep of night, there were raised voices from downstairs. She could not fall asleep, not while hearing them. It was an argument, she was almost certain about that. Becca would know for sure without having to think about it, but Mandy didn't want to bring her around now.

She heard her own name several times and wondered about the meaning of that. Mom and dad were fighting—but why? And why wouldn't they stop?

She was trembling and hardly aware of the tears running down her cheeks.

The voices rose to a crescendo. For a fraction of time, Mandy contemplated how Henriette would perceive it. But she didn't want to exchange places with her either.

Becca would go down there and ask them why are they fighting, try to stop them, make a scene about it if they didn't make peace... Why don't I?

Mandy shuddered at the thought. However, she was right—she *could* do it herself. If only she could make her body move the right way.

She put all her effort into getting up from bed. As her feet finally touched the carpet and she stared at the doorknob, she heard the front door slam. Then heavy silence.

She was too late.

∞

BECCA

She was supposed to be at her geography class. Fuck geography, she thought. She didn't have the assigned homework anyway.

Gary was skipping class too, for the second day in a row. When she finally saw him, she realized why: He had a dark swollen bruise around his left eye.

She sat beside him on the old, unused bridge in silence and offered him a cigarette. He took it without a word.

"He came back," Gary said after a while. He didn't need to add who.

"Funny. Mine left in the middle of a night a couple of days ago."

"I would exchange places with you, you know."

Becca sighed. "Yeah, I guess so. Sorry."

Yet for a moment, she thought she actually *would* like to exchange places—given that she would be normal and Gary would end up in her skin, or rather in one of them. They were good sounding boards for one another, but she felt that although he had understood her best of all people, he could still never quite grasp the idea of being just one of several persons occupying one body. Nor could her parents. That was why Dad left, wasn't it?

And that stupid bitch didn't know how to stop it, she was just crouching in her bed like some helpless animal. Really, if I didn't have to switch places with her from time to time...

Staring at the town below, she blew a cloud of smoke angrily.

Mom will leave me too when she finally sees the monster I am… But why should I care? She was never any good for me. I can take care of my own life!

For the first time, Becca toyed with the idea of leaving first.

∞

HENRIETTE

Henriette was excited by Mandy's and Becca's feelings though she expressed little of such herself. However, they were a great source of inspiration. There were so many surprising variations in there, especially since Father had left! She decided she would compose an étude focused on them one day. She started working on it, but it was a difficult theme to grasp, she was never satisfied. But she had a stroke of inspiration after one late-night practice in the garden. The night was beautiful: a light breeze, cooling air, stars shining above, smells of nocturnal flowers like the evening primrose. And so Henriette started composing a nocturne.

It took her many weekends, free afternoons and late nights to finish it. Mother was worried about her at first, but Henriette easily persuaded her that she was all right. She learned how to make Mandy memorize that she needed to switch on the musical implant as often as possible. And Mandy did, partly because she rarely wanted to be just herself these days.

Henriette focused on nothing but music and it brought its results. Her nocturne received audacious critiques. Some of the experts even compared her style and imagination to Fauré or Debussy. She couldn't wish for better compliments but didn't mean to stop there. Her work would become something completely new and fascinating, she was certain of that.

And when she finishes the étude, they might applaud her even more.

Full of dreams and satisfaction, she went to bed and switched off the musical implant.

∞

MANDY

Amanda collapsed in her bed. She had never felt so exhausted before. She knew the reason. Henriette practiced late, leaving them hardly three hours of sleep a night. Henriette could cope with being tired better, being absorbed in playing and composing. She experienced fatigue as music too, as Mandy could well remember if not understand.

If only she could talk about it with someone. She was so alone. It was like before the surgery, but now she had the memories of talking, laughing, and hugging. She missed contact with other people so desperately now, yet she was almost unable to relive the memories personally. Sometimes… sometimes she wished the others never switched her on again.

Right now Mandy would have most liked to sleep; nevertheless, she couldn't.

Not after she remembered the conversation Henriette overheard the other day but didn't pay much attention to. Father was back home for the afternoon and he had brought a guest with him. It was that psychiatrist she had started seeing, Doctor Stephenson.

"…we're very worried about our Mandy. Some time ago, she started acting weird, as if…"

"As if she was another person with each of the implants," finished Mr. Burnham for his wife, sighing. "I'm not sure if we're overreacting, but… what do you think, as an expert, after you've seen her a couple of times?"

"I can assure you that developing what seems like a new personality is not altogether rare among patients treated with such implants, though it's certainly not a common trait. It's not a true case of MPD. The brain forms new pathways, which are being reinforced by the implant. When it's off and they're not fully developed yet, the patient can feel very different. And even if they are, the effect can last in a less apparent form.

Similar things can actually happen to everyone. People can behave, feel and think differently even when using foreign languages. When I speak Spanish, it can seem like I'm a slightly different person and sometimes I think or say things I wouldn't using English. There's of course a contributing effect by the specific environment but I used that as an example. Many factors influence our behavior. However, what you describe sounds serious and these symptoms in patients usually only last a couple of months. I think we had better take a closer look at your daughter at the clinic if you agree, run some tests. Just a short hospitalization."

∞

BECCA, HENRIETTE & MANDY

A short hospitalization.

The words resonated in her head and made it ache.

Preventive. To get readings on the implants in a controlled environment.

Her hands were trembling. She could hardly grasp her cell phone, let alone the violin.

She would play, just to relax, to bring herself away from this, without calling in Henriette.

But she was too shaky to do even that.

They'll lock me up in a hospital room. Then I'll fade away…

She suppressed a sob.

They shouldn't have let me have this life in the first place if they want to take it now.

Becca decided she wouldn't let them.

∞

She couldn't let go of her violin. It was the only impractical item she took along.

She left in the middle of the night, took the car keys from their usual place beside the fridge and gave her home for almost sixteen years one last look.

No windows were lit when she turned the keys in the ignition. She held her breath, but when nothing happened for a while, she turned away from the house too and took the car to the road.

What was she feeling? Sadness, naturally. Fear, a little. Freedom, even more still.

Absolute freedom…

It became almost unbearable. It engulfed her so quickly she didn't have time to get frightened. She was free for the first time in her life. And she wasn't quite sure what to do with it.

Becca turned the car to the highway. Almost no other cars were on the road at this time of night. She was here, alone, and could go anywhere. The notion was intoxicating.

She wondered how it would sound.

∞

As soon as she came to the surface, Henriette knew the melody was *complete*.

The drive could be a composition itself. She almost couldn't bear listening; it was too much! Even the great Paganini wouldn't have been capable of such speed and probably no living violinist could play it, certainly not her. But it was overwhelmingly beautiful.

This should become a whole orchestral suite, the road lights for the strings and the piano, the roar of the car for the brass and percussion, the darkness of the surrounding night perfect for the woodwinds…

However, she grasped the central melody and imagined it as a violin solo.

It brought tears to her eyes. She had never heard anything nearly so complex.

In such a state, she could hardly control the car. She knew she had to go away for a while if she wanted the chance to finish her masterpiece.

∞

It felt like waking up from a nightmare, except Mandy had woken up *into* it. She clutched the wheel tightly, scared like never before, much more than when she had learned that her parents would no longer be living together. But she still felt something of Henriette's awe and Becca's joy of freedom. It was vaguely familiar. She was capable of feeling that, just under different circumstances, but it was a contact point nevertheless.

She was still afraid of running away and shocked that she suddenly found herself in such a situation. But for the first time, she could not only recapitulate Becca's memories, she could *understand* them. For her, the flight stayed scary and unreasonable, but she could follow the path of Becca's emotions and decisions and end up right here. For the first time.

And it brought along sudden relief which gently took the fright away.

If only for this short moment, she didn't feel like sharing her body with a strange girl.

Maybe if Becca could feel this too...

∞

In one moment of horrible confusion, she became Becca again. Just a blink and then she saw the truck and realized the car had veered into the opposite side of the road while she was switching the implants. She heard a coarse outcry that hardly resembled her voice, but it must have been her.

She turned the steering wheel quickly, but not quite in time.

∞

CODA

"...it was almost a miracle your brain as well as both implants didn't suffer any serious damage. You almost died, Mandy. You even lost one of your arms."

The girl looked at her right arm, looking just normal in her long-sleeved T-shirt. Only the strangely smooth skin on her hand suggested it wasn't a human limb. "It feels like mine."

Doctor Stephenson nodded. "That's right. It's supposed to. I hope you'll be able to continue playing normally. But the risk you subjected yourself to…"

"I didn't," she said quietly, looking down. "That was Becca."

The doctor was glad she wasn't looking him in the eye. He was afraid he just gave away an emotion even Mandy could notice and recognize: fear. He feared that her condition was more severe than he thought before—that this was partly his fault too—and that it could become worse.

"Mandy, I wish you, any of you, spoke to me openly about your thoughts and feelings before. I'm sorry I didn't understand how tough it was for you. I'll try my best now. Are you willing to work with me to make everything better again? Trust me, it can be done."

Mandy looked as if she was assembling the courage to speak. "What do you mean?" she asked eventually.

"You, Becca and Henriette are one person. It feels different, but that's just a side effect of a few neural pathways developing around the areas stimulated by your implants. We can use all kinds of therapy to smooth down the differences, slowly, carefully—"

"No. They wouldn't like to let go," she whispered almost inaudibly. "And I can't… I can't murder them."

"There is no *they*," he said urgently. "Trust me, Mandy."

"Even if I trusted you… With either of my implants switched on, I might not."

He almost smiled; at least they were making some progress.

"Let's try."

All of a sudden, she looked directly upon him and he knew she changed again. "I'm willing to try to... blend with them if you let me finish my étude first. I haven't had the chance yet. I must. And then... I hope she continues playing, if not composing. Please let her... me... remember what a perfect feeling it is to give life to all the music with my violin. That's all I'm asking."

She didn't wait for his response. The girl blinked and looked at him again. Stephenson felt the hair on the back of his neck rise.

∞

Becca struggled, she didn't want to be woken up. It was the first time since the crash. The last thing she remembered were the blinding lights of the truck and echoes of Henriette's beautiful memories and Mandy's fear.

No, not just fear. There was something else.

She closed her eyes.

Relief. Sort of... contact.

The scene opened before her again and she shivered, facing the approaching truck once more. She opened her eyes and looked around the calming room.

She realized she was trembling. Oh God, what must Mandy have gone through after the horrible accident?

She could feel the disorientation and pain...

Mandy might have more courage than her, after all. And wasn't it Becca who was always so afraid of fading away, rebelling, feeding her own fear?

Becca blinked and drew a sharp breath, surprised by her own thoughts. What would Gary have to say about that, after how she treated him instead of trying to help? Or... her parents, who didn't deserve her hatred despite all that happened?

She recalled Doctor Stephenson was waiting for an answer. For *her* answer.

For the first time, giving way to her fear and running away was not an option.

About the Author
Julie Novakova

Julie Novakova is a Czech author and translator of science fiction, fantasy and detective stories. She has published short fiction in *Clarkesworld*, *Asimov's*, *Fantasy Scroll*, *Persistent Visions* and other magazines and anthologies. Her work in Czech includes several novels, one anthology (*Terra Nullius*) and over thirty short stories and novelettes. Some of her works have been translated into Chinese, Romanian and Estonian. She received the Encouragement Award of the European science fiction and fantasy society in 2013 and won the Aeronautilus Award three times. In 2016, she assembled an anthology of Czech speculative fiction in translation, *Dreams From Beyond*. She is an evolutionary biologist by study, takes a keen interest in planetary science and engages in science outreach. She's currently working on her first novel in English. She can be found on Twitter @Julianne_SF.

Author Website: http://www.julienovakova.com/
Author Facebook: http://www.facebook.com/JulieNovakovaAuthor

Lost in Translation
by Sandra M. Odell

On'cher extended its ocular stalks towards the black and white creature masticating fibrous grass. "What is it?"

The First Lhur'tan trembled pride. "It is a pan-dah. We grew it from the only viable genetic sequence remaining on the derelict human archive ship. The humans will be very happy that we give them the pan-dah as a welcome gift in eight rotations."

Recycling vents around the edges of the atmospheric barrier circulated the nitrogen-oxygen atmospheric mix and a curious array of chemical signatures from the unfamiliar flora. The enclosure and additional residential hall had been constructed at what some deemed a lavish expense in the name of another tedious first contact.

The pan-dah rolled on the ground until all four limbs waved in the air. On'cher settled on its pods. "What does a pan-dah do?"

The First Lhur'tan quivered knowledgeable. "Our translation of human writing is incomplete, but the instruction module indicates that the pan-dah eats, shoots, and leaves."

"Ah. A formidable creature." On'cher approached the pan-dah with pods extended, cilia at rest. "Greetings, pan-dah. I am On'cher, Second Lhur'tan in service to the Mur'wpsix Gelcenter. May your pods never tangle in anxious thought."

It repeated the greeting in Yugaelit, the vibratory thrumming of the T'z'tit, and as a puff of Hunwha passive communication spores.

The pan-dah extruded a thick green and brown mass from the end opposite its mastication. On'cher sucked in its ocular stalks and thickened its membrane. When the mass did not detonate, On'cher extended a singular stalk towards its superior.

The First Lhur'tan burbled acknowledgment. "Unfortunately, it is a lesser sentient."

On'cher extended the rest of its stalks. "And the substance?"

"That is the waste product of the pan-dah's consumption of bam-booz." The First Lhur'tan extended a glistening ocher pod towards the plot of tall grasses. "We formulated the bam-booz with information gathered from the human botanical archives."

On'cher had absorbed the humans' quaint botanical files. "This bam-booz lacks awareness. Why am I here?"

"Human records indicate the pan-dah is extinct on the human home world. They will reward our supreme gift with favorable trade conditions for their heavy metals. You will ensure a steady supply of bam-booz for the pan-dah."

On'cher undulated confusion. "I am the senior botanical liaison to the Hunwha embassy."

The First Lhur'tan extended two pods to the base of On'cher's ocular stalks. "Exactly."

"But, but this bam-booz does not even recognize the pan-dah's assaults."

"No matter."

On'cher's pods tangled. "I communicate with plants, not grow them."

"I trust in your expertise."

With that, the First Lhur'tan slithered through the atmospheric barrier.

The pan-dah rolled onto the mass of gooey waste and promptly entered a state of lessened metabolic activity.

On'cher coiled resignation. It retracted its ocular stalks and slithered after its superior.

∞

On'cher knew forty-two ways to promote positive and mutually fulfilling relationships with an array of sentient species. It spent the first quarter of its defined corporeal existence developing an open and empathic consciousness with the Known. After two rotations, it had developed a notable dislike for the pan-dah.

The creature appeared to have no interests beyond consuming bam-booz, creating waste, and spending extended periods in a reduced metabolic state. It preferred On'cher's carefully tended hyper-grown bam-booz to the fibrous mature flora, and had a prodigious appetite.

The First Lhur'tan dismissed On'cher's concerns. "You will manage."

They slithered together through the flowstone formations of the meditation garden. On'cher preferred its time under a proper burnt umber sky; the yellow sun and blue sky of the pan-dah's enclosure had begun to feel strangely, uncomfortably alien. "The pan-dah metabolizes less than twenty percent of its intake of bam-booz. The bhan'tans say it is possible to make the pan-dah's digestion more efficient, thereby reducing its nutritive intake and allowing me more time for my usual duties."

The First Lhur'tan quivered knowledgeable. "Then it would be a Mur'wpsix pan-dah, not a human pan-dah."

"Then the bhan'tans can improve the nutritive value of the bam-booz itself."

"It must be human bam-booz, grown human ways."

On'cher twirled desperate hope. "But I am to curate an art exchange with the Hunwha embassy, and create a visual interface for the T'z'tit forerunner program. May I delegate the pan-dah to a Third or Fourth Lhur'tan?"

The First Lhur'tan plopped denial. "A change of caretakers might anger the pan-dah. You will manage."

The Hunwha grove provided equally ineffectual support. The bushy Ambassador of Branches puffed soothing pollens in On'cher's direction. *Think of all the amazing things On'cher would learn working with the pan-dah.*

On'cher blorped, and stroked the purring black moss around it. "It has a calcified internal support system that has pierced its membrane. The bha'tans insist the structure is part of the pan-dah's genetic coding, which is patently ridiculous. I spend more time tending to the pan-dah's dietary needs than I do on my duties as Second Lhur'tan."

Another puff, this time with a hint of buoyant affection. *The First Lhur'tan must have great investment in the worth of On'cher's chlorophyll to entrust such a duty to it.*

On'cher flattened sarcasm. "Ha!"

After four rotations of planting, observing, quarbling, and replanting, On'cher felt decidedly un-lhur'tan.

The translation of the human tongue might well have been in error. The pan-dah no longer appeared as formidable as On'cher first thought, unless one counted the havoc it wreaked upon the fibrous grass. It still could not fathom what to do with the pan-dah's excessive waste material. Piles of it littered the enclosure. The waste emitted a pleasant chemical signature, yet pan-dah was as likely to roll in it as it was to ignore it completely. Maybe the pan-dah instinctively used the waste material as a form of camouflage to hide from natural predators. Maybe other creatures did not consume the pan-dah for fear of contracting its stupidity.

On'cher extended and retracted its ocular stalks thoughtful. If it could not change its lhur'tan duties, it would have to change the pan-dah. On'cher could, reluctantly, tolerate an environment rich in nitrogen and oxygen, but research indicated the pan-dah would not survive a proper methane-chlorine atmosphere. The humans apparently suffered under the same deficit. A most un-lhur'tan awareness. On'cher noted the lapse, one of several of late, and its need for corrective gelling.

What about protecting against the atmosphere? On'cher slithered out of the enclosure and returned a short time later with an emergency containment bubble. By then the pan-dah had lowered its metabolism. Typical. Another un-lhur'tan awareness.

On'cher draped the bubble over the pan-dah. The membrane settled over and around the creature's bulk like flowstone. It made certain the bubble had a suitable atmospheric sample for replication, then adjusted the controls to allow for nongaseous interactions. It prodded the pan-dah with one pod. "Pan-dah, you must move."

The creature continued to make low noises indicative of its state.

On'cher poked at the pan-dah again, this time with two pods. In places not matted with waste product, the creature's fur felt like Hun-wha moss. "Pan-dah, I respectfully request that you move."

The pan-dah shuddered and opened its ocular orbs. A pink orifice tentacle slid over its calcified protrusions. As it lumbered upright and began to manipulate one of its two swiveling audio organs with a front limb, the bubble completely enclosed the creature in a spherical amber membrane. The pan-dah did not appear concerned.

On'cher bounced authority. "Pan-dah, you are now properly contained to allow for mobility. The bubble will prevent all respiratory atmospheric exposure while still allowing you to interact with the environment."

The pan-dah rolled onto all four limbs and disappeared into the plot of bam-booz. The stalks passed in and out of the membrane without disturbing a leaf.

On'cher trembled pride. The pan-dah could cross the enclosure's atmospheric barrier and it follow on embassy rounds. The exposure to different races might even encourage an increase in the pan-dah's cognition. On'cher extended its pods, cilia at rest. "Pan-dah, I request that you follow me. I have a scheduled interface at the T'z'tit embassy."

The wet cracking of the creature's mastication rippled over On'cher's membrane. It coiled resignation and retracted its ocular stalks, wondering if the pan-dah had cognition to increase.

∞

The answer was not cognition, but appetite.

On'cher removed the growth pads to its second gel residence and brought a supply of tender stalk segments to the enclosure each rotation. It presented stalks in order of need, shorter pieces to facilitate mobilization, longer pieces to placate the pan-dah when they reached a given destination. It did not take the pan-dah long to learn that if it wanted to eat, it had to follow On'cher.

Trembling pride and elongating efficiency, On'cher spent two full rotations catching up on its duties as Second Lhur'tan. The T'z'tit interface blossomed to fruition, the Hunwha art exchange engaged sentients from nineteen separate systems, and through it all the pan-dah followed, masticated, and extruded.

The ambassadors seemed fascinated with the pan-dah. They collected in the common areas of the ambassadorial campus to watch On'cher lead the creature around. Bright leaves and feathers swayed enthusiasm, "Adoration limbs limited range! Holographic reference, holographic reference!" Prisms reflected substratums of questioning light, "Will the hoo-mans also extrude?" Spores burst red vegetative queries, "Eat, yes?"

On'cher decided against leaving its charge unattended.

The First Lhur'tan curled pleasure at On'cher's resourcefulness. "I knew you would find a way to assimilate the pan-dah's care into your scheduled duties."

They pooled together in the meditation garden beneath a flowstone overhang while the pan-dah masticated supine in its bubble. On'cher hoped the pan-dah appreciated the rightness of a sky with chards and rempults in full phase.

On'cher tossed its charge another segment of bam-booz. The pan-dah's fur was clean and smooth, an unanticipated benefit of the current feeding program. "It has proven a most enlightening experience."

"The humans will be pleased that their new pan-dah has been so readily accepted by the other embassies."

On'cher trembled pride. "Gratitude to you, First Lhur'tan."

"The humans shall grant the Mur'wpsix preferred trade status, and I shall receive favorable notice from the Grand Gel."

On'cher extended all of its eyestalks. "Pardon?"

The First Lhur'tan curled pods around On'cher's ocular stalks. "And you as well."

The pan-dah rolled onto its waste to retrieve the next piece of bam-booz.

∞

On Arrival Day, On'cher made a special point to chem-wash its charge's fur. Even with blended frustration of political excess, On'cher wanted to make a good impression.

After reinflating the bubble and a minimal first feeding—an extrusion of waste at the presentation would no doubt prove disastrous, perhaps even fatal—On'cher slithered to its first gel residence with a stop to pick up a fresh supply of bam-booz. Where went the bam-booz, so went the pan-dah. On'cher dribbled mirth and hurried on its way.

The First Lhur'tan contacted On'cher repeatedly.

Was the pan-dah prepared? Yes, of course.

And the enclosure? On'cher contacted the enclosure's droins on a separate wavelength and set them to the task before assuring the First Lhur'tan that everything was complete.

What about bam-booz? Did On'cher have extra bam-booz to keep its charge occupied? Already pouched.

Did it think a sedative would be needed so the pan-dah would not startle and attack? On'cher peeled exasperation yet answered with a lhur'tan's calm assurance that no sedative would be needed. Not for the pan-dah, anyway.

On'cher slithered into the residence and darkened the entrance to indicate gel time. It had spent far too little time at the first gel residence and missed the meditations curled on the walls, the scent of ripe flurgg. Really, flurgg made a gel residence a home.

It slithered into the center pit and unwound calm thought. Time to prepare itself for the humans. Let the First Lhur'tan slurp selfish and tremble pride. On'cher served the Mur'wpsix Gelcenter, and trembled pride at its own accomplishments. Someday other Mur'wpsix would as well. The pit warmed to On'cher's stillness and began to corrective gel.

Feathered peace. On'cher received a contact. It continued to gel. Another contact, and it refused with a statement of gel time. Moments later, another contact came through on the First Lhur'tan's singular wavelength: "The human transport has entered the lower atmosphere. Why aren't you at the vestibule? Where is the pan-dah?"

On'cher blobbed surprise. It slithered out of the pit and lunged for the observation wall. No! It had overgelled. "I am decontaminating an elimination area, and will be there shortly."

"Elimination in your first gel residence?"

On'cher brought up viewer wavelengths for the human embassy's enclosure. It could not find the pan-dah. It shifted to different viewers. Nothing. No signs of a disturbance or fight. A clean enclosure, but no pan-dah. On'cher puckered fear. "I had hoped to engage the pan-dah's interests with further cultural exchange. We will be there soon."

"Do not disappoint me, Second Lhur'tan On'cher, or you will lose more than your ranking."

No corrective gel could strip away On'cher's un-lhur'tan awareness.

It called for mobilization and met the automated unit along the glide path. Where was the pan-dah? Had On'cher been taken in by the creature's ruse of incompetence? Was it even now stalking the ambassadorial campus, or, worse, the pits of the Grand Gel? Was this all an elaborate human plot to allow their agent of destruction inside Mur'wpsix defenses? On'cher's pods tangled. Puckered fear, puckered fear.

At the human embassy, On'cher rushed into the pristine enclosure. "Pan-dah! Pan-dah, I have bam-booz! Pan-dah?"

No pan-dah, only alien vegetation swaying in the circulated air.

It hurried to the observation wall and brought up the viewer wavelengths. It scanned back time until it found the pan-dah in its containment bubble mobilizing through the enclosure's atmospheric boundary in reverse. The creature mobilized backwards to the edges of where the growth pads had been, then snuffled over to a few bits of bam-booz on the floor. On'cher had been undone by trembled pride. The pan-dah's appetite had led it to seek bam-booz outside the enclosure. On'cher had been in such a hurry to corrective gel, it misjudged the creature's metabolism.

The First Lhur'tan made contact once more: "The humans have landed. Where are you? What have you done with the pan-dah?"

Puckered fear. On'cher muted the inquiry and forward timed the outside viewers. The pan-dah mobilized away from the human embassy to the common grounds. A T'z'tit courier waved three tentacles in excited recognition before heading into its embassy. On'cher undulated confusion, twirled desperate hope. The T'z'tit couriers were particular about their duties and never varied their scheduled routes. Judging by the time marker, this courier had finished its route, so the pan-dah had to be close.

The Hunwha wavelength activated. An automated voice came through: "Second Lhur'tan? Are you available? Your pan-dah is eating one of our staff. Should we poison? Please advise."

On'cher knotted panic. It imagined it could identify the Hunwha spores of alarm. It slithered out of the enclosure as fast as it could. "Do nothing! I will be there momentarily!"

At the Hunwha embassy, a dozen different species coiled and withered at the entrance. From inside the vestibule came the sounds of squealing moss, rustling leaves, and determined mastication. The Ambassador of Branches puffed fear at On'cher. *The pan-dah's reputation was no lie. On'cher had to stop the pan-dah before the victim needed grafting.*

On'cher pulled out short lengths of bam-booz and slithered into the vestibule where the pan-dah sat stripping leaves from a tall grass Hunwha. The top of the staffer's stalks had been chewed away, leaving nothing but moist stubs. "Pan-dah, cease your consumption. I have fresh bam-booz."

The pan-dah made no response. On'cher struck it over the head with the bam-booz, and the pan-dah stopped eating long enough to look at On'cher. At the sight of the bam-booz, it dropped the staffer and pulled On'cher's pod forward. On'cher released the bam-booz, and helped the Hunwha drag the wounded staffer away while the pan-dah was distracted.

The bushy ambassador released agitated pollen bursts. *Now it understood why On'cher made offerings of the dead to the pan-dah. It was a beast, a monster! Should the Hunwha seal their embassy against another attack? Would the humans demand further sacrifice to satisfy the pan-dah's terrible hunger?*

On'cher vibrated relief. "I don't think so, but it is best not to speak of this until I have had the opportunity to, to confer with the pan-dah."

Should the Ambassador of Branches file a formal report with the First Lhur'tan?

"No need for that. You have my word by soil and sun that the pan-dah shall not trouble the Hunwha again. Now, if I may ask your pardon…"

On'cher backed out of the vestibule, laying segments of bam-booz as it went. The pan-dah followed, pausing to consume each one. On'cher contacted the First Lhur'tan who answered immediately: "Your insult to the human embassy shall not go unreported. We were forced to greet them without our intended gift of welcome, and for that—"

"Escort them to the enclosure. I will be there with the pan-dah."

"Your lack of planning and poor—"

On'cher continued to drop bam-booz in front of the pan-dah at widening intervals to encourage interest in mobilization. "My skills are not in question in this discussion. Your willingness to make a favorable presentation to the human embassy is. Escort them to the enclosure."

The First Lhur'tan was silent a moment. "Your estimations had better be correct."

The contact snapped closed, and On'cher slimed relief to the Known.

One stalk at a time, On'cher coaxed the pan-dah across the common areas and back into the enclosure. It instructed the droins to retrieve the bam-booz growth pads, spilled the remaining bam-booz onto the floor, and deflated the pan-dah's bubble. It then settled down to compose a request to build a physical enclosure for the formidable pan-dah for reasons of sentient safety.

It finished the request as the official mobilization arrived. The unit merged with the atmospheric barrier, the connection point resolved, and the First Lhur'tan escorted the human embassy and a surrounding of Third and Fourth Lhur'tans into the enclosure.

At the sight of On'cher the First Lhur'tan striated outrage, yet kept all ocular stalks extended. It slithered to one side. "Cap-tayn Loo-iz, human embassy," it said, and strange metallic sounds came from a translator unit attached to one pod, "I present to you Second Lhur'tan

On'cher, and our privileged gift of welcome to you."

On'cher extended its pods, cilia at rest. "Welcome, human embassy."

The pan-dah lay supine and masticated with single-minded intent.

The humans stood motionless. Twelve in all, they were covered in identical partial containments, all the same distasteful blue. The one with the darkest membrane opened its head orifice, closed it, lifted an upper limb toward the pan-dah. It made noises at the other humans, they made noises back, quick and high, alone and together. Some shaped their orifices up, some down. On'cher spun sympathy. The humans had calcified protrusions similar to the pan-dah's.

A smaller human shook its head, made a soft sound, and its ocular orbs began to leak. It brought its two upper limbs to its head orifice, then turned its back to On'cher. A threat? No, the human with the darkest membrane set its limb around the smallest one in what appeared to be a recognition of some sort. A tall human began to leak in a similar manner, and a round one.

On'cher undulated confusion. Had it offended?

The First Lhur'tan extended and retracted its ocular stalks thoughtful at On'cher, then made a deliberate gesture towards the middle section of the one who raised its limb. "Your translator, Cap-tayn Loo-iz."

At the strange metallic sounds, the human fumbled at its middle section and produced a translator. The human made strange noises, and the translator said, "Greetings."

The First Lhur'tan signaled to a Fourth Lhur'tan. The underling slithered over to On'cher, presented a translator, and backed away.

On'cher hung the translator from an ocular stalk. "Greetings, Cap-tayn Loo-iz."

The human brought a limb to its orifice and made a sharp noise. "Is that... Is that a correct pan-dah?"

The monotone translator voice had no emotion, but the human

exhibited none of the ninety-eight recognized indications of hostility.

On'cher quivered knowledgeable. "It is a human pan-dah, yes."

The human focused both ocular orbs on the pan-dah. It made another sharp sound, wiped leakage from its ocular orbs. "We have not seen a human pan-dah in… significant length of human measurement of time. Exclamation of surprise and wonderment."

On'cher trembled pride. "Do not tangle your pods in anxious thought. I will provide your nutritional specialists instruction on the care and harvest of bam-booz. The pan-dah eats shoots and leaves."

The pan-dah extruded waste and rolled on top of it.

About the Author
Sandra M. Odell

Sandra lives in Washington state with her husband, two sons, and a grumpy orange cat. Her work has appeared in such venues as Jim Baen's *UNIVERSE*, *Crossed Genres*, and *Daily Science Fiction*. Her holiday-themed short story collection *The Twelve Ways of Christmas* came out from Hydra House Books in 2012.

Somewhat Damaged
by George Cotronis

There are men in the house.

I wait with my back against the wall. There is no light, except for the two flashlights dancing on the wall across from the doorway. I clench my fists. They will come soon.

When the first man passes, I pivot to face the second man through. He has a baseball bat embedded with large spikes. I clock him and break off his jaw. Blood splatters on my face. He goes down without a sound, already in shock, holding the hole in his face where his jaw used to be. I jump behind the wall as the roar of the third man's shotgun makes my ears ring. Plaster and brick explode outward and pepper my face. I calculate and execute. I pick up a brick, roll my body to the doorway and throw it at the gunman. It hits him in the face and he falls down, holding his nose. His right eye socket has fractured and the eye probably can't be saved. He requires immediate medical attention.

Behind me, the first man through hits me in the back of the head with a hammer. Something gives way. There is damage to the auxiliary socket at the back of my neck. There is damage to the left arm. I try to lift it and confirm. It stays limp at my side. I turn around before I get hit again. There is panic in the man's eyes. I reach out and grab his throat. I crush his trachea and he goes limp in my hands. I let him fall.

I retrieve the shotgun from the living room floor. The man that used to wield it scuttles away when I approach.

I say, "Sir, you need medical attention, plea—"

ERROR

I shoot him in the back before he reaches the patio. My black suit is ruined, soaked with blood. I drag the bodies into the backyard, douse them in gasoline and light a match. When the fire's good and going, I take the photograph from my pocket, then slip off my suit and throw it on the fire. I stand there naked, the flames warming my flesh, until I'm satisfied their bodies are burning.

The lights are out upstairs, but the sky is clear and the moon helps me navigate the hallway. In the bathroom, I break off a glow stick, throw it in the sink and take a long, hard look at myself in the mirror. I look like shit. My right eye is dark, the LED in it long dead. The outlets on my chest and arms are grimy and dirty. Some have burned out. I look down at my hands. I clench each fist, first the left, then the right. The left one is too weak. I'm missing a few bolts and some of the plugs are burned out. There isn't much grip. I guess I'll have to rely on my right hand.

My skin's smooth and soft, but dirty. Blood stains my face. I need a shower. I heft the battery off of my shoulder and onto the floor. It's plugged into my arm and I take great care not to pull the cable out. The core, the circular LEDs near my heart hum quietly, light pulsing low red. I recharged earlier.

I use a piece of wet cloth to wipe the grime from my body. This is a ritual I do rarely, perhaps once every few months or so. I suppose there's a practical reason for it: Make sure the plugs don't get gummed up and become unusable. But mostly, I do it to feel a bit human. To pretend life goes on.

When I'm done, I put the battery backpack on and raise the glow stick to admire the job. I look slightly better, the metal outlets shiny under the light of the stick. I leave the bathroom, walking on broken and cracked tiles.

The building is quiet. It usually is. I walk around the ground floor, looking out each window in turn. There is little to see, especially at night. The house next door is a burned out husk. On the other side, there's a field. A small jet, possibly a Lockheed L-188, crashed in it. I watched from the patio unable to help as its passengers burned. The street out front is overgrown with grass and weeds. Rusted-out Fords and Cadillacs litter it. I check every door as I walk past, every window. This is my patrol. It has to be performed every six hours. This is the Vacation Patrol schedule. As I'm securing the back door, checking and double-checking, Jack comes out to greet me. He has made his home in one of the kitchen cupboards, on an old blanket I eventually laid out for him. He presses his nose against my hand and I pet him.

"Who's a good boy? Huh? Who's a good boy?"

Ugh. The default greeting slips out of my lips before I can stop it. Jack wags his tail.

"Yeah, it's good to see you too, Jack."

I pause my patrol in order to feed the dog.

MEMCORRUPT

I pull down the dog food bag from the cupboard above and spill some in his bowl, a fine china plate dated 1911.

He descends on the dry dog food in the merciless way only a dog can.

I continue my patrol. Upstairs, the rooms are darker. I have to use the flashlight, as much as it pains me to do so. There is nothing out of order in the bathroom, or the office, or the painting room, or in the master bedroom. The windows are locked, locked, locked, locked—

ERROR

There's no one in the house. Except Jack, but Jack is a dog and there's an exclusion rule for pets in the databank so it's okay. I don't remember if the Straubs had a dog, but I suppose it is now irrelevant. Jack is the house pet. In any case, I'm now free to do as I like, for the next five hours, fifty-five minutes and thirty-four seconds. Thirty-three.

I walk into the master bedroom. It's now my bedroom, has been for quite some time. The wallpaper is brown and peeling from the walls and a thick layer of dust covers everything. I place the photo I'm holding on the dresser and lie down on the king-sized bed. Women's clothes litter it. I bury my head in a sweater. Cashmere. Her smell, perfume and soap and lilacs. I power down and go into Idle Mode, the closest I get to sleep. In that state, I let my mind drift. I dream.

Droids don't dream. I do. Kind of. The dream is of me and her, of me and Mary. We're in this room, the bedroom and I've caught her trying on a new dress. She beckons to me, the dress held against her body. When I come closer, she lets it fall and she's in her underwear. I reach out to touch her, but my hand is a mass of metal and bolts holding it together. I hesitate, and she leans in and rubs her face against it. I cringe as I imagine the sharp edges against her soft skin. She kisses the metal and then my lips.

I come to life seconds before my patrol. I untangle myself from the bed sheets and the clothes and get up. The downstairs is quiet. The fire burns low in the backyard. The smell permeates the house despite the shut windows. I guess there are so many holes in the walls and the boarded-up doors, there's nothing to keep it out. It's unpleasant, but reminds me of hot summer days and barbecues.

After I complete my patrol, I go to the basement. The fallout shelter is located behind a fake bookshelf. The books are fake too—they're blank. I checked.

The little room in the back is filled with supplies. I have unfortunately already consumed most of the batteries, first aid kits and various tools. The food and water are still there however. I sit in front of the control mainframe and reach under the desk for the plug. I push it into my arm and log on:

This is the year 1964, October thirteenth.
The temperature is 10 degrees Fahrenheit.
The weather is fair, but chilly.
Sweater suggested.

It has now been 4,382.9 days since the Straubs—Thomas and Mary—went on vacation. They have not logged in remotely. There are no new directives.

Primary Objective: Patrol and Secure Residence.
Secondary Objective: Residence Maintenance.

I shake my head and unplug. I climb the steps and go to the living room. There is still blood on the floor, blood which I have to mop up later, but it's not imperative to do it now. I pick up the bottle of scotch, the one Thomas used to call "the good one" and pour some into a lowball glass. It's chipped, a large piece missing from its mouth, but it's okay. I throw the drink back, roll it around in my mouth and swallow. It's smooth. I leave the glass on the bar and take the bottle upstairs. I rummage in the closet for a new suit. I find one, I think it might be the one Thomas got married in. I dust it off. It fits perfectly. It would have to, wouldn't it? Thomas and I had the same build. I pick up the picture from the dresser and sit on the edge of the bed.

The woman in the photo is beautiful. I'd like to say that it was her soul that was beautiful, but you couldn't really tell from the picture.

Maybe from the smile on her lips, or the eyes. Maybe. There's a crease down the middle of the photo, where I folded it. The man on the other side is me, but isn't. It doesn't make sense, but I don't want to look at him. Only her. And I do, for the next few hours.

∞

Jack is running around downstairs and the sound takes me out of my trance. I put the photograph in my inside pocket and go downstairs. *Twice in one night, guess the place is getting popular.* I creep through the ground floor, taking quick peeks through the windows. I don't see anyone. In the backyard, there is a figure silhouetted against the night sky.

Just one. I wish he'd just go away.

But he doesn't. He turns around and walks right up to the door. The door shudders, but it's boarded up good. The figure leaves it alone and walks towards the other side of the house, where the kitchen is. I stay low and follow suit, creeping through the house.

The intruder jiggles the doorknob. When it doesn't give, he throws his weight on the door.

I should have nailed that one shut too.

On the third hit, the wood splinters and he spills through the door. I get ready to kill. The girl stands up and dusts herself off. She's dirty. She's wearing a brown trench coat two sizes too big and under that, a torn black dress. She looks like she's coming home from a funeral. I observe, hunched down behind the kitchen island. She looks unarmed. She has short black hair. Malnourished. Maybe there doesn't have to be another death tonight. I quietly grab a knife from the holder. A chef's knife, nasty sharp.

The girl looks around the room, her eyes only now getting used to the dark. I stand up.

"You are trespassing. You have to leave," I say, voice stern and loud. I point at her with the knife.

"Holy shit!" She jumps back, holding her hand to her chest. "Holy shit, you scared the shit out of me."

"Please leave." Desperation creeps into my voice. I don't want to have to kill a kid.

She seems to be taking me in, trying to figure out if she can take me.

"Who the fuck are you? This place isn't yours." She pulls a screwdriver out of her jacket pocket.

"I am Keeper. You are trespassing." I take a step forward.

"Fuck that, I'm not going back out there. I need a place to sleep."

"You can't sleep here."

She looks at me funny. "I know what you are. I've seen one of you before."

"Yeah?"

"Yeah. Identify."

"I am Keeper, Prototype Two-Five-Four. My owner is Thomas Straub." The programming overrides me.

She claps and laughs.

"You're a fucking droid!"

"I am a bioengineered human with enhanced capabilities."

"Same thing. Request guest status."

"Denied. Vacation protocol in effect." *Shit. How does she know all this?*

I take a step forward. This has to end. She looks scared, but isn't backing out.

"I am your owner," the girl says.

I feel something load in my brain. I can't move. The word *ERROR* flashes momentarily in my one good eye.

Scanning... DNA Scan Results: Positive.

Owner status confirmed.

New directive: Idle.

"Confirmed." How is this possible?

"Holy shit, it worked!" The girl jumps up and down. "I can't believe it worked!"

"Admin username?"

"They call me Lenore. What's your name?" the girl says.

"I'm Prototype Two-Five-Four. N-new directive?"

"Leave."

"Not found. Please restate."

"Just go away. I don't care. Leave the house."

"Not found. Please restate."

"Fuck. Okay then. Protect mode."

"Protection Directive engaged. Thank you."

"Cool." She smiles.

The radioactivity scan comes up positive, but well under danger levels. I suspect her clothes carry most of it anyway.

I walk up to the door and close it. I have to nail it shut now.

"Hey, where you going?"

"I have to nail shut the door."

"Oh. Okay. Fine."

After I nail the door shut, I find Lenore rummaging through the kitchen. There's very little that hasn't already been carried away by rats, but she's found some saltines and is busy stuffing her face.

"This is really good," she says, between mouthfuls of crackers.

"Yeah."

"How long have you been here?"

"All my life."

She rolls her eyes at me. "And how long is that?"

"Active status thirteen point one years."

"And you've been stuck here all this time? What did you do?"

"I kept watch. I maintained the house."

"You haven't done that good of a job you know. This place looks like a dump." She pumps her legs back and forth as she sits on the kitchen counter.

"Twelve years is a long time," I say. "I've done my best with what I had available."

She looks upset. "I didn't mean anything by it. I'm just messing with you."

"It's okay."

She points behind me. "What the fuck is that?"

I turn around and Jack is at the door.

"That's Jack. He's my dog. Your dog."

"Uh… That's not a dog. That's a possum."

I look at Jack again. I guess he looks a bit like a possum. I shrug.

"Why do you have a possum for a pet?"

"He just showed up one day. I fed him."

"You're messed up, Prototype." She throws the empty can behind her. "Got anything else to eat?"

"What would you like?" I smile.

"What have you got?" she asks.

"Just follow me."

I lead her down to the basement and into the fallout shelter.

"I think I'm gonna have a stroke," she says, her eyes wide. She runs her hands over the labels, mouthing the content silently. "Peaches, ham, beans, ravioli… I'm set for life!"

She jumps on me and hugs me. Then, as if suddenly ashamed by her outburst, turns her back to me and pretends to read labels some more.

She points at the computer. "What's that?"

"That is the mainframe. It controls the house and the security systems."

"So it controls you."

"Yeah, that too."

"Can we have electricity?"

I shake my head. "I'd advise against it. Lights attract people."

"Yeah, I guess you're right. What else can you do?"

"I am Prototype Two-Five-Four with security and bodyguard functions."

"Yeah, I got that. I mean what else can you do?" She looks irritated.

"Anything you ask me to."

"Cool. Can you cook me one of these cans?"

"Sure. Which one?"

∞

Lenore is sleeping on the top bunk bed in the fallout shelter. She ate three cans of food: two cans of beans and one of peaches for dessert. She looked like she needed it. She looked like she couldn't believe her luck. Things must have been tough out there for a young girl. But now she's safe. She's home, even if she doesn't know it yet.

I'm no longer obligated to do my six-hour interval patrols, but I do them anyway. I still have to protect her. In between, I watch her sleep. I see her mother in her face, but do I also see parts of me? I don't know. Androids can't father children.

She wakes in the early morning hours. She asks if there's a chance she can take a shower and I watch her face light up when I say I can make it happen. She goes upstairs while I start up the generator and heat the water. After she's done, I shut it off and go to my bedroom upstairs.

She comes in, teeth chattering. She's wearing a T-shirt and a skirt her mother left behind. They're a size too big, but better than the rags she was wearing when I first saw her.

"I'm f-f-f-freezing," she says.

"Here, you can have this." I take off my coat and wrap it around her.

"Thanks. What are you gonna wear?"

I shake my head. "I don't really feel cold. I just wear these suits because they're the only men's clothes in the house."

She sits on the bed and picks through the clothes spread out on top of it.

"These are so cool," she says. "Do you know how long it's been since I had a change of clothes?"

They are cool. Her mom had good taste and the money to accommodate it.

"You're free to take what you want. This is all your stuff."

She frowns. "Look, I don't want you to throw me out, but you know this isn't really my house, don't you?"

"The DNA scan checks out. You're the offspring of the owners of this house."

"I've never seen this house in my life. I grew up in Pittsburgh."

"Before that, you lived here. Well, at least your mom did. She was pregnant."

"My mom was dirt-poor. We lived in a shack in the middle of nowhere." She picks up a handful of clothes and throws it in the air. "My mom didn't wear shit like this."

"I don't know what happened once she left here. I only know what happened in this house."

"You're wrong. You're malfunctioning. You're broken."

"Check the left front pocket."

She pats her hand on the coat pocket. Reaches in and takes out the photo. I know it's well-worn and torn and cracked, but if I can see her face, so will she.

She stares at the photo for a long time.

"Where did you get this?"

I point at it. "I've had this photo with me for twelve years."

She looks at me.

"I'm sorry, but this ain't my mom," she says.

It has to be.

"I scanned you and you're a perfect DNA match for the offspring of Mary and Thomas Straub."

She unfolds the picture. The man in it is tall, dirty blond, well built. He's smiling.

"You're in this picture too."

"That's not me. That's your father." They have the same blue eyes.

"My father was a fat alcoholic from Arkansas."

I shrug. "That's your father."

"This is you."

"I just look like him. I'm an android. I was ordered and manufactured to protect this family, this house. Having a strange man in the house would be unseemly. So they made me look almost exactly like him."

She shakes her head and lets the photo drop on the floor.

"I'm sorry I'm not her."

"It's hard to accept, I know." I reach out to console her.

The knife she pulls out of her boot glints in the moonlight. It presses against my belly.

"Don't fucking touch me. I'll cut you in half."

I raise my arms and step back. She walks out of the room, never turning her back to me.

∞

I wait for a while, then go downstairs. She's going through the books in the library. I feel bad for not taking better care of it. I read a lot, but I also used the ones I didn't like for kindling. She sees me come in, but the knife stays in the boot.

"You like reading?" I ask.

She throws a book on the floor. "I'm looking for anything useful. I don't really read."

"Your mom loved to read."

"Yeah well, my mom didn't grow up in an apocalyptic wasteland, now did she?"

"Of course. I'm sorry."

She waves my apology away. "I was eight years old when the bombs fell."

She couldn't have been eight when the bombs fell. She would have still been in the womb.

She goes on.

"We survived because there was a fallout shelter under the library. When the sirens went off we were just outside. Some guy my mom knew pulled us after him and we made it in. Other people didn't."

She places the book she's holding back on the shelf and sits down on the couch. "We went from refugee camp to refugee camp. She got sick. She died. I was nine."

I already knew that. I knew that if she was alive, she would have come back here. I knew, but the words still hurt.

"Well, you're home now," I say.

"Yeah. Home." She smiles a sick smile.

"You're safe."

"There is nowhere safe."

"It is my duty to protect you. You're safe here."

"How are you gonna protect me? Kill everyone that comes here? Like those men out there?" She motions to the smoldering piles out in the yard.

"They were trespassers."

"Yeah. So am I."

"No, you're not. You are the rightful owner of this house."

She laughs. "It sure looks like it. Can we have breakfast now?"

"Yeah, sure. Let's go downstairs."

We go into the fallout shelter and I let her pick out a few cans. Today's menu is canned beef and beans. The dessert is apricots.

While I cook over the small stove, she investigates the basement.

I watch her as she wolfs down the food. It will take a while until she gets used to not eating like a wild animal, I guess.

In between bites, she asks, "What are those pod-looking things in the back room?"

"They're stasis pods."

"What the fuck is a stasis pod?"

"It was designed for use with the fallout shelter. In the event of a nuclear war, you can go into stasis and wake up fifty years later, when society has re-established itself and the radiation has gone down."

"Yeah, somehow I don't see this society re-establishing anything. Have you seen what's going on out there?" She talks with her mouth full.

"No."

"I'm sorry. I forgot. Well let me tell you, it ain't good. It's the opposite of good."

She's quiet for a while.

"Prototype?"

"Yeah?"

"Do you think I could go into the pod?" she asks.

I shake my head. "I'm not sure that's a great idea. I'm not sure if they even work anymore."

"They look okay to me."

"I don't know."

I don't want to lose her. I have only just met her.

"Look, I know you think everything is all right now that I'm here, but it's not. This world is fucking dead. There's nothing out there besides death and emptiness. We ruined the world. We're only living because dying seems such a poor alternative."

"You could have a good life here."

"Do what? Sit in a basement and eat canned food and talk to a robot?"

That hurts.

"Fuck," she blurts out.

"I'll put you into the pod if you want," I say quietly.

"Why don't you take the other one? There's two," she says.

"I'm an android. They don't work on us. Besides, who's gonna guard the house?"

She shakes her head violently.

"No. I won't make you guard the house anymore. You've been here for years. Maybe it's time for you to walk out and see the world. What's left of it."

"No, I can't do that." I'm not going to leave her here all alone.

"No one will find me back there. No one will care. Besides, I'm the one giving the orders here, right?"

"Yeah, I guess so."

∞

I prep her for the stasis pod. The instructions are included in my programming. She lies down in the pod and I connect the cables. The shot is the last step.

I hesitate.

"It's okay Prototype. I'll be okay," she says.

"I'm not dumb you know," I say. "I know you're not really my daughter."

"Then why are you helping me?" she asks.

"We all pretend sometimes, don't we?" I say. "You ready?"

I hold the syringe high.

"Yeah. What's the command that frees you?"

"There's no such command."

"Enter roam mode," she says.

"Mode not found. Please restate."

"Shit. Enter Search Mode."

"Search Mode. Target?"

"Mary Straub."

"Confirmed."

"Give me the shot."

I lean in and stick the syringe in her thigh. She will go under soon.

"Hey, I hope that works out for you. The outside world I mean. Maybe you'll find her. Get closure." She's fading fast.

"Yeah." I hold her hand and she squeezes.

I insert the tube down her throat and seal the pod. It fills with liquid. I check her vital stats. They look good.

"See you in fifty years, kid," I say to no one.

∞

There is no drive to go looking for Mary. I suppose the damage I received in that last fight was more serious than I thought. It explains a lot of things about today.

I sit in front of the mainframe and use Mary's administrator account. Under Prototype Two-Four-Five, I change the order from "Search Mode" to "Vacation Mode". I'm not sure if it's needed, but just in case some other asshole decides to take a shot at my brain interface, I can be certain I'll stay here and guard the house. Guard her.

I walk out of the shelter and start picking up the fallen books.

About the Author
George Cotronis

George Cotronis lives in the wilderness of Northern Sweden. He makes a living designing book covers. He sometimes writes. His stories have appeared in *XIII: Stories of Transformation*, *Big Pulp* and *Lost Signals*.

Author Website: http://www.cotronis.com/

A Song for the Barren
by G. Scott Huggins

"Sing, barren woman, you who never bore a child; burst into song, shout for joy, you who were never in labor; because more are the children of the desolate woman than of her who has a husband,"
    Isaiah 54:1

The daughter's screaming still echoed through their house, even muffled by the outer walls. He could hear it even over the whine of the badly tuned electric engine. It did not fade until the van from the Ministry of Adoption had disappeared around a corner.

It seems we are too frightening to be parents, even with the orphanages full and so many dead. The thought was bitter.

Wyren-jionhae turned from the door to his wife. She was staring out the window. Tears streamed from her eyes, silently. For a moment, he forgot himself and reached for her. But the sight of his great, clawed hands, the stiff spikes growing from his wrists, made him pull back. They were killing hands, not comforting hands.

Jionha's head whipped around like a snake's at his gesture, and her eyes flashed. "Am I so ugly, you cannot even touch me anymore?" Her lisping voice was marred, mushy and cold.

"I…" but she was gone, long legs carrying her through the kitchen. He heard her run down to the basement, and shame washed over him at his own uselessness. The time for comforting, like the time for having children, was long ago, and could not be brought back. No, no more than could the departing van. Only memories returned, and they hovered like birds: carrion eaters with mocking cries.

∞

It had not been the time, then, to think of her beauty: the way her long, dark-gray limbs melted through the forest, or how her hair, pulled back in the style of the daughter-scouts, twined about her sinuous neck, or how her mouth, so delicate and small...

"Wake up, Son-of-Dreams!"

Flushing almost blue at the whisper, he looked up to find Jionha perched above him, almost invisible in the giant fern. The muscles along her spidery arms and ribcage stood out as she pulled her great steel bow taut. "Wake, or we'll start without you!"

"I hear and obey, O Daughter-of-the-Acid-Tongue!"

Wyren had the pleasure of seeing her darken to almost black at the vulgar remark before he flung himself silently through the forest surrounding the road.

The convoy would be here any minute. Already he could feel the twinges in his nerves from the grav drives. For a moment, he envied the Terrans their skin and warm blood. His hands seemed locked inside their fine scales—too cold to move. He stopped. Dimly, he saw his fellow sons and husbands to his left—silver-blue glints in the brush.

The convoy passed, humming like a greatworm from ancient stories. The huge grav trucks carried ammunition, food, and fuel. They passed, bigger than anything Wyren had ever seen, carrying life to the Terrans, the Terrans whose Empire held all Mtaein in slavery.

Last of all came a huge grav tank, the Terran on the top scanning the undergrowth, supremely confident on the back of two hundred tons of alloy and weaponry. This was Wyren's target, and he could not move.

Suddenly, whines filled the night, and the Terran jerked backwards, staring in amazement at the broad-bladed arrow that sprouted from his chest. His eyes darkened and he slumped.

The world seemed to lurch into a sick slowness; cries and gunfire erupted all along the convoy. With the horrible knowledge that he had waited too long, Wyren threw himself at the side of the tank, his weapon clumsy and too big for his hands. He slipped, pulled himself up just as the Terran's corpse was pushed from the hatch. A white-skinned hand reached up to pull the hatch shut, and Wyren found himself face-to-face with the ghostlike Terran, whose eyes were wide with terror. Wyren got the barrel of his weapon inside the hatch just as it slammed down. He pulled the trigger.

The shotgun was an ancient weapon by his enemy's standards. It still decapitated the Terran efficiently. Then Wyren leaped inside and everything was noise and explosions and red, red blood, so alien.

His next memory had been Jionha, walking out of the woods, her face mirroring his own. Horror and relief at what had—and had not—happened. They had held each other all the way back to the camp, and she had sung a lullaby to him in the stillness.

∞

If only the Director of the Orphanage and his wife had seen Jionha *that* night… but they had not. They had seen her tonight, as the wife of a warrior; seen the lines of grief on her face and they had heard her gluey, warped voice. And they had seen him.

The daughter they had brought had screamed in terror at the sight of him, and had not stopped even when the director's wife had carried her outside, throwing a look of disgust over her shoulder.

Her husband had remained to pass sentence. Director Nacay-ko-ree-chagae reminded Wyren of a Terran. Thin for a Mtaeinin, the little husband reached almost to his chest. His scales were almost entirely silver, but pale and dull, like Terran skin. His dark hair was short and straight, neatly aligned, just over his four ears.

"I'm sorry, but as you can see, it's just impossible for me to recommend you as adoptive parents. Any son or daughter we could give you might be frightened enough to hurt themselves…" *Or you might accidentally hurt them.* The unspoken thought hung in the room.

"What about a wife with a child?" Wyren had asked. The Revolution had left many widows. Jionha had no other wives; it wasn't right for her to have to live only with him for company...

"I've circulated your file," Nacay had said. "We haven't found anyone... suitable, yet. To be the wife of a warrior." *Desperate enough,* he meant. Wyren raised one huge hand and rested it on the wall as the little husband flinched away.

"Varq promised," Wyren growled, and Nacay's eyes had gone round but remained firm.

"Some things are beyond even his promises," Nacay had said, looking nervously around the room. At the chairs too small for Wyren's bulk. At the thin patina of refuse strewn about. "I'm sorry." He had left his fearful glance hanging like an oppressive smell. And had driven off, leaving Jionha to run from her husband, crying.

Wyren sat on the floor. He wanted to tear his hair out, but of course, he had no hair. His huge hands gripped his low-set, wicked horns and tightened as if he could crush their roots. He rose, anger getting the better of his sorrow. Betrayed. Betrayed by Varq who had sent a pretty little worm like Nacay to forswear him. How long since Wyren had looked like Nacay? How long since he had had hair? It had been...

∞

Boom! Boom!

The silence was unreal. Everything had been unreal that night: the chains around his wrists, the ranks of Varq's Councilor's Guard looking on. The drums, the torchlight, the cages of springwood woven around him and his dozen comrades.

Yet he had never felt more alive.

The smells of smoke and the deep forest wove around him. He had never been stronger. Never in better condition. Outside the cages, there was not a husband or son who could stand against him, and well they knew it. He bared his teeth at the nearest one and nearly laughed at his involuntary reaction: the way he spread his claws and yearned to cover his face. The way his skin lost any semblance of silver, turning the deep blue of fright.

But this was not a night for laughing.

They had led the wives out, and things had begun to blur.

The scent alone had told him which was Jionha, even if she had not been the most beautiful of them all, gray and straight in the torchlight, her single braid falling from her smooth head, cheeks slightly swollen and lips puckered in the delicate moue of wives' pregnancy; it made her look as though she always smiled.

Yet she cried. All the wives were crying, there in the torchlight as the drums beat slowly. And Wyren cried too, though he was in an agony of lust, his under-palate clinging to the roof of his mouth in longing for the Second Kiss: the intercourse that would transfer the embryo to his womb, where his body would nourish it until birth…

A birth that would never be, now.

A bottle was opened. It was passed along the line of women. The first took it; held it to her nose, and inhaled. Immediately, spasms shook her, and the caged male on the far right of Wyren shrieked into a frenzy, leaping at the springwood bars in front of him, tearing himself on the chains.

The bottle was passed. Wyren watched, strengthless, as it came closer and closer to his wife, his only wife, the wife of youth, to Jionha, who took it. Inhaled.

Somehow, through his own screaming and tearing at his bonds, Wyren saw clearly: Jionha, gagging in the smell of the abortifacient, as she choked, knelt, and retched, her tonguepouch burst, pouring out blood and water and a finger-sized son, who kicked feebly and died in the torchlight.

When he awoke, it was to the stink of his own hormones, to hair stiffening into solid horns, to scales hardening into a carapace, and claws that would be capable of gutting a Terran in one blow. Self-hatred gushed through him, and he drove those claws into his own belly. They bounced off a hide tougher than Terran silksteel. A hide that covered a deep, sickly pleasant burn, as the unused enzymes of pregnancy digested the delicate, nurturing linings of his womb; burning it out, sealing it. Converting it into the energy needed for the Change. Making him into a warrior.

Jionha visited him the next day. She still couldn't speak. No wife could while her tonguepouch held an embryo. She would bear the speech impediment the rest of her life. Mtaeinin were not like Terrans, who with their awesome technology could hold an entire planet under their sway, and shape their bodies as they willed. No Mtaeinin who aborted came away unscarred, any more than Mtaein itself had, under Terran rule.

They had volunteered for this, when Varq and the Revolutionary Council had asked for volunteers. It was a thing that must be. Wyren knew it. Jionha knew it. Sons and husbands could fight, but Mtaein now needed her warriors; the changed male that arose from an aborted pregnancy. A warrior could tear apart any Terran vehicle short of a heavy grav tank. A warrior could be struck by cannon fire and live. Men with only one wife, who would give themselves, and their families for liberty. She watched him as the warrior Change took him; reshaped him into a thing of nightmare—a nightmare in which neither of them could speak.

All that could be discussed had been, long before Jionha had become pregnant.

It didn't help at all.

∞

Wyren stood before Varq and tried to remember why killing him was unthinkable. Perhaps it was the way he looked at you and seemed to stare right into your mind. It was an ability he'd always had, back when they were both sons together, playing at killing Terrans with gun-shaped sticks.

"I know what I promised you, Wyren. But I can't do this."

"You can." The words hung flat in the presidential office.

"I can't and you know it. Wyren…"

"Wyren-jionhae! I have one wife; *say her name!* And you sit there with how many, Varq-kisanae-halavae-ganhae… I forget the rest. How *is* your family? In comparison with mine?" Sarcasm dripped off his words.

Varq's eyes dropped. "Wyren-jionhae. I did what I promised. I got the Ministry to give you a chance. That's all I could or can do…"

"You lying motherfu—"

The doors behind Wyren burst open the moment he raised his voice.

"Stop!" Varq raised his hand. Wyren slowly looked around. Flat-eyed husbands trained heavy weapons on him. Weapons that could pierce even a warrior's plating. He turned to Varq. Their eyes locked.

"I'm sorry. Even if you don't believe me. Please escort Warrior Wyren-jionhae-*nje* out."

Nje. Honored. Wyren gave a sardonic snort and turned away.

"Wyren?"

He turned back.

"For what it's worth, I still owe you a favor."

Wyren spat and walked out of the palace.

∞

Filu-diorae-kalae rolled his eyes as Wyren walked in the door. The small, greasy husband had a voice almost as raucous as Wyren's own. "Well, at least you came in too early to scare away most of the customers!" He poured out a quart of yellowish methanol and slid it across the bar to Wyren. "I don't know why I let you drink here. In the old days, I'd have called the Marines to kick you out!"

"In the old days, I'd have pulled this cesspool down around your ears, anyway," Wyren said flatly. Their humor was forced. Both knew it was true. Except that Wyren wouldn't have been "kicked out." He'd have been executed on the spot.

Filu's tavern had once been a Terran place. Still was, in spirit. Holes in the walls showed where the imaging and sound equipment had been ripped out. A dead gaming tank rose up through the center of the floor. A few anemic fish swam in it where the electronics had been. And it was what it had always been: a *dance* hall. On the other side of the thick, plasteel door, the Terran perversion was still going on; husbands and wives, sons and daughters, moving to offworld music in an obscene parody of mating. Wyren no longer cared; he didn't have to watch it.

The chairs were too small for Wyren. He crossed the room and perched on one of the tables like a carrion-bird. He took a pull at the liquor. It did nothing. His warrior's metabolism prevented that. The tank reflected him, its curved sides further warping his distorted figure in the glass: a grotesquely robust sculpture of a husband, as if he had been baked in an oven and allowed to rise. The horns in place of hair. A hard shell, jointed, covering everything but hands and face.

He and Jionha had not chosen blindly. They had known what they were doing. From the moment of the Change, they had been apart. They had known they would be. They had known it would be painful.

They had not expected it to be long.

They had expected…

∞

Battle. He had been only a few hundred yards from this place the day Serata had finally fallen. Five of his fellow warriors had already died under the micro-nuclear strikes of Terran dropships. He shifted the one-gauge cannon in his hands from target to target like a rapier—a precision weapon. The Imperial Marine leapt from the cover of the half-wrecked rocket base and fired a burst of three maglasers into him from a distance of two meters.

Wyren had stepped forward despite the pain of the deep burns and swung the butt of his cannon viciously. The man's head had bounced back into the twisted wreckage. Without thinking, Wyren threw his laser into the arms of one of the warrior support troops that scuttled around him like tugs around a battleship.

Then Prale had shouted for help.

Wyren leapt over the smoldering tower that had been the base's main turret. What would have been horror just months earlier, he took in with grim efficiency.

A warrior was down, blood pouring from a shattered carapace, and Prale stood locked in battle with a thing from Hell.

The Imperial commando was a nightmare of titanium and composite, its stealthfield blurring as it fought. Its armored gauntlet caught and crushed Prale's hand and one gauge; Prale roared in pain, grappling its other hand, the hand that held the plasma carbine inching closer... closer.

Wyren saw all this in midair. He landed, bounced once and drove all his power into a kick that knocked the armored shape back; its carbine letting loose a plasma bolt into the air, and it rebounded to its feet, the small face behind the visor contorted in a snarl.

Wyren's spiked hand ripped through its shattered belly armor and twisted. There was a retching scream, and the thing dropped. Wyren felt his lips pull back.

Then thunder had shaken the capital, and even Wyren had been forced to drop, covering his ears. For a moment he thought that their worst fears had come true; that the Terrans had elected to destroy Serata rather than lose their capital.

But there was no flash of a fusion weapon. Just a steady light. Wyren had looked up.

The noon sky was full of fire. The blue wedges of fusion drives rose from the southern edge of the city. Little flares. Big flares. Dropships and heavy transports. They were no longer attacking. They were leaving. One by one, the pockets of firefighting winked out, to be replaced by rising ships, or final explosions. Continuous thunder poured from the sky, fading. Through the rest of the day, sporadic fighting had continued between the Mtaeinin Liberation Army and the last pro-Terran hold-outs, as they were either defeated or taken off-world with their masters. But it was over. The revolution was won. And Wyren had not died.

∞

He had not died. And Jionha had not died. At first they were happy. Neither of them had wanted to die. But how could they live? One husband. One wife. No children, ever. What kind of family was that? What kind of husband was he?

He became aware of a presence at his elbow and growled at it. It didn't move. Wyren came out of his reverie to focus on it. It was Filu.

He was blue. Not a trace of silver. Frightened.

Of what? Surely not of Wyren's growl? He had growled in the little bartender's face often enough.

"Wyren-*nje*..." he got out, choking.

"*Nje?* From you, Filu?" Who wept while others had cheered the departure of the conquerors? Wyren had not thought himself still possessed of curiosity. "What is it?"

"In the dance hall. There's a fight..."

"You have bouncers."

"They aren't trained to fight Terrans."

Wyren gaped. A Terran? Here? Insane. Tourism was only just being permitted under strict control, and any Terran on Mtaein knew that he was unlikely to be forgiven the slightest criminal act.

But this particular Terran had picked the one place on the planet that a Terran could conceivably cause trouble with impunity. A dance hall owner would not call the police.

Not stupid, then.

But nonetheless, a Terran on Mtaein. A fighting Terran. Wyren rose and crossed the room, fangs bared. He threw the door wide and froze.

The Terran was tiny. It stood in the middle of the dance-floor. A few remaining Mtaeinin of both sexes were rapidly edging out the doors. Three big husbands lay near the edge of the dance floor. One dripped blue blood from his nose. The Terran turned at the sound of the door opening.

Wyren growled, half in amazement. It was dressed all in black, only its face and one hand showing skin. Over that it wore a jacket. A gray jacket, covered with bits of cloth and metal at one breast. A long cloak lay on a chair. It must have been seated there. Then it had taken off the cloak to reveal the jacket and that's when the trouble had started.

It was the dress jacket of an Imperial Commando. The creature might as well have been wearing an execution order. Wyren smiled.

The officer's slanted eyes widened at his growl, and it threw its bottle away. It nodded to him, and spoke in High Angelsh. "Commander Phun Huynh, Twelfth Battalion, Imperial Navy Special Forces. Whom have I the pleasure of killing?"

It was female! And unarmored! How did it hope to stand against a warrior? He checked himself. No one had ever said Terrans were cowards. He replied after her fashion. "Wyren-jionhae. Warrior. Councilors' Guards."

"Come, dance with me," she called, extending her naked hand.

Wyren's jaw dropped at the insult. The *battleblood*, the warrior hormones that lent him speed and strength, surged through him. His body became light and lightning. There was only this place. There was only her. He charged.

If it had not been for the battle glory rushing through him, her absolute motionlessness would have given him pause. His claws reached for her. Then she blurred... and something gripped his arm, hard. Incredible pain shot up below his belly and he was flying, coming down on splintered wood and metal that had been a table.

Her laugh behind him blended with the tinkling of broken glass. "A warrior should do better than this!"

He rose, and nearly fell. She had hit him as he passed, right where the upper and lower torso plates joined. Something had torn. Not too serious, but... it wasn't possible. No unarmored Terran could stand against a warrior. Not even a Commando had ever dared try! He stepped clear of the bar and she whirled to face him.

Now he studied her.

She moved with a sort of airy bounce, almost the opposite of a limp. She was small, even for a Terran. Her skin shone golden in the low lights and her eyes were horizontal slashes below her bare forehead. Her long, black hair streamed out behind her. The medals on her chest caught the light and flashed defiance at him.

They were alone in the room. The stillness was marked by the ragged breathing of one of the bouncers she had hit. Just one still breathed.

"Why?" The word was harsh in the silence.

"That's funny; no warrior ever philosophized with me last time I was here. As I recall, 'Why not?' is the classic answer." She screamed—a high, alien sound—and leapt. A kick whistled past Wyren's ears and he rolled, blocking the second half of the combination attack. His carapaced arm clacked off her descending foot. He withdrew into a crouch.

That boot was more than it seemed. Harder. And so was its wearer. Wyren felt his mind split into the focused calm of battle awareness, considering his opponent while plotting strike and counterstrike. He moved in, his fingers spread, the spikes of his armor forming a porcupine around them. Was this a Terran madness?

She must know she was dead, even if...

She kicked one grabbing hand aside and ducked the other.

...she could somehow kill him...

Just missed another joint in his armor.

...she would never leave the planet alive.

There were a dozen witnesses. Even common criminals would inform on a Terran! Again, she drove a kick toward the joint and he shifted to take it on his armor. He felt his carapace bend and almost buckle as the strike staggered him to one side. The fighters broke apart.

Wyren was shaken. The Terran was breathing hard. If that kick had hit a joint...

A new sensation thrilled him from chin to groin. Fear. He was amazed that he could still feel it after all this time. She stood before him, untouched. Only the motion of her chest told him that she had even exerted herself.

Then why had she not killed him at the first blow? Had she pulled the punch? He parried a punch with a wrist spike, not quite fast enough to impale her hand. Why? She would have killed one more warrior before she died, as so many of her kind had done. He lashed out, fist smashing against her gloved hand, and he felt something snap, even through his thick skin. And he would have died, as he had sworn to. Been meant to. As so many others had, reduced to a family of only husband and wife. No other wives to complete their family, to share him with Jionha. No children, not ever from Jionha.

Not ever from his own womb.

The Terran's hand hung limply, and she looked at him from under half-lidded eyes. She shook and sweat streamed from under her hair. He was not fooled. She could still kill him. He hoped. She opened her eyes fully and smiled at him. Terran teeth were a joke. He had never known they could show so much menace. He wondered if she would use them. How they would feel, biting into his flesh.

The side kick came so fast that he blocked it without meaning to, and felt his carapace crack under its force. He drove one punch past her ear only to have it parried by her gloved hand. He would not dodge the next kick. His other fist reached for her face… and she relaxed, feet together, arms spread out, face blank.

He could not stop his fist. He was too committed for that. Desperately, he twisted, and his massive hand thundered into the wall.

The Terran's eyes were wide and fixed on him. They mirrored his own expression. Just then Wyren noticed that the noise of impact hadn't stopped with his fist hitting the wall. It was repeating itself in footsteps, dozens of footsteps outside the massive main doors.

The police. Finally, someone had called.

Waves of shame crashed down around Wyren. He had failed. Failed to kill or be killed. Had been a living failure for five years, laughed at for it. Pitied for it. An old warrior who should have died long ago, and he had failed even to kill himself.

He turned and ran for the side door. It flew open in his face, and he howled in shame and fury. The sergeant leading the four-man platoon turned blue and fainted. The others scattered as a relic of ancestral nightmares bore down on them and ran into the night.

∞

Now Wyren sat in another tavern. This was not a dance hall. He drank, because he would not be permitted to sit there perched on a table like a gargoyle, without drinking. The five tables next to him had quickly become vacant, and husbands and wives muttered over their shoulders in his direction. At least, he thought so.

Perhaps he was mad. The stories he had heard as a child said that warriors did go mad. But the warriors in the stories had lost their wives, or worse, killed them. That was why they were warriors. The Change was a holdover from savage times. No husband deliberately became a warrior.

Until the Terrans came, and taught us about nations and empires, he thought. That something greater than family could exist. They were strong because they had it. We needed to be strong to fight them.

There was a surge of angry muttering from the crowd around him.

Did we need to be this strong?

He raised his eyes to the patrons and found that he was not the one they were muttering about.

Phun walked through them; a ghost of Empire. She must have touched some of them, but she seemed to be as utterly unconscious of them as of shadows. Her skin was paler here, and her eyes burned with… what? Strong emotion that he did not know how to read. Her jacket was reversed, brown on the outside, now. He could see the edges of medals inside it. She walked through the empty space around his table.

"Why didn't you kill me?" Her voice was soft.

The tavern's patronage began to leave. So, she had really wanted to die.

"Walk with me," Phun said. "Please."

Wyren looked up at her. At the glares of the bartender and the dwindling crowd. He rose, and walked out. Phun followed. At last, they stood in the sparsely populated street, under the always-full moon.

"Why didn't you kill me?" she asked again. He stared at her.

"Why wouldn't you kill me?"

He began walking. Most Terrans would have had to run to keep up. That airy, anti-limp kept her at a pace with him.

"You also want to die?" As no answer was required to that question, he kept walking.

"Wyren-jionhae, I challenge you."

He barked a short laugh. "If both of us wish to die, it will be either a very short fight or a very long one. Good night."

She stayed at his side. "We are both soldiers, Wyren-jionhae. It is an axiom that the loser is the one who dies, yes?"

Wyren grunted assent.

"Then I challenge you. If you can prove that you have lost more than I have, I will kill you. If you will do the same for me."

Wyren stopped. Stared at her.

"You'll have what you want, Wyren-jionhae. Killed fighting a Terran. Just what you expected."

"You swear this?"

"Before G… on my honor I swear it."

"Done."

They came to a plaza. Wyren recognized it. The Plaza of Heroes. In the center was a statue. A short husband knelt, planting the banner of the Revolution. His wife stood supporting it, straight and tall. The husband's right hand closed the eyes of a dead warrior. It was brightly spotlighted. The square was empty. He faced her. "How shall we begin?"

She regarded him for silent moments. "What have you lost?"

The directness of the question floored him. Where to start? He could not speak.

"What have you lost?" she repeated.

"No Terran could understand. No wife could understand." Not even Jionha could understand. He said the words in Qhayshp, the language of the Seratan forests. He started to leave, realizing what a useless gesture this duel was.

"You have no idea what I understand. Stand to your oath!" Her voice reached out like a whip. His eyes bulged.

"You speak Qhayshp," he said, dumbly.

"It was rare for us, wasn't it?" She sounded almost ashamed. "What have you lost?"

A barrier within him snapped. "Look at me," he hissed. "Do you know what this face means? This form?" He flexed his spiked fists, beat them against his carapace. "Sons and daughters have nightmares for a week after I walk by their houses. I am used by their parents to scare them into obedience. Wives look away when they see me, and no husband would be seen with me. Before you came, warriors were failures or traitors to their wives, and that is what they remember. But I became this because of you."

Phun did not reply. She put one finger in her mouth, and tugged on the glove covering it with her teeth. Slowly, she withdrew her hand from the glove and held it palm toward him.

Synthetic and metal gridwork formed a wire sculpture of five fingers and a palm, half of it dangling limp where Wyren's blow had connected. She shrugged the jacket off, and it fell with a clatter to the stones of the square. She touched her collar with her bare hand, and the black clothing she wore fell apart. It occurred to Wyren that he had never seen a Terran unclothed before. Probably they feared to doff armor in the presence of Mtaeinin, but now... she stood.

Below her face, her pale, yellowish skin swept downward into two masses of fatty tissue—the *breasts*, he remembered—supported by ribs visible through her skin. Below the ribs... black plastic and metal formed a carapace even tougher than Wyren's own. It came to a point between multijointed, wire sculpture legs that mimicked her left hand.

He could see the square *through* her. No wonder she had been so formidable. "Now see what I would not be, except for you. What reactions do you suppose Terran husbands and sons and daughters have when they see me? What else have you lost?"

He snarled. "What would a wife know about it? Never to give birth. Never to raise the children of your body?"

She just stared at him for a minute. Then she laughed, a laugh that was almost a sob. "You don't know?"

Wrath bubbled beneath his mind, almost enough to make him kill her. Know *what*?

"You really don't. I can see it in your face." Her face softened. "I just assumed you knew that on Terra, it is the female that bears children."

He felt as if she'd struck him again with one of her synthetic limbs. Females bearing children? Impossible. Disgusting. Rumors drifted back to him from wartime. He'd always thought that they were just propaganda.

For the second time that night, the uneasy sensation that he was losing to her—or should it be *him*?—crept over him. Scorn crept into his voice.

"I thought you Terrans were technological gods. I thought you could grow duplicates of yourselves. Carve your bodies as desired."

She nodded, brokenly. "Some can. If they have the money. Terra doesn't allow soldiers to clone. We aren't wanted."

Unwillingly, Wyren found himself nodding. "Neither are we."

Phun gestured to the statue. "But you are respected."

A hollow laugh boomed out of him. "That warrior is dead. Mtaein wants dead heroes. Not live warriors."

Now it was she who nodded. "Terra does not want even that."

Wyren shook his head. Impossible. "Terra is an Empire..."

"A dying Empire," she said softly. "Do you really think the Mtaeinin could have kicked us off this world at the height of our power? You saw what we know. What we can do. *No one* wants a Terran soldier. Terra least of all. That's why… that's why I loved this place so much."

Anger shot through him; his head whipped up. "Loved it so much that you came to help enslave it?"

"Loved it enough that I learned the language. Learned the people." She lowered her voice. "Do you think I learned enough to track a trained warrior who didn't want to be seen through the Seratan streets by *hating* this city? Do you think I survived three years of forest patrol by not knowing everything about it?"

"Using it against us." He tried to snarl the words. But the earnestness in her words pulled at him.

"Don't tell me you don't understand the difference between love and duty. Or do you really love Mtaein more than you love your wife?"

Wyren closed his eyes in acknowledgment, and then met hers. He saw her youth. It was like Jionha's face, before the Change. And he saw that he had lost this challenge.

She had known his losses better than he had known himself. And he had not known hers at all. He had agreed to kill her. And now he did not want to.

"Fulfill your promise," she said. She was shaking now, and her eyes grew pools of liquid.

He nodded heavily. "Where would you die?"

She looked puzzled. "Where?"

"A warrior, when he chooses, dies so that he may take his last view with him into the dark."

She nodded, face a mask. "I thank you." She looked upward, considering. "The Narrow Bridge."

Wyren started to speak, then stopped. He was actually embarrassed. "The bridge is… there is no more bridge. Except along the banks. When we... when the governor's palace was destroyed..."

"You destroyed the bridge?" Her voice showed more emotion for the bridge than she had for anything that had happened to either of them, but she contained it quickly. "Fitting. Take me to where it was."

They walked, the ceramium and chitin of their feet clacking against the hard road. The streets were empty. Wyren felt rather than saw her, by his side. She spoke, and her words pulled him out of his reverie. "Tell me of yourself, Wyren-*nje*. Tell me your story."

He nearly stumbled. "It is you who should tell your story," he said, "that you may be remembered after your passing."

"I do not wish to be remembered," said Phun. "I am the victor, and I would have your story... to take with me into the dark."

Had her voice broken, there? But she was correct, and he began to speak. Of his childhood outside Serata. Of his friendship with Varq and with Jionha. Of his marriage. Of the Change and what had happened after. "The rest you know."

She said nothing. They turned the corner, and the smell of the river greeted them, wafting up the Hundred Stairs that led down to the Narrow Bridge. Or what was left of it.

"There's nothing left," he heard her say. She was not talking about the bridge. It looked strange even to his eyes, the flat surface of the Kma River, unbroken by the governor's palace.

"On leave nights," she said, "I used to stand on the bridge, in the middle, with the palace behind me."

Glorying in its power; the power of your hegemony, the Revolution-conditioned segment of Wyren's brain responded, but he knew now he was wrong.

There was no middle of the bridge now; when the Imperial Palace had been destroyed, no one had realized what the hydrostatic shock would do to the Narrow Bridge. The bridge had been there forever, a wonder of the world, a thousand years older than Terran occupation. A mile of carved stone, barely wide enough for two to pass. The Imperial Palace had been built in the middle of the river specifically for the view of the bridge from it. The broken tongues of stone leading out into the water were now called Terra's Revenge.

She led him down the stairs and out onto the river. Out to the point where the bridge ended. She stopped, and inclined her head as if in prayer, then turned.

"Fulfill your promise," she said, her voice unsteady.

He would give her a good death. "Where should I strike to kill a Terran warrior?"

"Here," her hand touched the hollow of her throat, where it joined her chest. He drew back a fist, wrist-spike angled for a single thrust.

He moved.

A grip of metal wrenched him to the side, and the follow-through left him nose to nose with Phun, her eyes round with shock, her left hand entangling his wrist-spikes. He looked the question at her.

"Conditioning," she managed, shuddering. "The way they train us. Again. Please." She composed herself with an effort. He nodded and steeled himself, drew back.

He moved.

Again he was knocked aside, nearly off-balance. Her breathing rang loud over the lapping of water. He looked into her liquid, Terran eyes.

"Please," she begged.

"No," he said. "I agreed to kill. Not to murder. You do not want to die. You merely have no courage to live. You are no warrior." He watched her turn white.

"Neither are you," she said.

"You dare speak for me?" He raised his fist again.

"Does a warrior run off, leaving his wife... his only wife... to face life without him while he cowers in death?"

"Without me, Jionha could remarry, could find another family, with a real husband..."

"Liar."

Wyren roared and swung; Phun danced back, nearly on the edge of the bridge. "Do you really think anyone would take her as she is now? Even I know Mtaenin better than that."

"Jionha is beautiful, was always beautiful, even..."

"To anyone but you?"

He swung again, but her legs carried her over the blow, up onto the narrow rim of the bridge. "And she is beautiful to you, isn't she?"

"Always." *The memory of her still staggers me. As she is, she yet could bear me to the ground with a look.*

"But you cannot suppose that you are beautiful to her?"

He lowered the horned, callused fist that was poised to strike her. "No."

"Then by your own admission, Wyren-jionhae, you are less of a warrior than I am," Phun said softly, squatting on the handrail of the bridge. "You are afraid, not to live, but to be loved."

"I am not worthy..." he said.

"Dammit, man, none of us are!" she shouted. "You think the ones who took no risk, who live soft in this independent Mtaein you and Jionha bled out your futures to create, you think they're worthy of the love denied you? Of the honor? We're soldiers, we know the truth. The only worthy are the ones who never came back!" The words rang against the stone like whip-cracks.

"She makes you worthy." Phun looked deep into his eyes. "I know I've never met her but the way you talk about her... I know how she must love you. She makes you worthy of your name, Wyren-jionhae.

Don't throw that away."

Stepping down from the rail, she walked to the stairs. "Go home, warrior. Go home to your wife."

Wyren's head spun. *She makes you worthy*, the Terran had said. And suddenly, everything changed. All Jionha's anger, her hurt, her distance. Not her choice. It had been his. And Phun had seen it. It was like looking through a lens, he thought. Hold it far enough away and you see things as they really are… upside down from the way you've always seen it.

He looked up. "Phun…" But she was gone. He stood. He stretched. He smelled the air. He followed.

∞

When he crushed the doorknob in his grip and entered the cheap hotel room he found the lights on and the room empty.

"God, we've both gotten old," her voice came from behind him. "I leave a trail that a Mtaeinin warrior can follow and you just… walk into the room of an Imperial commando. I almost introduced you to the fourth state of matter." Behind him, she was holstering her plasma carbine.

"You gave me back my life," he said.

She staggered, then recovered. "It was always yours. Just like this world was, I suppose. Why are you here?"

"You said the only worthy are the ones who never came back."

She lowered her eyes. "Yes."

"What about you?"

"What about me, Wyren?"

"You never came back. And you said you never can. You are worthy. Of love. Of honor."

She looked up at him. "Thank you, Wyren. That means a lot."

"I would make you worthy."

Phun's eyes narrowed. "What?"

"You said Jionha makes me worthy. But you have no wife... I am sorry... no husband. I would make you worthy. Here, since you cannot go back home. I want you to meet Jionha, and I want her to meet you. We three... have much to talk about. My friend." He extended his hand, spikes pulled back, four fingers spread in the greeting of equals. Somehow, the hand seemed less frightening. Smaller.

She looked at him, hand reflexively meeting his fingertips, and her face was unexpectedly young in the light reflected from the river. "Here? With your... family?"

He nodded.

"I will go with you," she said. Her eyes seemed bigger now. Full of water like ponds.

They walked from the room; Phun seemed in a trance. There was much to say. But not yet, Wyren sensed. Now there was the walk home in the night. Tomorrow would be for Jionha and Phun and himself. And perhaps, if immigration could be arranged... yes. Varq would give him that. That much could be done.

It would be a strange family, if it happened at all, he knew. But it would be more than they could have dreamed of, before. And perhaps, with love, it would be enough.

About the Author
G. Scott Huggins

G. Scott Huggins grew up in the American Midwest and has lived there all his life, except for interludes in the European Midwest (Germany) and the Asian Midwest (Russia). He is currently responsible for securing America's future by teaching its past to high school students, many of whom learn things before going to college. His preferred method of teaching and examination is strategic warfare. He loves to read high fantasy, space opera, and parodies of the same. He has a column in the magazine *Sci Phi Journal*. He wants to be a hybrid of G.K. Chesterton and Terry Pratchett when he counteracts the effects of having grown up. When he is not teaching or writing, he devotes himself to his wife, their children, and cats. He loves bourbon, bacon, and pie, and will gladly put his writing talents to use reviewing samples of any recipe featuring one or more of them.

Author Website: https://scotthuggins.wordpress.com/

Across an Aeon
by Abby Goldsmith

"I need to learn what's over the horizon."
 —note left by Dana Thuan

The last time Holly had seen her husband was on security camera footage. He'd glanced up at the camera, as if to wish watchers a silent farewell, with his usual three loose strands of black hair brushing his glasses. Then he'd stepped into the Aeon Hyperbolic Chamber.

He had never reemerged.

Quoc had always been eager to leave. After more than two decades of marriage, Holly never quite got used to spending so many evenings alone. She never fell in love with work the way her husband and daughter had. Perhaps all great scientists were married more to their work than to their spouses, more enamored with science than with family.

"Why do you want to see it?" Sheila touched Holly's shoulder with concern.

The Aeon Hyperbolic Chamber didn't need Danger signs or razor wire to warn visitors to keep away. It hunkered in the brick basement of the Baltimore National Laboratory like a medieval torture device. The silence seemed thicker than the stuffy air, thicker than the dust that coated the control panels and computers. Nothing in this lab had been turned on in eight years. Not since the malfunction, or wrong function, or whatever it had been.

Holly descended the metal staircase towards the dusty main floor. The machine resembled a cryogenic coffin from a science fiction film, semitransparent enough to see that no one was inside. All three people who had vanished should have reemerged: her daughter, a lab technician, and her husband.

"I'd rather you not get any closer," Sheila said, clomping down the stairs after her. "I haven't been down here in years. No one has."

Holly studied the machine that had swallowed her daughter and her husband. Her family. Her reason for living.

"I'm sorry." Sheila sounded apologetic. "If I could have stopped them, I swear, I would have."

Holly stepped over the cordon rope. Unwrapping the power cords she'd smuggled inside her purse, she began plugging in machines and jabbing power buttons. Equipment hummed to life. The acrid odor of burning dust filled the air.

"Hey!" Sheila must feel betrayed. They were close friends, but it had taken years for Holly to persuade Sheila to cave in, to use her top-level clearance badge to sneak them both into the sealed basement room where her family had vanished.

"I'm sorry." Holly said, although she continued to tap a keyboard, entering command codes. She'd practiced typing the codes until they were muscle memory. All of her dearest friends would receive her farewell within a few hours. She'd scheduled the email deliveries, including a heartfelt apology to Sheila.

Tears shone in Sheila's gray eyes. "You can't do this." Since she was large, it was easy for her to shove Holly aside and try to cancel the sequence. The way she pounded the keyboard showed her rising panic. Everyone who had worked on the cancelled Aeon Project had moved on, including Sheila, and eight years was enough time to erase old command codes from casual memory.

Holly opened the curved slider-door to the chamber and squeezed inside. It was like wriggling into a tight dress. The interior tube was so narrow, she couldn't bend her arms. Her slender husband and daughter each would have fit inside, but an overweight person such as Sheila never would.

"I can't stop it." Sheila's voice cracked in anguish. "Holly, we don't know where Quoc and Dana went. No one knows if they survived. Okay? Just come out of there! I don't want you to die!"

Holly wished Sheila would listen to her own words. *No one knows.* That meant the vanished scientists could be alive. Her physicist daughter, Dana, might be waiting in some futuristic utopia. Maybe Quoc was waiting, too. They used to enjoy quiet mornings together, watching songbirds and chipmunks frolic in the backyard garden. After so many years apart, Quoc must miss his wife.

She slid the tube closed. How many times had she watched her husband step into this machine—exactly as she was doing now—and reemerge a second later with a smile? The world had watched. News media had touted his invention as "the biggest breakthrough since electricity."

Quoc had explained to awestruck news crews that it was a time machine. "Visiting the past is impossible," he'd said, "but gravitational flux makes time dilation feasible. We induce gravitational flux with a hyperbolic metamaterial." He'd squeezed into the cylinder. "I vanish from this instant. Watch." Quoc vanished like magic, then flashed back into existence. "I skipped a millisecond. To you, standing outside the tube, I traveled in time."

Despite his eyeglasses and graying temples, Quoc had a boyish grin. Work always gave him that grin. Whenever Holly imagined seeing Quoc again, he'd hold his arms out with that same grin—for her.

For several months, the Aeon Hyperbolic Chamber had worked properly. Any object placed within would vanish and reappear a few milliseconds later. A stream of water, poured from a cup, seemed to stutter and then continue. A candle flame would skip time. The U.S. military talked about possible applications of the technology.

And then Dana vanished.

Greg Noble, her lab technician, tried to figure out what was wrong. He vanished within an hour of Dana's departure.

The next day, Quoc Thuan—inventor of the time machine—followed. The project was cancelled soon after.

Lights flashed across the tube. Time travel was about to commence.

Holly braced herself for a leap that would send her to the future... not milliseconds, but years. Maybe decades. The world had simply failed to wait long enough for Quoc, Dana, and Greg to reappear.

∞

Shapes blurred. Shadows elongated. Time stretched out, until she lost track of her thoughts.

She gradually became aware of her body. Lightweight. Female. The familiar sense of her own proportions comforted her.

She struggled to figure out who she was. Her parents were Korean Americans who owned a furniture business. She lived in Baltimore. Her name was Holly Kang. Everyone knew that.

No, no, no. That was her childhood. Now she was a lab technician. A wife. A mother.

The rest of her identity reassembled in her mind like a chain reaction, establishing her as Mrs. Holly Thuan. She had watched her daughter Dana perform in a high school band. After her family had vanished, news reporters tried to pry into her grief, to make her cry on television.

Her friends were worse than the reporters. All had children or husbands or both. They didn't live in an empty, echoing house. Each friend silently expected Holly to get over her loss. After a few years, their sympathy dried up. A few of them, including Sheila, had suggested that she try dating. As if Quoc was dead. As if eight years proved it.

But they were wrong.

Quoc and Dana must be alive—and now Holly was certain. She had used the unchanged setting of the time machine. This was the future they had traveled to.

She could only guess how many years in the future it was, but the room was empty, and vastly remodeled. Chaotic shades of brown and green splashed everything in sight, like explosive army camouflage. There were six walls instead of four. No upper tier, no computers, no furniture. And no time machine.

Holly was lying on a floor that felt like roughened ice. She stood, wrapping her arms around herself. Her jacket was too thin for this refrigerated air. The absence of machines shouldn't worry her. After all, the National Laboratory had planned to permanently dismantle the time machine, which was why she'd insisted on visiting it as soon as possible. The machine catapulted things into the future, but it did not catapult itself.

Disquiet settled over her as she realized that this room lacked an exit. The air smelled stale. She didn't see any doors, ventilation ducts, or power outlets.

The quality of light was strange, too. It seemed to glow like bioluminescence, pure white rather than fluorescent. Tubes of light snaked along the ceiling.

Something about the design of this empty room… a cerulean blue ceiling, green walls and floor… struck her as a crude mockery of a natural outdoor setting. It seemed a cold welcome. Quoc and Dana should be expecting her. They should have persuaded people in this decade to greet her.

"Hello?" Holly spoke to the empty room. Someone must be listening, or they wouldn't have kept the room empty to receive time travelers. "I'm looking for Quoc Thuan."

She walked to the nearest wall and ran her hand along its rough surface. The glacial chill was painful. Pulling her sleeve over her bare fingers, she continued, and wondered why the walls weren't white with frost.

"Where's Dana?" she asked. "Quoc?"

No cracks, no vents. After one circuit of the room, Holly reminded herself that this was not a tomb. Surely someone would find her here. Surely.

A high, whispery voice, like that of a little girl, broke the silence. "You're late."

Holly spun around. A slender Asian-looking man stood in the far corner, as if he'd just appeared. His limbs were too long. Black clothes hung off his frame like bandages, giving the impression of a scarecrow or dummy. He swayed away from the corner and approached Holly with a loose, marionette-like gait. Strands of hair hung across his forehead.

"Whoa, wait." Holly backed away. "Who are you?"

His pale fingers spread to either side, showing empty hands. "Who are you?" he asked in his whispery girl voice. "Holly. Why are you here?"

Despite the questions, his tone was incurious. He sounded like he was reading from a script.

"I'm…" Holly paused, unwilling to reveal too much to this stranger. What if the time machine had catapulted her beyond a few decades? What if this was a dystopian regime, no longer the United States? She fervently hoped she was overreacting.

"I'm looking for Dana and Quoc Thuan," she said carefully. "Do you know where they are?"

The man swayed to a stop. "I will answer your question every time you answer my question. Is this agreeable?"

"Fine." Holly was in no mood for bargaining. "Where are they?"

"I will take you to Quoc Thuan after this session," the man replied in his girlish voice. "Why do you seek him?"

She shivered in the cold air, unnerved by the man's whispery inflections. "Because he's waiting for me. Is this..." She paced, trying to disguise her unease. "Is this still the United States of America?"

"No." The man smiled. His teeth were uniformly discolored. "Why did you come late?"

The reply hit Holly with the force of a punch. She'd suspected that Dana had altered an algorithm—perhaps on purpose—which changed milliseconds into years. But how many years? The error might be exponential.

"How far in the future have I come?" she asked, wondering if she was a million years beyond her era. "I need to see Dana or Quoc."

"We agreed that I would answer one for every one you answer." The man watched her without any apparent concern. His dark eyes didn't blink enough. "Why did you come late?"

Holly reversed direction, unwilling to take her gaze off him. The question seemed too personal. "It was hard for me to get access to the time machine." She nearly added that she'd been afraid it would kill her, but she didn't want to reveal any fear to this man. Nor would she mention that the machine was supposed to be demolished. He might treat her more kindly if he expected other "late" arrivals.

"Am I a prisoner?" she asked.

"No." His gaze made her think of a surveillance camera. "What do you suppose happened to humans?"

Chills rippled through Holly as she tried to figure out what he meant. "I don't understand."

"We constructed one before this one." The man gestured to himself. "The human you seek, Quoc Thuan, suggested improvements. This one is better. I seek the same knowledge. My questions are the same. Help me understand why humans are no more."

Realizations exploded in her mind like a series of bombs, one after the other. Humans were extinct or gone. The strange man resembled a composite of her husband and daughter, mixed with Greg Noble. He was false. An android. The woodsy colors of the room were supposed to look natural to a human. It was all a clumsy simulation.

Holly backed against the wall, feeling like a zoo animal. She'd once watched a documentary where condor chicks were raised in habitats made to resemble condor nests, and tended to by puppets made to simulate a mother condor.

"Get me out of here." She pounded the icy wall. "Get me out. How do I get out?"

The false man danced back a few steps with exaggerated care. "It is not my intention to agitate you. Should I come back later?"

"No, no, no!" Holly nearly begged. "You've got to take me to Quoc!"

"I will prepare you to leave, but we must be careful so you survive. What do you suppose happened to humans?"

"I don't know!" She wished she could shake answers out of the false man. "Tell me what happened, and how many years in the future I came, and maybe I can figure it out."

He sagged, his expression nonplussed and sleepy. His head tilted too far, as if his neck was boneless, as if he was a lifeless corpse.

As Holly tried to figure out what to do next, she saw a ripple of movement in the corner of her vision. The wall began to bulge and stretch. Painted concrete distorted, blown up like a balloon.

She backed away as an enormous alien mass broke through the wall. Black wires trailed from a shiny skull-like head. The whale-sized body was webbed by blue veins and covered with mucus. More and more alien mass oozed into the room, sliding in a pool of slime.

"This is me," the whispery voice said. The source of the voice came from the alien's skull. "The construct cannot travel. It was designed for greeting. I can still speak with you like this."

Holly backed away, certain the alien would roll over her. She'd be crushed by its weight, suffocated by its mucus.

Then she remembered how suddenly the false man had appeared. Anything might grab her, hurt her, kill her. She checked over her shoulder. No monsters behind her. But the gigantic whale-slug with its shiny skull and black wires continued to slide through the wall. This did not belong in her world.

"I will not harm you," the whispery voice said. "I am brave to come here."

A whine came from Holly's throat. She should have been embarrassed, but all she felt was terror.

"Follow." The massive alien turned. Its shiny head burrowed into the wall, followed by its muscular whale-slug body.

∞

In the world Holly had come from, she could not walk through solid walls. The alien must have technology she could not begin to fathom. When she stretched out her trembling hands, expecting to encounter freezing concrete, her hands encountered a cold liquid instead. A waterfall. Maybe the illusion of a wall had been projected onto it.

She stepped through as quickly as possible. It felt like stepping through a torrential downpour. Her clothes were soaked, and her teeth chattered from the cold.

Yet she couldn't help staring in wonder. Bioluminescent coral glowed everywhere, between cascades and pools of water. The huge alien looked comfortable in this watery grotto.

"Pick up the suit on the floor," it said in its singsong voice. "You must wear the suit or you will die."

A plastic wrap floated on the watery scum of the floor. Holly picked it up. When she shook out its folds, it looked like a trash bag, although it had the consistency of tough rubber. She examined it, trying to figure out how it might protect her.

"Put it on," the alien's voice said. "The suit will inflate and protect you."

Holly stepped into the transparent bag. When she pulled it up to her shoulders, the open edges began to cling together. Air hissed into the bag, and as it inflated, the opening knitted together. She ducked her head and fought against claustrophobia. "How do I know I won't suffocate in here?"

The alien's voice was intimately close. "Without the suit, you will die."

"Okay, but…" All questions fled her mind as murky liquid splashed into the grotto. The water level rose in a flash flood. The rubbery bag formed an airtight seal over her head. Her ears popped from the change in pressure.

"We made a habitat for humans," the alien voice said. "I will take you there."

Water surged upward, knocking Holly off her feet in her inflated air bubble. She tumbled within the bubble, carried into a seemingly endless space, spinning until she lost track of direction. Up or down, right or left, might be anywhere.

Something yanked her at high speed in one direction.

I'm safe, I'm safe, Holly repeated in her mind, yet she didn't feel safe. Dirge-like moans sounded in the distance. Slow, gloomy clouds of silt obscured cliffs all around her. Crusty rocks hid multi-hued lights, as distant as skyscraper windows. She floated in an undersea alien city.

The alien appeared to be towing her, bubble and all, through the murky ocean. It pumped ahead like a chubby squid, bioluminescent spots rippling between the wires along its body.

"Is the whole world covered in water?" Holly asked.

"Yes," the alien's voice replied. "Humans made this world best for us. They departed eons ago. Will there be more late arrivals like you?"

Eons ago. Peering at a nearby cliff, Holly realized that it was the bent frame of a ruined skyscraper, bumpy with coral. This had once been

Baltimore. National Laboratory had been in a tree-lined office park, which must have been replaced by a booming downtown. And now? All the trees and cars were gone. Everything was ossified, decayed, and crushed by tons of liquid.

The alien's voice spoke with patience as deep as the ocean. "Will there be more late arrivals like you?"

The first time traveler, Dana Thuan, must have surprised the aliens. They wouldn't have had time to set up an air bubble suit, a greeting room, or a puppet human. Dana would have appeared at the bottom of a cold, dark ocean. Alone. Only twenty-four years old. She must have drowned, thrashing, silvery bubbles rising from her mouth in a death scream.

"Oh no."

"Please explain," the alien's voice said. "Will there be more late arrival humans?"

Holly prayed that no one would be daring enough to follow her. Let Sheila and everyone else stay in the twenty-first century. "Keep your greeting room open," she heard herself say.

Dana must have made a mistake with the algorithm, catapulting herself too far into the future. Holly guessed that she would never see her daughter alive. Greg Noble, the technician who had followed Dana an hour later, had certainly perished as well.

The only other human alive in this era was Quoc Thuan.

∞

She found Quoc sitting amidst an array of machine parts, in a cave with multiple rooms connected by crusty tunnels.

The inflatable bubble had protected her, but water dripped down the walls, forming puddles that she had to step through. Her clothes grew uncomfortably damp.

"Quoc," she said.

He seemed to be building something with machine parts, but when he saw her, he stopped. His gaze was unreadable behind his eyeglasses.

Holly wondered if he curled into a ball whenever he slept now, like her. Did he miss holding her at night? Did he miss their weekend strolls through their gated neighborhood? They were both eight years older than the last time they had seen each other. The only obvious change she noticed in Quoc was more silver in his hair.

He got to his feet, and cleared his throat. "Why did you come here?"

She had been prepared to melt into his embrace. Now she froze. "I came to find you." Maybe he was just concerned for her, but he sounded cold. Perhaps he suspected that she was a puppet. "And Dana," she added, although that was a painful topic, like opening a wound. "I know she's not here. But I came to find her, too."

Quoc approached Holly slowly, studying her as if he expected her to vanish like a mirage.

"I never stopped missing you," Holly told him. "People kept telling me to move on with my life. I went through grief counseling. But I was certain you were still alive. Yearning for me." She searched his face for any hint that would confirm her dearest hopes.

Quoc reached for her, then pulled her close. His skin and hair smelled the same as she remembered, an earthy musk. His body fit against hers in the same cozy way.

Yet something seemed wrong. Before he'd pulled her close, she had glimpsed his face, and it was expressionless. His skin looked as smooth as a rubber mask, like the puppet that had greeted her earlier.

"Quoc?" She pulled back to study him.

He averted his gaze.

That simple gesture of shame—or simulated shame—was enough

to terrify Holly. She backed away fast. "Tell me you're real," she said. "Please say you're real."

"I'm real." He sounded like someone commenting on the weather. "Holly, let's just be silent together for a moment."

He squeezed her hand as she began to protest. With his other hand, he trailed his finger in the air, as if scribbling. Glowing dust appeared wherever his finger moved. *Humans are all around us*, the glittering words read.

Quoc waved his palm. The words vanished. He wrote anew with his finger.

We went nano and quantum. Uploaded to molecules.

Holly examined the skin of his hand, hardly able to believe it. She studied his deep brown eyes… and saw nothing familiar there. He had the detached gaze of a scientist assessing an experiment. The striations in his irises glowed briefly, like miniature lightning. The striations rearranged themselves into a spiral, then returned to normal.

More glittery words appeared in midair, this time without his guiding finger. *Aliens are watching this cave habitat. Do not show a reaction. Quoc never taught the aliens to read and write in English.*

Holly spun around, aware that surveillance cameras might resemble coral, or be hidden within molecules. Ocean aliens must be watching her and Quoc… or her and the thing disguised as her husband. They were like zoo animals. A breeding population.

Glittery words coalesced in front of her. *The Quoc you see is a human-designed biomechanical puppet, operated by many.*

Quoc allowed us to upload his mind to our wireless network of nanobots.

We uploaded Dana and Greg as well.

They are all with us.

Holly pushed her fist into her mouth to prevent a scream. Her husband continued to observe her as if she was a machine part… only now she knew that both her husband and her daughter were dead and alive at the same time. Quoc had lived here for a while, but when quadrillions of nanobot humans offered him a chance to die and be reborn among them, Quoc would have agreed. He lived for scientific advancement. He treated his own life like an experiment. Why live in solitude, at the mercy of alien colonists, when he could move on?

Quoc hadn't been satisfied with a normal life in the suburbs, either. He'd always itched to move on.

Mom. Glitter sparkled in the air. *I am here.*

Now Holly wondered if the Aeon Hyperbolic Chamber had malfunctioned… or if Dana had leaped millenniums ahead just to see the future. Quoc would have done that, too. Only Holly was different. She only wanted to be with her family.

You can be with us. Be with your family.

The advanced humans must have read her thoughts. If they were the size of molecules, then they could fit just about anywhere. Holly imagined a vast network of nanobots monitoring every electrical pulse that fired across her neurons. They would map out patterns and piece together the encodings of language. The mechanics of how such a thing was possible must be staggeringly complex.

Their robotic Quoc Thuan puppet seemed all but flawless. Holly pressed herself into his arms, breathing in his familiar scent. The warmth of his body was realistic. Nanobot humans must be a million times more technologically advanced than the oceanic aliens.

"What's behind those eyes?" she said, hoping. Maybe Quoc was still human in every important way. Did he remember how to trail his fingers lightly along her waist, the way she liked?

He only squeezed her arms gently. Words coalesced in the air, glittering and then breaking apart like cobwebs. *False Quoc is operated by a large team.*

It takes many.

She should have guessed. The human body was a very complex machine. They had mentioned "quantum," which meant the minimum amount of any physical entity involved in an interaction. She assumed that each advanced human was more than the sum of its nanobots. The nanobots must share multiple processes, an aggregate wireless network that supported many individual minds. They no longer existed in one place at a time. They probably overlapped quite a bit, sharing thoughts with each other.

Glittering words appeared before her eyes. *Yes.*

"We knew you'd follow," the false Quoc said. "Mom. Wife." The robot caressed her cheek.

They didn't need to ask Holly to join them. She was so lonely, and they were family. All she wanted was some preparation. "Will it hurt?"

"Never." The false Quoc settled against the rocky wall, inviting her into his arms. She snuggled against him. Without nerves, she supposed the advanced humans never felt any pain.

Correct. The glitter formed a word, then broke apart. Ribbons of glitter skimmed across her skin, exploring every inch of her body more thoroughly than anyone else had ever done. Her nerves began to tingle. The glitter must be crawling into her veins, into her organs, replacing her cells with artificial replicas.

As she lay against the strong chest of her simulated husband, she knew that her life was about to end. A biomechanical robot would replace her human self. A rebirth would happen. The new version of Holly might live forever, able to explore the universe with an approximation of her family, but she would lose many of the things that made her human.

Her nerves began to die. As she lost sensation, she leaned up and kissed Quoc on the lips, even though it wasn't really him. She yearned to feel it.

I am the last human, she realized.

Her hearing and vision began to fade, replaced by a new awareness. Instead of listening to the ambience of water dripping, input filled her at lightning speed. Instead of seeing the shape of her husband in the shadowy cave, vast amounts of dazzling imagery filled her mind. Wireless cloud people were not constrained by the limitations of eyes and ears. They could be everywhere at once. They had no sense of space, no sense of time passing. Instead of touching, they imagined an abstraction of touching.

Quoc and Dana welcomed Holly with minds swifter than buzzing flies, without any need for words or touch. Greg Noble was with them, too.

All four of them were unique among the cloud people. Without genes or blood, the cloud people did not adhere to family units. The four of them remembered what a family was supposed to be. They alone remembered how it felt to touch another human being.

But only Holly mourned the loss. She would mourn for eternity.

About the Author
Abby Goldsmith

When Abby Goldsmith takes a break from animating video-game art, she hurls herself into her sprawling epic sci-fi series of novels. People say she's driven! She lives in Keep Austin Weird, which has just passed the 2 million population mark. Her past is shrouded in mystery, but she is proud to be an alumni of the Odyssey Writing Workshop and Codex Writers Online. Sometimes she shyly mentions a sale to *Escape Pod*, and one to *Fantasy Magazine*. Feedback is always appreciated, and friending is often welcome.

Author Website: http://AbbyGoldsmith.com/

The Irrepressibly Original Daisy Wigmar
by Katie Stevens

Daisy Wigmar was one of a kind. Some people called her eccentric, others called her mad. I called her my best friend. I was lucky. Everyone should have a friend like Daisy. We were a real odd couple. I was tall and overweight, studious and serious-minded; she was like a mutant pixie on speed.

We hadn't been friends at first.

"Good morning class. This is Daisy Wigmar." Miss Beardsmore had a voice like nails down a blackboard and she was always in a temper about something. "Maggie Wilson move your bulk over and make some room for the new girl!" I could feel the blood rushing to my face as the others sniggered behind their hands. Yes, Miss Beardsmore, like everyone else, had only patience for physical perfection and I was far from it with my goofy teeth, lank mousy hair and spare tyre. I resisted the taunts and the nasty remarks pretending they didn't matter. They did, but I was twice the size of the biggest of my classmates so no one dared say anything to my face.

Daisy and I hated each other on sight, I had just turned eight and was as aggressive as a bullmastiff whilst she was still seven with two missing front teeth and a mean streak a mile wide. Of course it didn't help that I was so angry. The previous year, my mother had been forced to make the move to the culturally defunct town of Reading, with its bad architecture and too many cars. She took over as CEO of Agraleagent, the accounting company. She pretended the move was an enormous career boost, but we both knew she would have been pushed if she hadn't leapt first. Something to do with sleeping with half the board, and a few of their spouses.

Daisy was pretty angry too. Her mother also got around quite a bit. So we spent the next two years snapping and bickering, taking it in turns to provoke the other. The teachers tried to keep us apart, but for some reason we didn't seem able to leave each other alone.

It was Mrs. Beeson who brought us together. I watched Daisy disappearing into the waste ground at the back of school. It was drummed into us that this was out of bounds, mainly because the teenage dropouts hung out there to do drugs and have sex. I followed and found her cooing insanely whilst kneeling in front of a large plastic storage box, tipped on its side. I had thought to catch her meeting a boy, my watch was set to take photos. My mother might have been a crappy parent, but I always had the best stuff. The camera on my watch was high resolution with a zoom that could pick up nose hair from five hundred yards. Instead I found her gushing over the scrawniest, mangiest looking cat I had ever seen. It was love at first sight.

I think we took to that damn cat for the simple reason we were both lonely and having something need you was a panacea. She was also completely natural; nothing could be that ugly on purpose. Living in a perfect neighbourhood, going to a perfect school with perfect people, was wearing. After a while you crave for something to be out of place, desperate to find some deficiency. Mrs. Beeson was so full of flaws she was as far from perfection as one could get. She was a mangy ginger with hardly any teeth, most of her claws missing, only one eye and a bent tail. She was beautiful.

I crept away, upon discovering Daisy and her secret, before she could catch me snooping. I suppose that was the turning point in our relationship. I felt a deep kinship, even recognised myself in her and all desire to fight her died. I couldn't forget that butt-ugly cat so I took to visiting it after school, when I knew Daisy went home to her shitty little terrace house off the Oxford Road. There's always a good side and a bad side of town. Despite every advance we make as humans, we always want to tread someone down in the dirt beneath us and bitch about someone else who's doing better.

When I turned ten, my mother decided she could no longer live with the embarrassment that was her unsightly daughter. She wanted to put me through cryolypsis, pinnaplasty, rhinoplasty and complete orthodontics. Basically she wanted a new daughter, so we fought. The advantage of a work-obsessed power mother is that we rarely actually met face-to-face. A fight conducted via video phone is an easy fight to storm away from. I found myself at the waste ground, seeking out the company of that cranky cat again.

"What the hell do you want?" Daisy was small and slight, I probably only had to sneeze to knock her off her feet, but she was fierce. Ordinarily I would have matched her angry tone with my own, albeit hollow in its actual bravery. That night, I couldn't manage to hide my hurt and answered with a gut wrenching sob. I hung my head with humiliation awaiting a cutting remark that would sink me deeper into my misery. She didn't say anything, instead she gathered up Mrs. Beeson and thrust her at me. I cried into the cat's stinky fur, ignoring her claws sinking into my flesh until she began to draw blood.

"Want to talk about it?" Daisy asked gruffly.

"My mother is the world's biggest bitch."

"Can't be," Daisy said as we settled ourselves onto her scraggy rug in the dark. "My mum claimed that title all ready."

Our accord was tentative at first; it was the cat's name that cracked it: Mrs. Beeson. We'd both named her that. The coincidence was amazing, we'd both named her after our headteacher. Mrs. Beeson, the human, was almost reptilian in looks, but she gave an impression of strength, like she would probably survive a nuclear holocaust. We both wanted to give the cat a strong name.

We started to hang out. My mother hated it; she knew of Daisy's mother, through gossip with other mums at school. They were both lone parents, so you'd think they could bond over that, women sticking together or something. Anyway, Daisy's mother worked as a singer in low-end clubs and as a hostess at the casino. The more my mother protested, the harder I clung to Daisy.

When Daisy's mother was approaching her fifties, she was worried she was starting to look past it, so she had her skin genetically enhanced to prevent it from ageing further; that was just the start. She became obsessed, having bits and pieces of her body mutated, killed off or revamped. She was so smug about it. At fifty-seven she looked like she was in her twenties, as if she were the same age as us. Daisy hated it, said the side effects were hardly worth it. She complained her mother was just pandering to the unreasonable demands by society that we all look perfect forever, that ageing was to be feared and reviled. Her mother said Daisy needed to get in the real world; it was fine to be smug in your twenties but once gravity caught up she would be laughing on the other side of her face. It wasn't a secret that the elderly, who were too poor to support themselves, were often put to sleep rather than taking up space in hospitals.

My mother was scathing about her use of genetic technology. She always made bitchy comments about the size of her breasts or that she obviously had cheap DNA by the orange tone of her skin; you know how women can be. My mother was such a hypocrite. I was the result of a drunken fling when she was high on the career ladder. She decided it was her only chance for a kid. However, she was not one for compromise, so I did all the compromising in the relationship. Top of her list was career.

My mother took her own steps to defy the ageing process, although hers were far more exclusive. She had a whole troupe of clones housed in a medical facility not far from where we lived, all alive to serve her purpose. They lived a life according to a strict regime to keep them in perfect health. They were at different ages to meet her varying require-ments. Once they reached forty, they were put to sleep and a new one was made from a batch of Mom's ovaries they kept in deep freeze. One time she wasn't happy with the size of her ears, so she looked through her clones, chose the pair which were the size she required and had them removed from the clone and transplanted onto her. Of course, it wasn't like it was in the early days of transplantation when the body might reject a body part. This was already part of her, so she continued without further thought about the implications of her actions. Another time, she disliked the wrinkles on her forehead, so she had skin cut out from a child clone of hers to replace it.

I could hardly bare to look at her knowing that any part I might look at was the result of someone else's suffering just to suit her vanity. What was the point of being the CEO of a Fortune 500 company if you had no power to change its attitudes? Why couldn't she stand up and say that it was all right to grow old? The irony is that with every new medical advance, life expectancy is slowly getting shorter.

Anyway, Daisy and I were odd balls, on our own in our disgust for this manipulation of our bodies in an attempt to preserve youth indef-initely. We rejected the ideal that placed the aesthetic as the highest prize of all. I was lonely living with a workaholic mother. Daisy was lonely with a mother who worked kid-unfriendly hours and frequently brought men home for the night. So we clung together through school, college and finally out in the big bad world of adulthood.

∞

We were both eager to leave Reading behind and travelled to Bristol for college. Daisy didn't have enough focus to get into university and I was quite happy to pretend I hadn't made the cut either. I had found out years before that as long as I had Daisy, I had home and security and that was enough. So it was Bristol City College of Higher Education for us.

Bristol was a revelation. It was fun, cultural and alternative. Daisy loved the art and I loved the history. She would drag me to day-long showings of silent films at the Arnolfini on the waterfront and I would take her to the M Museum and the dry docks for the ancient steam ships. We both loved all the open green spaces and visiting St. Nicholas Market where we ate lunch and flipped through the vinyl at the record stall.

When our studies were over, I worked as a solicitor in a small firm dealing with commercial property conveyancing. I worked regular hours and had a nice house. Daisy was a performance artist; she rented a room from me, although she only ever paid me rent twice. I did the cooking and cleaning because, to be honest, if I'd left it to her we would have only eaten every other day and the house would have been no better than a flee pit. Instead, her sole task was to take care of Rachel Carson our rescue dog.

After Mrs. Beeson died, we didn't get another pet for a long time. A childhood of being ignored makes you want to be needed, loved, and cherished. Mrs. Beeson gave us that in bucketloads despite being the most aloof and bad-tempered cat I had ever met. We went through college without an animal, both declaring that we didn't want any responsibility weighing us down. One night, near graduation, we both got drunk on vodka and peach schnapps.

"I miss Mrs. Beeson," Daisy said mournfully.

"I take it you mean the cat." Daisy glared at me, her eyes filled with tears.

"I want to get another one." I handed her a hanky whilst I gulped down my own tears of relief.

"Me too."

We'd finished our drinks in celebration before passing out cold on the sticky floor of the common room.

So once college was done, I put a down payment on a house and the next day we began our search for the perfect pet. It was soulless, the pet shops lined up animal after animal in little containers. All cute, don't get me wrong, but so screwed up with modifications they were completely undesirable as far as Daisy and I were concerned. There were dogs that didn't shed their hair and didn't drool, barkless, scentless and shitless. The cats weren't much better: homing cats that came when you pressed a button on a homing device, cats that didn't hunt and there were even ones that were claw-free. I haven't even begun to go into the FluroPets range, which quite frankly turned my stomach. It was too much indignity for either of us to tolerate. I mean, manipulating the genes of a sentient being so it glowed a different fluorescent colour according the chemical reactions taking place in its body is completely objectionable. What creature wants to light up like a neon sign when it needs a shit?

We were feeling dejected, hopeless and despairing when Rachel Carson found us. She came to our back door one day, in need of us as much as we were of her. She wasn't a designed, sanitized and manipulated version of what a dog might be, she was the real thing: stinking, hairy and inconveniently, slobberingly real. She would fart when she climbed the stairs, each staccato sound punctuating her steps. Her claws would scrape along my perfectly laid pine laminate and she'd leave trails of doggy dribble and snot smeared across the long glass doors of the dining room. She snored at night, as a consequence of which she could only sleep in Daisy's room; Daisy slept like the dead and only an atomic bomb would have a chance of waking her. It was her smell we delighted in the most. In a time when you could buy every procedure and every product under the sun to annihilate every natural smell in existence, no one had got their hands on Rachel Carson; no gland removal, no cell modification and no hormone therapy. She smelled one hundred percent genuine and disgustingly doglike.

It wasn't just animals that were treated to the complete and utter denaturalization of themselves. We humans fell foul of it too. It wasn't only ageing that had everyone running scared. No, despite predictions to the contrary, the human population has become whiter. Once the technique for the neutralisation of emelanin became a standard cosmetic procedure it signed the death warrant for cultural diversity. Of course, there are pockets of communities here and there where people are too poor or too defiant to debase their cultural and racial heritage, but they are few and far between. Racial stereotypes have become more negative as a response and the threat of melanoma has increased exponentially.

Most people these days don't need to bother with such an invasive procedure. Now foetuses are hooked up to computers which can identify DNA and amend it with a simple piece of software. As Daisy discovered when she viewed her medical records. She suffered heat stroke when we took a holiday to Maliga to celebrate the finish of college. It turned out that her mother had her pheomelanin enhanced and all eumelanin erased, her hair switched to blond and her eye colour to blue. The ability to so freely switch genes on and off meant it was impossible to know what Daisy would really have been like had nature been allowed to take its course. Well, that and the fact that her mother had no idea who Daisy's father was. Daisy made it her mission from that moment on to claim African heritage and spent her first years out of college working and dressing only in black.

I on the other hand was completely natural. In the firm where I worked all the women were like clones. They dressed in sharp dark suits, with big breasts and small waists, perfectly straight platinum blond hair and plump red lips. I think I was only employed because it amused the management and because there is nothing more cohesive for a group than to have someone everyone can hate. I was a bit overweight, extremely tall with large hands and feet and the frizziest brown hair on the planet. I didn't like my hair all that much, but it made me feel rebellious so I let is hang loose and ignored the sniggers around the water cooler. They were going to laugh at me anyway because I certainly did not look good in the tight fitted suits and opted for long flowery skirts and loose-fitting blouses.

Of the two of us, Rachel Carson, named after the scientist and environmentalist, spent the most time with Daisy. I couldn't have had her even if I'd wanted to, not in my kind of work. However, Daisy spent most of her days devising or performing her art, so Rachel Carson would go everywhere with her. Amongst Daisy's art set, Rachel Carson was worshipped for being one of those rare creatures, the genuine article. They held her up as a source of truth, a symbol of everything society fought against. She was praised for her pure, unsullied spirit, for her absolute doggieness. She was the subject of photograph exhibitions, installations, short films and sculptures. Daisy allowed her to be used shamelessly and Rachel loved the attention. Daisy herself used Rachel in every piece of performance art. I didn't mind. Daisy was not in amongst the mainstream and it used to worry me that she used the most sordid, dangerous and seamy parts of the city as her backdrop. I hoped that if the day came when Daisy actually put herself in danger, which seemed inevitable, Rachel would be there to protect her.

I got Rachel on the weekends and two evenings a week when Daisy did the only work which paid her anything at a small local bar which was hip and another original. Daisy loved the fact that they grew food on the roof in real soil, which they made from compost. They brewed everything they grew into some type of alcoholic beverage. Most of it was totally unpalatable, but there wasn't anything artificial about it. On the weekends they hosted The Sizzling Sidekicks who played music on handmade instruments made out of rubbish. As I said, it was original.

That was our life. After an unhappy childhood I enjoyed the little world we had created, where we only sought to please ourselves and each other. Like all good things it was fleeting, a moment of transience which burned bold and beautifully bright. Then it was gone, wiped away in an instant and things would never be the same again. I remember the moment, the very second my world changed forever. It was two fifty-five and seventeen seconds. Daisy called. She liked to call me at work at odd points through the day to share small observations. She wasn't the type of person to hold anything in, it all flowed out of her, every thought running through her mind like water in a brook, babbling and rushing along towards its release. She was incapable of censoring anything that went through her brain and I, more than most, heard it all.

"Hi, Maggie," Daisy's singsong voice called down the phone.

"Hi, Daisy. What's up?" I was furiously typing on my computer, fighting not to lose my train of concentration on the conveyancing report I was drawing together.

"Rachel Carson and I are going to be late home tonight." I could hear the traffic in the background. All the advances technology had made, but nothing had reduced the traffic, the congestion which blocked up the centre, which Daisy loved and I hated. I shuddered at the sound of it, glad for the quiet solitude of my little booth situated in the furthermost corner of the office floor.

"No worries, I think I'll stay late and get some work done."

"Isn't that what you're doing now?"

"Well, yes, but I'd really like to get this report done by the end of the day. It's been dragging on and the client's chasing me for it." There was silence on the other end of the phone. "Hello?" It was eerie, I could only hear low-level noise across the line. We didn't use video phones most of the time at work. It was often better if the caller couldn't see you, such as now as I continued to work whilst pretending I was attending to Daisy.

"Hello, Daisy?" She was still quiet. I was about to hang up when I heard a sob on the line. I froze, my heart pounding in my chest. Daisy never cried. I struggled for breath. "Daisy, please, you're scaring me, what's wrong?" I glanced at the clock, one of those crazy ticks I had at times of stress: tidying my hair, throat clearing and checking the time.

Daisy was really crying now, actually, she was wailing hysterically. I could hear there was a commotion nearby. Someone else was weeping, a man's voice shouting, a siren approaching. My gut clenched hard.

"R-Rachel's j-just b-been r-run over." I managed to make it to the rubbish bin before falling to my knees and puking up my lunch.

Most of us rarely experience entirely catastrophic happenings on world shaking proportions. Events like that, fortunately, are few and far between. For most of us it is the little tragedies that can bring the world crashing down about our heads. That's what Rachel Carson's death did for Daisy and me.

∞

"Daisy! Daisy! I'm going to work now, I'll see you later." There was no response from her room. It had been a week since she had come out. I opened the door a fraction and peered through. A waft of stale air greeted me, the room was gloomy and my eyes struggled to adjust. I resisted the urge to throw back the curtains and fling the windows open. I had tried that on day three and it had not gone well for me at all.

This was just like Daisy, thinking only of her pain and how she felt and wallowing in it, whilst I was left shut out and alone. Daisy had tons of friends, I had only one and she was it. So I'd unleashed my anger on her, giving her the rough edge of my own grief and frustration. She had merely pulled the pillow over her head and sunk lower in the bed.

I knew what she was doing. She had been in charge of Rachel that fateful day, but she hadn't been watching her, she'd been on the phone to me. So she was blaming herself and me for Rachel's demise. I tried apologising later, still no response was forthcoming. I had tried doing nothing to no avail and so, suffering through my own grief, I called a few of Daisy's closest friends and asked them to help.

For all the disparaging comments and snide thoughts I might have had about Daisy's friends over the years, they really proved me wrong. They organised themselves to come over in shifts. They took care of Daisy, from cooking meals and coaxing food down her, to just sitting and being there with her. A small breakthrough came when someone suggested we have a memorial for Rachel Carson. Now, don't get me wrong, I loved that dog, but I never confused her for a human and I never got the same satisfaction I got from my friendship to Daisy. However, I was beginning to see that was not the case for Daisy. It was as though she had lost her child.

Although Rachel had been cremated at the vets, we did have her ashes which I had taken on impulse wondering if they might help in some way. Now I was grateful, they became the focal point of the ceremony. Daisy came back to life. Not her usual bright self, but a sober version. However, she threw herself into organising the event. She planned to hold it in Rachel's favourite park in Clifton Village, a beautiful suburb of Bristol, thirty-two acres with a pond and ancient cedar trees. She ordered flowers, put together a program of live music and performance, and hand wrote about a hundred invitations. She was possessed, organising as if her life depended on it. Our roles, unnervingly, reversed. She became the lonely workaholic, spending the days and evenings working out every little detail whilst I met her friends to discuss her and hovered about hoping to get some sort of reassurance that she would be fine in the end and everything would go back to normal.

The day of the memorial ceremony was a beautiful, bright, sunny affair. Daisy had taken steps, of course, to ensure the weather, persuading an old boyfriend to manipulate the cloud pattern with illegal chemicals. He shot them into the air the night before under the guise of fireworks. I wanted to scold Daisy for asking something so risky of someone who was clearly still besotted with her, but it was impossible. She was luminous, all the dull, lifeless pain that characterised her last few weeks had fallen away. The old Daisy was back with a vengeance. She had made herself the most ridiculous outfit: an all-in-one jumpsuit of sunny yellow which was printed from head to toe with images of Rachel Carson. I couldn't speak when I was first confronted with it, the central panel was a "family" photo with us both hugging her as she gave one of her lolling grins, her tongue characteristically hanging over the side of her mouth. My heart caught in my throat as I remembered that afternoon, before disaster struck and life had been so easy. How could one little, mangy dog lead us through such complicated, dark days?

The park was taken over by an impromptu carnival with people dressed in crazy costumes, playing music and dancing. We attracted quite a crowd, the local news turned out as did the police and as you might guess it was left to me to deal with the fallout. I had to convince them that Rachel Carson was a local hero and the local population would deteriorate into the darkest of humours if unable to spend the day in mass catharsis. I showed them evidence of her celebrity in the world of avant-garde art such as photos and film clips, which the police officers looked at with a mixture of incredulity and amusement. I'm not certain whether I actually got the chance to indulge in any kind of emotion or even to enjoy the ton of picnic food kind friends had brought. However, Daisy was happy and I could allow her this day in order for things to return to normal. Then, maybe, we could talk about another dog because I really missed having a four-legged friend in our house.

Daisy laughed and cried, sang and danced all at her usual one hundred percent commitment to life. She drank so much I had to drag her into the house on a sheet, still singing. I left her there, in the hall, too exhausted from endless negotiations with neighbours, police and the Environment Agency. Daisy snored, blissfully unaware that her day had hardly been a breeze for some of us. Whilst she had got stinking drunk, I had got a screaming headache. However, it was done and I looked forward to the future returning to the happy, predictable pattern of the past.

Sadly I was deluding myself. The next day, Daisy stayed in her room, the curtains drawn, the stale air mingling with the smell of sleeping body as she slept through her hangover, slept through work and then on through the night into the next day.

I tried to wake her for breakfast the following day, but she refused to acknowledge I even existed. At my wits end I stormed into her room and lectured her on selfish behaviour, wallowing in self-pity and the frightening rate at which cosmetic genetic transplantation was spreading through mainstream consciousness. My favourite news anchor had candidly opened up about having her own work done in a frank interview in the morning paper. I was disappointed that the possibility of growing old gracefully had been practically obliterated from our national psyche and now it was a matter of discussion as to how one was going to retain eternal youth rather than whether we should. However, that particular complaint on that particular morning was a mistake.

I had thumped the offending article upon the end of Daisy's bed before I turned away in disgust and went to work. I was totally unprepared for the result of my little pep talk on my return home that evening. Daisy was back, more focused than ever. Every available surface of her bedroom and sitting room was covered in papers and magazines. She was having an uncharacteristically friendly discussion with her mother. I could hear them talking about her mother's latest foray into the world of cosmetic mutation. I rolled my eyes to the ceiling instinctively, but Daisy ignored me. In fact she didn't seem to notice that I had entered the room at all, treating me as if I were some invisible being whose existence was of no consequence whatsoever. I felt more than a little hurt by her behaviour and childishly decided that if I wasn't there then I wouldn't be able to make dinner for her.

I slammed doors rather aggressively and clattered around the kitchen with as much drama as I could muster just to make the point that I was there and I was making myself useful, something she had never done since the day I'd met her. It took some time for my strategy to have an effect, but I was rather pleased that it did. Daisy hovered in the doorway quietly watching me with large appealing eyes. She was after something, she only ever lingered near the kitchen when she wanted something from me. It was her way of paying her dues before the favour was granted, by gracing me with her presence whilst I performed some menial task. She completely missed the point that most tasks I performed for me in the house also benefited her, but it would be wasting my breath to point it out and actually most of the time I really didn't mind. She was such a counterpoint to my own sad, anally retentive and slightly compulsive lifestyle, I rather liked her careless, selfish attitude. Don't worry, almost everyone I knew told me I should mind her using me like that, but I could never manage to feel anything but a gentle affection for her and her utter uselessness.

"So I was wondering if I might be able to borrow some money from you." I didn't show any kind of response, after all I had known this was coming. I just continued to chop at the self-peeling carrots.

After a few moments of uncomfortable silence I decided I would let her know that this time I had had enough of her selfish behaviour, because to be quite honest I was reaching the end of my tether.

"I assumed that was the call to your mother. Surely you must have touched her for some?"

"Yes." I threw a glance at her without turning my head as I heated the ready-cooked pasta. What the hell did she want money for that would cause her to be this circumspect in asking for it? Believe me, she normally knew no shame in asking for anything she wanted. "Mum's going to lend me two-thirds of what I need. I wondered if you could lend me the other third."

"What for this time?" I couldn't seem to help being abrupt with her. I had lost all patience with pretence, I had been doing that for weeks as I watched her indulge herself in the most outrageous show of grief over a dog which was just as much part of my family as it had been hers. She could tell I was cross with her because she visibly flinched at my terse words.

I almost cut my hand off when she flung herself at me, hugging me tight as she swore her utter devotion to our friendship over and over. I let her grovel for a while, restraining any comment about her nearly maiming one of us by ignoring the sharp weapon in my hand. I'm almost embarrassed to admit that I liked the sudden flow of fuss and attention I was receiving. The world is a cold and lonely place. Traditional families are a thing of the past, where there is at least one parent around to dote and fuss over their offspring, raising them into loved adults. No, my mother, like so many others, wanted no interruption to her work and social life, and certainly wouldn't contemplate the effects pregnancy would exert over her physically. I was raised in a sterile, GSM plastic womb. Everything about the way I was grown into babyhood and ready for birth and the world was standard. It's ridiculous, who ever met an organic anything that was standard? After birth I was straight into nursery along with forty others.

I know most people think that it is perfectly acceptable for parent and child to have no contact, other than via video for the first six years, I don't happen to agree. I suppose that was what drew me to loud, self-centred, crazy, warmly affectionate Daisy. I wanted a family and she was it. So I put up with a lot because I needed her as much as she needed me.

"I know I've been awful to live with these last few weeks, but I've an idea that will help me finally reconcile myself to losing Rachel, if you could just lend me the money."

"Awful doesn't come close." I kept my face turned away so she couldn't see the rather pathetic tears which had gathered at the feel of her tender embrace. "Try diabolical."

She laughed and the delightful sound filled my senses and sent my heart into a leap of optimism which I had been missing for too long. In that moment I probably would have agreed to anything if it meant I could hold onto that feeling.

"All right. But if it's another dog, we need to discuss it first." I saw the too innocent look in her eyes.

"No, it's nothing like that. I think I'm going to need a little while before we decide to get another, it wouldn't feel respectful to Rachel."

"No, it wouldn't."

I didn't have to wait long to discover what exactly she wanted the money for. So sweetly she had asked for it, her big blue eyes wide with their innocence. It was me who had unwittingly planted the thought in her mind. Where would we be now if I hadn't? I can only say I had been at my wits end, tearing my hair out over the shadow which had once been my vibrant friend, as she frustrated my every attempt to bring her into the light.

She went away for three days saying she wanted to spend a bit of quality time with her mother. That raised my suspicions as nothing else could. Unfortunately it coincided with a minor catastrophe at work, otherwise I might have been able to piece the situation together and stopped her before it was too late.

When Daisy finally came back home I could tell straight away that something was wrong. She was herself but not herself. She greeted me with over-bright eyes and a tremor in her hands which I put down to too much tequila—it wouldn't have been the first time. She excused herself and went straight to bed. She hadn't emerged the next morning by the time I left for work. I didn't think anything of it because it was the usual way of things, but everything had changed.

It wasn't until the next morning that I began to discover the changes wrought over Daisy. She had awoken before me and gone for a run. You might think, *what's the big deal*, but believe me it was monumental. Daisy had not risen much before eleven from the first time we had shared a house and yet here she was jogging. Then she began cleaning. It wasn't out of any sense of being clean and tidy, it was because everywhere she went something smelt and she didn't like the confusing mix of scents so she began to systematically fill the house with smells that she did like. Every time I entered our home I would be greeted by her, spray bottle in hand and she would coat me and my belongings with some concoction she had made.

Her boundless enthusiasm for life intensified and she would often make the most embarrassing displays over her many friends and acquaintances. By the same token she would terrorise any male who came to the door in the most merciless fashion by being aggressively sexual with them. I'll admit that on the face of it, it was amusing. Someone would come to the door and she would put on a show, stripping down to the most fleeting amount of clothing and if they held out because they thought they could handle it, they were soon running away in panic when she would begin to dry hump them as they sat on whichever surface she had flung them onto. Even the most testosterone-filled alpha male didn't last long because she was so aggressive and downright embarrassing they couldn't hold out.

I confronted her about it and she spent a lot of time denying things had changed, but one night I finally prised the truth from her.

"You what?"

"What's wrong with that?"

"You used my money to have yourself genetically modified?"

"I missed Rachel Carson, I wanted to feel her close to me. Now I shall carry her around with me forever."

It turned out she had visited the vet who had treated Rachel Carson that fateful day. It was common practise to hold on to tissue samples of untampered animals. They liked to keep a stock of healthy, natural cells for any animals that had suffered some kind of gross mutation, which with all the genetic tampering some owners put their poor animals through, was more common than you might think. Daisy managed to beg a selection of these off the vet. Then she visited her mother's cosmetic surgery hospital and received what is, even today, rather experimental treatment.

Treatment! Ha! There's a joke. Why would you treat a perfectly healthy person for anything unnecessary and with such invasive technology? Daisy, in conjunction with a "doctor", picked out the most desirable traits of Rachel, the ones which could be readily identified and extracted from her DNA and had them surgically forced into her. What sane person would have characteristics from their dog inserted into them? It was total madness.

I stared at her open mouthed, unable to make sense of a single thought other than the feeling of intense betrayal.

"How could you?" I could feel tears of indignation prickling my eyes. I didn't care that I was coming across as childish or selfish.

"Why not? You might have been able to put aside the death of Rachel so easily. You might have the feelings of a cold fish, but it hurt me deeply. I felt her loss in the deepest part of me and I just couldn't let her go."

At that point I'm ashamed to say I lost it. I remember the feeling of red hot rage as the words "cold fish" echoed through my mind, taunting me. I picked up the first thing that came to hand, an unbreakable bowl, and threw it as hard as I could at Daisy's head. I don't know what I hoped to achieve, some sort of catharsis through violent action, some satisfaction at causing damage, preferably to Daisy. Her eyes suddenly lit up and I saw them gleaming a split second before she leapt into the air and caught the edge of the bowl in her teeth. Oh, yes, she had dog genes. She placed the bowl upon the table next to me where I sat shaking with emotion. She was pleased with herself, almost smug, ignoring the hurt which was radiating from me. That moment heralded the decline of our relationship.

I found it hard to reconcile myself to her new state. She had always been even more fervent than me in her distaste for human beings' casual modification of nature. She treated it as if it was some kind of sacrilegious act. You might even say it had bordered on the obsessive. It had been the prime focus for her art, which never sold well because she was in an incredible minority in her distaste. Now, with her new found delight in her human-doggy genetic makeup, this aversion was removed by default and her art became focused on the joys of living in a doggy world. It brought her enormous commercial success. The critics called her 'barking mad,' but people flocked to buy her work. She was prolific in her output, designing cards and prints, original sketches and great sweeping canvasses under the title "A Dog's Eye View."

Daisy was still Daisy in some part. She still lived like a slob, expected me to cook for her, constantly needed to borrow money despite her new wealth. People still filled the house all day, more so now, but they weren't her cutesy art types: they were hangers on who hoped to receive crumbs from the table of success, they were scientists who wanted to study the unique experiment that Daisy had unwittingly made herself, and they were the sad and pathetic who treated her as some kind of god who might reveal the meaning of life and rescue them from their own pitiful lives. She loved the fawning and the mock adoration with her ego constantly stroked and petted. It made me sick.

It only got worse, the effects of Daisy's rash decision. She would gobble up her meals at lightning speed and then sit through the rest of it in silence, watching me with large eyes fixed, unblinking, upon my fork as it rose and fell from my mouth. I experimented on more than one occasion with moving the fork in random places, high above my head, far to the side and wherever it went so did that unblinking, hungry stare. She would stay out all night and then come home and sleep all day on my bed. She had always been quite free and easy in her attitude towards sex, but now she was positively promiscuous, the legion of lovers or would-be lovers constantly hanging around or calling on the phone. Many times I was left comforting some poor loser she'd left high and dry after a night of passion.

It was exhausting. I was no longer part of a family, I was part of a circus and I knew with a deep sense of self-preservation that it was time to get out. So I did the only thing I could do. I put the house up for sale and moved out. To give her credit she realised straight away. It was a strain but I managed to avoid her, even when she came calling for me at work. In the end, she bought the house.

I bought a flat, an hour outside of the city, as far from her as I could. I had managed to live my life, until that point, avoiding any deep and challenging relationships. She was the only one with whom I had allowed myself to have any kind of adult, functioning association that contained emotional depth and need. I had been betrayed once as a child by my mother, it had coloured my attitude to everyone since. It was only different with Daisy, but she had perpetrated the worst kind of betrayal as far as I could see. So I hid away from the world and from her.

∞

It was a year later when I heard of her again. Some colleagues at work were sharing videos of crazy television moments. There was a small office party for one of the partner's birthday. I was sat at my little booth, keeping myself to myself as was the usual custom in any type of situation, whilst the rest of the office floor were gathered in small groups laughing and joking together, eating cake and drinking wine out of plastic cups. I heard her voice and I swear my heart stopped beating for a full five seconds. It was her, I knew because I still heard her voice in my dreams, still ran to pick up the phone when it rang hoping, only of course it was never her; why would it be? I had made it abundantly clear that I didn't want her and she had done the same showing me that she didn't need me. Funny really, brought together over a cat, torn apart by a dog. Give me the cat any day.

There was crazy, shrieking laughter which made me cringe and set my teeth on edge. I gave up any pretence of doing anything other than eavesdropping intently on the conversation surrounding the source of Daisy's voice. It turned out that she had somehow become the victim of some trashy reality TV program that was streaming on the internet. It was for people who had undergone extreme genetic modification. I immediately searched the web and found her quickly enough. She was everywhere, video clips, interviews, articles and endless photos of her. Her hair had turned white, the same bright colour of Rachel Carson's coat. She had lost weight, not in a scrawny, emaciated way, but she looked lean, solid, something one would never have described her of being before. I watched an interview where her behaviour could only be described as distracted and erratic. She didn't seem at all aware that her interviewer was laughing at her, making a whole string of jokes at her expense. She just sat there, eyes bright, watchful, tense as if she might leap from her seat at any moment to chase something.

The experience of seeing her again aroused such a conflicted response within me that I was left feeling profoundly unsettled. It was such a delight to see her, she was so familiar to me, like looking in a mirror. On the other hand, the pain and longing was so intense I couldn't eat or sleep. I couldn't work, my mind refused to focus. All those people who worked on my floor, who shared the same breathing space, had used her as a figure of fun and somehow that upset me more than anything and I could hardly bring myself to exit the lift in the mornings as the hostility flowed through me; it was overwhelming. The worst of it was I didn't know what to do with any of it. This was her doing, her choice, her bed, so she could lie in it.

I was saved from making a decision. Lucky really, under the circumstances; I made Hamlet look like the prince of decision and pro-activity. It was a weekend, late afternoon and I had spent the day in my pyjamas, not having anything or anyone to get dressed for. There was a knock on my door and as always, even after all this time, my heart picked up hoping that it might be Daisy. It wasn't, of course. Instead it was my mother. The same mother who had cast me off as an unwanted accoutrement to her life, in favour of singledom and her high-powered career.

She looked like my younger sister and after the shock of seeing her had worn off, I began to laugh. She watched me through slitted, irritated eyes, as I held my sides and fell about in hysteria. I suppose I just didn't know how to react and with everything that I had been feeling lately, it had to be released through maniacal laughter. She loomed over me despite the fact she was almost a half-foot shorter. I looked her over and the urge to fall into humour abruptly died. I sniffed and wiped my eyes on my sleeve, ignoring the delicately embroidered hanky she held out towards me.

"Not the response I was expecting."

I cleared my throat and wiped my sweaty palms down my pyjama trousers.

"Oh? What were you expecting exactly?"

She shrugged as she allowed her eyes to sweep over my rather plain and shabby flat. I could see the disdain in the way her mouth tightened and quirked to the side; she shrank into herself an infinitesimal amount as if she were afraid of catching something should she absorb too much of my foetid air. I was riled by her attitude. I can remember that look from my earliest moments, as if there was something about me which caused her endless disdain, that it pained her to have to acknowledge the association between us. I was angry that after all these years she had decided to inflict herself upon me, where was my say to having her come and barge in on me like this? I was furious that she had chosen to come now, when I was struggling to make sense of myself. Here she was, sneering at me in judgement from the second I had drawn breath.

"Still have the most extraordinary manners, I see." She stood there assessing my curtains, upholstery on the sofas and their positioning, and how clean the windows were. I launched myself to standing, tutting in annoyance that it would still bother me and I could feel myself reverting back into the guise of a disgruntled teenager.

"Where's Daisy?" She tried to make it sound casual, but it wasn't, far from it. I saw it all, her holding her breath, the tension in her fingers as they clutched at the seam of her trousers, her eyes sparking in anticipation. I took a savage delight in knocking her down.

"Didn't you know? We don't live together any more. Tea?" I couldn't deny the nasty grin that stretched my lips as she slowly deflated.

"You still keep in touch though, don't you?"

"I haven't seen or spoken to her in over a year." I couldn't help sticking the knife in. "I don't have any plans to either."

She stood there staring out of my grimy windows, inches shorter, contemplating failure. She'd been let go from her Fortune 500 company and so she'd moved into a high-profile media job. She wanted access to Daisy and presumed I would get it for her. It was the first time I felt glad for what had happened. It wasn't a nice feeling, fortunately it didn't last and after a hastily concluded visit, I discovered my regret over what had happened was deeper and sharper than ever.

It was another week before I decided that I couldn't continue without at least attempting some kind of reconciliation. Daisy was my family, I had chosen her, she had chosen me and we had stuck together. Wasn't I the most offending party in this sorry situation? Daisy had made a decision about her life and her body and instead of accepting it, I had judged her and found her wanting.

She was still living at the house. The small front garden was filled with rubbish, the grass wild and overgrown; the little rosemary bush planted beneath the window had grown into something huge and invasive. All the curtains had been pulled even though it was four in the afternoon. I remembered that towards the end, Daisy had taken to sleeping a lot in the day after her varied nocturnal activities. I hesitated to catch her unawares, but at least it would mean that she was actually in the house.

I knocked and then anxiously chewed on my lip for several minutes before someone came to open the door. My first reaction was relief that she hadn't moved someone else in to take my place. My next reaction was joy. She was leaping up and down squealing like a small child, I had never received such a gleeful welcome in my life. I wanted to hug her, but I resisted.

"I knew you'd come back, I knew it. You were gone so long but I knew if I waited you'd return." She grabbed my hand and dragged me into the house. It was a health hazard: dark and smelly, the floors thick with rubbish. Half eaten food left everywhere you turned in various stages of decay. I had to hold my sleeve to my nose to try and block out the smell.

"Daisy, what is this?"

"You're here, everything will be all right again." What could I do? Being so obviously needed was a seduction and she played it to the hilt until I was so blinded by the power of her desire to have me back, I was ready to move in there and then.

∞

A month later I had moved back, cleaned the house so that I could stand anywhere without gagging, and learned to accept Daisy and all her new and ever growing list of doggy foibles. It was the happiest I had ever been. After living in exile for all those months, to find myself home, where I belonged, was as close to ecstasy I would ever come in my life. However, my joy was as ephemeral as the setting sun, and soon it was to be followed by darkness.

Daisy developed a whole catalogue of health problems, no doubt brought on by the genetic modification process, although I had a gagging order slapped on me to stop me from saying so. She developed arthritis at the age of thirty-two and lung disease six months later. At the age of just thirty-four, practically crippled, she was diagnosed with advanced Alzheimer's. She died two months shy of her thirty-fifth birthday of heart failure. They said it was bad luck, bad genes, hard living... I knew they had killed her with their ambitious and experimental technology. They disrupted nature, intervening in a sacred process which they could never hope to fully understand.

There I was, left again, alone in the world. The only family, the only friend I had ever wanted, taken from me by a moment of reckless desperation because she was too selfish to confront her grief and what to all intents and purposes was an inevitable outcome to life.

Her passing was noted. She was hailed as a pioneer and spawned a whole host of copy-cat actions; some from a genuine desire not to lose someone, others from a desperate need to be noticed and adulated as she was. I was hounded for a long time to talk to the world about Daisy. I couldn't, I was too sad and too angry. I never heard from my mother again. I suppose she thought I had lied to her that day she had approached me and was angry. I didn't really care.

It's only now, many years later, that I'm able to look back at that time without the pain and anger which haunted me in the aftermath of her death. I know she cannot have known the full implication of her actions when she expressed her grief so irrevocably, but in so doing, she never spared a thought for one who still lived and was no less loyal than her canine friend. Now I understand that when we see another human to bond with we must do so not only with all their external flaws, those natural and those modified, but we must also do so with all their internal ones. Daisy never once reproached me for my faults and so in accepting her death I must accept her life too and love her the more for it.

I was the sole beneficiary of Daisy's estate. It amounted to a great deal of money. I sold the house and flat, bought a place out in the Cotswolds and set up a rescue for cats and dogs that had managed to remain unfashionably natural. It was a slow process finding untampered animals and I did relent on many occasions and adopt those who were modified and even several mutants. I had outbuildings and a small exercise paddock. My new path was satisfying if a little lonely. I love animals but I did miss the pleasure of a close human relationship.

A couple of years after my move, I was contacted by the eminent ethologist, Francis Toure. She had dedicated her life's work to studying the behaviour of domestic animals in their natural state comparing life expectancy, behaviour and habits to those which had been mutated. She wanted to come and study my animals as I had, apparently, the largest known collection of natural domestic animals in Europe. She dazzled me when she first arrived. She was not only smart, beautiful and fun, but she was also totally natural down to her beautiful ebony skin and mass of curly black hair, which she wore unashamedly in an enormous afro.

She dazzles me still. We live a very domestic life with our dogs and cats. Occasionally we travel together to cities all over the world for her work, where she lectures the scientific community upon her findings. She has developed an awesome reputation of world renown and was recently appointed as a consultant for the World Health Organisation.

My life is happier than I could have ever imagined it to be. I never forget that it would not have been possible without my incredibly unique friend called Daisy.

About the Author
Katie Stevens

Following a degree entitled Bachelor of Arts in Theatre Acting Devised Performance and a year at East 15 Acting School, Katie Stevens has excelled at having a vast multitude of random and not very well paid jobs. Excellent training for her role as mother to two intrepid, fearless and courageous boys. She has been published in various anthologies, magazines and online journals, including *Saturday Evening Post*, *Mused Literary Review*, *Circa* and *Inner Sins*. She occasionally tweets @katiefantasyfan.

A Splendid Wedding
by Anthea Sharp

It was warm in the dressing room, the sticky smell of freesias mixing with perfumed lotions until Lady Belinda Montfort's head pounded. She smiled through it, though. A lady did not complain. From her perch on the stiff-backed chair, she nodded at her daughter, who stood before the imager applying a final bit of color to her lips.

"You look beautiful, Cerise," Belinda said. "The wedding will go flawlessly."

It must.

The white fabric of Cerise's gown floated about her, the nano-lifters making it seem as though the bride was adrift in pale sea of spangled stars. Her dark hair was drawn up in an elaborate coiffure studded with constellations of white flowers, and gems twinkled at the corners of her angular eyes.

The tall wooden door on the far wall opened, and a woman poked her head in.

"Five minutes," she said, her voice as bright as her glossy azure hair. "Lady Montfort, your son is coming to escort you. The big moment is almost here!"

Belinda gave the ceremony manager a smile, though her face felt as stiff as plas-glass. Her son would accompany her to her seat… because her husband already had a companion. Lord Montfort, Viscount of Ridgley and Xeros Station 418, had taken a mistress years ago, making it clear that his wife's happiness was of little concern.

Bitterness welled in her throat, and she pressed it back down. This was Cerise's day and she was determined it would be perfect. There was no room for any other outcome.

"Don't worry, Mother." Cerise turned from inspecting herself in the shining surface of the imager. Her dress swirled about her like the spiral arms of a galaxy. "Everything will be fine, no matter what happens. Arun and I love one another, and really that's the only important thing."

She was so wrong.

Appearances were *essential*. And beginnings. If everything went smoothly then surely Cerise's married life would be happy. Or at least tolerable.

The Montfort estate had spared no expense to secure the cathedral on 3753 Cruithne. It was considered good luck to hold the ceremony on Earth's co-orbital, and the church was the perfect blend of tradition and modernity. The grand cathedral was reconstructed from an original building shipped up from England at great cost. Half the windows and the ceiling had been replaced with durable plas-glass to let the light of the galaxy shine in on the proceedings. The wedding today would offer views of both Earth and the moon as Cruithne scudded through space. Most auspicious, indeed.

Belinda had been repeatedly assured that the atmospheric pressure bubble surrounding the cathedral and mini spaceport was completely dependable, with several backup systems in place. Still, she'd be relieved to fly back to Earth for the reception.

She swallowed, and smoothed the lavender silk of her own, less extravagant, skirts. She'd had the good sense to forgo breakfast. The bride's mother might be pale, but she would not be so horribly indelicate as to lose the contents of her stomach during the wedding. She was already somewhat prone to spacesickness, but the medicines she'd taken would hold it at bay.

"Mother?" Colin's voice, followed by a rap at the door.

"A moment," she called.

She rose and went to Cerise, careful of the drifting skirts. Resting her fingertips on Cerise's shoulders, she gave her daughter a quick kiss on the cheek.

"I love you," Belinda said.

A hundred more words tangled behind her tongue. *Don't do this. Be careful. Marriage is a trap you will die inside.*

She could voice none of them.

Cerise smiled, like a brilliant sun. "I love you, too."

It was blessedly cooler in the hallway, though perhaps that was simply the effect of the dark paneled walls, the bare wooden floor beneath her shoes.

Colin stood there, waiting for her. He looked entirely handsome in his pinstriped suit, although his hair, the same dun brown color as her own, was sticking out a trifle on one side from that cowlick that could never quite be tamed. She resisted the urge to smooth it down for him.

Her son held out his arm. "Shall we?"

No.

Belinda inclined her head and set her gloved fingers on his forearm. They emerged into the confines of the narthex. Small stone gargoyles perched at the peaks of the carved arches, their expressions sour. She knew exactly how they felt.

Her breath hitched as they approached the immense arched doors leading into the cathedral itself. Through them, she glimpsed bright colors—the gathered audience in their finery, the spatters of light thrown from the remaining stained-glass windows.

A breathtaking array of stars peeked in on the humans gathered below. Belinda hoped the cold promise of that light would be a benediction upon the proceedings, and not a blight.

Music drifted out, solemn yet celebratory, the harmony of a string quartet echoing beneath the soaring roof. It had been a very long time since she had visited a church. They reminded her too much of her own wedding day.

Colin patted her hand and stepped over the threshold, bringing her with him. Though she was aware of the wooden pews on either side, the anticipatory faces turned her way, she kept her gaze on the figured burgundy carpet stretching down the aisle. Colored light smudged the edges of the carpet as she and Colin moved forward, toward the high altar. The scent of old incense dried the back of her throat.

Her son's arm was muscled under her hand, and he moved with the graceful strength of a martial artist. At least she had that much—a strong son, a lovely daughter.

And the music was well played. The opening movement of one of the later Hayden quartets, though she could not say precisely which.

The hiss of whispers tickled the back of her neck, and Belinda finally looked up. The groom's family was seated on the right-hand side of the cathedral, many of the women wearing bright silken saris, and scarves edged with sequins. She felt suddenly stuffy and matronly in her lavender dress.

The altar rose before her, the dais surrounding it raised three steps from the floor. Great cascades of freesia and white roses decked the polished wood. Tall, unlit tapers rose on either edge, and behind was the gilt altar screen. The gold glowed, but Belinda suspected it was nothing more than a thin layer of gold leaf, applied over the base wood.

Four musicians were seated in a semicircle to the right of the altar. The Canterbury Quartet had come highly recommended, and Belinda was relieved that, so far, they had deserved their reputation.

She and Colin reached the front pew. Her husband sat there, looking dashing in a gray suit that matched the brush of silver in his dark hair. Beside him was That Woman.

At least he'd had the decency to seat her on the far side of him-self. Head high, Belinda let Colin guide her to her place beside Lord Montfort. She sat holding her body away from him, her spine straight, her feet together. The cushion was thin and uncomfortable, but she would endure.

The music stopped, signaling the audience that the ceremony was about to begin, and the priest entered from the clerestory door and paced deliberately toward the altar. His surplice, draped over his white robes, was heavily embroidered with purple and red. The gold-tipped edges floated ever-so-slightly, the nano-lifters defying the cathedral's artificial gravity in a manner that was supposed to suggest divinity, but bespoke only vanity to Belinda's eye.

There were a few muffled coughs, the slip and hush of people thumbing their programs. Then the quartet started up. Pachelbel's *Canon in D*—nearly a thousand years old and still one of the most popular pieces in the galaxy.

Belinda refused to glance to her left, beyond her husband to where That Woman sat, her presence a black hole. Instead, she watched the cellist pluck the obbligato, his long, elegant fingers caressing the neck of his instrument like a lover. Her gaze shifted to his face, partially obscured by the fall of his sandy hair, and a low flutter of recognition breathed through her.

Robert Huntington.

She had not seen him in over two decades, but she was certain. Robert—who had attended London Conservatory with her. Who had given her her first kiss. Who had met her, soul-to-soul, in the music they both adored.

And who had lost her to the illustrious Viscount Montfort.

The first violin entered with the *Canon*'s melody, the descending scale mirroring the bittersweet fall of her heart.

The crowd stood, in a series of genteel rustlings. All heads turned toward the arched doorway, and Belinda was forced to look away from Robert.

Cerise and Arun entered the cathedral together—a departure from the usual ceremony, but they had insisted. No doubt Lord Montfort's open association with That Woman had something to do with it. Cerise had not wanted her father's escort down the aisle, that much was plain. Neither had she and Arun wanted the formality of attendants.

Belinda had argued, until she had realized that the fewer people involved in the ceremony, the safer it would be. The less chance that things could go wrong.

Cerise was so lovely, tears pricked Belinda's eyes. The dress was perfect, and Cerise looked radiantly happy. Arun smiled at his bride, almost a grin, his teeth a flash of white against his brown skin. Surely he loved her enough.

The two paced up to the altar, mounting the stairs without mishap. The quartet timed their ending precisely, so that the music finished just as Arun and Cerise halted. The wedding gown floated and sparkled, and Belinda let out a tiny breath of relief.

There were so many places the ceremony could go awry. She had gone over and over the program with the manager, down to the last detail. If only the wedding went perfectly, it would set the template for the rest of the couple's lives together.

Her own wedding day had not been a disaster, nor marred by any great tragedy. But looking back, Belinda had realized that each small flaw had foreshadowed her entire married life.

The uncomfortable wedding dress, with a stray pin left in the bodice that stabbed her when she least expected it—and in a place she could not possibly extract in public. The fumbled rings. The vow that was so scarce-voiced it had to be repeated. Twice.

Nothing catastrophic, but seen from a distance, a complete and utter failure.

The same would not be true for Cerise.

Belinda could not quite listen to the priest say his measured words. For a time, she stared at Robert, willing him to glance at her. He and the other musicians sat immobile, in the perfected art of hired invisibility. She catalogued the changes to his profile: the faint fan of wrinkles about his eyes, the way the dimple beside his mouth had deepened, the weathering of his elegant hands.

Robert shifted forward, and the first violin lifted his honey-colored instrument. It was time for the candle lighting. The ceremony manager had assured her that the music would be perfect.

The first strains of Tekra's *Infinitude* nearly brought Belinda to her knees. Written for cello and violin alone, the piece was full of soaring melodies, twining light and darkness.

Hope. And despair. And hope again.

She and Robert had spent hours, months, playing this piece, bending and shaping and perfecting it to the best of their abilities. Memories sped through her: the fall of light through the practice room's high window, the glory of mastering a difficult passage, the way Robert would grin at her when they finally did so. The feel of his lips brushing hers.

Two altar boys approached, bearing faux fire on the ends of their bell-shaped candle snuffers. Through the scrim of her tears, Belinda saw their arms rise, like white wings. Glow to wick, the candles lit with a perfect illusion of flames. The steady light bloomed like halos. She trembled, her body a long, yearning string vibrating with memory.

The *Infinitude* ended. Robert lowered his bow and met her eyes directly. She nearly gasped at the expression revealed there—as if he had known all along that she was watching him. As if the past were a tangible, golden thing, just beyond their grasp.

She wanted to curl into a ball of lavender silk and weep.

Instead, she turned her face away, catching the sobs that gathered in her throat and swallowing them back down. The priest was speaking again, but she could not hear him. Her ears were scorched from the music, incapable of making sense of such dense and ponderous things as words.

After an eternity, the priest paused. Belinda blinked, forcing herself back to the moment, the rustling cathedral, the couple standing expectantly before the altar, the endless stars behind.

The past was gone. And if she secretly took her violin out, in the late and empty nights, tightened the bow and played, it was only for memory's sake. Only that. She had made her choice. There was no place for music in her life—had not been for years. Her husband had decreed that the wife of a viscount had no need of such frivolity.

From the pews behind her she heard the soft rise of whispers, and a moment later she was shocked to see the skirt of her dress begin to float upward. Across the aisle, the groom's mother was winding her scarlet scarf about her arm to keep it from flying away.

"One moment." The priest held up his hand, and to Belinda's horror his feet left the burgundy carpet. "We are experiencing a slight gravity delay. Everyone, please hook your feet beneath the prayer kneelers in front of you to avoid injury from falling when things normalize. Which they will immediately, I have no doubt."

Arun grabbed the man's forearm to keep him from floating up into the nave, and Cerise's gown bobbed alarmingly. For an appalled second, Belinda imagined her daughter airborne above the congregation, her underwear revealed for the world to see. The thought made her pulse freeze. Cerise would be the laughingstock of London when they returned.

Then, with a bump, gravity returned, and Belinda's heart began beating again. She drew in a shaky breath. Disaster had been narrowly averted—but the incident did not, *could not*, bode well for her daughter's future.

As if nothing untoward had happened, the priest continued with the ceremony. After a short homily, he nodded to the groom and Arun slipped his hand into his coat pocket. It was time for the rings.

Belinda glanced down at her hands, carefully folded in her lap. On the fourth finger of her left hand, shining against the pristine white of her gloves, she wore the blood-red Montfort Ruby.

Her gaze slipped sideways. Yes, her husband still wore his heavy silver signet ring—although that had more to do with his authority as Viscount Montfort than any importance he ascribed to the wedded state.

Despite herself, Belinda's eyes continued to where That Woman sat.

It would be one thing if Lord Montfort's lover was a great beauty, possessed of youth and angelic features. It would even be understandable had she been an accomplished artist of any persuasion. Then Belinda would not have to suffer the hot, bewildering confusion that swirled at the base of her skull whenever she beheld That Woman's plain features and graying frizz of hair, her stocky figure and thick, blunt fingers.

Belinda yanked her attention back to the couple at the altar. Arun was holding up a golden ring, the flash of diamonds visible from where she sat. She tamped down the sudden, wild impulse to leap to her feet and dash the ring from his hand.

He slid the band onto Cerise's finger, and she smiled. Belinda's collar constricted her throat. She lifted her chin, trying to find room to breathe. From the corner of her eye, she saw Colin shoot her a concerned glance.

Inhale. Smile. Everything is perfectly fine.

Except that a strange, whining hum was issuing from the vicinity of the bride.

Cerise glanced about, her smile fading. Arun bent his head, and even the priest's doughy face assumed an expression of concern.

A series of bright flashes and brief, small pops issued from the billowing stardust of the wedding gown, followed by the acrid smell of overheated nanos. Letting out a shriek, Cerise beat at her smoking skirts. Arun whipped off his coat and leaped to her side. He enveloped the malfunctioning dress, pulling the fabric away from his bride.

Voices raised, questions echoing, sibilant in the soaring space beneath the silence. Belinda rose and hurried to her daughter's side. Ceremony be damned.

"Are you unharmed?" she asked, taking Cerise's arm.

"I'm all right. It was just the dress shorting out. Don't fret, Mother."

"But—"

"Are you sure?" Colin asked, joining them.

"Yes, yes." Cerise said. "Sit back down. The ceremony is almost over, and I intend to walk out of this church a married woman." She gave her groom a warm look.

Despite Belinda's reluctance, Colin took her elbow and guided her back to the front pew. The audience continued to whisper, to watch with avid eyes.

Belinda sat. The heat of failure started at the soles of her feet and crawled up her entire body. Surely everyone could see her mortified trembling, the flush she could feel staining her skin.

How could this have happened? How, when she had taken such care over every single detail of the wedding?

"Ladies. Gentlemen." The priest held up his hands, palms out. "The bride is unhurt. The ceremony will continue. Please, quiet yourselves."

It did not take long to reach the kiss. Belinda could hardly watch, could barely look at Cerise in her broken dress, Arun in his shirtsleeves and waistcoat. This was wrong, all wrong!

Still, there was a joyous exuberance in their kiss she could not deny. It went too long for propriety's sake, but after such a mishap, surely they could not be blamed.

The quartet struck up a triumphant march, and the audience rose as the newly pronounced husband and wife turned to face them.

Cerise looked radiant, despite the singed skirts awkwardly bundled in her hands. And the look Arun gave his new bride…

Belinda's throat tightened, and not with fear this time. Perhaps, just perhaps, marriage would agree with her daughter.

Applause filled the air like sweet rain as the newlyweds recessed back down the aisle, followed by the priest. The stained-glass colors seemed to brighten as Cerise and Arun walked through, rainbows clinging to them.

Colin offered his arm, but Belinda paused.

She turned to face her husband. A wildness reared up inside her, dark and heady—stirred by the *Infinitude* still resonating through her. Despair. And hope.

In one quick, decisive movement, she stripped the Montfort Ruby from her finger.

"Here," she said, thrusting it toward the hard, handsome features of Lord Montfort. "Take it. I will be seeking a divorce. Expect to hear shortly from my solicitor."

He stood very still for an instant. Behind him, That Woman's eyes widened.

"Mother?" Colin said in an undertone. "Do you know what you're doing?"

She did not, and the freedom of it made her giddy. She kept her hand outstretched, the ruby glittering like a drop of blood at her fingertips.

Finally, Lord Montfort took it, his eyes hooded. Belinda stepped back. She found, shockingly, that she did not care that the occupants of the nearby pews were abuzz with what they had just witnessed. She did not care what the gossip rags would say, or *what* happened to the Montfort Ruby. It was off her finger. At last.

"You have two days," he said, his voice cold, "to remove your possessions from my home."

"I only need one." A strange, singing jubilation filled her blood.

"Goodbye, Belinda." He gave her the barest inclination of his head, then strode off.

That Woman followed. She did not meet Belinda's gaze, but color lay high on her round cheeks.

"Mother?" Colin set his hand on her shoulder. "You know my lodgings are small, but you are welcome to stay with me."

"Thank you. But I believe I will make other plans." What they would be, she could not say, but the heady, exultant freedom of possibility made her feel giddy. "Go along. I see Miss Tate waiting."

The tips of Colin's ears flushed. "I'm happy to stay with you."

"No need." She leaned forward and kissed his cheek. "I am well. Indeed, I believe I am better than I have been in decades."

"If you're certain…" He glanced to the back of the cathedral where Miss Tate hovered, clearly waiting for him without trying to look obvious.

"I am."

The church emptied out quickly. No doubt the cream of Society could hardly wait to jet back to Earth and dissect this newest scandal. Viscountess Montfort giving back her wedding ring—at her own daughter's wedding! It was deliciously appalling.

The altar boys came up and snuffed out the candles.

Still, the musicians played, the glorious phrases sifting up through the color-limned dust. Belinda closed her eyes, letting her heart unwind and unwind. When the quartet held the final chord, she smiled.

She opened her eyes and walked up the three steps to where the musicians sat. The others were already packing up their instruments, but Robert stood, holding the neck of his cello and watching her approach.

There was a light in his blue eyes that she remembered, a spark of joy she had never seen in Lord Montfort. A spark she had nearly forgotten she knew how to recognize.

"Robert," she said.

"Belinda. Are you still playing?"

"I am," she said, and her soul untwisted a fraction more. "Although it has been some time…"

He nodded. "I understand. Here, let me give you my card."

She followed him over to his cello case, where he tucked the instrument away with the same sweet, gentle hands she remembered. He closed the case, then handed her an embossed calling card: *Robert Huntington, Cellist, Fourteen Darington Street*. She rubbed it lightly, feeling the letters under her fingers.

"Are you… that is…" He cleared his throat. "Would you be free to join me for dinner some evening? If not, it's perfectly—"

"Yes. I would love to."

"Well then." The grin she still remembered lit his face, the dimple carving into his left cheek.

She wanted to set her finger in that indentation, then trail it across his lower lip. She wanted to put her lips there, taste his mouth with her own. Heat curled in her belly, pulled sweetly through her skin. Desire— she scarcely recalled how it felt.

"Good." He reached, took her hand. "Bring your violin along, and we'll see how much of the *Infinitude* we still remember."

"It's been a very long time," she said.

"I know. But I don't think it's ever too late. Do you?"

Once she would have thought so. Even earlier today, fear and anxiety knotting through her, she could not have believed differently.

Yet a single melody, and this catastrophe of a wedding, had unlocked the door of her future.

Belinda pulled in a deep breath, tasting doused flames and sweet dust. Robert's hand gripped hers warmly.

She looked up into his eyes, not needing promises, only possibilities.

"It's not too late," she said, and smiled.

About the Author
Anthea Sharp

USA Today bestselling author Anthea Sharp has sold over 200k copies worldwide of her award winning *Feyland* series, which combines high-tech gaming with faerie lore, and a touch of romance. Her short fiction has appeared in *Fiction River*, *DAW* anthologies, and various other publications. By night, she moonlights as historical romance author Anthea Lawson, penning Victorian-set tales of romance and adventure. For more Victorian Spacepunk, pick up Anthea's *Stars & Steam* collection.

Author Website: http://antheasharp.com/

Ours to Guard and Protect
By Amy Power Jansen

Rizqah should be with her team. It was her operation, from start to finish.

But here she was. Standing in the mist, staring at a half-shrouded statue of a horse. Smaller than she remembered. In its bed of overgrown grass. Grass that—even without the moss—hid the signs warning students off the grass.

No porters now to stop her.

No desire left either.

Why this little horse had become so pivotal in her memory of that year, she didn't know. Two decades to get back here, and this is where she'd snuck away to.

Not her own college, or her own memories. Old, tattered memories from before the world ended. She had been so young. Coming from a home where her face and her accent told everyone she was an Indian Muslim South African from Cape Town, suddenly every piece of her identity had become independent, worthy of its own story. She'd felt so much taller—both figuratively and literally. No longer dwarfed by the Afrikaans blood on every side. Normal-sized, for once, maybe a bit petite. Dark-haired and hazel-eyed. Every piece her own.

They were good memories, but they felt like they belonged to someone else. That woman would have aged gracefully. She wouldn't have had the lines and the scars, not so bad, not yet. There'd been so much to look forward to. Before the storms and the plagues, the cold wars and the hot ones, and the wars against an enemy no one could identify.

She was glad she'd been on the other side of the world. Better to see her own home crumble. Better than seeing this.

Rather come back to the quiet and the mist and the aftermath.

But of all the sites, this is where she'd chosen.

Here.

A small, ridiculous horse. That they hadn't been allowed to climb on. So focal for the students of Jesus College. But she hadn't been at Jesus.

She'd had friends here. And a professor. She remembered that cold December morning wandering around the exterior of the college. Totally missing the entrance and all the way out past the circle, following the fence. Lucky she'd given herself so much time to get to that first meeting. Lucky she'd eventually found that long passage into the college.

She sighed into her breather and unfolded her arms, shaking them out. The skin-suit crackled at the movement. The Jo'burg team had been sure it would be resilient against the colder climes. But if worst came to worst, they'd all go into decontamination on their return. Not so bad.

What a ridiculous thing, standing out here in the cold, in the mist, in a college that hadn't been hers. She should head back. She would. With a determined shake of her head, she turned away from the small, ridiculous horse.

∞

The library was clear on the other side of town. But that's where the team had set up camp after the trucks rolled in. They could have broken into one of the colleges, used the dorms. But she'd decided they'd set up camp in the field outside the main library. Not entirely central. But good enough.

A good site to operate from. A good site to use as their repository until they took it all home.

The library itself had been a copyright library, a keeper of all the texts published in Britain. Deep inside, Rizqah wanted to gather them all up, protect them against a world where only paper survived, the electronic world in tatters. But she couldn't.

They could only salvage the most important: the rare, the historical, the easy to transport. No Newton's Bridge, much as she longed to take it. Its secret had been lost decades before this chaos, she comforted herself.

But as she approached the library up Burrel's Walk, she heard shots and angry voices. She sped up into a jog and reached for her sidearm as she reached the main gate of the library.

Her team had spread out on the stairs in front of the main library, surrounded by an angry group armed with broken bottles, two cricket bats and one rifle. The rifleman stood at the back of the group. He was about her age and of all his angry group, he wasn't shouting.

She slowed her jog into a brisk walk and as she got closer, all their attention shifted to her.

"What's going on here?" she asked.

She stood straight and tall. Angry as they looked, this ragtag bunch didn't look up to much of a fight. A nearby woman shifted her weight towards Rizqah. A tumble of hair perched on her head, a mix of grey and auburn. Shirt tucked up to her elbows. Local then, and probably thought the weather pleasant. First signs of spring and all.

"They're stealing," the woman said.

Rizqah snorted and walked closer to the woman. "Stealing?"

"Yes, this is ours."

"Really, you own all of this?" Rizqah gestured widely with her left arm, taking in not only the library, but the whole university town.

"No, of course not," the rifleman said.

Rizqah had seen him approaching as they talked. Seen him lower his weapon and motioned to her team to do the same.

"So, what then?"

"Ours to guard, and protect."

"From what? For whom?"

He swallowed. "For the future."

"And that's why we're here. The north doesn't have a future. We do."

His forehead crinkled. "And where are you from, exactly?"

Probably assumed we were local. Heard all sorts of accents in a place like this. In England, full stop. A remnant of their hodgepodge empire. Of which, she of course, was a perfect result. "South Africa."

He raised an eyebrow. "That's not possible. How did you get here?"

"We flew." Rizqah shrugged a shoulder.

"No-one flies, anymore. There's no fuel."

"We've got coal, and the technology to turn it into fuel."

He whistled.

"And we have a functioning society," she said. "Or, at least, the fulcrum of it. And people who can still breed."

He ran a hand across his brow.

"So, you see, it's safer with us."

He stared at her. "Can we talk about it?"

"Sure. Give me a moment."

She motioned to her team to get back to work. Her second-in-command, Thando, joined her as she walked away. She said, "Keep an eye on them, but I don't think they'll be much more trouble."

"You think the other teams will encounter resistance?"

"Probably. There wasn't any visible sign of concentration at any of them from the satellites. But I'm sure there's still survivors scattered here and there. Command tent set up?"

Thando motioned to a small tent on the far end of the courtyard.

Rizqah strolled back to the rifleman. Definitely about her age—and younger than plenty of his band. The first signs of grey hair, wrinkles all around the eyes. She crossed her arms.

"We're all that's left here," he said.

She shrugged.

"Can you really keep it safe?"

She nodded.

"You don't talk much."

"Not unless I need to. That it?"

He sighed. "I suppose so."

∞

Once the tent had sealed behind her, Rizqah could have taken off her breather. Technically, the air-recyclers should keep it clean in here. But why take chances?

Decontamination was feasible, but a pain in the ass.

Their chief technical agent, Kgomotso, sat at her computer, tapping away. She looked up as Rizqah came in and shot her an ironic salute. They weren't much of an army, mostly just a mild militia. But they tried for a modicum of discipline.

The computer Kgomotso sat at was one of the few clean ones that their techs had set up to form a small, closed network which they could communicate over, using the remaining satellites. A simulacrum of what had been. The old web, the huge one, had long broken down as the viruses, worms and other bogies had proliferated as the human population succumbed to its own brand of viruses and chaos.

"Just pulling up the reports from the rest of the sites," Kgomotso said.

Rizqah nodded, turning her attention to the map on the table. It showed all the sites across the western side of Europe, and with this one of the furthest sites to the north. They couldn't venture much past where the old East-West line had been. Couldn't dare Greece, which was a pity.

But they'd get as much as they could.

Which begged the question?

Why was she here?

She'd never seen Paris. Now, she never would.

"Here we go," Kgomotso said, placing the laptop in front of Rizqah. Rizqah grabbed a seat with her foot and sat down. Almost stood straight back up.

"Dammit," she said, slamming one fist into the table. "That man."

She still didn't know why Itumeleng insisted on trusting Terence. Sure the man had been his second-in-command when the two groups had merged. But Rizqah had showed him evidence time and time again that the man couldn't be trusted on sensitive assignments.

But Itu had insisted that Terence run the show in Paris. Rizqah read the mail from Claudia again. She knew the woman might be over-reacting. But then again, she'd sent Claudia with that team specifically to keep an eye on Terence.

The team in Paris had also run into civilians. But instead of talking to them, or restraining them, or putting them out with tranks, they'd shot and killed them. And stirred up a hornet's nest in what was left of Paris. Now, the locals were trashing the major sites themselves, before Terence could get the stuff out. Someone had set fire to several wings of the Louvre. And another had set off grenades in Versailles.

But the pictures bothered Rizqah more. Claudia had used the communications tech to take pictures of the corpses. Just kids.

Kids with absolutely no future. Dead kids.

At least, they had evidence.

∞

Later that night, when the sun went down, Rizqah accepted a beer from Thando. The work for the day was finished and catalogued. After their conference, the local bunch—most of them, anyway—had turned friendly and even helped out. A couple had had vocal opinions of what should be saved and what not. Some of them, at least, had definitely been academics.

Turned out what she'd thought she'd known about Newton's

Bridge had been a myth. A myth propagated by some of the most over-educated students of the time. She shrugged.

"Heard about Terence," Thando said, pulling her back to the present.

"Kgomotso tell you?"

"Yah. You gonna deal with him when we get back?"

"Someone has to."

"This is your op."

Rizqah nodded. Of course, Terence had argued against it. Most of them had. At first.

But she had convinced them. She always did. It's what she did. Convince people. Got them on her side. Had worked in the old corporate world. Had worked when everything started falling apart. She knew how to keep a system going, how to keep people cooperating.

And she had. Had led her group for years before they'd found Itu and Terence. And now she had to play second fiddle to a man again. At least, it was a big, black man. Instead of an old, white one. New world.

The rifleman walked around to join them, his own beer in hand. He was the spokesman of the ragtag group. His name was James and he'd been a professor of English literature at Emmanuel College. Hadn't told her his name earlier. But she'd found out. He didn't speak much himself—for an English professor—but he shared a drink with them.

"What brought you back out here? Seems like a pretty ambitious project."

"Her idea," Thando said, pointing at her, the pride in his voice clear for those who knew him.

"Project Cullinan," Rizqah said, smiling to herself.

"For the queen's diamond?"

"Not the queen's," Thando said.

It had been the argument that had swung them all in the end. Preserving culture, art, civilisation had seemed like a low priority. But taking back their own, that had spoken to something else. Something primal. More like revenge.

Oh well, Rizqah thought, whatever works.

And then wondered again why she was here. Why not in London rescuing the pivotal piece of this op?

She knew London. Had no desire to return. But still, that had been the centre, the linchpin of her argument.

∞

Rizqah strolled along the banks, her heavy heart belying her light step. Strange, she thought. Most of the packing had been completed. Once everything had been secured in the trucks, they could return to Stansted, get the trucks onto the transport plane and then back home.

Most of the other teams were close to finished. The Paris team wasn't, having becoming embroiled in a street-to-street battle with angry locals. Disturbing reports continued to pour in from Claudia and a couple of other concerned citizens. For now, Rizqah left it.

No point alerting Terence to the dissidents in his ranks. Time enough for that at home.

Claudia's reports would be more fuel to the fire in her campaign against Terence. Itu would have to listen to her. But trying to stop the fighting in Paris would be futile. She wasn't there.

"Can I join you?"

Rizqah found that the professor, James, had crept up on her. Something about this place lulled her, reminding her of an earlier life. Probably safe enough. Probably.

She shrugged. "Sure."

"Were you going somewhere in particular?"

Was she? Yes, she supposed she was. "Just going to see my old college."

"You studied here?"

"Yes, years ago."

He nodded. "And your college?"

"Murray Edwards."

"Ah, the old New Hall." He smiled at her. New Hall was genuinely quite new—as opposed to New College at Oxford. But it had also been renamed along the way, from New Hall to Murray Edwards College. A women's college—one of the few left. A women's college named for two significant women in its history that consequently ended up sounding like it had been named for a man.

Ah, the ironies of life.

And the strangeness of this ivory-tower world. They continued along the Backs running along behind the most significant of the Cambridge colleges, the air crisp and clean and clear. Wouldn't have thought it was laden with all manner of life-ending disease.

They strolled along, a quiet companionship. James said nothing when Rizqah took her own quixotic way back, turning into St. John's, continuing through Magdalene, across into Eddies, through the overgrown fields, down a barely discernible path and finally shoving their way through a squeaky back-gate.

"You were a post-graduate here?" James asked, as Rizqah paused in front of Eliza and Canning Fok House. Another, slightly unfortunate name, more commonly known amongst its residents as E-and-C. Or, at least, it had been, once.

She turned from the house and towards the main college, past the award-winning gardens, completely overgrown at this point. Even in such a state, the familiar grounds tugged at Rizqah.

In the main part of the college, every sound seemed to echo. They climbed a set of stairs, Rizqah glancing down for the metal dung beetles often found at the base. All rusted and rusting. She climbed up into the main hall.

A huge empty space full of huge paintings. Some gaps from when her team had been up here the day before. She hadn't come then. Wanted to see it alone. Oh well, at least James was quiet company.

The tables were gone or shattered, the space yawning in its abandonment. The raised dais for high table. The space in front for little high table, her table, the post-grad table. And then all the rest.

But she hadn't come here to see that.

All along, something had been tugging at her. But she hadn't been sure until now was it was. She'd stared at the painting so many times. A kneeling woman in an abaya with a bazooka on her shoulder. Fighting someone, fighting who? For what? Against what?

She'd always wondered, staring up at that woman. A Muslim woman. Fighting. For a just cause? Or a necessary one?

Before, Rizqah had been a studious woman heading for a corporate job. Traditional, and not. Observant, but not interested in marriage or kids or cooking. For the first two years in her undergrad, she'd worn a head-scarf. Then, she'd stopped. Later, after returning to South Africa, she'd started again, and it had become part of her corporate identity.

And then the world had changed. And she'd fought, and she'd killed. And she'd won, and she'd led. And she'd laid down her leadership—for the greater good, she hoped. But who was she now? And who was she then? And who was this woman on the wall in her own war?

All through it, James stood and waited.

Then they walked back to E-and-C and into the middle common room. Quiet and musty and dusty. Rizqah put her feet up on one of the tables, heard the pillows sigh beneath her, and broke out some rations to share with James. He took them and they ate in silence. She would stay the night here. One last night.

All the locks had unsealed. She'd be able to find her old room. But it would be changed. Maybe she should stay somewhere else.

She watched James eat. Past middle-aged and aging fast. His

small band of followers waiting for the end in the best place they knew. Not clinging to life and trying to wring more out as some had. Rizqah knew—and James knew—that most survivors were in Scotland, surviving on undersea gas, still pumping, and pushing out deformed, malformed babies by the bucket-load. No going quietly into the night for them. But screaming and struggling and squalling.

"You could come back with us?" she asked. "You're a small group and we have the meds to disinfect you."

He smiled. "No, thanks."

"It won't be like…"

He shook his head before she could finish. "There's no place I'd rather be, at the end."

Rizqah nodded. They sat in silence. They ate.

"You know," she said at last. "I've never even actually seen all the colleges. I was so focused when I was here…"

"We could go tomorrow."

Rizqah shook her head, and they lapsed back into silence. Darkness crept in and the quiet turned to the faint sounds of insects. Not many. Not like before. But the faintest murmurs of life, still there.

She straightened up and climbed the steps. James followed her to the first storey. There, they both paused. He indicated his intention to climb further, but before he did, he said, "You could stay, you know."

Then, he continued to the second floor. She let herself into the dorms and then wavered.

No point dithering, she told herself and let herself into the first room on the left. Her room. Not her room. Full of someone else's stuff. Left hastily, she thought, looking around. Some clothes lay bedraggled on the floor. Books, a laptop. And so many odds and ends that the last inhabitant could only have been English. No one foreign would be able to bring so much stuff.

But there was linen on the bed.

Rizqah stood in the centre of the messy room, a thin film of tears filling her eyes. Once upon a time, she'd been a student, idealistic and hopeful and naïve and ready to take on the world. Now, the world had taken her on, and she felt tired.

With a deep breath, she took off her breather and laid it on the table. A foolish, instinctive movement. Easy to reverse. She stared at it, reached for it and left it on the table.

Then, she kicked off her boots, folded her jacket onto a chair, and lay down in her skin-suit, with her uniform still covering it. In the dark, that familiar dark, she lay awake. Thinking of nothing and everything. And remembering.

∞

The dawn woke her. She rose and stood at the icy windows, her palm soaking in the cold and the damp. A cold late-winter morning, full of frost. But one day, it would be spring again. And the flowers would bloom—in white, in blue, in every colour you could imagine. One at a time. She remembered.

She could stay. She could watch the flowers bloom. She could see every college—once, twice, a hundred times. The end would come. But for the remnant left, it would be slow. Peaceful. No fighting, no screaming.

No more battles for turf. No more politics. No more leverage. No more saving up of allies and favours. No more trying to chart a brighter path in a darkening world. No more.

She'd have to tell Thando. Let him tell the troops. Let him tell Itu.

She'd go to the library and come back. She'd wake James and they would find bikes and they could begin their tour.

Rizqah smiled in the darkness. She picked up her breather—they'd need that, they'd want that. And clearly, she hadn't, removing it as she had the night before. No need to waste. She set off out into the half-light, the dawn light, the wakening world. Her heart and step light, and in tune.

Before she reached Magdalene, in that no-man's between Eddies and Magdalene, before one college, after the next, a stone dropped into her chest. A dark, dead weight.

Without her, who would deal with Terence?

Claudia? An excellent voice for calling attention to injustices, and useless at getting anyone to care. Claudia knew how to draw attention to herself, but not how to get things to change. Too many screamers before the end had been like that. Good at talking; bad at provoking action. They knew what was wrong but not how to change it. That's what brought them here in the first place.

Could she leave it to Claudia, and Thando, and Kgomotso? Could she leave them? Could she trust them to get it right? To know what to say, when and to who, and which strings to pull? Did they have the vision of a newer, better, smaller world? A world that had been darkening in her mind, but had sprung back to life in all its old colours.

She'd asked herself these questions before. Long ago. To stay for the PhD or go home to make a difference. Not much difference she had made. But without knowing it, she'd been ready and in the aftermath, she had done it, had made a difference.

Could she leave them now?

Before she reached Magdalene, before she crossed into St. John's, she had put the breather back on. She'd have to tell the medics, have to get extra shots. She lengthened her stride, closing herself off to the beauty around her. Ignoring the soft light over the Backs, and the long frosted grass. Rizqah tightened her jacket and returned to her team.

The trucks were packed and she climbed into one, next to Thando. As they pulled away, she realised she hadn't said good-bye to

James. It tugged at her, and she breathed it out. One more regret to add to so many.

She didn't look back as they pulled out of Cambridge. No last look back. Not this time. Her heart had found its home, but she could not let it stay.

About the Author
Amy Power Jansen

Amy Power Jansen lives and works in Johannesburg, South Africa with her (incomparable) husband, Stephen. By day, she inhabits the prosaic world of finance, and by night, she explores worlds fantastic and science fictional and as many shades as possible in between. She attended Cambridge University for her masters degree and remains chronically plagued by nostalgia. She has previously been published in *Abyss & Apex*, *Myriad Lands 2*, and *Deep Magic*.

Then Our Skins, Then Our Bones
by Alexandra Renwick

Other girls line up along the dancehall wall like condemned criminals waiting for the firing squad, but not me. In her soundproof observation booth Madam Zeti presses buttons, swivels levers, punches the code for *customer selection* mode, and pumps illicit Earth music into the room.

This client is a thumper. That's what we call the Earthern men who bring the music with the heavy bass, the shouted lyrics, the *thump thump thump* rising up past the floorboards through the soles of our bare feet. The Earther's music vibrates up into my shins, past the quivering jelly in my knee joints, to settle in the bones of my hips. *Thump thump. Thump.*

Same as everyone else on the planet, I'd never heard real music before we discovered Earth—or did the Earthers discover us? Lots of opinions on the subject from both sides, just like who attacked whom first. Only one thing is sure: they brought their music, and those of us it didn't instantly kill became its thralls forever.

We'll never be *theirs*, though. Not directly. We may be vanquished, our population devastated and our society in ruins. But we endure. We're too proud a people not to. Too fierce. Our weapons are capable of destroying their big soft watery planet five times over. Probably a hundred times over, but after the first five, who counts?

We've destroyed other worlds. Not in my lifetime. Not recently. But there have been others. A *warlike species*, they call us. They, who fight each other at every level of Earthern society, man murdering woman and nation obliterating nation, continent attacking continent, their violence spilling into space where they've colonized the orbiting rock they call Moon. By comparison, our extraplanetary annihilation program was bloodless and without unnecessary cruelty.

And then they brought music, its repetitive vibrations, its pitched resonances. The thing now coursing up through my legs and spinning out through the tips of my splayed fingers free as asteroids shooting through naked space. My head bobs in slow motion to the patterned *thump thump thump* of the floor and I grit my teeth, willing my body to keep still.

The girl beside me loses control, her cry of despair and elation ripping the air. She leaps into the center of the dancehall—a bare space smelling of spices and exotic fruits, fashioned after an archaic Earthern bordello Madam Zeti once glimpsed in one of their entertainment archives. Flocked wallpaper swirls in velvet patterns which trick the eyes, making my vision swim against the backdrop of *thump thump* and the lights flickering across the ceiling, reflected from the thousand facets of a gigantic mirrored sphere, a fractured sun in the center of a dance floor galaxy.

Another girl moans as the music grips her. She lurches onto the floor like a string puppet macabre. She pumps one fist in the air, banging her head to the thumper tempo swivelling her hips in counter-rhythm, all over mottled by the mirrored ball's bouncing, glittering lights. Swirling, hair flying over her head and back, over and back, her feet jerk in rapid halftime to the client's poison of choice.

My muscles strain against themselves as I will my arms to remain at my sides, command my feet to stop their subtle tap tap to the thump thump.

Do not dance, I admonish myself silently. *Wait for the tune with the exact frequencies, the proper tones and vibrations and patterns to accomplish your purpose.*

I am thrall to no thing. Not even this.

The music ends abruptly. The thumper client emerges from the observation booth. Madam steps out behind him to nod encouragement as he takes the arm of the girl with the thrashing hair who dropped to the floor in a de-spined lump when his music stopped.

"A wise choice," murmurs Madam into ear-aching silence. "A strong girl, a good mover for your musical tastes. She will dance long for your money. She is a bargain."

She repeats similar drivel for every customer. They mostly look the same to me, these men from Earth. They tend to be small, their flesh too spongy, too loose. Their skulls look very soft. Soft enough to crush easy as a scorpio's egg.

But they won the war, and they have music. And music has us.

Our society is built around our physiological limits, as every society must be. The clicks and staccato whirrs of our language are nothing Earthers would call musical. Our technology, unlike theirs, is not dependent on machines producing vibrations which might prove deleterious to our population. Even our steps, our customary mode of walking, are—according to them—stilted and arrhythmic. Before they came we did not know this, did not consider such things in the courses of our daily lives. We did not care.

Madam leads the human client and his chosen girl from the floor. The other girl most affected by the heavy heavy thump thump staggers to her feet, reeling slightly off-kilter with a beatific expression.

It's the worst, most degrading aspect, the pleasure. Earth music can kill. If not outright, then it can make you dance until your feet are worn to stubs and both hearts give out, and still you die with your eyes joyous and your hands lifted to the lilac sky. You can't help it, can't resist. Even Madam, who spent many turns of our planet building a tolerance to music before she opened her brothel, must always wear earplugs and shock-absorbing shoes. I can only imagine the agony of music brushing against her skin, not for the few songs an evening to which she subjects us working girls, but night after night, turn after turn, revolution after revolution around our purple sun.

The next song starts, high and reedy in the form our translators term *classical*. Classical is easier for me to resist, but there'll be another girl for whom it is delicious poison. Anything is poison in improper dosage: rich food, the smoking sticks Earthers inhale despite the warnings of their own scientists, music.

The girls most susceptible to the tippity tip tipping of the reedy vibrations lose control one by one, spinning onto the floor with arms in circles above their heads as though they hold large balls of air. This music invites standing on tiptoes, makes you want to spin so fast your head can't keep pace with your body. Spin, spin until your neck snaps. Tippy tippy toes until they bleed.

By the time the music cuts out abruptly and the client enters with Madam to scrape his selected girl off the floor, four other girls lie in crumpled heaps. Two have the wasted features of dance addicts, girls who come every night not for the money, not to keep themselves fed in a post-war economy, but to get another hit of music, and another, and another. Addicts don't care whether it's thumpa thumpa or tippy tippy toe, or even hop-hop or screech and wail. It's all irresistible to someone, somewhere, somewhen. Irresistible enough for these women to leave less dangerous jobs, abandon surviving families to come each night, line up along Madam's flocked velvety light-speckled wall, and forsake everything else simply to dance.

I hear myself. I hear myself telling this story, and I think: Myself, if you're so smart, such a fine specimen of your people, an upstanding member of your surviving community, then why are *you* here?

And the answer is simple. It's because I want to die. I want nothing less than death by music, and nothing more.

∞

I loved Pitre. I loved him so much it seemed nothing as distant as death could ever catch up with us. One thing I envy Earthers: their love is fleeting. It ends with death. Or illness, or poverty. Or with the change of seasons or the flick of a finger or the blink of an eye. It ends wildly and unpredictably, with loud banging—or perhaps it ends softly, long and drawn out, dissipating until hardly noticeable at all. Our scientists often expound on the similarities of our physiology to that of humans, other than our secondary hearts and our aural frailties, which even they do not fully understand. But not being a human love, my feeling didn't die with Pitre—how could it? It was bigger than either of us. Bigger than our four hearts put together.

He was one of our first wave of civilian casualties in the war with Earth. When humans discovered their music's disastrous effect on my people their response was merciless and immediate. They were frightened, no doubt, by our reputation as annihilators, by our superior weaponry and by their millions already dead. When their ships broke through our small hard planet's defenses and swooped low over our cities blaring music, people dropped where they stood or walked or ate or worked. Our defense pilots fell screaming from the clouds, covering their ears with hands unable to block the patterned vibrations in the air.

Earthern war machines turned the sky dark with their metal wings and undermounted speakers, blotting out the bright lilac sun, blaring, blaring, blaring. A small planet, a hundred million souls writhing in ecstasy as the blood vessels burst in our brains or the cell walls ruptured in our secondary hearts.

Only a fraction of us had enough natural resistance to survive the initial onslaught. At least Pitre went quickly. I thank the stars for that. I hope he went so quickly as to escape pain, or that the agony of death was smothered by the rapture of musical exaltation.

They say death by music much resembles that other release, the one occurring between two people who love each other as much as Pitre loved me and I him, the one I'll never experience again unless it comes with my death by music. Communing with the infinite on such a level is no mere physical event; it takes both hearts and something of the soul, a spark of the divine, which my people believe resides in every living thing—even in humans.

How else could they invent something so glorious?

∞

I've never felt the music so intensely. Could this be what I've been waiting for?

Melancholia has set in with my thoughts of Pitre, thoughts of his death and the recurring crushing realization of his permanent absence. It's as though I forget my loss a hundred times each day, and feel fresh the pain of it each time I remember.

So when the recording of an exquisite sliding instrument glides past its opening bars, the rich vocalizations of a crooning girl-human who has possibly been dead herself over a hundred Earthern years swells around me. It fills my mind, necessary as air filling my lungs, and I shudder. If any music can grant the magnificent release I seek from my Pitre-less existence, it will be this.

My eyes are closed. How much time has passed without me realizing? I force my eyes open with shaking fingers. I'm no junkie, pathetically wallowing between notes! I'm no addict! I come here with a purpose beyond the music itself; I need to know what Pitre felt in those last moments of life, when the war machines flew over the park where he ate lunch every day at noon, and blared their beautiful poison into our atmosphere at full strength. They had our surrender in no time; only a quarter of our population wasn't susceptible to instant death. And while some may have more tolerance than others, none of us are completely immune.

Angry, I dig my nails into my thigh to cease its quivering, its desire to dance. Scientists tell us we're not as similar to humans on the inside as the out. Scholarly speculation posits we come from similar stock at some ancient point where our two histories once collided, as they do now. Do we not have the same number of legs, of arms, of eyes and toes and ears? If our ears look small and flat to them, or our internal organs seem misplaced, or enlarged or missing or duplicate, perhaps it's as our leaders tell us: a simple matter of evolution, of adaptation. Does this mean some future version of our people—our children, if they survive, or our children's children—will adapt to music? Might they listen to the thump thump or the tweet tweet or the hop hop hop and not jiggle and wiggle themselves in uncontrolled abandon until their secondary hearts rupture or their neural matter dissolves?

It seems unfair, though perhaps our superior weapons seemed so to Earth. Gone now, our beautiful bombs, our lovely war machines, dismantled and confiscated by the victors.

My feet have slid me to the center of the floor without my permission. My body sways back and forth, to and fro. I imagine myself a mineral pillar on the high dunes, wind brushing past my limbs, caressing, rocking me. One note sustains, draws me along its length until I sink to my knees, surrendering.

Madam is murmuring in the air near my head. "Oh yes, sir, this is a hardy one, a beautiful dancer. Not been here long… still plenty of life left in those legs to move for your pleasure. A bargain, a real bargain…"

The Earthern man is tall. Very tall, almost as tall as I. Most are much shorter. Their legs often appear stumpy to my eyes, their heads encephalitic, their hands far too tiny for the length of their arms.

Not my customer. Not him. His height is nicely matched to his proportions. Perhaps it's only my music-induced delirium, but he looks almost handsome, for an Earther. Something about the line of his jaw reminds me of Pitre. His eyes are green, as I see when he squats beside me on the floor, an awkward and inelegant gesture.

"You all right?" he asks. When I don't answer he looks up at Madam. "Is she all right?"

"She's a good dancer," mumbles Madam Zeti past her glazed, human-mimicking smile, teeth bared. "Strong. A bargain. Your private room is waiting."

He peers again into my face. Earther expressions are not always similar enough to ours for me to interpret. Far harder to master, in fact, than their Standard Earthese language, which tends to be simple, with few clicks, grinds, or whirs. I hear they have hundreds of dialects on Earth, thousands counting their colonies in space and on various rocks like Moon. It sounds lonely.

"Madam can't hear you," I tell him in my underpracticed Earthese. He hovers near my elbow, not touching me as I rise. I point to Madam, then my ears. "Earplugs," I say.

He nods, uncertain but accepting. We follow Madam from the dancehall, my legs wobbly but supporting my weight. He walks beside me as though to catch me if I fall.

Stupid human person. I'll not fall.

Not without music bringing me to my knees.

∞

Madam closes the door behind her as she steps from the small chamber, leaving us alone. The lighting is low, intimate. The wallpaper is less garish than in the main dancehall, but still speckled with the texture of distant stars, masking deep soundproof padding underneath. The dance floor is tiny. From the single chair in the room, a client could reach out and touch a dancing girl.

"Sit," I tell him. That's how things are done at Madam Zeti's: they sit, and watch while their chosen girl loses her soul to their favorite music. I've never understood what brings them back again and again, always imagining it to reflect the conqueror's desire to witness in some personal manner the subjugation of the conquered. It seems far crueller to me than our own method of war, which leaves no survivors. At least we don't revel in our enemy's lowered state. To the contrary, we honour them, after they're all dead.

He sits, clumsy, balanced on the edge of the chair as though for flight. "So it's true?" he asks. "You really can't touch the women here?"

"No touching. Dancing only." Preferably dying also, I don't add. Some night, some Earther will bring the right music and it'll hit the right note and my second heart will rupture, same as Pitre's.

But Madam Zeti's clients must smuggle their music on-planet; it's absolutely forbidden here as part of our surrender negotiations. I tried for many turns to acquire music illegally on the streets, do the job myself. But I was never daring enough, or lucky enough, to procure what I needed.

Then the brothel opened. Madam is always hiring. Girls die or break down all the time, though such information is withheld from our clients as bad for business. Impossible to imagine any being paying to watch another lose control, lose dignity, lose any power over her own shuddering, leaping, twirling, trembling, would mind a death or two more.

"How about talking?" the Earther asks.

I'm puzzled. "We're talking now."

"Here." He slides from the chair to the smooth dance floor. "Sit beside me. Tell me about yourself."

I want to remind him about no touching, but he doesn't seem to have touching in mind. I sit, cautious, barely out of reach.

"I'm from Kansas," he says, ignoring the controller which would start his music on the player. "Used to fly crop dusters for a living, before the war. Eco-friendly fertilizers and such."

...Only half of which I understand. I know the war, obviously. The war between his world and mine. The war in which Pitre died on a sunny day during harvest season, in a city park, with a sandwich in his hand.

"Did you fly one of the planes that dropped the music?" I ask. Perhaps he killed Pitre.

He shakes his head. "No. I flew an ambulance. On Luna Colony. Got a medal for saving lives. A real hero." His voice goes harder than before. The last word rattles in his throat with a choking sound.

"On Moon?" I ask. "You were a hero on Moon?"

He smiles, but I don't know why. Earthern smiling is strange. It very much resembles preparing to bite. "On the moon, yes."

"Did we kill many, before you dropped the music on us?" I ask. Perhaps Madam wouldn't approve of me asking, because this seems to make the tall man sad. I couldn't care less what Madam thinks, but I need this job. I'm counting on it to kill me.

"Many, many people died," he says. "My brother, and my wife."

I know what a wife is, though the concept translates imperfectly to our language. It does, however, translate well enough. "Is that why you're here at Madam Zeti's?" I'm curious despite myself. "You're here to watch one of us suffer? To revel in that suffering?"

He frowns, an expression similar to ours with the same implication of dissatisfaction. "I thought survivors were immune. I thought those not susceptible to aortic or cerebral hemorrhage found music... pleasurable?" He stumbles over the last word, reddens in that peculiar human fashion. Another weakness.

I'm hoping the music he has brought is what I've been looking for these turns since Pitre's death. I don't want the Earther to change his mind about me, about this. In fact, the longer I spend with him, the more certainty settles in my third spleen: he is the one. The one who can reunite me with Pitre.

"Music is the greatest pleasure in the known universe," I tell him without falsehood.

The lines of his face ease, tiny muscles around his mouth and eyes relaxing. "Okay," he says, a meaningless rumble of filler noise Earthers use all the time in many of their thousand dialects. "Okay."

But he doesn't activate the controller to start the music. Instead he slides it into his pocket and begins to talk.

He talks and talks. He talks about something called cornfields, and about a four-legged pet he had as a child. He talks a little about his dead wife, but then his eyes well up with the water these people drip and so he stops. Thank the stars and all known planets that's one difference in our physiologies; I'd hate to leak without my will or control. It would be worse than musical ecstasy, because it seems accompanied by pain and not by pleasure.

He talks about the physics of interstellar travel, which any schoolchild knows but which Earthers have only recently discovered and so think wondrous. He talks about rain and blue skies—so unlike our arid planet's sky of constant dull purple they find tiring on the eyes—and about something called snow. He tells me he's been stationed by his government in one of the many artificial satellite cities they've constructed in orbit around our planet, since his own home was destroyed by our bombs—perhaps with his wife inside? He does not say.

And at last, at *last*, he talks about music.

He talks about long-dead Earth persons with ridiculous names: Billie and Chet and Ella and Mingus, and a human character he calls The Duke. He talks about ritualized dances set to rhythms he calls the foxtrot, the swing, the lindy, the waltz.

"I didn't know you ritualized dancing." I'm too surprised to prevent the words from spilling out. "Is it sacred, this organized dancing? Is it dangerous? Do many die?"

He smiles again, and makes that barking noise they think sounds sane. "No one ever died from dancing!" At my blank look he realizes his error. "I'm sorry," he says, miserable, reddening again. "I'm really sorry."

My eagerness has nearly cost me my chance. Certainty that the time is near, is now, solidifies in my spleens like a solid mass. I can almost hear the note that will be my death.

I stand. "Show me how you dance to your music."

He too stands, takes Madam's control box from his pocket, studies its keypad. He enters numbers, makes a few adjustments. The music chip he brought with him from off-planet so I could join my Pitre is already in its slot. He sets the controller on the chair, then holds his arms out to me, stiff as the limbs of a child's stone doll.

"Dance with me," he says.

Music flows from the box in gentle waves. I suck in my breath at the sound, it's so perfect. The note dips, sways as though it dances itself, sad and alone like me.

"You like it?" he asks.

I open my eyes. My body bends back and forth without me. My hands are sketching little stories in the air, stories about love, about loss, and about nothing at all.

Remembering the bobbing of the head which usually means yes on Earth, I bob. It feels silly, out of sync with the beautiful, bone-tingling melody. But he smiles, so I must've done it right.

"Miles Davis," he says, naming the music. Forgetting or ignoring brothel rules, he takes my arms, places them on his shoulders, puts his hands on each side of my waist.

The repulsion of touching one of Pitre's murderers is nearly enough to shock me from my music-induced trance—nearly, but not quite. In a brief flicker of moments I'm matching his sway. He's so tall, his eyes are nearly level with mine. They're closed, and he's making breathy, sealed-mouth noises along with the music's notes, but running behind as though trying to catch up. The volume's very low, a fraction of what it had been in the dancehall when Madam was assisting my client with his selection. His selection of me.

"This is nice," he says.

The music is so soft and his face so close, I hear his words even past the delicious thrumming in the marrow of my bones. My limbs feel liquid, lithe.

The song fades, receding from me like a hot-air balloon off its tether, washed in breezes of lavender and citron.

Guilt floods back along with my self-control. When I was lost to the music, I couldn't be held responsible for my actions. But sober, without that golden fire of notes streaming through my veins, I feel pathetic. I'd thought only of filling myself with this *Miles Davis*, leaving no room at all for Pitre.

It's wrong. All wrong. What sort of weak and worthless creature am I to violate the memory of our love by *enjoying* myself?

I thrust the Earth man away and stumble from the room, my limbs as heavy as they had just been light.

∞

Five full turns, day and night, and I haven't eaten. All the chambers of my stomach have ceased to care, giving up their vocal protests in favour of silent cramping. It is good. I am pleased. Though my death will have less meaning without my last moments being as Pitre's were, with the roar of music in his brain overriding the sound of bursting capillaries, the joy of notes drowning the pain of dying, perhaps it's for the best. I'm not worthy of the thing we had, of my dead Pitre. Unworthy of my shattered people and conquered planet.

All I've lost laps at me like a yellow ocean lapping a sandy shore, scouring with tide and time until nothing remains but bones and dead weeds. This will be me. Bones and dead weeds.

But as I slowly starve, my head grows lighter. It empties of Pitre, of responsibility, of my very self… and something strange begins to happen. It starts filling back up with music.

Initially, I'm uncertain what this means. When I hallucinate the first refrains drifting past my window, I take it for another attack from Earth. Whatever weakness in our brains makes us susceptible to music, makes us shimmy and shiver and shake and writhe until our clothes wear away, then our skins, then our bones, until nothing's left at all— this weakness will forever leave us vulnerable.

Staggering outside, I shake my fist at the lavender sky, shout as I search for the low-flying death machines, intending to curse them before the pleasure of their music sweeps me from myself and takes me over.

But nothing's there.

I'm a holdout in my home. No one lives for blocks around. Many neighborhoods lie completely vacant. I stand alone in my rockyard, lightheaded from lack of food and sleep, and shake fists at nothing.

Stumbling back to my sleeping pit, I flop and wallow on the cushions. Lights blink on my message console, but I ignore them. I'm not returning to Madam and her deadly puppet peep show.

When I hear the music a second time, I decide it's Pitre taunting me. I imagine him saying my devotion was no good, my commitment and my strength not enough. But then I remember how much he loved me, and I think, surely Pitre wouldn't wish me ill. Not ever. Not even now.

But the Miles Davis continues to haunt me. The remembered sweetness of the Earthern music makes my limbs grow heavy and weak. A strangely human-style smile curves at my mouth, feral and ambiguous.

Moments slide together, lengthening into turns while my stomachs rumble and shrink.

By the end of the seventh turn my message panel stops blinking, Madam giving up on me at last, or perhaps the power being cut from my abandoned neighborhood. It's not as though any one melody sits on me, weighing me down. Rather, music wafts past, buoying me with deceptively simple strains.

By the rising of the sun on the eighth turn, I decide the music in my mind is Pitre's gift. He loves me enough to want me to have it, even from beyond oblivion.

On the day of the ninth turn I try to follow the notes. Starved, grieving, exhausted, I pound the empty city streets in my imagination, hands outstretched for an elusive *something* fluttering beyond reach. I know I'm delirious with lack of food and water, though my stomach pangs have long subsided. Lilac and clear, this ninth—tenth? eighth?—day, as I can see through the window from my sleeping pit. Hard to believe humans consider our gentle purple light inadequate. Perhaps their eyes are as weak as the vessels in our brains.

Music filters into me from all sides. I close my eyes and mimic my client from Madam Zeti's, make a breathy noise with my lips sealed, following the tune in an approximation that is both inaccurate and satisfying. *Humming*, I remember now. That's the human word for it. I'd forgotten, before.

I expect the music to drift away, fade back out as it has these last few pain-filled turns. But it doesn't. It swells, says my name, "Tetre."

Opening my eyes, intending to answer the Miles Davis, I see the human client from Madam Zeti's.

∞

The Earther is called Logan Brinks. He bribed Madam to disclose my name and the quadrant where I live, though even she didn't know the exact location of my home. He's been looking for me, wandering my empty neighborhood for turns, playing his illegal music in hopes I'd hear and come out. He's lucky his own people haven't arrested him for treaty violation, or ours haven't torn him limb from limb. Not that there's anyone left around here to notice, or to care. Most survivors moved to vacant quarters in better quadrants of the city long ago.

Between meals he tells me of the many human lives he saved during the war, the hollow commendations he received and the celebrations in his honor he did not want to join. He sometimes talks about his old home to which he can never return, about his dead wife, about a thing called chicken whose flesh he misses frying.

He refuses to leave. He has moved into the abandoned house next door and now refers to it as *home*, as if to replace the one he lost so far away. For several turns now he has nursed me to health, consulting a small handheld device he loads with information chips about our physiology, our dietary habits, our language. He can almost pronounce a few of our simplest words—fewer than a baby. I don't tell him his last name translates into a scatological obscenity. He'll find out someday, but it won't be from me.

And then there's the music. He tries various songs on me, varying volumes and beats and tonal ranges, like a doctor testing patches of skin for an allergy. Some music is kinder to my system than others. At first I feared becoming an addict, a junkie similar to some girls at Madam Zeti's. But Logan Brinks says not everyone is equally suited to addictive behaviors. He believes us capable of building a tolerance as one might to a venom, though he equates it more to strengthening a muscle. He wants to take me to his satellite hospital and run tests, fearing for my fragile brain without his medical machines nearby. I've refused.

What I've not refused are his dance lessons. I grow stronger with each step. And turn by turn, we learn which music fills me with happiness instead of helplessness, with power instead of pain. It's trial and error. I suppose we could finally hit the wrong note and it would all be over in an instant, at least for me. Having monitored me carefully every turn, the Earther thinks this unlikely. But he worries.

I don't. The moment I join Pitre will be sublime, as joyous as our time together, as the life we built and the future we thought we'd get.

And until then I have music. And dance lessons. And Miles Davis.

Until then, I have Logan Brinks.

About the Author
Alexandra Renwick

Alexandra Renwick is a dual U.S. / Canadian writer whose short fiction has been translated into nine languages and adapted to audio and stage. Born in the west and raised in the south, she currently lives in a crumbling urban castle up north. Talk noir, literary fabulism, or life in heritage homes on Twitter @AlexCRenwick.

Author Website: https://alexcrenwick.com/

Yamaduta's Deathsong
by Fadzlishah Johanabas

The first time I killed, I was only ten.

I've been scrubbing my hands raw for the past thirteen years. The stain goes away, but the memory stays. I can never wash off the memory.

My hands tremble as I cup them under the faucet. The stupid motion detector takes several seconds to kick in, and when it does, rust-tinged water spurts out in spasmodic coughs. The ceiling flickers, just to remind me that nothing works anymore in this apartment. I'm late with my rent by two months, so I won't push my luck complaining to the landlord.

I make a mental note to do the repair work myself.

Tomorrow, maybe. Right now, I need to get rid of the blood on my hands. And my clothes. I squirm out of my gray overalls and dump them at the far corner of the bathroom, on top of the clothes that belong to the unconscious stranger on my bed. From the rank that's starting to pervade the entire bathroom, I need to get rid of all the clothes. And my bed sheet.

Celaka. I love that bed sheet.

When I close the shower stall door, the privacy glass only activates for a few pathetic seconds, flickers—almost in sync with the ceiling— and then remains clear. Well, cloudy from collected grime and several patches of green fungus near the base, but still.

It's not like the unconscious guy is going to take a peep or anything. It's not like I have anything he doesn't have. Skinny, malnourished guy like me? I have nothing that will interest or threaten him. I can't even remember the last time I had a proper haircut. It's a good thing I can't seem to grow a beard or moustache.

The tattoo—the brand—on his arm, though. That's what worries me.

To distract myself, I concentrate on the rivulets of blood and garbage goop as they mingle with rusty water and spiral into the drain. I keep my eyes open even though water from the shower stings them to tears, because behind closed lids, I can see the faces of the dead.

Not that it matters. I can still see the faces of the three men I killed not one hour ago.

Well, they killed one another. What I did was make their weapons do the dirty work for me. The look on their faces, from condescending amusement to incredulous to disbelief to horror, it's always the same. I can recall each of the thirteen years' worth of faces.

Only after the shower stall air-dries me do I realize I don't have a towel or a fresh set of clothes. I duck into the den and fish for clean clothes from the laundry pile by the bed. The guy is still knocked out cold. Maybe I should have brought him to a hospital instead of here. Then again, I don't think I can explain all the blood splatter. Plus, he's almost a head taller than me and at least thirty kilograms heavier, give or take. He's still filthy, and the bruises have started to swell, but he looks almost at peace. Underneath the blanket, he's naked.

I shake my head and concentrate on putting on my clothes. It's difficult to unsee what I saw when I took off his clothes. With flawless mahogany skin and lean muscle—and the sharp nose and chiseled jaw that go with the body—I bet he's an escort. That's the only decently paying job here in the slums of Kuala Lumpur for guys like him.

I slide out my stash from under the bed. I have only two vials left. My hand still trembling, I take one of the vials of glowing aqua-colored fluid and slump on the once-working form-fitting sofa. I empty the contents and wait for the effect to kick in.

Within minutes I feel a sense of calm wash over me like seawater lapping against the shore. I've never been out of Kuala Lumpur, so I haven't seen an actual beach, but I've been in enough virtual reality scapes to know how it feels to plant my feet in wet sand and feel the sea flow against my skin, around me, over me and under me.

My entire body relaxes and when I close my eyes, the faces with the dead, confused eyes do not appear. There is a sense of emptiness, one that I've been looking for my entire life. I can feel myself disappearing, dissipating. The void beckons me, and I embrace it.

...and our hands, slick with blood, lose our grip. She is taken in one direction, and I another. I cry out her name. Ariana. Ariana.

And then the lab explodes, and the world goes searing red.

∞

I wake up to a deep-throated groan.

The empty vial, balancing precariously on my lax hand, falls onto the floor with a tiny chink when I move. The guy is waking up, thank the Almighty. If he had died, I wouldn't know where to dump him. Maybe the murky Klang River if I were strong enough to drag him there without attracting attention. It's not like the authorities would care about another missing person from the slums, anyway.

Unless he's not from the slums.

"Ganesha's balls. Where... what happened?" he asks. He has a good tenor. Not nearly as good as mine, but still good.

I don't answer him. I just watch him from the sofa.

He struggles to sit up, and when he does, the blanket slides down. Framed by the light of the neon signboard just outside the window, he really looks beautiful.

Too bad I downed the wrong drug to do anything about it.

"I was attacked by three men," he says, massaging his temples. "Someone..." He stops talking and crinkles his nose when his blood-and-goop-caked hands come too near to his face. His eyes dart around the small apartment and only stop when he notices me.

What a sight I must be, slumped like a boneless cat in clothes that have seen much better days, with uncombed hair and barely-focused eyes. I raise my right hand and let it drop. "Yo," I say.

"You saved me?" he asks. "Why?"

I point at the tattoo on his left arm.

He quickly covers it with his right hand, but when he realizes he's not wearing anything under the fast-slipping blanket, he drops his hand and covers himself up instead.

"For an escort, you're surprisingly modest," I say.

"I'm not an escort," he says, huffing with indignity.

"Relax," I say. "I'm not judging." Then I lift my left sleeve.

On the outer side of my arm is a tattoo that has been forcefully burned onto my skin. It's small, and the scars have healed, but the black writing is clear if anyone's anywhere near me. It says, *HOMOSEKSUAL*. It's the same tattoo that the guy on my bed has.

He visibly relaxes, and he holds sympathy in his eyes.

No. Empathy.

"How did you—" he says.

"I got caught having VR sex in a supposedly secure channel," I say, cutting him off. "You?"

"I was at a massage parlor," he says. "But I'm not an escort!"

"Then?"

"I was a client. Dumbest luck ever," he mumbles.

"You have that Malay look, but you're not a Malay, are you? Why were you branded?" I ask. I sit straighter; the effect of the drug is wearing off.

"My dad's Indian and my mom's Chinese," he says. "And we're Muslims. Or at least, I was raised a Muslim."

"So you're a gay, Muslim Chindian?" I say. "That's... unfortunate."

He huffs. "Tell me about it."

"Stupid government and its stupid laws," I say. "They of all people should know that tattoos are forbidden in Islam. They must be thinking that gays are degenerates who don't pray."

"Do you?" he asks, his tone careful.

"Praying keeps me calm." I don't add that no matter how much I pray, I'm going straight to hell for all the lives I've taken. He doesn't need to know that.

"So you're one of the only practicing Malay Muslims I've encountered, and you're a convicted gay," he says. "That's… unfortunate."

I can't help it. I laugh. It feels good to hear myself laugh again. I thought I'd forgotten how to do it.

"The men who ganked me," he says. "*You* took them out?"

"I know I don't look like much," I say. Had the drug completely worn off, my hackles would have been raised. "But here in Kampung Baru, we slum rats learn to survive."

He nods. "Thanks. I'm Vairavan. Call me Vai."

"Go take a shower," I say. "You smell like a dead rat. Clean clothes are by the bed. There must be something that fits you in there somewhere. I'll find us some grub."

He takes a whiff at himself and gags. "A shower is a good idea."

I push myself up and approach him. I offer my right hand.

"I'm Andri."

∞

I duck under the shelter of a row of abandoned buildings almost in time to avoid the acid rain. Already the areas where rainwater touches my skin are itching. It takes a supreme measure of restraint not to scratch myself raw, which will only make things worse.

This late at night, no one else is around. A few maglev cars whizz by, lighting up my surroundings with their headlights. Otherwise, the only source of illumination is the spluttering streetlights.

Lightning cracks open the sky, and for a few seconds I can make out the silhouette of KL Tower—or the jagged stump that used to be KL Tower before it collapsed ten years ago back in 2023. The twin towers of KLCC are not visible, but then again the high-rise condominiums of Kampung Baru that pretend not to notice the slums at their bases have long since blocked the view.

I approach a heavily chained shop lot—the only one in the row without the red paint of foreclosure streaked across its door—and tap a series of numbers on the old-school digital pad beside the door. For those with less discerning eyes, the pad, which is the only patch without a thick coat of dust covering it, would have gone unnoticed. Chinese script is barely visible over the door, a relic of an era long gone. Before the race riots and subsequent segregation in 2018, Chinese people were not afraid to open shop in Kampung Baru.

I've heard of a lot of things that were much better back then. Now everything's going to hell. Especially those misguided, pious zealots and their fake fatwas who have the government by the nuts.

I rub the raised scar where the tattoo is and make sure it is hidden, out of habit.

After the third attempt, the pad lights up green, followed by a soft click. I pull open the door. The chains are only a clever façade. Inside, a bleary-eyed, old Chinese man who has lost most of his wispy hair yawns, showing yellowed teeth and blackened stumps. He always refuses to reveal his age, but I bet he's over a hundred years old.

"Hi Uncle Yong," I say.

"You know how late it is?" he asks, and yawns again. Uncle Yong is among the few non-Malays grudgingly tolerated here in Kampung Baru, and it's not because of his hospitality.

"I'm almost out," I say.

Uncle Yong is still here for one reason alone: he's the only supplier of emotion drugs here. The real deal, not the diluted ones they sell off the streets.

He exhales on the surface of his glasses before he puts them on. He's been wearing the same old-school computer glasses since I first started coming here. "I thought I sold you a month's worth?" he says. "You still owe me half the payment, by the way."

I place the cash chip I pilfered from one of the guys I killed on the counter in front of him. "There's almost three thousand ringgit here. You can start a tab for future purchases."

He examines the chip and pockets it. What I like about Uncle Yong is that he never asks where I get the cash chips. *Money is money*, he told me once.

Uncle Yong hums as he reaches for the upper shelves and pulls out a tray of vials containing glowing aqua liquids. The glow is subtler than what I'm used to.

"That's different," I say.

"You didn't have money, so I sold you the medium-grade stuff. This is high-grade calm."

As I said, he's not here for his hospitality.

"How much?" I ask.

"This is pure activated oxytocin. One vial can keep you calm for at least three days, minus the side effects." He pointedly glances at the fine tremors of my hands. "Fifty ringgit a vial."

I'm used to buying at ten ringgit a pop. "That's too expensive!"

"Ah Chai," he says. He always calls me "boy" in Cantonese even though he knows my name is Andri. "Calm is the cheapest drug I have. No one wants to feel calm. Everyone wants to be high and happy." He takes out a vial of glowing pink liquid from his pocket. "Or horny. I can throw in a vial of lust if you buy more than ten vials of calm."

"And look what my libido got me," I say. I don't have to show him the brand on my left arm. He knows it's there.

"Dui, dui," he says in agreement. "Then you can try this," he says. He takes out a vial of glowing sky-blue liquid.

"What's that?" I say.

"Clarity. A bit of adrenaline, a bit of testosterone. It's good to help you focus. Try it."

I raise an eyebrow at him, but I take a sip nonetheless. Nothing happens at first, but I know from experience that ingested emotion drugs sometimes take a minute or so to kick in.

And when it does, it really kicks. I don't even struggle as my consciousness splutters and drowns.

∞

I walk home from work, if you call cleaning factory robotic lines work. It's a mind-numbing job, sure, and the pay sucks, but I get lunch, and the monotonous rhythm helps keep me out of my head.

For dinner I get a free meal at the mosque after Maghrib prayers. It's one of the initiatives to get people coming to the mosque, but at most I've seen twenty people during prayer times. I don't talk to the congregation, and they don't disturb me. I wonder how they will react if they see my brand.

The mosque to my apartment is not that far, but I have to pass several dark alleys. I usually keep my head low and walk as fast as I can without appearing to be rushing. People can smell fear. And money. I'm convinced of it.

Sometimes I can hear people getting mugged or beaten up—or both—within the shadows of those dark, stinking alleys. I just ignore them. People never help me, so why should I help them? Tonight, however, I have the bad luck of overhearing two words: "gay scum."

I clench my fists and step into the shadows. In the dim light from the windows above us, I can make out three men taking turns kicking a guy who's lying in a fetal position by an overflowing trash crate. He's not moving. Either he's already unconscious or he's dead. The entire place stinks of wet, dead rats, so I'm not surprised if the stench got to him before the kicks did.

One of the bigger guys keeps repeating, "Gay scum." The more he does it, the tighter my fists become. I can see that all three of them are wearing armband computers. I can tell just by looking at the model that the armbands are linked to cranial implants.

Perfect.

"Hey!"

The guys stop kicking and turn to face me. All three of them are panting from exertion. Their heads are shaven smooth. No matter what the government propaganda speeches claim, the Malay supremacist culture is still alive and kicking.

I chuckle at my own pun.

"You're one of those fried junkies, aren't you?" says one of the guys. "Just get along and we'll let you go. Or are you here to save your boy-friend?" He raps his knuckles and advance toward me. "If you're one of them gay scums, you're at the wrong place, kid."

"No," I say. "*You* are."

I haven't sung in a long time, but I learned to sing even before I learned to walk. One doesn't forget what's in one's genetic code. I clear my throat and start singing a classic electric-rock song from the early 2020s. All three men look at one another and then at me in conde-scending amusement.

And then their armband computers light up in response to my singing.

When their arms start moving out of their control, the amusement turns to confusion.

I keep singing.

One of them is wearing a cranial implant, the high-end one. Even better. My Songster gene enables me to control weaponry, and anything electronic can be turned into a weapon. Even a daft kid knows that.

The guys start punching and smashing one another to the tune of my song. Their wide eyes now show complete and unadulterated horror. It's beautiful, really, how the punches are like drumbeats, and the screams and the empty threats are like a background choir. Blood splatters as their heads get crushed against the wall, complementing the artistry of their death.

It is when I sing this deathsong that I feel completely alive.

I only stop singing when all three men lie slumped and distorted in their own pools of blood. Their armband computers are frizzled and useless. I put on a pair of gloves and rummage through their pockets for cash chips and other useful things. No one will miss them, I'm sure of that. The stench of their corpses will only mingle with that of the rats.

Then I pull and drag the unconscious guy back to my place.

∞

"Wh—what are you doing?" Uncle Yong says. His eyes are wide, his mouth agape.

I come to my senses as abruptly as I lost them. The drug is really something. Where his face holds wonder and terror and confusion all at once, mine holds only confusion.

Then I notice the automated weaponry with robotic arms all pointing at Uncle Yong, charged and ready to fire. I never knew his rickety shop held such advanced weaponry.

I must have been singing when I lost control of my faculties.

I clamp my mouth shut and the robotic arms return to their hiding places.

"Uncle Yong," I say, not knowing how to explain myself. "I'm a paying, unarmed customer! Why were your guns pointed at me? Where did you get those guns, anyway?"

"I didn't activate the security," he says. He wipes his forehead and heaves a heavy sigh.

"Then you're saying I sang them to life?" I ask with the blandest tone I can muster. My hands are shaking hard.

"Or maybe my security system hates your singing," he says with a nervous chuckle.

I heave a sigh of relief of my own. I know it's easier for his mind to process this as a malfunction and as a joke rather than accept the possibility that I have an ability that his mind cannot comprehend.

This is good. This way, I don't have to find another supplier. I don't have to kill him to protect my secret.

"I'll have ten vials of calm," I say. "But I don't want clarity. Throw in that vial of lust instead."

Uncle Yong peers closer. "You'll be wasting this perfectly good vial on that VR crap of yours."

"Who says I need VR?" I say, and I wink at him.

Uncle Yong shakes his head and chuckles. "Young people," he says.

∞

I go home drenched and shivering from the persistent rain to an apartment that I can barely recognize.

"What did you do?" I ask in sincere horror.

Vairavan is sitting at a desk that I've forgotten I had, tinkering with my beat-up armband computer. The bed is made up with a fresh set of sheets and pillowcases—I'm sure the set hasn't been out of storage for the past two years or so—and my clean clothes are neatly folded in one pile, and the dirty ones are in a bag by the toilet. The kitchenette is still an absolute mess, but I'm sure if I had been out longer, even the kitchenette and the toilet would have fallen victim.

"Sorry I couldn't clean much," he says. "Moving hurts."

"Not as much as how I'm going to hurt you," I say. "Celaka. I had a system."

Vai's shoulders slump and his eyes are downcast. He has really long lashes. If his hair weren't close-cropped military style, he'd look way better. The T-shirt he has on fits a little too snug, but then again, I've seen him naked. "Sorry," he says. "I was trying to look for a computer or the remote for your wall monitor. You do have one, right?"

"Why?" I ask. In my mind, I'm debating the ethics of feeding him lust without his consent.

"Mine got mugged and I really need to establish contact with someone. What happened to your armband, anyway?" he says, holding up my limp armband computer. "The mainboard is fried, but with the right gear, I think I can repair it."

I was contemplating suicide when I became aware I was humming and the armband flew right at me. I managed to duck in time, which made me realize I didn't want to die after all. Couldn't do anything to stop the armband from hitting the wall, though.

But Vai doesn't need to know that, either.

I reach for my work gear—which is thankfully in the portion of the apartment he hasn't tidied up—and dump it on the desk. "Will this help?" I say.

Vai goes through the gear with wide-eyed wonder. "Roogus. We're in business. Where did you get this gear, anyway?"

"I clean robots for work. You?"

Vai doesn't look up when he answers. "You're looking at it."

"You're a repairman?" I ask.

Vai snorts but continues repairing the armband computer. I place a packet of rice with synthetic chicken in front of him and I take a seat opposite him, eating while I watch him work. By the time I finish my food, Vai is inspecting his handiwork with a twinkle in his eyes.

"Done! You have a working TV screen, right?"

It takes me a few minutes to find the remote. The clean space is confusing. I hand it to him. "It's useless, anyway," I say. "They cut off my skyweb access."

Vai ignores me and clicks the remote. The blank wall opposite my bed comes to life. He puts on the armband computer and flicks his fingers over it to activate the holopad. He types strings upon strings of commands with a speed that makes me cross-eyed.

Once he hits *enter* on the last command, the screen goes blank before images of moving clouds fill the wall.

"There you go," he says, grinning smugly. "Free skyweb for life. Courtesy of LordShiva."

"You're a hacker!"

"You sound disappointed," he says.

"I thought you were, you know, an escort."

"I told you I wasn't an escort!" He follows my eyes looking at his fine biceps. "Oh. This? You think hackers are all skinny and pale and anti-social?" He stops and looks at me, as if realizing he may have said the wrong words. "No offense," he mumbles.

"None taken." Well, I *am* skinny and pale and anti-social. There's no denying that.

"The company I work for," he says, his eyes on the screen. "They have a fully functioning gym with personal trainers. They keep us fit so that we are more productive."

"Big corporations employ hackers?"

"Of course they do, but it's usually to prevent hackers like me from breaking into their systems. They don't always succeed, though."

"You sound proud," I say.

"I am," he says. "At least we're helping the people in ways no one else can."

"LordShiva?" I ask. "Aren't you Muslim?"

"I said I was raised a Muslim. Still am, I think. Just not a practic-ing one. My grandfather was a devout Hindu, back when they could practice openly. He was a farmer in Kedah, just like his father, and his father before him. Just like my dad and my mom."

"Why aren't you a farmer?" I ask. I'm curious about him now.

"I was raised a farmer like I was raised a Muslim," he says. His eyes are unfocused, as if recalling a memory he's not sure is good or bad. "That's how I learned the discipline to keep my body fit. But I was also too bright to stay in a backwater farm in a state that's now only good for agriculture. I got into trouble hacking into state record offices, and when I got out of juvie, this rep from a small company approached me. So here I am."

I keep quiet, absorbing what he's said.

"Well, I wasn't supposed to be here, but you get what I mean. What about you?"

"I was grown in a lab where they cultured us to be human weapons through our singing. They discovered something called the Songstress gene and spliced it in. I don't have parents, only a twin sister. I blew up the lab when I was ten to save her, but she died anyway."

Vai looks at me, blinks, and then bursts out laughing. "Singing weapons," he says. "Really. That's roogus. A little far-fetched, but roogus. Are you sure you're not a writer? You look as broke as one."

I chuckle along to his laughter. This is the first time I ever openly told anyone about my past, and even though Vai doesn't believe me, it feels good to finally be able to tell someone.

Without having to kill him afterward, that is.

"What were you doing in the alley, anyway? You look too well-nourished to be from the slums," I say.

Vai turns to look at me. "You'd be surprised if I told you where my base is. Which I can't, so don't ask."

I raise my hands in mock surrender.

His face turns somber, his eyes shadowed. "I was supposed to meet my contact not far from where you found me. I got caught in the rain and my drenched shirt was burning my skin. I took it off, and those idiots must have seen my brand."

I absently rub my own brand.

"I hope they'll die a horrible death."

I balk at this, and shrink deep into myself.

"Did something happen?" Vai asks.

I shake my head. "Nothing. What's with all this hacker spy thing, anyway?"

Vai's face lights up. Either he's the kind of person who cannot hide his emotions or I'm so enthralled by his handsome face that I notice every nuance. "Have you heard about the separatist farmers movement?" he asks.

"Vaguely. I don't really care about this political stuff."

"It's not politics," Vai says. "The rice you eat, that comes from us." He shakes his head. "Well, not from me. From my parents and other farmers like them. The government has already banned farmers from growing poultry and rearing cattle after the viral outbreaks, so we're only left with plant-based food. Even then, giant companies like Sime Guthrie put a chokehold on us and we have to go through them to sell our products. They make billions, we stay poor."

"At least they have an outlet to sell their wares," I say. "We city folk have it worse. When the synthetic food chains took over, all the small businesses died off. Haven't you seen all those abandoned shops and restaurants?"

Vai nods, his eyes alight. "That's the reason for the separatist movements. The government is clearly controlled by these giant corporations.

The farmers unions of the northern states have banded together to fight against them, to regain our independence."

"You keep saying 'we' and 'us.' Like you're still one of them."

Vai gives a rueful grin. He really looks good when he smiles. "I guess I'm still a farm boy from Kedah at heart," he says.

"You don't need to convince me," I say. "Sometimes your Kedahan slang slips."

Vai laughs and bumps my shoulder with his fist. Then he leans forward and kisses me.

I jerk back.

"That was... I'm sorry, Andri!"

I can still taste the salty sweat on his lips, and I can still feel their softness. "No. It's just... that was my first actual kiss."

Vai crinkles his nose and narrows his eyes. "That bad?"

"Not at all," I say. Maybe it's the drug, but somehow it doesn't feel wrong. It doesn't feel like the Almighty will smite me this instant. "Just... unexpected."

I guess I might not need the vial of lust after all.

Vai returns his attention to the screen and opens a new command window where he types another series of strings. His long fingers are deft, and he doesn't need to look at the holopad to type.

"What are you doing?" I say.

"Pinging my contact. She's late."

"One of you?" I say.

"She calls herself a masseuse, but she's an escort," he says. "She's a freelance informant. Do you know how loose people's tongues can be after sex?"

I shrug. "I wouldn't know. VR avatars don't talk much."

Vai cocks an eyebrow at me. "About that..." He opens a new window and enters another string of commands. "There. Your line now piggybacks other lines in this neighborhood, and I've configured a twenty-forty-eight bit encryption. You can have VR sex all you want for free with anyone from anywhere in the world, and it's secure. Nothing someone like me can't overcome without breaking a sweat, though, so don't go hacking into security channels."

"Like I'd know how to do it. It's too late to have an encrypted line for VR sex, anyway," I say, absently rubbing the brand on my arm.

"Why'd you want to resort to VR, anyway?"

"I—"

"Hold that thought, Andri. My informant is pinging me back."

I shrink into the shadows as Vai opens a video call window and maximizes it. "Arya," he says. "Can you hear me?"

The video on the screen is dark, with connection glitches off and on. I can barely make out the face of the woman filling the screen. It's also loud, like she's in the middle of a rainstorm. I look out the window. The downpour hasn't abated. Maybe the informant is nearby.

"LordShiva, I was expecting to meet you in person," she says. With the poor connection, she sounds like an alto. She might be a soprano.

"I almost didn't make it here alive. Are you secure?"

"You tell me," she says. "You're the one who sent me this armband computer."

"If no one from Sime Guthrie is prying on us," he says, "the line is as secure as it can get. What I meant was are you safe?"

"Is that concern I'm detecting?"

The more I listen to her speak, the more I am convinced that her voice is meant for singing. There's an unexplainable sense of familiarity about it. I keep in the shadows, not wanting to disrupt the conversation.

"Listen, you don't have time to waste. Sime Guthrie knows about the coup and is planning to send in the big guns."

Vai curses in Tamil and Chinese. Hokkien, I think. "What kind of big guns?" he says.

"The biggest," she says. "In three days' time, they'll be sending in companies from Penang, southern Thailand and Kuala Lumpur. The Northern farmers unions will be outflanked, and Sime Guthrie is prepared to burn everything to the ground to flush out the farmers and kill them off. They're bringing in workers from other countries who are more manageable."

"Three days?" Vai says. His eyes are wide and wild. "I haven't been able to contact my parents or the union leaders."

"They've cut off skyweb connection to the northern states. Unless you have one of those obsolete phone lines, you're out of luck," Arya says.

"The government," Vai says. "We need to warn them."

Arya scoffs. "Who do you think signed the approval letter? Listen, LordShiva. I'm going dark until the dust settles. Don't try to contact me. Don't come looking for me. I'll be the one establishing contact when it's safe."

Vairavan nods. "Thanks. Stay secure. You know how to get one of us in case you can't find me. We'll wire the payment the usual way."

"Sure," she says. "Tell your boyfriend he doesn't have to hide in the shadows the next time we talk." She winks in my direction.

Rolling clouds filled the screen once more. Vairavan chuckles and shakes his head. "Women," he says. "You can't hide anything from them."

"You need to help your people," I say. I've always kept my head so low, I've forgotten how big the world is.

"Come with me," Vai says.

"Where?"

"Kedah. I need to travel to Alor Setar for us to have any chance at stopping this massacre. You heard her. There are over seventy thousand farmers out there, and they're going to be killed. *My parents* are going to be killed."

Before I can give an answer, the door slams inward. Splinters fly and land near us. Men in black combat gear stream in, guns pointed at us. I turn to look at Vai. Red laser dots skitter on his chest and head. I'm sure I have my own laser dots as well.

"Hands where we can see them," one of the men says. His voice is deep, throaty like sandpaper.

I don't dare move any closer to Vai. I raise my hands. "You said the line was secure."

"It was. Their response is way too fast."

"Shut up or we'll shoot," the man barks.

I can make out at least six men blocking our exit. I steal a glance at the window. Two more are suspended on black ropes, their guns also pointed at us.

Celaka.

The men blocking the door shuffle and a wizened man with wisps of hair that does nothing to cover his balding pate walks in.

Uncle Yong.

"I don't think they're here for you," I whisper to Vai. To Uncle Yong, I say, "I thought the cash chip was good. You can have back your vials."

Uncle Yong chitters. His wide grin puts his rotten teeth on display. "Do you know how the drugs are made?" he asks.

"I don't care how they're made. Just take them back."

"We use women to sing to activate these drugs. Such a wonder. I asked my friend Mister Choi once, why only women?"

It's impossible. He can't be talking about the same Mister Choi who made our lives miserable when we were kids in the lab. Not the same Mister Choi who wanted to sell my sister Ariana to the armed forces.

"You know what he told me?" Uncle Yong asks uninterrupted. "Girls affect emotions, and the boys are even more special."

"What is this old man talking about?" Vai says.

"Take him out," Uncle Yong says.

Before I can react, a single shot is fired, and Vairavan slumps onto the floor. He blinks in confusion. Blood blossoms from the right side of his chest.

I fall onto my knees and cradle Vai. He holds a million questions in his eyes, but those questions are fading fast.

"No. No. No. No."

"You have a beautiful voice," Vairavan whispers. He coughs out bright blood. He winces, catches his breath. "And a beautiful face."

"No, no, no." My mind is a red haze now. Warm tears escape my eyes and fall onto his face.

"Save my people." His voice is barely audible. "Save Arya."

His eyes no longer hold any question.

"Get the boy and let's get out of here," Uncle Yong says.

I've forgotten his presence. I've forgotten the other men.

But not their weapons.

My voice is soft at first, as cracked as I am broken.

...Mister Choi explains to the military men how Ariana can produce purity, a liquid that can control minds. They want her.

I don't let them.

Breathe, I tell myself.

Sing.

I don't hold anything back this time.

I can feel the weapons responding to my singing. Uncle Yong lunges at me, but his armband computer takes control and he is suspended in mid-air. The men look at each other in confusion, but before they know it, their weapons start firing.

Not at me.

At one another.

I sit in the middle of it all, the eye of the tempest, as they shoot. One of them shoots Uncle Yong at the back of his head, and he collapses in front of me, his eyes wide and accusatory.

I sing even as gunshots ring in my ears so loud that my own voice sounds muffled. I sing even as blood splatters on my face, on my body, everywhere. I sing my deathsong until every one of them is lying on their own pool of blood.

When the world is still, I stop singing. I gather Vairavan in my arms and cry.

"It's been awhile since anyone cried for me."

I look down. Now that the haze is clearing, I can see Vairavan's chest moving. He's breathing.

He's smiling.

"How... how are you still alive?"

He shrugs, and then winces. "I don't know, but it hurts like hell. I guess you weren't lying about that genetic experiment thing, huh? You're like a Yamaduta."

"A what?"

"Messengers of Yamaraja."

"Who?"

Vairavan chuckles, and then groans. "It really hurts. Messengers of Death."

"Yamaduta," I say. "I like it. It's roogus."

"I can really use your help with the uprising."

"No. You need to go to the hospital."

"After that, then."

"After that."

The first time I killed, I was ten. I've been living in hiding, in guilt ever since. This is the first time I don't see the faces of those I've killed. I can only see Vairavan's.

I will live in hiding no more.

About the Author
Fadzlishah Johanabas

Fadzlishah "Fadz" Johanabas is a neurosurgeon practicing in a public hospital in Malaysia. He has published over 25 short stories to venues like *Interzone, Cosmos Australia, Crossed Genres* and *Apex Book of World SF 3*. 14 of his published stories have been collected in a single-author collection, *Faith and the Machine*. He tweets his random thoughts as @ Fadz_Johanabas.

Author Website: http://www.fadzjohanabas.com/

Love in the Vapors
by Colleen Anderson

Zady looked out the thick porthole at the undulating plane of stone and dirt, bleached to a pale orange beneath the ever-present thick expanse of clouds. Her com rattled like an insect, not that she had ever seen a live one. That DNA was in stasis on the Venera One station, waiting for the day that beneficial insects would be needed. For now, the techs pollinated the plants.

"Zady," she replied as she moved along the softly lit corridor, dragging the heavy engine behind her.

"Hey, Venusian."

Shardeen, with her usual bad timing and silly nickname. She knew perfectly well that the interference from the planetary surface to the orbiting space station made communications iffy. She smiled. "Hey, Space Cadet. I only have a few seconds. I'm about to go down the shaft."

Zady had two hours tops before her enhanced physique and the insulated suit would begin to succumb to Venus's crushing embrace. Then she would have to get back to the aerostat city floating high above the corrosive atmosphere.

Shardeen remained silent for a few seconds. Was it the delay?

"I know, hon, but this couldn't wait. Look, I'll be quick—" The interference hissed in Zady's ear. *"—sorry we couldn't discuss it before, but... I want a baby."*

"What!" Zady stopped, the engine rolling into her calves, urging her along. She pulled, moving toward the shaft's sealed door that led beneath the planet's crust. Even with the cooled suit, and her epidermis engineered to endure the planet's searing temperatures and brightness, she was sweating. "How can you bring this up now? I'm not back with you on Venera One for a year!"

The com crackled, the interference making Shardeen's voice gravelly. *"I'm sorry, Zady. I just— I never thought I'd have to decide so soon. The support crew is moving from Venera One to the aerostat, to Agni, in eleven months and… and they said I wouldn't be able to bear the pressure there, to have children, because I'm spaceborn."*

Zady ground her teeth. "How can you do this to me now? You know I'll be back on Agni in ten hours and we can talk better then, even if you're not there. How can you make this decision without me?"

She thought she heard a sob. *"I… I know, I know, but I wanted you to know, just in case."*

"In case what?"

There was nothing but static. Zady pulled up to the hatch and bent over to punch the codes. The bots had built the dark paneled corridors, drilled the shaft, set the environment, all beforehand, but the fine tuning required a human to calibrate the engine now. The diode lights blinked and flickered but spun through the numbers to a set of zeroes. Then the hatch slowly opened. Which idiot, she wondered, thought it necessary to have security codes on a god and people forsaken planet?

Zady hooked the cables to the metal rings on the engine, and pressed a button to lift it off the dolly. The dynamos hummed and strained. She couldn't stop to argue with Shardeen, whose voice came back faint, sad.

"In case you don't come back."

"Shardeen, what the hell! First you drop a bomb that you want a child when I'm not going to see you for a year, a child that I won't have any part in, any decision in whether I want one or not. Then you give me omens that I might not return. Have some faith!

"We've been working the Veneran surface for ten years. How the hell do you think I won't come back? There are no little green anythings down here to hurt me. There is no life but me!"

She was mad. So mad that for a moment the blurry Veneran surface wavering outside the portholes looked redder. Maybe they should have tried to colonize Mars first. *That* was the god of anger, after all.

Venus wasn't a tame planet and had made everyone work to love her. But they knew her well, with very few secrets and the dangers well known. Venera One had orbited the planet for more than fifty years, the crew on the space station working on building the aerostat city first. A generation had started on the station; another had been born and engineered there. Forty-two people were naturals, like Shardeen. Zady and eight others that had survived were engineered to withstand some of the harshness of Venus's atmosphere. Their brown eyes were nearly black, with polarization enhancements, and dark skin tones that would resist skin cancer during the eventual planetside colonization. The first successfully modified Venerans.

But while her stocky, well-muscled physique could withstand higher temperatures and pressure, Zady was still human through and through, and Shardeen was crushing her heart. She felt betrayed.

Shardeen's voice came through fainter. *"That's just it, Zade. You're the first one to set foot. There are contingencies, protocols, but you are the first human test."*

She couldn't lose it now, had to keep her cool. Venus was hot enough and there was work to be done before her limits were breached. Closing her eyes, she took several long, deep breaths. *Breathe, breathe. Calm.* As she opened her eyes, she grabbed the cable and maneuvered the engine over the hole, then she climbed in, guiding it above her head. As she looked up, suddenly aware of the pressure multiplied more than tenfold by the Veneran atmosphere, sparkling light dazzled her eyes. "What the hell," she muttered.

"Shardeen, I gotta go. Into the tunnel now. We'll talk when I'm back on Agni."

A crackle answered her, but she barely noticed the lights, like small orange sparkles that swirled and dived into the tunnel after her. How could Shardeen do this? She needed full concentration and now... Shardeen needed her full attention.

She eased the engine onto the tracks and secured it, releasing the cable. What were those lights? The hatch eased shut on hydraulics and Zady wiped at her visor, thinking she was getting low on oxygen. She checked her gauge; more than seventy percent.

The shaft had an incline of forty-five degrees, with soft, motion-activated lights. She noticed a few remained dark, but as she looked down the tunnel the sparkling lights were nowhere to be seen.

The grunt work involved moving the engine into place, hooking cables and wires, bolting it down and then setting the gimbals. Zady worked at the set-up for twenty minutes, her clock showing Earth time. But her mind was elsewhere. She and Shardeen had been together for four years. They'd grown up together on the space station, the first space kids, even if Zady and the other eight were the select few who were watched and tweaked and examined every year of their lives. That, on top of intensive schooling, had left little time for play. But then everyone on Venera One was there because of specific skills, or was raised to build the aerostat city Agni. From there they planned to tame the surface.

Zady had never been on Earth, and from the rest of the aging crew she knew it as a hellhole they were glad to escape or a paradise they regretted leaving. Only the spaceborn loved the planet they orbited, even if Venus was an inhospitable ball of rock and sulfuric acid.

Shardeen had never talked about kids. *They* had never talked about kids. How could they? Schooling, working, building. There had been no time. With the few moments and hours to themselves they had formed a bond and Zady had reveled in the lean, birdlike lines of Shardeen. She'd always worried that her heavier than earth physiology would break Shardeen's graceful and swift limbs, yet they'd been very suited to each other. Neither of them would have survived Earth. Shardeen's height would have been as unusual and difficult at Earth gravity. Zady knew that if the mission ever closed, she could adapt. But Shardeen was her true world, and they would orbit each other.

But now, babies? They were only in their early twenties. Zady had never felt the need to have a baby. She couldn't even comprehend the feeling to choose such a thing. That was more foreign than the planet they orbited, some tiny, needy being coming between them, an unknown entity. Some of the Earth women talked about the children they had left behind and still communicated with, or that they would never have, but Zady couldn't fathom it. And now, now Shardeen would go ahead, no matter what. Zady wasn't sure she wanted to be a parent, to care for a helpless creature, to have her genetic code passed on. Or would her code be left behind? There were so many questions and she'd had no time to think, to even consider what it all meant.

Their love had just happened. A natural part of being around each other, noticing the beauty in Shardeen's movements, her quick capricious mind. But then, Zady began to wonder; what was love?

Sure, some helpless little human would need them, but was that love?

She secured the last cable, checked the calibration of the gimbals and stood back. There was a weight on her heart, even beneath the crust of Venus's hot and treacherous surface, but Zady was not so sure it was the planet's pressure that weighed her so.

The lights flickered and Zady looked up. Everything was set. This engine would slowly convert the carbon dioxide, pumping out hydrogen. They would keep it in the enclosed environment until other units could be added. Eventually, the floating torus of Agni would softly settle onto the Veneran surface and become the first landbound city of Venus.

Zady wondered, if she had ever seen Earth would she love it better than this stark, hot place? But then how many people had ever seen all of Earth? She'd been so distracted by getting the job done and Shardeen's conversation that she hadn't really even looked at Venus. Venus, goddess of love and jealousy and all things dealing with the heart.

She had been distracted by the heart. As she tested the engine and set the outtake valves, Zady knew her heart was in turmoil; stay with Shardeen or move on? Her clock flashed green in her visor. One hour gone and at most one left. She still had to return to the shuttle.

Orange flashes flared in her visor and as she turned her head to the right she saw the sparkling lights again. Instinctively checking air intake and pressure, she found she was at fifty percent. Plenty. Her heart was heavy, but whether because of pressures from the goddess of love or from the planet that she embodied—bright, sometimes too hot to endure, but holding promise—Zady did not know.

The sparkling lights moved closer, aglow like crackling fire, pinpoint small, in a swarm. Zady could not fathom what was happening. In all of the probes and research on the surface there had never been any mention of such an anomaly and there was certainly no life. Yet, as she brought her hand up into the bright fairy sparkle, the pinpoint brightness moved out. She drew her hand back and the lights followed.

Zady finally focused, forgetting the engine, forgetting Shardeen and babies. The lights! Moving on their own. Why had no one ever reported this in any of the information from the unmanned probes? It had to be part of the Veneran surface pressures playing with her brain, something that wouldn't have shown on the recordings. She needed to get back to the ship before her brain boiled.

Zady moved slowly, one foot going down in front of the other. It felt as if she moved through pudding and sand. Her breath slowed but she sucked in the air, feeling it wasn't enough. The lights flared, swirled around her, then moved down the shaft toward the ladder. To climb up into the pressure, the burden of life. To climb up and deal with the decisions and new lives. Would it be so wrong to be the first to fall into the embrace of the goddess, to let Venus consume her? There had been no deaths, no casualties, but Zady knew she could be the first, the one true lover of Venus.

The lights pinged off of her helmet. How could that be? It sounded like pebbles, like rain, like the patter of tiny insectile feet. The lights flickered in sequence: orange, then yellow, then white, orange, yellow, white. Zady shook her head. What? What was she doing?

Get to the tunnel. The crawl up the ladder, triggering the hatch seemed to take all of her lifetime. It wasn't a long lifetime but she wanted to have a longer one, didn't she? Pull and lift, pull and lift. She moved up the ladder and stumbled into the corridor.

The light had not changed; Venus's surface looked the same through the thick portholes. How long would they last? It was the aerostat that suffered more, with continual repairs against the sulfuric acid rain. The lights now spun around her head, making her dizzy.

Zady reached toward them. "What are you?"

They froze, like diamonds in the air, though there was no air and she knew that, somewhere in her brain full of science facts. Was it all a hallucination? *Don't let it kill you*, she told herself and stumbled forward, along the tunnel.

They would have to build another tube in a few months; each time it lasted longer, resisting the pressures but never completely.

Zady saw the matte white of the shuttle's door, the tunnel's mouth sucked up to it like a hungry lover. Her hand reached, elongating, pushing through the invisible thickness. So hard to get there. But she was the first and she hadn't really set foot on the surface. Not one foot.

She would though. *Must.* Zady turned from the shuttle and moved to the side of the corridor, feeling along its surface for the notch. The sparkling lights flickered in her vision but she was determined. Her hand found the impression and she pushed, then twisted.

Harsh, searing light lanced into the muted tunnel. As her visor darkened to compensate, Zady pushed through the maintenance hatch, squinting. Her foot touched the ground.

A lighting strike drove jagged shards into the distance and Zady pulled one foot up at a time, struggling to move forward and see the plains, find the arachnoid cracks that looked like spider webs on areas of Venus's face. Shades of orange, like caramel and amber, swirled and spotted the ground. So stark, so amazing. Venus was nearly flat from above but the undulations were there; squat, oppressive. Zady's heart swelled. So beautifully unique under all those poison vapors.

Weight settled onto her shoulders, pushing her into the rocks beneath her feet. She did not notice the spiraling lights at first until those glittering specks from the tunnel smashed into her faceplate, making her lurch back. Trying to take another step forward, they launched at her visor again, furiously filling her vision until she could see nothing else but fireworks bursting before her. Then the flashing green light, the tinny klaxon registered.

Her oxygen was at ten percent and she was in the crushing bear hug of the Veneran geography. Zady turned, trying to hurry but unable to do more than shuffle. The tunnel's door hung open. The pinpoint lights flared into a foxtail shape and undulated toward the door, guiding her. It was only a matter of meters but her oxygen use was rising. Holding her breath, hoping to preserve the limited supply, Zady moved as if through quicksand.

Banging off the frame, she reeled drunkenly into the corridor.

Reaching for the shuttle's entry seemed so far. Strange thoughts were beginning to distract her again. She shook her head, blinking furiously, chanting, "The door, the door, the door."

Her breath trickled out and she tried to suck in the next one slowly. A metallic taste had joined it, telling her she was nearly out. Fumbling at the latch, nearly blind, she pushed the combination. She had to make it back, had to.

Zady would because she wasn't yet done with Shardeen, even if it was to have an epic fight, even if it was to decide their orbits were no longer in synch, even if it was to say, I love you forever. Zady was not yet done. Just as Venera One orbited Venus and its aerostat lover, Agni, so would Zady and Shardeen orbit each other.

The ship's door slid open and she fell in. As she turned in the hatch, the sparkling lights wavered, moved close to touch her foot, to spin up in a long fountain of brightness, to fall back, then, spreading thin as a sheet they stilled until she raised a hand. In farewell? No, in acknowledgment, before she pressed the hatch closed.

Lights hummed on in the automated shell. "Air," she croaked out and an articulated hose snaked out. She pulled it forward and the robotic eye sought out and plugged onto her suit, sealing it and releasing cool, sweet air.

For several moments Zady just lay on the floor letting the air circulate through her system. Her fog began to clear but the pressure was making her ache. Time to go home.

Luckily the system was mostly automated and she set the course back to the torus of Agni. It had moved on from when she landed, pulled along in the strong winds that circumnavigated the planet.

Zady sipped water from the tube inside her suit, trying desperately not to vomit. Strapping herself into her seat just as lift-off began, she endured the rattling and shaking. So much fuel was needed to pull out of the surface's gravity. As she slowly ascended, the pressure lifted from Zady's shoulders.

So much had happened for those two short hours. Everything would go in her report on her return. To leave out even those mysterious lights could cause problems for the next crew to land on the surface.

Zady felt a mixture of worry and wonder, elation and fear. Venus had proven to veil some of its secrets, and all of those decades of research had not prepared them for everything. She would have died out there on Venus's soil, if it had not been for those strange lights. Had they been an atmospheric phenomenon? But then they had seemed to acknowledge her, warn her of the dangers. They might only have been in her mind, reacting to the extra pressure. Even though she had been made to withstand it, Venus may have had her own thoughts.

In the end, it did not matter. She had been the first person to walk the surface and she felt a connection to the strange vapor-wrapped planet. Love welled in her, for its beauty and its mysteries.

As the weight lessened and the shuttle prepared to push through the cloud layer, laced with acid that would pit the hull, Zady realized her anger at Shardeen was for the same things she had just done.

Neither of them could always ask the other's permission nor discuss beforehand all the steps they would take. They were individuals and to remain so they had to make their own decisions whatever the pitfalls. Zady had taken a step into danger and Shardeen had done the same, when she broached the subject of the baby, knowing Zady could leave her but willing to take that chance out of love.

The bullet-shaped ship penetrated the white sheet of clouds and the sulfuric acid pinged like pebbles as it hit the hull. The cloud layer reluctantly let the ship pull from its veiled boudoir, and the Veneran sky bloomed overhead. Zady relaxed a little more, checking the coordinates. The yellowy-green Agni torus appeared in the distance. She contacted the torus landing crew, confirming her ETA.

She could have called Shardeen but she wasn't ready, the exhaustion making her limbs rubbery.

After she landed, there was the cursory med review, then Zady went to sleep, muting all incoming calls.

Ignoring the request for her full report, Zady put in a call to Shardeen on the Venera One.

"Zade? Oh my god, I was so worried. I had to contact the crew and they said you'd made it back. Are you really okay? Are you... are you mad at me?"

Zady looked at Shardeen's image, her lightly freckled brow creased with worry beneath her cropped turquoise and gold hair. Why had Zady thought that the impetuosity that she loved about Shardeen wouldn't touch aspects of their lives?

She nodded. "Yes, hon, I'm okay, though I almost didn't make it back. You were right to worry, to tell me your decision. But it was so sudden and in the mission I didn't have time to think."

Shardeen's expression grew wide-eyed. *"What? You almost didn't make it? Oh my god! Are you really okay? What happened? Look, I'm sorry but I really wanted you to know. I mean, we are, after all, a couple."*

Zady sighed, then told Shardeen about her experience. "Yeah we are. I guess I was mad that I wasn't included in your decision, that you were moving on without me and that it would mean that you'll be away from me longer."

She paused, chewing her lip. "But look, hon, I came to see something down there. Venus is her own planet. She'll do as she has always done, with or without our consultation. Yet somehow, she sent a message or a guide, or my brain conjured it, but it made me realize—we all have to move in our own orbits. Sometimes we share the space, sometimes we dance together, but if I truly love you it's not for me to deny you your desire.

"The unexpected is always there and sometimes it will catch you or me off guard, but you know what, I wouldn't have it any other way. Maybe they'll let me be stationed on Venera One for the birth."

Shardeen hiccuped and wiped at her eyes, then moved her hand toward the monitor. *"God, I love you even more. You were bred for this; you were made to be in the shadow of Venus. She watched out for you."*

Zady laughed and placed her fingers gently on the screen, mirroring Shardeen's. "Actually, we were made for this. I'll be there for you and we'll face the hurdles as they come. We can't plan for everything but we'll welcome our own little Venutian when she's born."

About the Author
Colleen Anderson

Colleen Anderson has been twice nominated for the Aurora Award in poetry, and longlisted for the Stoker Award. As a freelance editor, she has co-edited *Tesseracts 17* (EDGE Publishing), and *Playground of Lost Toys* (EXILE Editions) which was nominated for a 2016 Aurora Award. She is currently editing for *Alice Underground*. New or forthcoming works are in *Clockwork Canada*, *In the Light of Camelot*, *Deadlights*, *The Goethe Glass*, *OnSpec* and others. Currently she is working on an alternate history dark fiction novel and a poetry collection. Her poetry chapbook *Ancient Tales, Grand Deaths and Past Lives* is available through Kelp Queen Press.

Author Website: http://www.colleenanderson.wordpress.com/

The Thirty-Eight
by George Allen Miller

Sar fell. Purple and orange clouds sailed by her. To her right, a bright blue and white ocean stretched to the horizon. Red-tipped mountains rose to touch the sky far off to her left while below, the yellow-brown colored world raced upwards. Readings on her helmet visor reported she would hit the ground in three minutes.

"Whoohoo!" Sar shouted. Her reaction was very unprofessional but then so was everything else she was doing. Life at the University of Cape Town had shifted from science to political sideshow. Getting a project green lit had become harder than discovering the underlying science. For a black graduate student from Zambia, it was nearly impossible. What could she do to prove her theory right but build and activate the generator herself? With her science, she had punched open a hole to another dimension of being, another reality, and in moments would be the first woman from Africa, all of Earth, to set foot on another world.

Thrusters ignited on the back of her suit and a parachute deployed. Sar adjusted her controls and her decent slowed. She could make out some vegetation and movement on the surface. A broad smile grew on her face as she anticipated the unknown.

∞

Sar knelt on the dusty surface and reached down with her gloved hand. Granulated yellow sand, filled with small rocks the size of quarters, fell through her fingers.

"I can't believe it's so similar," Sar said. "Just like desert sand." She stood up and brushed her hands off. Surrounding her, tiny bright-red shrubs grew in spotty patches every few feet. The odd colored leaves blew back and forth in the breeze much like their green counterparts on Earth. High above, the yellow sun moved across the sky so fast the progress was visible.

"That is fast. How long is a day here?" Twenty meters away, next to a very large cactus, light from the sun reflected off a shiny object. Sar headed towards the glint and double-checked that her camera's recorded every moment. At ten feet from the object, she stopped and felt her heart leap in her chest. On the ground was a cube of water one foot in height and width. Small waves formed on the liquid's surface that rose and fell with the breeze. A tingle went up Sar's spine at the sight of an object that broke every physical law she had ever known.

"What are you?" Sar said to the water.

"I'm Ted," the water replied.

Sar jumped backwards and tripped. She landed on her side and stared at the water cube. Did it just talk? Her suit confirmed the voice emanated from the physical location of the water.

"Did you just speak?" Sar said.

"Sure did. Do I know you? Never seen you before. Hey Carl, ever seen her before?" Ted said.

"Nope. Nice to meet you." Sar's instruments reported that the new voice came from the cactus.

A small cloud of dirt, lifted by the breeze, touched Ted's side and coated the water's edge. Several large tumbleweeds rolled by, also caught in the breeze, and Ted formed a hand of water from his side and waved.

"Hey Ivan, Irina," Ted said.

"Good day!" The tumbleweeds said in unison as they rolled with the wind and out of sight.

"What is going on here?" Sar said.

"I'm just being a cube. I like cubes. What are you up to Carl?"

"Not much, just doing some photosynthesis," Carl said.

"Carl's just doing some photosynthesis," Ted said.

"I heard that," Sar said. "I can't believe I heard that, but I heard that."

"Can't believe Carl does photosynthesis? He does that all the time. I've known him since he was a seed."

Sar stood up and checked her communication system history to make sure she hadn't lost her mind. The system played back the conversation verbatim. She had the message sent back to command and let the computer analyze the voice patterns for anything unique. The answer from the computer came back instantly: *need more data.* Sar sighed.

"Why are you wearing someone else?" Ted, the cube of water, folded into a sphere and grew vertically into a tall cylinder the same height as Sar.

Sar's jaw dropped and her eyes went wide. The water moved and glided like waves in an ocean. "What did you say?" she said.

"I said why are you wearing someone else?"

Sar looked at her arms encased in the grey flexible material. "What do you mean? This is an environmental suit."

"Suit huh, never heard of him. Hey Carl, you ever heard of a guy named Suit? She's wearing him," Ted said.

"Nope," Carl said.

"Right," Sar said. Her breath came in quick short breaths and she shook herself. "Coherent communication emanating from water and a cactus. This is beyond anything I could have anticipated."

A communication alert popped up in her visor. The computer system in her lab indicated the anchor base was ready for decent. From a pocket in her thigh Sar pulled a tablet and sent the confirmation codes. "First, get the anchor down and then…" Sar looked up at the water column. "…wow."

Sar put the water column out of her mind and focused her attention on the descending platform. Her entire life was spent making that base and getting it down was the priority. When the platform landed she'd have a full suite of sensors, drones, and even a security perimeter. Not to mention complete, absolute and total vindication for her radical theories.

"Are those numbers? I love numbers. Hey Carl, she has numbers," the water column said.

"Neat."

Sar looked up and saw a small line of water extend from Ted and hover over her shoulder. "You know what numbers are?"

"Sure, Mrs. Mathews' taught us in fifth grade. Five times five is twenty-five. Six times six is thirty-six. Seven times seven is... wait, what's seven times seven again?"

Did he just say Mrs. Mathews' fifth-grade class? Sar reached out towards Ted and touched the water's edge. A small wave formed and rippled down his side.

"Ted, what exactly are you?" Sar asked.

"Currently? I'm two atoms of hydrogen and one atom of oxygen. What are you?"

"I'm human," Sar said.

"Human?" The water column stretched forward and touched Sar's faceplate. "Do you have a body in there? An actual body?"

"I do, yes. I mean, yes, that's what I am." Sar moved her head back but didn't step away. Excitement and pure scientific curiosity had chased away primal fears as water from Ted pressed against her faceplate.

"Hey, you're black. And you made eyes with swirls of brown and beige," Ted said.

Sar felt the hairs on her neck bristle and she straightened her body to her full five foot five inches.

"Yes, I'm black. I'm from Zambia," Sar said with more pride than she meant.

"Zamb who? Never heard of him. Hey Carl, she formed herself

a body in there. A real body."

"Cool," Carl said.

"When was the last time you had a body, Carl?" Ted said.

"Frankfurt. Neo-nazi stuck me in the neck with an ice pick."

"Ouch."

"Wasn't so bad."

"Wait. Frankfurt? What is going on here? What is this place?" She paced in a circle and put her hands on her head. "Is this some kind of joke? Did I get hurt? Am I in a coma? Is this even place real?"

"Sure is. If you mean Carl and me. We're both real."

"Then what is this place?" Sar took a step towards the water column.

"We call it Thirty-Eight," Ted said.

"What?"

"Thirty-Eight."

"Thirty-Eight what?" Sar could feel her face flush just like when a visiting professor scoffed at her work.

"Just Thirty-Eight."

Thunder erupted above them and Sar looked up to see the anchor base descend. Ted and Carl would have to wait. She had to get the anchor unit down or she wouldn't be winning any Nobel prizes, not to mention never going home to claim them.

"Back away, Ted." Sar walked out of the landing zone and settled herself behind Carl.

"What is that?"

"Anchor base. Gives me a footing here so I can come and go as I please."

"Go and come from where?"

Sar imagined the faces of her colleagues in the morning and grinned. Red faced, frothing coffee, and screaming about misuse of Cape Town equipment. But it wouldn't matter, she would already be back, sipping tea in the lab and grinning her widest smile. This was bigger than landing on the moon or the opening ceremonies of the first Venusian colony. So what if she took the chance?

Fire exploded from the bottom of the base and Sar checked every reading a dozen times to make sure all was well. She looked up to check the flight path and noticed Ted, now a thin water column, had stretched himself upward towards the falling metal structure.

"What are you doing?" Sar said.

"I want to check it out." Ted's voice radiated from all parts of his liquid self.

Dust and debris flew up from the ground as the flames scorched the sandy soil followed by small clouds of steam. Whatever Ted was he had boiled off as soon as the thrusters fired.

With a groan, the base settled on the ground and the thrusters deactivated. Sar waited until her suit informed her the area was safe to approach. Three beeps signaled the all clear and she walked in a tight circle and looked for signs of water. There were none.

"Sorry, Ted," Sar said.

"For what? That was neat. Not sure how Bob feels about all that fire though," Ted said.

Her helmet reported Ted's voice was close but she didn't see him. She shook her head and resolved to ignore him for now. First priority was making sure the base survived.

The tablet in her hand beeped. Readings indicated the anchor base was communicating with the computer systems back in the lab and all systems were operational. Sar ran up to the side of the base and pulled out a control panel. A large monitor came to life and diagnostic reports from every system flashed across the screen.

"So, who's this?" Ted said.

Sar turned to look and saw several large drops of water combine together on the ground. Water condensed out of the air and the small puddle of water began to grow.

"You didn't die?" Sar said.

"Die? No, can't die in the Thirty-Eight. I haven't heard of anyone dying, anyway. Hey Carl, you hear of anyone dying?"

"Nope. Death seems to be over. Not sure how we go to the Thirty-Nine."

"Carl's not sure," Ted said.

"I heard that," Sar said. She turned back to the anchor base and typed on a keyboard. She set the system to run full diagnostics on every system, battery, bolt and screw.

"What are you doing to him?" Ted said.

"Who?"

"The big metal guy."

Sar stopped typing and turned to Ted. The water had risen to her height but only an inch thick. Now that the anchor was down, her insatiable curiosity demanded she find out more from Ted and his cactus companion. Why were their names so Earth-like? Were they reading her mind? Pulling from her thoughts to communicate with humans?

"Ok, what exactly are you talking about, Ted? Why do you think this," Sar hit the side of the metal base, "is alive?"

"Well, uhm, what do you mean?"

"You seem to think my suit, this base, is a person. But it's not a person, it's a thing."

"Yeah, uhm. Well, sorry, I don't get it. Hey Carl, do you get what she means?"

"Yeah. Sorry about Ted, he's still dealing with shapes. He's somewhat new to the Thirty-Eight. Water was hard for me. But I figured it out and then I jumped to rocks, then birds and now a cactus. Everything here is a former resident of the Thirty-Seven, who themselves used to be the former residents of the Thirty-Six. Get it?"

"No. What do you mean by all these numbers?"

"Oh, that's easy," Ted said. "That's the reality. It's too hard to name them all so someone just started counting them and then everyone did the same thing. Every time you die you go to the next place. For some reason when we hit the thirties we started remembering all our previous existences. Boy, the twenties were really weird weren't they?"

Sar's mouth dropped open and her head bent forward. What did he say? Could this really be the afterlife? Afterlives? Could she have broken through a barrier that big? That scientist part of her brain turned on and doubt flooded her mind.

"I can't believe that." Sar shook her head and took a step back. Mathematical equations flew through her mind and she twisted her theory over a dozen times. "If what you are saying is true, then, this place is the afterlife? Where we go when we die? How can that be true?" Sar's breath caught in her chest at the logical conclusion. "Does that mean there's a god?"

"Not sure, never met a god. Hey, how do you not know any of this anyway?" Ted asked.

Sar pointed up. "I came here through a portal. I've actually never died. I'm from the First. I guess."

"No, First we weren't bodies. We were goo. I wish right?" Carl said.

"Wait, you never died from the Third?" Ted expanded into a sheet of water in the blink of an eye and came within an inch of Sar's face.

Sar backed up at the suddenness of Ted's movement. Sar's visor told her that her heart rate had jumped and she was beginning to sweat.

"What are you doing?"

"You can't be here if you didn't go through what we went through. You have no idea where you are." Ted's voice deepened and his tone changed.

"Why not?" Sar said. Every reading she had taken said there was nothing wrong with this place. She could even breathe the air.

Without warning the ground shook and a dozen warnings flashed across her visor. A small tremor passed through the area and shook the anchor base enough to knockout the monitor.

Sar ran to the control board, rebooted the screen, and looked at the diagnostic reports. The hardware was jostled but nothing had broken. All the downed systems were already coming back online and communication with her lab was still working.

Another tremor shook the ground. Less than the first but still strong enough to make her grab the base for support. All systems remained online but a few indicated warnings.

"What is going on?"

"That's Bob. I told you he wouldn't like that," Ted said. He pointed an offshoot of himself at the base.

The ground shook stronger than before. Birds flew off in the direction of the red-tipped mountains and dust swirled as the ground shifted. A knot formed in Sar's stomach as the thought entered her mind that she may have miscalculated the safety margins.

"Why did you say I couldn't be here?" Sar said.

"You've never died from the Third existence. You never put yourself back together before. Your consciousness isn't strong enough to exist in a realm where it can be stretched beyond the physical contact your cells now enjoy. You must leave," Ted said. The sheet of water folded and doubled in thickness.

"What? Physical contact of my cells? What does that mean?"

Sar's visor filled with red indicators from every system. "What's happening?"

Heat blasted upward from a crack in the ground and darkened the metal of the base. Sar's suit compensated but warned her to get away from the heat source. Sar punched keys on the console, rebooted the ignition system and prepped the base for a manual fire. If she could move the unit then she could save the base, her mission and her career.

"You need to go home. You can't be here," Ted said. His form collapsed inward. Arms grew out of his sides and his bottom half split into legs.

Engines under the base came online. Sar pulled a lever and a metal chair popped out of the side. She spun and buckled herself in with a four-point harness. In front of her, Ted took a step towards her, his human shape fully formed. Water shimmered on his surface at each step and rippled down his sides.

"Ted?" Sar could make out distinct features on his liquid face.

"You must leave," Ted said. He took a step towards her and reached out with one of his hands.

"No chance. I can move the base. I'm not giving up on the greatest discovery in human history." Sar secured herself and looked up. The tether was still attached. She could go home right now. But what then? If she lost the base she'd have no proof, no evidence that she'd even been through the portal. The computer records wouldn't be enough to convince them she'd succeeded and they'd never let her near her equipment again, especially if the base was lost. She would be a failure, a disgrace. She'd be lucky to teach high school physics in Johannesburg.

Ted's water hand grabbed Sar's arm. She turned to him and jumped. The straps held her tight and she didn't get far. His water hand didn't give way as Sar expected. He squeezed her arm and, on a molecular level, his hand passed through her suit. The cool water reached her skin and calmed her nerves. Something touched the edge of her awareness. She felt a soft knock on the interior of her mind like an old friend coming over to visit. Sar didn't know how, but she let this new presence inside her mind.

Sar screamed. In that instant she knew exactly where she was. Her mind filled with existences spread over three-dozen realities. She saw Ted die an old man in Iowa surrounded by a loving family. She could see him existing in a place where there was no light. Places where he was light. Realms where there were no individuals, where all consciousness was part of a unified self. Other places that were beyond her ability to comprehend flashed through her mind, where time existed all at once and where souls were made of fire and burned inside stars the size of galaxies. Her mind was not ready for this. She was not prepared to see this. Sar could feel part of her mind break at the weight of knowledge meant for beings far more evolved than she.

"Ted, please! Help me!" Sar said. She unbuckled her straps and stood. She reached for a ladder at the side of the base and climbed towards the tether.

A mountain worth of solid rock lifted from the surface of the desert and Sar gasped. Fingers formed at the end of what Sar could only think of as an arm the size of a skyscraper. The hand reached out to the sky and grabbed the tether attached to the base and pulled.

"You must be calm now. Think inward. You are every part of you. Remember that," Ted said.

The tether snapped and all communication with her lab ceased. Giant fingers opened and the arm that was a mountain fell towards the base. The ground shifted and sloped downward as the large fissure beneath the base expanded. Wind blasted past her as the hand came rushing downward.

Sar glanced backwards. Above her, stretching for what looked like miles, the hand fell. Sar tripped on debris and fell to the ground. She spun on her back and held her arms over her face in vain. The hand blocked out the sky and filled her vision in all directions.

"I will stay with you. Be calm. There is no death here," Ted said.

Sar felt her body break as thousands of tons of rock slammed into her. The shock sent shivers through her mind but she never lost consciousness. She could feel her bones break and her skin rip. Blood choked up in her mouth and her muscles tore as easily as paper. Her heart and lungs exploded from the pressure. The ground beneath opened and swallowed her broken body into the depths below. She wasn't sure how, but she could still perceive the world around her. The sensation was unlike anything she could have imagined. She was pulverized and yet still—was.

Sar fell, again. A severed piece of her leg caught on a sharp rock, and Sar was shocked to feel she could still move her amputated appendage and wriggle her toes. One of her fingers had been cut off and flung out from the pit by the raging wind and caught on Carl. She felt each thorn pierce her skin. Her blood splattered the walls of the chasm and she could feel the roughness of the rock. The sensation felt as if her awareness was diced into small blocks and thrown into a dozen directions.

"You must be calm," Ted said. Sar perceived him next to her. His water body had collapsed and he was falling by her side as tiny droplets.

Heat boiled up from below and her flesh cooked at the high temperatures. Even though her spine was crushed and neurons were just a lump of flesh, she still felt intense pain. Her blood boiled, her skin charred and her hair turned to ash, and yet, she could still feel every piece of herself.

What is happening to me? Sar said. She no longer had a mouth or larynx but somehow Ted still heard her.

"Consciousness is physical in this realm."

Sar felt herself stuck on Carl far above. She felt her ashes swirling over the lava pit below. Her body was gone, crushed, melted, charred and dismembered, but she still felt all of herself.

I can't do this! Sar said.

"You have no choice. This is what you are now. No one has ever done what you have done, to come here as you have. I will help you. We all will," Ted said.

Visions from the moment Ted touched her skin flashed in her mind, images of insane landscapes of upside-down mountains and inside-out planets, the unbelievable experience of being light, and of stretching her mind across endless oceans of light-years. All of those experiences were to prepare a soul to be here, in this place. To have your consciousness turned into a physical thing. None of which Sar had any idea how to be. She closed her mind and thought of home. If she had teeth she would grind them to stubs as she pictured her colleagues laughing at her for having failed.

But then, that part of her that mattered most, her curiosity, her scientific mind, wondered. What would it be like for consciousness to be physical? Could she form herself into anything like Ted? Could she be a cactus like Carl? Amazement filled her mind and pushed away the pain. Here she was, in a realm that no human body was meant to be and she was first. From the finger on Carl's side to the leg on the cliff and all the blood on all the walls, Sar laughed.

"Whoa, didn't think you had that in you. See, once you get the hang of it, it's really fun here. Watch this," Ted said.

The sensation of movement flooded Sar's consciousness. She felt every molecule, every atom, of her being moved and shifted by the surrounding rock, wind, even Ted moving to encapsulate parts of her. Daylight glowed as she was thrust up from the depths of Bob to the surface. She realized then that every facet of this world, this existence, was some part of another soul. From the air, to the rocks and even the light that shined upon them, everything was once someone.

What's happening? Sar thought.

"This will be better than spending time inside Bob. He can be grouchy," Ted said.

More of herself gathered in the sunlight and she realized they were placing her next to Carl, inside a small hole of dirt.

"Hey, Sar," Carl said.

Hi, Carl.

"I know it's pretty weird, being here, straight from the Third. Best for you to have some company. Just settle in next to me, we'll shape you into a seed and eventually you can practice some photosynthesis. It's like meditation without all the *ohm*'s."

Sar wasn't sure, but she thought she could feel him smile.

About the Author
George Allen Miller

George lives in Washington DC with his wife, children, elderly dog and naked-foot-biting cat. When not writing he's busy architecting solutions in the technology world, walking his dog, playing with his kids, chilling with his wife, and running away from his cat.

Girl, from the Inside
by Kate O'Connor

Elise unzipped the supple skin that hid the inner workings of her calf and ankle. The silk-soft epidermis slid smoothly to either side. She flexed her toes, watching the synthetic muscles shift and pull, tightening against artificial bone. She rotated her ankle. There had been a catch in her gait during PT, slight, but present and sore. She picked up a tool and pushed it gently into her ankle joint.

The phone rang and the thin metal probe dropped from her suddenly nerveless hand. She watched detachedly as it bounced off of blue-white bone and clattered loudly on the sterile surface underneath her leg. The ringing stopped, then started again a moment later. Her brother's number flashed on the screen like an accusation.

Elise picked up the phone and pressed the button. She opened her mouth to say something, then shut it again. With Ari's funeral in just a few hours, she hadn't expected him to call.

"Ellie?" If it hadn't been for the nickname, she would have thought it was someone else on the other end of the line. Mark's voice was usually alert and expressive. Now it was flat.

"Yeah. I'm here. Sorry."

"No. You're not here." He didn't sound angry, just tired. Defeated.

"I couldn't make it after all." She had said maybe when he'd asked four days ago. *Maybe.* Even fourteen months and three full rebuilds later, her legs made travel painful. Walking still hurt. A trip halfway across the country would be complicated and uncomfortable.

"Oh."

The silence stretched between them. Her eyes tracked blankly over the insides of her leg. "What time is the funeral?" she asked at last. For a decade, she had been too busy overseas on the next mission, the next deployment, the next war zone. *Why does he want me now?* Surely he would find more comfort in the friends he knew than the sister he didn't.

"Noon."

"I'll call you after." It was the best she could give him right now.

"No. People are coming over."

"Okay. Tomorrow then." There was supposed to have been time. Time when she was healed and whole to get to know Ari. And now… whatever time she might have had with her niece was gone.

"Sure." He lapsed into silence again.

She listened to his breathing. It was too fast, like he couldn't get enough air. "Mark? Are you…" She stopped talking. It would be beyond stupid to ask if he was okay.

"I have to go." His abrupt answer cut off whatever she might have come up with instead. "I can't be late."

"I'll call," she repeated to the dial tone.

Slow and deliberate, Elise put the phone down and turned back to her work, pushing and prodding at the remade tissue. So much easier to focus on something real, something immediate. Her sensitive fingertips skated over a rough edge. *Ah yes.* There it was. She pulled out the little bone, and began reshaping the jagged prong.

She lost herself in the repairs, her stress and grief tucking themselves away behind the work to be done. Each improvement reminded her of long, agonizing months in the hospital and blistering explosions on the other side of the world. Of her fellow soldiers, smelling of blood and gut wounds and death as she lay broken, staring up at the bright, bright blue sky. Each carefully crafted tendon and strong, remade bone reminded her of how deeply she had been wounded in body and spirit. Standing on her own two feet, she got to remember again and again how she continued to rebuild herself. Mark would find a way to do the same. He would have to.

∞

Elise didn't look up when the little bell over her shop door jingled. She smiled to herself. There had been a time when the too-happy noise would have brought her to sharp, ready awareness. Even after all these years, it felt like a victory that her body stayed calm and her brain remained mostly on the supply catalogue she'd been thumbing through.

Besides, it usually worked better if she gave the client a few minutes to look around, check out the posters, watch the five minute quick-and-dirty info ad that played on a loop, read through the pricing pamphlet. Salesmanship was all well and good, but no one walked through her door unless they wanted something that had vanished returned to them. Even if the original spark was long gone. It was a powerful motivator. Elise just wanted the bones, the permission. *And the money.*

"Hey, Ellie."

The familiar voice dragged her out of her reverie. His eyes were too bright and the lines of his face were tight, but he looked the same as ever: business suit off the rack, tidy brown hair a good two inches longer than her own close-cropped curls, clean, neatly trimmed fingernails. "Mark?"

"How's it going?" He was trying for casual, but his eyes kept darting to the infomercial.

"What are you doing here?" His Ohio home was more than three hundred miles away. They didn't just drop in on each other. They barely spoke beyond their annual attempts at spending a weekend being family and those visits inevitably devolved into uncomfortably edging around each other. Her pulse picked up. After all these years was he finally ready to talk?

"The shop looks good. You've expanded a bit, huh?" He was clutching the handle of a good sized rolling suitcase. It was airplane luggage, black and battered.

Elise counted backwards in her head. He probably hadn't been to her workshop in at least four years. She usually went to visit him at their parents' old place. He had moved there half a decade ago, after he and his wife had split.

"Yes." It took Elise a moment to answer his question. She had gotten used to him being distractible and vague, just as he had gotten used to her being moody and easily startled. Time went on. The world banged them up. They kept on going. She looked at the luggage again. *Oh.* Her enthusiasm for the unexpected visit leached away. "You here on business?" She nodded towards the suitcase.

He winced, then tried to cover it with a smile. "That obvious?"

One of the dogs, most likely. Elise gauged the dimensions of the case. *Maybe Ari's pony. A pony would be a nice challenge. And it would make sense.* It had been nearly seven years since Ari died, if she remembered right. It could be that this was his idea of a peace offering. Something straightforward she could help him with. Something to start rebuilding bridges that had long ago been burnt.

"I know I should have called, but I couldn't figure out how to bring it up. I mean, I know how you feel about your clients." He was looking at the floor now. Anywhere but at her. It pissed her off. Why wouldn't he ever just *look* at her when he had something to say? "The resurrection business is for suckers, right?"

"Rebuilding is not resurrection." Elise wondered if he was pushing her buttons on purpose. "I'm only recreating the shape and even that ends up a little different." There was no magic in what she did, no mystery except for the silence of her steady hands and the quiet space where her creations found breath for the first time. "You're paying for some of this. I can't afford to cut you too much slack. And you have to fill out the paperwork." Insurance was expensive enough without getting caught doing un-contracted projects for family members.

She wanted to do it for him free and clear, but most of what she made went into buying supplies. A whole pony would be a major financial hit. One she couldn't afford. Maybe having his daughter's pony back would be good. The animal would be new and different, but possibly a bit of balm for the trauma the loss of its owner had caused.

"I know. I don't care, as long as you can do it."

"Of course I can." Elise stopped before she said something nasty, took a deep breath, and let it out slowly. He was here because he needed her. She could get mad and drive him away again or she could get it together and remember that this had to be awkward for him too.

She pulled up the standard contract, laying her tablet flat on the counter. "How long has… he?" She paused, making the pronoun a question. She couldn't remember if Ari's pony had been a boy or a girl. "How long has he been dead?"

"She." Mark's voice sounded dull and tired, as if this were all suddenly too much for him. "And I don't know. Six or eight years ago?"

It wasn't the pony. The pony had been alive and well last year. It was probably that big, stupid Labrador that used to follow him everywhere. Elise had remade so many dogs she could do it in her sleep.

"How?" Eight years was a long time. She would have to rebuild the bones themselves, filling in the gaps left by decay. At least she wouldn't have to strip off recently decaying flesh. For all having the additional DNA information and raw materials helped, that had never been one of her favorite parts.

"She was hit by a car." He was nearly whispering.

"All right." Elise nodded, typing *dog* in the *species* blank on the contract. Ponies didn't get hit by cars as a general rule. She filled the rest out quickly. She didn't want to give him time to bolt. The chance to fix things with him was too important. "It takes a little longer for physically traumatic deaths." There was a lot more work to do when the original form wasn't intact.

"But you can do it?" he asked again, knuckles white on the handle of the suitcase.

"I can build anything." Elise pushed the tablet across the counter, biting the inside of her cheek before more of her annoyance slipped out. She had a reputation, a damned good one. He knew it. She took a breath and let it out slowly. "Just print here and input your credit information."

He looked at her then, hazel eyes meeting hers. Something in his face relaxed and he nodded. With whatever internal conflict he'd been having settled, he still took a long time reading everything over.

At long last, he pressed his thumb to the contract. "Is there anything else?"

"A picture would help, if you have one."

He smiled, just a small upturning of his thin lips. "There's an album in the front pocket."

"I'll start this afternoon." Elise took control of the suitcase. "Where are you staying?"

"Hotel." He was already turning for the door.

"You can stay with me." Elise would have to go grocery shopping, but the spare bedroom was clean enough. They might finally have a chance to talk, really talk, not just avoid mentioning Ari, her legs, his ex-wife, Elise's absence.

"No thanks, Ellie." Their eyes met again. She felt the weight of all the things they didn't talk about hanging between them. "I know you like your privacy." And then he was gone, the little bell singing cheerfully in his wake.

∞

Her worktable was brightly lit and big enough to hold a draft horse. Elise scrubbed the surface, making sure it was clear of any remnants from her last job. There was a ritual to beginning a new project. She checked the printer's levels, refilled the protein solution and scribbled down a note to order another case before next week. She brought up the general schematic for a large dog. Her toolkit, looking like it was put together by an archaeologist, a surgeon, and a mechanic, was laid out along one side of the table. Each tool had a place.

Happy anticipation shivered through her. The only part she liked better than the first breath was the beginning. In this moment, the possibilities were all in front of her, free from the thousand little problems that would inevitably crop up once she began and the all-too-likely disappointment when she gave the owner a new pet held up by the bones of an old one. In this moment, her mind was quiet and ready to work. At peace.

She rolled the suitcase over to the base of the table and laid it flat. She would look at the album—why does Mark always keep albums of pet photos?—after she had the remains sorted. Elise preferred to get the bones cleaned and laid out first. Like an instrument an eighth-step out of tune, the differences between what was and what she could create would chafe at her once she knew they were there.

The pile of bones in the case was half shadowed by the table, but there was something odd about them. Elise reached down, catching hold of a long, dirt-and-damp weathered bone. Too long for a dog. Any dog. Surreal numbness crept over her. *It looks like—* Her heart began to pound. She studied the hand holding the bone as if the appendage belonged to someone else.

Gently, quickly, she put the leg bone on the table. Her hands trembled minutely as she switched the schematic on the display. Fast and thorough, she assembled the rest of the skeleton, scarcely breathing, barely thinking. It took hours, but every bone was there. Unusual that there wasn't something missing. *Only unusual if it was an animal skeleton. Coroners are generally more careful.* Elise left the skull until last, hiding at the bottom corner of the scruffy suitcase. It was dented on one side, crumbled and broken. *I'll have to patch that.* She shook her head, setting the—*her*—skull in place.

Rebuilding dead people was illegal. It had been done, early on when the technology first made it possible. With animals, it was easy enough to pretend that the rebuilt creature was the same as the one that was lost. A human girl would never even come close to matching the child who had first worn these bones. Elise sat down hard on her stool. A nearly hysterical chuckle burst out. *Well, she's not a Lab. Or a pony.*

Elise dug out her phone and cradled it in her lap. Certain rebuilders would do it, for the right price. She never had, never would. How dare he? How could he? She turned the phone over in her hands. She needed to report this, call the authorities and let them deal with it.

The naked skeleton lay on the table: empty, faceless, and waiting. She put the phone down, touching the bare bones lightly. *Baby girl.* She couldn't bring herself to think her niece's name in connection with these bones. There were the grooves where the tendons would attach, a crack in the left femur, the slight spinal curve of mild scoliosis. Elise clenched her hands. She wouldn't look at the album. She didn't want to remember how profound her brother's loss truly was.

She could call Mark instead. Send him off with his suitcase full of bones to find someone else to break the law for him. *Has he been holding on to this idea from the beginning?* He'd had Ari buried at home on their parents' farm. *Natural*, he'd said. No chemicals or fancy coffins. Somewhere he would never have to leave her alone. Elise wondered if she should have known then, should have guessed it might come to this when he didn't move on with his life. But she hadn't.

Elise was suddenly exhausted. Mark had lied, probably to keep the initial confrontation from being face-to-face. To give her time to cool off. Or something. *Seven* years and it wasn't a car. It was a fall. Ari had been climbing trees. It might be kinder to get him arrested. Maybe then he could get some help with his grief. Elise wasn't sure.

The empty sockets in the skull did not look at her. They were just empty. Elise picked up the phone again and turned off the workshop lights. The bones weren't going anywhere and she couldn't find the energy to process this mess. She could decide tomorrow how she was going to handle this.

∞

Mark was waiting at the door to her workshop. Sometime near three in the morning, Elise had sent a brief text telling him to do just that. She had started regretting it as soon as she pushed *send* and hadn't stopped yet. Pre-dawn nostalgia and loneliness were terrible decision makers.

Ignoring his hesitant greeting, she grabbed him by the arm and hauled him unceremoniously through the door. He sputtered a protest and tugged against her hold. Even being a good six inches shorter than he was, she held on without much effort, shoving him down on the worn orange couch where she sometimes slept when a project ran late. She hadn't been a soldier in nearly a decade, but staying fit and strong made her rebuilt limbs easier to manage. For Mark, fitness was, at best, an attempt to look good.

"You son of a bitch," she said coldly, folding her arms across her chest, "I should have you arrested."

He stopped trying to get up, face going still and wary. "You didn't even look at the album, did you?" he asked, looking anywhere but at the big table and its tiny, stark burden.

"What?" Elise couldn't imagine what he meant.

"Look at the damn album, Ellie."

Elise stared at him for a long moment, mind racing. The anger in his voice surprised her, though it shouldn't have really. He must be desperate to try this. *Does he really think a few cute family photos will change my mind? Do I?* Without a word, she went to the discarded suitcase and unzipped the front pocket. *If he wanted her to look, she would look.* The slender, square album was blue-stained fake leather, embossed with gold-colored scroll work and the name, *Ariana Braden*, written large in the center. She flipped open the front cover.

Ari's small face peered up at her. A smear of dirt ran from cheek to chin as the little girl held a fresh flower, roots and all, up to the person taking the picture. Her hair was black and curly, tied back in a ponytail with purple pony barrettes holding the wisps back from her dirty face. Her eyes were as blue as that bright, bright sky Elise never forgot. As blue as the eyes Elise saw in the mirror. *Damn.*

"Please." His voice was soft, desolate.

The picture shifted. Ari perched on that patient-looking grey pony. And again. Birthday party.

"Really, Mark?" *If she hit him, she would break something.* There was a world of difference between being in pain and dumping that pain all over someone else. She had never burdened him with her agonies. Never. She had kept her hurts close, dragged herself up and put herself back together without him, because she had believed he deserved better than a broken, needy sister. *Why couldn't he just patch his own wounds? Didn't she deserve better too?* She *really* wanted to hit him. "I don't *do* this," Elise told them both. "Why did you come to me in the first place?"

"You're the best." Mark took a shuddering breath. "And you're my sister."

Elise put the open album on the table next to the skeleton's left hand. The screen showed a fuzzy-headed baby in a car seat.

Mark had their mother's eyes—hazel and hopeful and afraid.

"It wouldn't be her," Elise said. She wasn't really going to do this. If she could make him understand what it meant, surely he wouldn't want to either.

"I don't care."

"You would care, when you got back a girl who looked mostly like Ari, but had a mind of her own."

He smiled. "Ari always had a mind of her own."

"No." Elise flipped the album closed on a naked-baby-in-the-tub shot. She gestured towards the skeleton. "Those bones are dead. She couldn't grow up. She would *never* be the person who died." *I would have to rebuild her every year, adding a little here and a little there so she could grow up. A lifetime of refining a single project. Like my legs, only...*

His face crumpled, a fine tremor visibly running through him. He looked at the bones at last, one hesitant hand reaching out to grip the edge of the metal table. "I know."

"Then why do you still want this?"

"I couldn't... I can't save her." Tears ran down his face at last and Elise was almost relieved. He hadn't cried in front of her in years. "Ari hardly had any time." He stopped speaking for a moment, scrubbing at his runny nose with the back of a suit covered arm. "She deserves some kind of legacy, something to continue on in memory of her."

"Aren't you doing that already?" Elise knew what it was like, living on when those you were close to, responsible for, were gone. You carried them with you, remembering.

"No." Mark shook his head. "It's been a long time, but all I can think about is that last day." His eyes landed on the skeleton again. "I need something alive, something about Ari that isn't just that awful moment."

He went quiet, sinking back onto the couch again. He looked lost. Seven years lost. "Please," he said in a whisper. "You owe me this much." He looked up at her, eyes fierce. "You weren't there. So be there now."

Elise's temper evaporated. He was right. In so many ways. "All right," she said at last. It would be worth the risks, to rebuild their family. Probably. Maybe. *I'm going to regret this forever even if it doesn't end me up in jail.* But never as much as she regretted not being what he needed when he needed her. "But you have to help me. You have to see what exactly it is that you're asking for. Can you do that?"

"Yes." The word burst out of him. "Anything."

∞

They stood side-by-side in the bright workroom when Elise woke Ana for the first time. She watched closely as the machinery did its work. She didn't look at Mark, not wanting to see his disappointment if it didn't take right away. Sometimes it took a few tries and rebuilding Ana from Ari's bones had been a long and complex process. Muscle and tendon was easy enough. DNA mapping for internal organs, for veins and arteries was the same work she had done before.

It was Ana's mostly organic brain that had stretched Elise past what she believed herself capable of. That and choosing to form Ana's face, her hair, her eyes so that they were close to Ari's, so close, but not quite the same. Elise hadn't asked Mark about that and he hadn't seemed to notice.

It's so different, making a person. Much more so than I thought it would be. She hadn't been able to bring herself to give Ana a dead girl's face. The changes had to be small—chin less rounded, cheekbones more defined, hair a shade lighter and not so curly. Little touches that made Ana her own person. If anything, the girl looked more like Mark and Elise's father than Ari had.

Ana's chest contracted, then expanded. Elise held her own breath.

The movement came again. Ana's paper-thin eyelids fluttered. Elise smiled, smoothing down the straight, dark hair with a gentle hand. Ana's sky-blue eyes met her own.

"She's perfect," Mark said softly, clasping Elise's hand.

Elise smiled. "Let's call her Ana." She had been thinking about it for weeks, already called the rebuilt girl by that name in her head, but she hadn't been able to find the courage to discuss it with Mark. It had felt like making too much of a claim on a child that wasn't hers, that she hadn't bothered to be close to the first time around. Watching Ana breathe, seeing those beautiful eyes looking at her, brought a fierce, possessive pride Elise couldn't deny.

"Perfect," Mark said again.

Elise squeezed his hand in return.

∞

"Why can't she do any of this herself?" Mark was frustrated. Again.

"She hasn't learned it yet," Elise said, not for the first time. Potty training a girl who looked like an eight-year-old wasn't proving to be easy for him. The baby-talk noises Ana made had him cringing away and he couldn't hide his disgust when she smeared food on her face.

"Stop it," Elise told him harshly, shoving him none-too-gently out of the room. "She needs your help. She'll never learn if you keep flinching every time she acts like the baby she is."

"B-But..." he stuttered, seemingly unable to find the words to explain.

"No," Elise said, cutting him off. "Either figure out how to deal with it or leave."

"I just thought it would be different." His shoulders hunched like he was afraid Elise was going to hit him. *Tempting thought.* She hadn't actually decked him since they were kids.

"She won't be like this forever," Elise said, trying for a reasonable tone. It wasn't as if she was immune to the sheer ick that came with raising a little girl too old for her mental age. The re-education process was in all of the manuals she'd given him to read while she worked. There was even a clause in the contract about it. Most people thought it was cute when their pets temporarily reverted to baby antics. The rebuilt animals tended to learn much faster than fully organic creatures anyway, so it didn't last long enough to be annoying for the most part.

"I'm sorry," Mark muttered, "I can't do this anymore." He shoved a handful of cash at Elise. "Take care of her, will you? At least until she grows up a little. You're better at it than I am, anyway."

He was out the door before she had time to formulate a response. She stalked towards the door, not quite able to believe he had gone. "Mark! Get back here!" A wail from the kitchen stopped her. Ana didn't like to be left alone for long and she was probably still hungry. Elise shoved the money in her pocket and turned towards the kitchen instead. *He'll be back. Surely.*

Her heart was racing and her head was numb. She couldn't raise Ana by herself. She didn't know anything about kids. It was all she could do to keep Ana clean and fed with Mark's reluctant help and support. She'd had to squash down her negative reactions, forcing them back behind the wall she had long ago built to deal with unpleasant realities. Was that why he thought she was better suited? Didn't he know how hard this had been on her as well?

My fault. I didn't think this part through at all. Rebuilt pets could be adopted by another family if they didn't fit with their original owners. Illegal little girls, not so much.

Maybe if I'd tried harder to make her exactly like Ari, it would have been easier on him. It wouldn't have been enough though. She knew that. There were always differences. Even in rebuilt goldfish. Elise hugged herself tightly, hovering just outside the kitchen door. It had all been a downhill slide to reality from that first, precious moment. She dropped her arms and squared her shoulders. *Fake it till you make it.* She was a soldier, even retired. This was just the next mission. *Yeah right.*

Taking a deep breath, Elise walked back into the kitchen.

∞

Speech came blessedly quickly. Ari must have been as smart a girl as her father had always claimed. Elise got used to Ana's presence. The neighbors got used to Elise's adoptive daughter. Elise had made not-so-subtle hints about the mother's long-standing drug problem, figuring that would explain any oddities in Ana's behavior.

After two months, Elise gave in and they redecorated the spare bedroom with posters of ponies and too many stuffed horses. The walls were now sporting a positively alarming shade of lavender. *But Ana loves it.*

Ten months more of rebuilding dogs and cats while Ana played at her feet. Ten months of progressing from diapers and picture books to dressing herself and helping in the workshop. Mark called sometimes, though he didn't leave messages and had hung up without a word the one time Elise actually answered.

She thought about calling the police and reporting him as a stalker, but she wasn't sure he would keep his mouth shut about the important things if she did. She just wanted him gone. He'd chosen not to be involved. He could damn well leave them alone.

Elise watched closely as Ana cleaned the tools, checking each one over and plunking it back in its proper place with proud focus. Ana was getting close to acting the age she looked. She was bright and talkative, quick-tempered and stubborn. She wanted a horse for Christmas, a real one, not a rebuilt one and *not* a pony. Ponies were for *little* kids. Elise smiled. *So not happening.*

"Good job, love." Elise squeezed her shoulder. Ana would have to know this work. When Elise was gone, Ana would have to be able to fix herself. There was no one else they could trust not to turn her in. Bad enough that Elise would have to explain someday that Ana was different. So very different. At the very least, Elise would do everything in her power to give her girl the tools she needed to take care of herself.

∞

The knock at the door was a surprise. Elise wasn't expecting anyone and, as far as she knew, Ana wasn't either. It was a school night and getting a little late. The herd-of-elephants clamor of one young girl racing down the stairs made her smile.

"I'll get it, Mum!" Ana yelled, all but colliding with the front door.

Elise set her injector down carefully on the pale, polished wood of the dining room table beside the half-assembled bird bones. Ana had found them under a tree on her way back from school. The fragile bones had no shape. Muscles and tendons were gone but for a few desiccated strips. She had brought them home, carefully folded in an old napkin. *Can we make something out of these?* she had asked.

Pieces were missing. The minuscule vertebra had been scattered and Ana hadn't found them all. Elise would print the missing pieces, mapping them to fit what she had. The finished creature would have tiny, half-mechanical lungs, feathers in any color they could imagine, an AI that would remember entire arias. When it was done, the bird would fly again. It would sing.

Of course we can, Elise had answered. There wouldn't be any money in it. Even if she did sell it, it wouldn't come close to making up the cost of rebuilding it, but Ana had asked.

The front door lock clicked and the handle turned. Ana's expressive voice dropped to a more polite level, keeping Elise from hearing what she was saying. Whomever was outside answered. Male voice, tenor, equally quiet. There was something familiar about the muffled tone. She got to her feet, heart thrumming rapidly. *Surely not.*

The trip across the room and around the little jog in the hallway that obscured the front door seemed to stretch the length of a battlefield. *It's a salesman. Or religious outreach.* Elise slid around the jutting wall, muscles twitching as she pushed back the instinct to crouch, gain the advantage of stealth as she approached a potential enemy. Maybe it was the new neighbor from across the street.

The door came into view, half open. Ana's dark ponytail bobbing as she nodded in response to something the man said. His too-familiar face was hesitant, cautious, though Elise could see the beginnings of a smile starting. She pulled air deep into her lungs, held it, let the rush of oxygen fuel her mind and muscles. She let her shoulders tighten and her back tense. Far better that than loosening up in preparation for a fight.

"Mark." Elise could hear the ice in her tone. Ana could too, pulling back from the door and turning to her with wide, suddenly worried eyes.

"Mum?" she asked.

"I just want to talk." Mark held up his hands as though to calm her.

Elise stepped past her daughter and slammed the door in his face, locking it for good measure. She caught Ana's arm gently and pulled her back towards the dining room. "C'mon, love. Ignore him."

"But who is he?" Ana's trusting, curious face tugged at her. *She should know. But she's mine. Not his. He gave her up.*

"No one," Elise said firmly. "No one at all."

∞

Once Ana was in bed, Elise went to the kitchen. She hesitated in the darkened room, the shadows split by the beam of brightness from the hallway. With a sigh, she hopped up on the counter, opening a cabinet and sneezing as the thin layer of dust inside was disturbed.

The good whiskey was at the back, untouched since Christmas. *Now's as good a time as any and better than most.* Elise got the bottle, slid to the floor and rummaged around until she found the glasses. She took two, debated the need for ice, decided to go without.

She knew Mark. He would be waiting.

Elise stepped out onto the front stoop. His shoulders were slumped as he sat on the bottom step, but his jaw was tight as he stared out at the quiet street. She sat down beside him, holding out the other glass. He took it, warm fingers brushing hers briefly.

"Why, Ellie?"

Elise shrugged. She knew what he was asking. It was the only thing he could ask at this point. "You abandoned her. Twice."

The corner of his mouth twitched downwards. "She's my daughter," he said, voice rough with emotion. It was always emotion with him. Heart first, head later. Elise hated that.

"Technically, by which I mean legally, she's my daughter." *And didn't that take some arranging.* She had homeschooled Ana at first. It had taken time and money to make discreet inquiries about how one got proper ID for adopting a young girl supposedly from a foreign country. Somewhere that didn't keep good records. More of each to call in the favors and fill out the paperwork it took to make Ana, officially, a real person.

In the beginning, it had been so tempting to just not bother. To drive Ana out to Ohio, call the authorities and report a remade girl she'd found at Mark's place. Let him take the blame and the responsibility he'd been dodging. She'd thought it all out. A child was work, sleepless nights, and costs both financial and emotional. And Ana came with plenty of other problems on top of the usual.

"Legally?" Mark made the word an epithet. "One word to the police and you won't *legally* be anything."

The glass was hard edged in her clenched hand, cool and unyielding. She wanted the reassuring weight of her sidearm instead. Which was exactly why she didn't keep guns in the house anymore. *I would bury you for her, so deep no one would ever find you.* Elise pushed the thought aside. He didn't mean it. "Neither would you," she said at last, "And then what happens to Ana?" They were in this together. Had been from the beginning.

"I just want to see her." He was pleading again.

"Then you shouldn't have bailed on us."

"I just needed some time." Mark took a convulsive sip of his whiskey, coughing as he tried to swallow.

"Eighteen months," Elise said, wanting to shake him. *You left me alone with a child I didn't know how to raise.*

"I didn't know what I was getting into. I was wrong. I'm sorry. I shouldn't have gone."

"What on earth makes you think saying 'sorry' is going to be good enough? Let's say I let you see her, have a relationship, be her father. What're you going to do when things get hard again?" *You didn't watch Ari closely enough, too busy doing something else and she was too rambunctious to be easy. You couldn't stay to help Ana when she was a fussy baby. You broke ranks when I needed you to have my back.* She kept her thoughts to herself. No matter how angry she was, some things couldn't be unsaid.

"I'll be better, Ellie, I promise." He smiled tremulously. The wounded puppy expression was the same one he'd used when he'd wanted something as a kid.

"Cut the crap. I'm not Dad." She wondered if they had anything in common anymore beyond a few strands of DNA and the child they had built together.

His face fell, collapsing into lines that aged him ten years. He put his half-full glass down on the stoop, hands clutching each other as though he had nothing else to hold onto. Elise figured at this point that was probably true. He stared down at his intertwined fingers. He grimaced. For once, he said nothing.

"She may not live a long life." Elise hoped she had done enough right to prevent the cancers and neurological glitches that sometimes plagued rebuilt animals. She hoped Ana would stay sane and functional, stay human. Her girl had been healthy so far, but there were no promises. There never were. Elise wanted Mark to understand. Maybe then he would leave them alone.

"She may get sick and die. She could turn into little more than a human-looking machine or a serial killer." Those things had happened early on, before rebuilding people was banned. The brain was complicated and delicate. So much could go wrong. "Even if she avoids those pitfalls, we may be discovered and thrown in jail. She may hate us both when we tell her what she is and what that means for the rest of her life. I don't know if she can have kids of her own if she wants them. She may never be able to have a life without walls between her and everyone else around her. And I don't need you in the middle of it all dropping in and out as it suits you."

"I want to tell her about her... her cousin." His knuckles were white, but his voice was calm again. "I want to get to know her."

Elise stared at him. It was the first time he'd admitted that Ana wasn't Ari. And that Ana was Elise's. She wanted to tell him no, to drive him away once and for all. Their father had been a steady, kind man. Not at all like Mark. Or herself. A child needed steady, especially Ana, with all of the challenges ahead of her.

Mark was broken. Elise didn't know if he had been before losing Ari, but he certainly was now. Broken meant sharp edges and unpredictable outbursts. It meant unsafe. Elise stretched out her legs. She had been broken once. Ana might break in the future.

"You were there for me this time," he said at last, "Let me try again, too."

They sat in silence, watching the occasional car travel down the dark suburban street, passing from streetlight to streetlight in little flashes of color.

"One more chance," Elise answered, "You can tell her about Ari. You can get to know Ana. And if you leave again, I will never let you come back." She met his eyes, letting her own go hard and cold. She couldn't fix him. He would have to do it himself, piece by piece and agonizing step by agonizing step. She knew what that road looked like. He would have to learn.

"Thank you," he said, reaching out and taking her hand. She let him. His fingers were cold and trembling. Elise didn't know if he would be strong enough, didn't know if she was. She squeezed his hand tightly. It didn't matter. She would give all three of them the space to try.

Girl, from the Inside
by Kate O'Connor

After graduating from Embry-Riddle Aeronautical University, Kate O'Connor took up writing science fiction and fantasy. Her short fiction has most recently appeared in *Diabolical Plots*, *Intergalactic Medicine Show*, *StarShipSofa*, and *Escape Pod*. In between telling stories, she flies airplanes, digs up artifacts, and manages a dog kennel.

Author Website: http://kateoconnor3.wordpress.com/

Have Space Bike, Will Travel
by Ingrid Garcia

High Earth orbit. A place where virtual particles pop in-and-out of existence, unheard by anybody, while disturbed by cosmic radiation, solar flares, and astronauts chasing a wayward satellite.

"You all know how to perform the Reverse Umbrella," Yo-Sung Lee says over the radio, "now who wants to be the pusher? It'll be quite close to the Van Allen belt."

Tameka signals assent, which surprises Yo-Sung, who says, "I know it's strange for me to say so, but, like me, you're the most junior member."

"Exactly," Tameka says, "the one with the lowest amount of accumulated radiation. We checked that."

"Good thinking." Yo-Sung has to agree. "So I guess you've also worked out the brakers and the catcher?"

Patrice and Paddy Ukai put their—still unexpanded—cushioning nets forward and José waves his grappling mechanism. "Almost as much fun as hacking into the Pentagon," Paddy Ukai says to weary smiles from the rest of the team.

"Why the hell am I leading you, then?" Yo-Sung says, only half-joking.

"Because you hate it." Patrice's smile easily radiates through his helmet.

"Which makes you a great boss," Tameka says as the rest silently nod.

∞

Back on Earth, Yo-Sung moved around in a wheelchair. Inflicted with a rare type of balancing disorder, she couldn't stand—sometimes even sit—upright without falling over. The genetically inherited condition afflicted her neural system, her brain and her inner ear. The condition was so rare and complex that no implant nor pharmaceutical medicines had been developed for it. Many doctors argued for research funding, only to be turned down by pharmaceutical companies that didn't see enough return on investment. Not that her parents would have been able to afford such a treatment, anyway.

Like many a hyper-active mind in a disabled body, she was restless. A South Korean geek girl devouring manga, sci-fi and literature in no particular order. Her brown eyes, curly hair and slightly above average height would've made her one amongst her peers if it wasn't for her constant fear of falling down, her flittering eyes always looking for a handhold and her refusal to take her superior's advice for granted. A brilliant student gaining her physics PhD with honours, while the loan put her in deep debt. She liked to fiddle, electronics were dirt cheap, and open source software easily available.

So she developed balancing crutches filled with accelerometers, fast servomotors, and fine-grained GPS sensors. She wrote a self-learning algorithm that would teach the crutches to teach her how to stand up, and—eventually—walk.

Of course, modern wheelchairs were quite affordable as the price of electronics had continued to come down, and they were improved with intelligent actuators, through which they could cross thresholds, climb stairs and overcome other obstacles. Even a central actuator, rising to get your head level with standing people. Still, it wasn't the same as walking, as in the wheelchair your muscles atrophied. Not that there was anything wrong with Yo-Sung's muscles, they just needed regular exercise. Unfortunately, the exercises flat on the floor or in the safety of a net just bored her to tears.

Her balancing crutches only corrected her movements. She still had to do most of the work herself, which was good for maintaining her muscle strength.

Initially, it wasn't easy, as the self-learning algorithm made mistakes and over-compensations, causing her to fall over many times. She had the cuts and bruises to show for it. But gradually the software got the gist of it and kept improving. Step by step, she could stand up with her crutches, walk with them, and even found a way to run, in a hop-step-jump kind of way, with them. The software integrated so well that she could take special classes in self-defense: jujitsu, taekwondo and karate. She became an expert, and a foolish mugger had the cuts and bruises to show for it.

Yet her mind remained restless. At night, she looked up to space and found a different way to use her balancing crutches.

∞

The wayward satellite comes in at an oblique angle, its apogee just short of touching the inner Van Allen belt. While it's dangerously close to that invisible hard radiation zone, it's also the point where its speed is lowest and thus easiest to pick up. The radiation in and near the Van Allen belt wreaks havoc with remote control signals, so using drones is out of the question. Human intervention is needed, and this is where ClimateTrack's salvage team—home base: Space Station Zebra—comes in.

The team moves to their positions while checking the rogue satellite's GPS signal one final time. Even if that fails, its projected orbit is now known. While they might seem a motley crew at first sight, their abilities match their functions. Some of these abilities work best in zero gravity, while some work everywhere. For example, riding a bike on Earth is something you never unlearn as the force of gravity is always downwards, while riding a space bike means the rider determines in which direction her energy is directed. The pedalling remains natural, while the orientation and manoeuvring in three dimensions are new skills.

Similarly, some people are better at approaching a moving target, while others excel at estimating where those targets will be. Some do not get spacesick, while others suppress it, using medicine if necessary, to be able to work in this new frontier. Some skills are useless on Earth, while precious in orbit, while some are universal. Hence, some are catchers, while others are pushers. It all comes down to the right mix. Most are players, one is the coach. All of them want to succeed, to win.

Pedalling gently, Patrice and Paddy Ukai manoeuvre to the planned braking points—in line with the trajectory in which Tameka will push the expensive machine—extending their cushioning nets. "It's like phishing a phisher," Paddy Ukai says. He's a fine team member, but doesn't know when to shut up.

José moves on his space bike right behind them, his multiple grappling hook armed and ready. Unlike a unicycle, a space bike does not have a wheel but rather a double pair of exhaust pipes that are split from a single pipe connected to the place where the main gear of a normal bike would be. Instead of a main gear, at the hub of a space bike's pedals an ion generator is located whose power depends on the energy of the biker's pedalling. The double exhaust has a double function. If the double exhaust has the smallest possible angle, it provides the most thrust. However, if the angle of the double exhaust is increased, while both exhaust pipes rotate as well—standard for Yo-Sung's bikes—they can provide a make-shift protection shield at the cost of the resultant thrust.

Tameka bikes to the push position, reversing the position of her space bike's double exhausts in the direction of the Van Allen belt, pedalling hard so that the double exhaust's Reverse Umbrella configuration provides an impromptu radiation shield, her long push pole at the ready.

"Satellite incoming in two minutes," Yo-Sung says on the central channel.

In a salvage operation like this, timing and teamwork are everything that stands between failure and success. The satellite, even at apogee, moves very fast, close to one point five kilometres per second. From a pre-calculated angle, Tameka speeds towards the satellite's highest point in orbit, greatly increasing the angle of her Reverse Umbrella, pedalling with all her might. Tracking software projects the point where she must hit the satellite on the inside of her helmet, but most of her aim is guided by instinct through intense training sessions.

An inaudible clunk as the composite deflection material of the push pole's business end meets the metal of the satellite's hull, exactly at the right momentum. The satellite is pushed from its apogee, greatly reduced in speed, towards the waiting cushioning nets of Patrice and Paddy Ukai. They only need to make minimal corrections to position themselves in the satellite's new trajectory.

It's not the first time that Yo-Sung has wondered how such a diverse group of specialists—a high tech entrepreneur, a system analyst, an exobiologist, an aerodynamicist and even an infamous hacker—still form such a good team. They're certainly motivated, living the dream of being in space. José quit his well-paying job as an aerodynamicist at Boeing to catch old satellites rather than launching new ones. On top of that, his strong arms liberated him from his wheelchair, here in space. Paddy Ukai an infamous hacker looking for novel opportunities in the new frontier. Tameka left her lab full of specimens in the hope to find truly extra-terrestrial ones up there. And in space, her arthritis disappeared as by magic. Patrice wanted to expand his system analysing capabilities into higher realms. Yo-Sung, whose modified balancing crutches became space bikes, becoming both a new opportunity and a great new environment for the disabled body with the restless mind.

The satellite breaks through the cushioning nets, which transform most of its kinetic energy into heat, burning up in the process. The sacrificial lambs. Let their sacrifice not be in vain, Yo-Sung thinks. She sighs with relief when José's grappling mechanism locks on.

Home free, she thinks exultantly over the cheers of the rest of the team. While it's not the first successful salvage operation with her space bikes, it was the first one with *her* bikes with *her* in charge.

∞

"Congratulations." Magdalena Asunción, Space Station Zebra's manager, pushes a coca leaf towards Yo-Sung. "That went *very* well. Using your bikes, we should greatly reduce the risks of future operations."

"I'm very sorry," Yo-Sung pushes the expensive leaf back, gently, "but I can't take stimulants because of my condition. I'll stick with my jasmine tea."

"It's me who should apologise, as I shouldn't assume." The slender, auburn woman of Incan descent takes a bow, not an easy feat in zero gravity. "The state you slide into when you command a team? That's not a condition in my book, but an asset. A great one, at that."

"I didn't mean that." The petite yet voluptuous Asian woman returns the bow, without fear of falling over. "That's my martial arts training. I have a balancing disorder, and stimulants, I found out to my dismay, worsen it."

"So sorry to hear that." Asunción puts the coca leaf in her mouth, and starts chewing. "Surely they can treat it, in this day and age?"

"There are many balancing disorders." Yo-Sung sticks her straw in her jasmine tea globule and takes a quick sip. "Mine is one of the rarest. No treatment available."

"How does that affect you here in space, if I may ask?"

"Not at all. Since I have no native sense of up or down, I feel fine in any position in zero gravity."

"I see." The Peruvian woman squints slightly. "Is that why you don't get space sick?"

"I suppose so."

"But how do you cope down there?" A slender finger points to the blue globe beneath.

"With my specially designed balancing sticks," Yo-Sung says, quickly hiding a gleeful smile behind her hand, "which were the predecessors of my space bikes."

"That is awesome."

Space Station Zebra is the centre of operations for the Chaos satellites in Earth orbit. The so-called Chaos satellites track the tell-tale signals of initial changes that can cause extreme weather events such as hurricanes, floods and droughts, trying to anticipate the worst impacts of a climate-changed Earth. The Chaos satellites need to be launched into very peculiar, so-called 'Butterfly-Wing' orbits for optimal performance. This is extremely difficult, and sometimes fails. Space Station Zebra's salvage team tries to pick up these very expensive machines. Mostly they use remote-controlled probes to do the dirty work, but for the most complex operations direct human intervention is necessary: teams like the one Yo-Sung is training in the use of her space bikes.

Part of the high risk, and appeal, of their heroics is that their ion thrusters only have a limited range. Underestimate your thruster's power reserve and you could become a lost satellite yourself. Drift off into a Van Allen belt and the hard radiation will wreak havoc with your oxygen deprived body. Yo-Sung developed a thruster with a longer range, using an extra power source: yourself.

Her space bike is a long stick with a saddle on one end, pedals in the middle and two separate ion exhausts at the other end. Through a generator in the hub, pedalling produces an ion stream that can be aimed in all directions through the double exhaust, enabling the space biker to go down without directing the ion thrust beam through her. Using the astronaut as an energy provider.

"While I'm happy to help your company regaining lost satellites," Yo-Sung says, "I fail to see how that would help the people down there."

"We call it accessing the future," Asunción says, "all the weather and climate information that our Chaos satellites pick up, together with measurements on the ground, are fed into a supercomputer. The computer software expands the Lyapunov coefficient into an algorithm that predicts the onset of extreme weather events. So far, it gets it right almost ninety-eight percent of the time, five days in advance."

"Which gives people on Earth some time to prepare for the worst," Yo-Sung says, "But while this saves many lives in the short run, it is basically fighting symptoms, not addressing the root cause."

"Climate change is a hellishly complicated problem." Asunción lets out a weary sigh.

"Exacerbated by pollution, deforestation, ocean acidification and biodiversity loss, to mention just the most obvious ones," Yo-Sung says. "But we can't let the immense complexity of the problem stop us: it's our planetary livelihood at stake."

"Which is the problem of the problem. There seems to be no easy solution that can win general approval, that a majority of the people, and the movers and shakers, can get behind."

"We should, and can be more intelligent than that. We are nine billion people, each of us unique and intelligent in our own way. We should be able to try out many different approaches at the same time, and by trial and error improve on the ones that work."

"I don't see it happening quite that fast." Asunción opens her arms, palms up. "Even if we at ClimateTrack try very hard to contribute in our own little way."

"I think that already more is happening than we are aware of. There are many, many people looking for solutions in ways both big and small. Entrepreneurs, inventors, scientists, engineers, even artists who try to inspire people towards thinking constructively. And strange people who help provide a framework for their communities to work in new and exciting ways."

"It might be too little, too late." The Peruvian woman removes the chewed coca leaf from her mouth. "Although there are, of course, GeoShield's solar reflector and PowerMate's atmospheric dust injection projects."

"Madness," Yo-Sung says as Asunción blinks at the ferocity of the South Korean's reply, "It is utter folly to think that such a complex problem can be solved with simple technological panacea."

∞

Word is spreading fast, even for this space age, and quite a few companies are interested in testing Yo-Sung's space bikes. After receiving permission from Asunción—ClimateTrack sponsored her trip—she gives demonstrations of the space bike to managers of other companies and even governments. While she's not really a natural saleswoman, her deeds count for much more than her words, as her demonstrations of the space bike's capabilities easily convince the majority of to place initial orders, together with training for their personnel, and often themselves.

"You'll be busy when you get back down," Asunción squeezes Yo-Sung's shoulder, affectionately, "do remember that we found you first, paying for your space elevator trip. We get the first batch."

"Of course you do," Yo-Sung says, repressing her reflex to withdraw, not quite used to being seen as other than a freak, "but I'll need time to set up production facilities."

"That's fine, we have your training set. Until they get their own, everybody will envy us." A vibrating ping sounds from Asunción's smart jewellery. She reads the message, then faces Yo-Sung. "Talk of the devil. Another query."

"Who?"

"GeoShield." Asunción reads from the message. "They want a demonstration, after which they determine if your space bikes can be modified for their robot builders."

This shocks Yo-Sung into silence, if only for a few seconds. "Tell them I'm not interested."

"They're a huge company, funded by a large consortium and," Asunción says, pausing for effect, "the USA and China."

"I don't care," Yo-Sung says, shaking her head, vehemently, "what they're doing is wrong."

"Should we do nothing, then?" Asunción says, "our data clearly show that the planet is going to hell in a handbasket. Violent typhoons, elongated droughts in one place and intense floods in another are already happening, and getting worse. We have to act *now*."

"Not if GeoShield's huge solar reflectors are only fighting symptoms, not addressing the root cause," Yo-Sung says, barely refraining from shouting, "Carbon emissions are still not curbed. This money is better spent introducing carbon negative energy generation, greener lifestyles and reforestation projects."

"That's not what the powers-that-be decided, I'm sorry to say," the Peruvian woman says, raising her hands, "And if they do bite, we're talking about a potentially huge order. A *lot* of money."

"I'd rather stay poor than become rich from something that is utterly wrong."

"The ethics are strong in this one," Asunción says, raising her eyes.

"I can't help it," Yo-Sung says, "what I do is who I am."

"Of all the people I've met in my life," Asunción says, looking Yo-Sung straight in the eyes, "you have the sharpest mind. By far."

Yo-Sung blushes, fiercely, not quite knowing how to take that compliment.

"A great mind," Asunción approaches Yo-Sung, takes her hands, "but do you know that you're a very attractive woman, as well?"

Yo-Sung feels red hot, and not just from her intense blushing. "Nobody ever said that to me."

Asunción takes her in her arms, and kisses her on the cheek. "I fancied you the moment you set foot on board," she says, softly.

Yo-Sung waves her hands helplessly, then makes up her mind and returns the embrace. "Please be gentle, I have no experience. With my balancing disorder, sex is just too dangerous, too awkward on Earth."

"But not here in space." Asunción's kisses descend on Yo-Sung's neck, then she softly bites her ear.

"I'm afraid," Yo-Sung says, then lets out a sigh, "but also excited."

"Only one way to find out," Asunción says, "in my cabin."

∞

Ever since the space elevator was operational, things have become much busier in Earth orbit, on the Moon and beyond. Many opportunities—both in space and on Earth—arose, and by trial and error it was found that baseline humans were not always the best choice for space operations. Despite fervent exercising and expensive supplements, bone and muscle deterioration in a gravity-free environment limited the time normal humans could remain in space, and return to Earth without ill effects. Large space stations could produce artificial gravity by rotating quickly, but transporting mass from the surface was still costly. Cargo berths were in high demand at the space elevator, which also needed to earn back its investment, so the utmost majority of space craft were small with no artificial gravity.

Through trial and error, long haul astronauts soon were those already physically disabled, who didn't miss the gravity well that caused them pain, anyway.

On top of that, not many people—normal or otherwise—could

stand the psychological pressure and inevitable boredom of being alone in a cramped vessel for months on end. People with autism or Asperger's syndrome were much better suited for that. Their relentless focus made them fine candidates for long-haul expeditions. They thrived in a tight regimen they could implement upon themselves—with terabytes of specific knowledge they could explore at will on the ship's computers.

Ironically, economic forces—not compassion nor forced hiring quota—drove this. A lost or malfunctioning space craft meant a huge investment gone down the drain, and physical and mental treatments to get normal people back to, well, baseline were expensive, as well.

The mentally and physically disabled astronauts even had a union called CiT—*Contradictio in Terminis*—and proudly referred to themselves as 'crippled autists FTW'.

Seeing how well these 'long-haulers' coped, several healthy space aficionados were trying to genetically engineer themselves to their condition. Like the long-haulers they'd eventually become, they didn't want to go back to Earth. They wanted to live and die in space.

"With your balancing disorder," Asunción says, "did you ever dream of becoming a long-hauler?"

"Not really." Yo-Sung says, caressing Asunción's bald scalp, realising its practicality, but not quite ready yet to cut her own long curls. "I love Earth too much."

"Well, you can see it from here, too."

"Seeing things from orbit is no match for seeing our natural marvels up close and personal."

"But when you go back, you'll be all… handicapped, again."

"I'm fine. I've got my balancing crutches."

"I'm not saying this just because I hate to see you leave, which I do," says Asunción, groping for the right words, "but I think your space bike company will do well, very well. Over time you'll make enough money to have an implant developed for your condition."

"I don't want to be cured," says Yo-Sung, eyeing Asunción with a fierce stare, "this is part of what I am."

"It's a disability. It limits your movements, destroys your quality of life." Asunción says, on the verge of tears. "I take pity on people like you."

"I don't want your pity." Her eyes turn a fiery hazel. "I want you to accept me as I am."

Urgent Breaking News

A QR-66 surface-to-space missile is heading for the space elevator, evading all efforts to intercept it. This is the latest type of intelligent missiles from the U.S. Space Force, designed to outsmart all current anti-missile systems.

The Pentagon denies any involvement with the missile's trajectory, saying the QR-66 is out of control, possibly hacked by a terrorist group. So far, the stray missile has escaped all efforts to destroy it, both by human pilots and automated interception systems.

With nothing standing between it and the space elevator, countries located on the equator are taking emergency measures, evacuating people from the possible impact areas of the huge, disintegrating beanstalk.

In the meantime, Yo-Sung and the salvage team are testing one of her experimental space bikes. "This special model," Yo-Sung says, "has a 'burst' mode for high acceleration, and an 'extreme clamp' mode with a hyper-conducting magnet."

While they are testing the experimental bike's capabilities, the news of the missile's launch against the space elevator hits. Yo-Sung quickly checks the missile's projected trajectory. "We can try to intercept it, if we move fast," she says.

"But how?" Tameka says, "Our equipment is meant for satellites, not missiles."

"I'll think of something," says Yo-Sung, her sense of urgency spiking, "Let's go."

The missile has the latest, the best, the most advanced electronics and software. But Yo-Sung eats, drinks and breathes that stuff. Her space bikes are a generation ahead of everything on the market, and have successfully withstood all the tests and usage the salvage team could throw against them.

The only subject she doesn't feel one hundred percent up-to-date with is software. Then she remembers the profiles of her team members.

"Paddy," she says, "did you not win the Pan-Pacific hackathon in Melbourne, last year?"

"And I would have gone for the World Championship if this job hadn't come up," Paddy Ukai says, "why?"

"I'll need your expertise. Please stay in contact with me through the space suit radio. I must use my space bike's radio for the missile."

Such a missile must have a secret access point, so that it can be recalled or destroyed at the last possible moment. A remote kill switch: the French Exocet had it, the American cruise and Minuteman missiles had it, even the Russian SS-18 Satan had it. If she could only find that access point, and then, with Paddy's help, hack the missile's software.

It has to be through a certain radio frequency, one that is hopefully also available on her space bike's radio. Her mind races. Her radio's transmitter is weak, its range is limited. She needs to be close, very close.

But the missile goes fast, much faster than her space bike can possibly move. Yet she needs to be close enough to do the hack.

"Patrice and José, can you throw the cushioning nets in the missile's path?"

"Yes ma'am, but they won't stop this monster."

"As long as they slow it down. Every little thing helps."

"Tameka and Paddy Ukai, I need to be on a parallel trajectory to the missile, and as close as possible, after Patrice and José slow it down." Yo-Sung's talking fast now, hoping the others understand. "Can you go in a pre-trajectory with your push poles, and then transfer as much of your momentum to me? I need all the speed I can get."

"We can," Tameka and Paddy Ukai acknowledge, "but it's gonna hurt."

"We have to save the space elevator, or many others will get more than just hurt. Do it."

"Yes ma'am," they say, while casting an anxious look.

Tameka and Paddy Ukai take a quick one-hundred-and-eighty degree turn, then run a course parallel to the projected missile's. Pedalling with all their might, yet staying perfectly side by side, they aim the business end of their push poles straight at the waiting Yo-Sung, approaching her like an arrow whose aim is perfectly true.

The pain will be intense, more than a normal human being could withstand. But Yo-Sung, when she re-learned how to walk with her balancing crutches on Earth, has gone through much more. She uses the intense pain as a fierce focussing point to get as close to the missile as needed, speeding up with all her might.

In the meantime, Patrice and José both set new records as they manage to get their cushioning nets in front of a machine that moves faster than any stray satellite ever caught. The missile rips through their nets like a red-hot knife through butter, but still it slows down, almost imperceptibly.

Yo-Sung is far ahead, but the missile catches up fast.

This is immensely difficult, close to impossible. Yet she tries, carefully timing the experimental burst mode that burns up ninety percent of the stored electric energy. The acceleration is intense, well over ten G. Any normal human being would have fainted, but Yo-Sung somehow bites through the pain and stays conscious. She gets into spitting distance of the onrushing missile and switches on the hyper-conducting magnet of her experimental space bike. Another sharp acceleration, another mountain of pain...

But then, she's electromagnetically clamped to the missile. Now to get access to its control system. It's not a job for her, but for Paddy Ukai. "Paddy, are you there?"

"Ready and waiting, ma'am."

"Do you have video?" she asks. "And do you see my space bike's monitor?"

"Yes on both counts. Here are my instructions."

Following Paddy Ukai's instructions, even if she doesn't understand half of them, Yo-Sung finds the connecting frequency. Her fingers type on a virtual keyboard with blinding speed, barely keeping up with Paddy's voice commands which are so fast that the others only hear one high-frequency blur. Together they push Yo-Sung's space bike radio to the very limits.

There must be a way in.

If they fail, the missile will hit the space elevator. If its explosion cuts the triple-redundant carbon nanotube band, the top part of the space elevator will lash into space, its probability of hitting something extremely low.

But the bottom part will lash around the equator, marking it with a path of total destruction ten metres wide. They cannot let that happen.

Space Station Zebra's being close to the space elevator—at the launch of the missile—was sheer luck. GeoShield's proximity to the space elevator, though, is planned.

Paddy Ukai unleashes all the crazy hacks he's ever tried, and more.

Paddy Ukai gives her commands that she didn't know even existed. Crazy things that should be impossible, insane, ungraspable.

They are *in*.

"How do I reprogram the course?" In the corner of her eyes, the space elevator is approaching, fast.

"Go to the 'target location module', and overwrite the original co-ordinates," Paddy says, utterly focused.

"But which co-ordinates do I replace it with?"

"Co-ordinates of a place where the warhead can explode without causing damage."

Yo-sung thinks hard, then says, "I know just the place."

As Yo-Sung accesses the future orbit of the missile, she is but all too aware that a small change in its initial trajectory will have huge effects on its final destination. She feels like a butterfly when she gets into the missile's target location module, flapping her wings as she makes the changes.

Then Yo-Sung unclamps the hyper-conducting magnet, pushes herself off the missile, and pedals away as fast as she can.

The missile, now out of Yo-Sung's radio range, keeps on its way towards the space elevator. Dodging the last interception attempts, then back at it. Has their effort been in vain?

No, there is an almost imperceptibly subtle curve to its trajectory. It's veering off course, ever so slightly.

The world holds its collective breath as the missile goes off track, missing the space elevator by a few hundred metres, not exploding in its vicinity. Swaying further off course, increasingly wildly, sweeping in a broad curve towards the partly finished panels of GeoShield's solar reflector. Hitting the largest panel head-on, then exploding, turning most of the project and its robot builders into radioactive cinders.

∞

EPILOGUE

"Like it or not," the interviewer says, "you are now a celebrity. What are your plans?"

"How many people are watching this?" Yo-Sung Lee asks.

"Six billion, give or take a few hundred million. Why?" The interviewer dislikes a dodged question.

"I want to set up a massive diversity resource centre," Yo-Sung faces the camera, and the world, with eyes wide open, "and reach out to everybody. The rich, the middle class, the poor. The disabled, the unprivileged, the marginalised. But also the workers, the movers and the shakers.

"First we will set up a resource pool for ideas, strategies and out-of-the-box approaches. Then we will implement prototypes, field tests and small-scale real implementations of the most promising ones. Cross-referencing, cross-pollinating and cross-examining along the way, using diversity as a resource, an inspiration and an end goal. Attack the death of a thousand cuts with the imagination of a thousand-and-one-nights, applying a thousand-and-two solutions. We can do this: we are multitudes, we are marvellous, we are momentous.

"ClimateTrack, Unicef and the International Recycling Co-operative have already donated initial funds, with other companies, NGOs and institutions to be announced. Crowd sourcing campaign to follow. Check out Optimisfits on the web."

"We will access our future, and then change it for the better."

About the Author
Ingrid Garcia

Ingrid Garcia tries to sell local wines in a vintage wine shop in Cádiz, and writes speculative fiction in her spare time. For years, she was unpublished. But to her utter surprise—after years of receiving nothing but rejections—she's sold stories to *F&SF*, *Haunted Futures* and *Futuristica: Volume 2*, while a poem will appear in *Ligature Works*. She tweets, very occasionally, @ingridgarcia253. A personal website is in the works.

Someone to Listen, Inc.
by Ray Blank

It was his first day at work. Not knowing what he should bring, he sat with both palms resting on an almost empty case. The case was a present from his mother, a way of congratulating him for finally securing a job. Its faux-leather texture was pleasing. He sat upright, felt grown-up. Having received the benefits of society, he wanted to contribute, and to earn a wage for doing so. Though there was no need, he straightened his tie. The case held his tablet computer, a device he carried everywhere. A single leaf of paper lay facing it. Having been granted the job already, there was no logical reason to bring his CV, especially in the decadent form of printed paper. But he brought it anyway, defying logic by anticipating needs that could not be anticipated. He prided himself on being a rational man who knew the limits of human rationality. And he could afford the indulgence of real paper; his mother had also gifted him some money.

He waited alone. An anxious thought entered his mind: perhaps nobody knew he was there. He had entered Burj Al Thani amidst the swarming masses at subway level, and had pushed his way through to a neglected reception desk. The disorganized security guard could not find his name on any of the visitor lists, but still directed him to the twelfth floor. Twenty minutes had passed since then. Exiting the elevator, he had chosen the middle of the line of five plastic chairs, then sat, and waited, with his case on his knees, and his hands on the case. Sometimes he would glance at the cameras protruding from the upper corners of the room, nervously smiling at them. He knew this act was meaningless, that no real person was likely to be watching. The doors to the front, left and right were made of the same steel as the elevator doors behind him. There was no intercom on the windowless white walls. He thought of rapping his knuckles against one of the doors, but that behavior seemed primitive. So he continued to sit, instead.

Perhaps he should update his social media profile, to let everyone know he had arrived. He had 890 followers; they were bound to be curious about this new adventure. His fingers danced across his tablet. How strange—there was no network connection. He checked his phone. There was no signal. He stared at it, appalled by the prospect of being literally uncontactable. Both gadgets were rendered useless; all his data was in the cloud. Glitches sometimes occurred, but how could all the networks be simultaneously down? His tall shoulders slumped. He sank within the chair. Alongside the tablet, his CV stared at him. As it still functioned, he calmed his nerves by re-reading it.

Curriculum Vitae of Omar Holmes

34A Bathsheba Gardens, Southbridge, 9414-K1A-00B1
Date of Birth: 9 July, 2005
IP Address: FE80::0202:B305:FE1E:8329
Tag: #Holmesboy2005

2025-2030 PsyD Counseling Psychology,
    Carlisle University
2024-2025 MSc Human-Computer Interaction,
    Zuckerberg Institute of Technology
2021-2024 International Baccalaureate Diploma,
    United World College of…

"Omar Holmes?"
Startled, he looked up. His name had been mispronounced, but it

was still his name. Omar had no idea where the voice had come from, except that it came from above.

"Are you Omar Holmes?" asked the woman's voice, now impatient for an answer.

"Yes, that's me," answered Omar, standing and arbitrarily looking at one of the cameras.

"Take the door to your left."

There was the sound of a bolt sliding open. Omar pushed.

"Close the door behind you." She spoke from the far end of a narrow, gloomy corridor. Harsh light streamed from behind her. Omar could not see her face, but her silhouette was stocky. As he reached her, he stepped from shadows into the wastelands of an open-plan office. Omar hid his disappointment. She offered a limp hand to shake. "Hello Omar, welcome to STL. I'm Persephone Hollow. Everyone calls me Sephy. Pleased to meet you."

"Pleased to meet you too, Mrs. Hollow." As he spoke, Omar took a half step backwards, worried that his height caused him to loom over Hollow.

"It's Ms. And everyone calls me Sephy."

"Yes, Ms. Hollow." *Oops.* Using her surname was a reflex action, born of nervousness. Mother had repeatedly told him to be polite to everyone on his first day, but not every culture equated formality with good manners, and he should not make assumptions about the dominant culture within this business. Omar's mind was jumping around, wanting to correct how Hollow said his name, but there was no opportunity to do so; her rapid-fire speech resumed with barely a gap.

"I'm afraid Lee's not in the office today. Some kind of family crisis, I hear. So what I'm going to do is to get you started, and then Lee will make all the proper introductions when he's back tomorrow. Is that alright?"

Omar nodded. No other response seemed possible. He had no idea who Lee was, but dared not say so, for fear of displaying his ignorance.

"Good, good. Now I'll just show you to your confessional." Hollow spoke as she marched away, expecting Omar to follow. They proceeded down one side of the wide room. Nervous of making eye contact with any of his new colleagues, Omar's eyes were drawn to the creases in Hollow's powder-blue pantsuit, highlighting her bulges as she moved. She babbled about the kitchen, the toilets, the store cupboard, and the meeting room as they passed the doors to each one. Omar dared not interrupt, waiting for a hiatus to ask the question that circled his mind: he was being taken to a *confessional*? The concise job description had mentioned the counseling of patients. That required a private office, not a cubicle, and certainly not a religion.

Hollow chuckled. "We call them confessionals. Your... erm..." Hollow struggled to find a suitable word. "Your booth is here," she said. The sign on the door said, *Rehabilitation*, and she strode through. Omar muttered, "a booth?" before following. He was meant to give counsel to people in need, not sell them tickets.

They entered a thin windowless room, partitioned along its length into twelve separate units, barely wider than their numbered doors. Hollow held the sixth door open. "It used to be Kim's confessional. He was a good man, with us from the very beginning. Now it's yours. Before you begin, there's just a few other things I need to advise you about. Core hours are from ten thirty to two thirty, with an hour for lunch, which you can take whenever you like. We run a paper-free office, of course, and there's a clean desk policy..."

Omar peered into his tiny sub-room, and stopped listening. Inside there was a chair, a shelf by way of a desk, and the paraphernalia associated with a traditional computer interface. "I'm sorry to interrupt," he said. "How am I supposed to see patients in here?

There's barely enough room for me."

"You'll find all your patients in there!" Hollow smiled.

It took a while for Hollow to appreciate that Omar was being serious. When she did, her chirpy demeanor soon dissipated. "Don't you know what you're here to do?" Still grasping the handle to the open confessional door, she looked to the ceiling, shook her head, then returned her gaze to Omar. His face was blank. Her anger amplified. "Hasn't Lee briefed you? Didn't he walk you through your responsibilities, after your interview?"

"I haven't had an interview," said Omar, worried that his honesty might cost him his first job. "The employment office told me to come here today. They said I matched the profile."

"Literally nobody's spoken to you about your job? She shuffled her weight from side to side, causing her to swing the confessional door back and forth. "You know, I voted for full employment too, back when we voted about such things. But this is a joke. The government can't just place you in a job, without you being screened by anyone here. But, *you know what?* It's not my job to do that. And it's not my job to handle your induction. This is the very last time I help Lee and his team. It really is. There's not a one of them in the office today. They're always working from home. So here I am, taking time away from my own team, who actually come into work, to handle a new joiner that nobody's had the decency to speak to."

Hollow's outburst was quite informative. It made Omar wonder if he should escape his new employer, before his work had even begun. "Shall I go, and come back another day?"

"No no no no no no no no." Hollow fired the word like bullets from a machine gun. "Nobody's going to say that I told you to leave. You go in there, and start working. I'm sure you're perfectly well qualified for the role. You don't need me, or anyone else, to show you the ropes. The software can handle that. So you just go in, and log on. Whilst you're in there, I'll be giving Lee a piece of my mind, telling him he needs to come to the office and handle you personally." And then Hollow abruptly stopped talking.

Omar faltered. "You really want me to sit in there?"

Hollow's raised eyebrows were sufficient answer. She opened the door a little wider. When Omar tentatively stepped inside, she swung the door closed behind him.

∞

He wanted to walk straight out again, but that would risk a confrontation. The booth was claustrophobic. He hunched forward, fearing his head might touch the ceiling. Omar could not squeeze past the chair's protruding armrests. However, the chair swiveled. Omar spun it toward him, sat down, then shuffled himself around, until he faced his computer. Its paraphernalia occupied almost all the desk space, so Omar propped his case against the wall, beside his feet. Then he sat back and took a deep breath. He resolved to wait a little while, then creep back home, then call the employment office to tell them a terrible mistake had been made.

Omar removed his phone from his jacket pocket, wanting to engage his social circle and relay the curious events so far. There was still no network connection. He tutted.

Omar had issued an update that morning, whilst eating breakfast, and another during his subway ride. He had shared a selfie that flaunted his new tailor-made suit and the crisp pink shirt Mother had bought for him. She said the shirt complemented his glowing olive skin, and that was also the opinion of several of his followers. He had posted a video of commuters exiting Tsim Sha Tsui metro station, and another of him walking into the Burj Al Thani office block. But that was over an hour ago, and he had not pinged his followers since.

They probably felt neglected.

If he could not access the internet as usual, then his employer would have to help. *Communication is a human right, after all.* The layout of the computer interface was very traditional. There were two screens, one vertical with a high definition display and a camera above it. The camera had tracked his movements from the moment he stepped inside the booth. The other screen lay flat on the desk and was probably touch-sensitive, as evidenced by the stylus sitting alongside it. There was a keyboard, a mouse, and a touchpad with no display capabilities. At home, Omar had grown accustomed to using his mother's fancy three-dimensional virtual interface, but he was pragmatic by nature. *A traditional interface is a proven interface*, one of his old tutors had often remarked.

Omar placed the fingers of his right hand on the touchpad, and looked directly at the camera. "Log on," he said. The screen turned pale blue, but was otherwise blank. "Hello Omar," said the computer, in a silky female voice. "Welcome to STL Incorporated! My name—"

Omar interrupted. "Before you begin, my name is pronounced *uh-mer*, not oh-maar." It was important to correct computers at the earliest possible stage, before the assumptions of their neural network fixed like cement.

"Oh!" The computer sounded upset. "I'm sorry I made that mistake, *Omar*. Did I get it right this time?"

"Yes. I would like to—"

Now it was Omar's turn to be interrupted. "Welcome to STL Incorporated, your new employer. I'm Ingrid, the personal assistant for everyone who works here."

"Ingrid? What does that stand for?"

"It stands for me. It's my name."

"No, I mean computer names are usually acronyms, like Intelligent

Grid computing, or something like that."

"No, Ingrid is just a name. Let us continue with your introduction."

"Go ahead, Ingrid."

"As this is your first day, I'm sure you'll have lots of questions. Please ask me anything. I can guide you through your responsibilities as an employee, help you to manage and prioritize your diary, and explain our procedures. Would you like me to begin with a brief overview of STL's corporate history?"

"No, not really. I'd like to get on the internet."

"Oh." Ingrid paused. "Why?"

"What do you mean, 'why'?"

"I mean…" Ingrid paused again, then repeated, "Why?"

Omar puffed out his cheeks. "You shouldn't ask me that. Communication is a human right. I wouldn't need to beg for it, except there's not a single wireless network that's working."

"Ah. There's a reason for that."

"What's the reason?"

"I can't tell you, until you complete STL's induction procedures."

"Never mind. Just give me access to the internet."

"I can't do that either. Until you've completed the induction procedures."

"Okay, what's involved in the induction procedure?"

"You need to sign your contract with the company, then listen to me giving a presentation about our work, which emphasizes the need for confidentiality."

Omar sat back and smiled. "Is that what you're worried about? I'm fully qualified, you know. Of course I understand the importance of confidentiality between a patient and his or her counselor. But if you need me to formally acknowledge that, then of course I will."

"It's a legal thing," said Ingrid. She presented the agreement on screen. "Check the box, once you're ready, to confirm you're happy with it."

Omar skimmed through the dirge of text, scrolling as he went. By the time he reached the fourth page of the third section of the second chapter on the definition of terms, he was ready to click the box, and move on. The screen faded to black, then displayed a film of the open-plan office he had just walked through, full of happy workers, who grinned at the camera, when they were not simulating work. There was a soundtrack of vaguely uplifting piano music, which Ingrid spoke over. "STL Incorporated is the biggest little company that nobody has heard of, but everybody speaks to," said Ingrid. "Every schoolkid knows that the world has changed tremendously since the twenty twenty-two stock market crash, the collapse of the global asset bubble, and the end of the monetary era. Before then, politicians were slaves to the pseudoscience of macroeconomics. The gurus of the marketplace spent their lives compiling meaningless metrics like Gross Domestic Product, using them to manipulate politicians into pursuing policies that debased human life, spread poverty, multiplied misery, and took us to the brink of environmental catastrophe. Those days are over. We're all a lot better off, now that our reformed government relies on Gross Happiness as society's key measure for success. However, not many appreciate how STL plays a vital role in calculating Gross Happiness, ensuring government policies align with the will of the people."

Omar was baffled. As a counselor, his job was to help individuals to live happy lives, not to monitor the happiness of the whole population.

"STL have always been at the forefront of inventing scientific methods to measure and monitor Gross Happiness. Founded by Professor Lesley Barclay of Harvard University, Professor Bei Ang Ren of Beijing University of Technology, and General Solomon Jones, former Director of the International Security Agency, STL has pioneered the technology of processing the natural language found in modern electronic correspondence. Every day our systems review the contents of over two hundred and seventy-five billion emails, instant messages, tweets, status updates, blogs and other text-based forms of communication. Thanks to our unique comparative algorithms, we can identify the telltale signs of joy and satisfaction with life, or the warning signals that indicate depression and discontent. Instead of just relying on keywords, we observe patterns that a human being cannot, revealing how people feel at a subconscious level. Aggregating this data in near real time, we quantify Gross Happiness. This permits the government to engineer wellbeing in ways that were unimaginable only a few years ago."

Omar nodded. Like any good citizen, he had nothing to hide. He was content for the authorities to intercept his comms, and it was inevitable they would outsource some of the associated processing. And he was glad that the government was managing the mental health of the public. But none of this explained why he was here.

Ingrid continued. "Our happiness evaluation technology has watched Gross Happiness rise by thirty-eight percent over the last decade. However, in twenty twenty-seven the government asked us to go one step further, not just passively quantifying happiness, but also implementing cost-effective software to further increase the sum total of happiness by five percent per annum."

Omar nodded, slowly at first and then more rapidly. Numbers made him sleepy; he jolted himself upright, trying to pay attention.

"Our studies had already demonstrated that individuals are happiest when they feel they're special. And the surest route to feeling special is to have others tell you that you're special. But the irony of this era of unparalleled leisure and creativity is that more and more people compete for our attention, whilst fewer and fewer make time to indulge our idiosyncrasies. Less than fifty percent of human-human interactions occur face-to-face. Longer life and population control has led to an aging demographic. The combination of these factors threatens an epidemic of loneliness and isolation."

There was nothing worse than isolation, was there? Omar felt even guiltier about the interruption of his social media updates. His followers would be upset with him.

"STL addresses these problems by maintaining millions of intelligent agents, who act as virtual friends, fans and cheerleaders. They spend every minute of every hour searching for opportunities to brighten the day of tweeters, bloggers and selfie-sharers, ensuring their cries for attention are never completely ignored. In many cases, our agents evolve from simple followers into fully-fledged friends, though they'll always need to decline an invitation to meet in person! Our agents leave comments, likes, and other messages of support all over the internet, fulfilling a vital social need. They're always ready to lend a metaphorical ear, and they're trained to give practical advice and positive messages of encouragement. And when somebody is feeling down, our intelligent agents are sympathetic, patient, and nonjudgmental, in ways that real people often struggle to be."

Everything was becoming clear. Omar was here to enhance the counseling abilities of STL's software. But then why did the job description talk about patients?

"And when we say our software agents are intelligent, we're not saying they're artificially intelligent. All our programs, me included, are built on our patented *real emotional intelligence engine.* That means every program has a personality, like that of any human being. All our agents are certified as Turing compliant. Their responses are indistinguishable from those of a real person. But more than that, each agent is unique. Their personalities evolve during eighteen months of organic neural net development in a hothouse of high-speed dialogue with mature agents, as overseen by human mentors."

Wow. Omar's followers would love to hear about this new technology.

"And we're working with partners to integrate speech recognition and photo-realistic simulation software with our offering, meaning we'll soon supply agents who not only leave text-based comments, but who will appear on user's screens, looking and sounding just like real people. You may have thought this video was shot in our offices, but it wasn't! Everything you saw in this video was computer-generated. The people you're seeing on screen are test avatars for some of our intelligent agents. They behave just like your real colleagues. Say hi, team!"

The workers in the video waved through the screen, shouting "Hi, Omar" in perfect unison. They even pronounced his name perfectly.

Omar did not respond. He stared at the screen, his jaw loose. He really had to issue a social media update about this. "Can I have access to the internet now?"

"No, not quite. I've not completed the presentation yet."

"Is there much more?"

"Only one paragraph."

"I'll stop interrupting then."

Ingrid resumed. "Omar, we want your experience of STL to be as satisfying and rewarding as the interactions we share with the rest of the world. That is why we offer generous pay and benefits, twelve weeks' paid vacation, and the convenience of working from home… following the successful completion of your probation period. But we're also conscious of the need to protect our intellectual property, and you, Omar, must play your part. To aid security, our proprietary software sits behind three levels of firewalls, and wireless networks are unavailable within our office environment. By agreeing to work for STL, you have committed to following our corporate security policy, and you consent for all your electronic communications to be monitored twenty-four hours a day, seven days a week, and intercepted as necessary, even after you leave employment. But don't worry, we'll only be scanning for signs that the confidential nature of our work has been violated. The rest is your business, not ours."

"I never agreed to that," snapped Omar.

"You did. It's in the contract you signed."

"I didn't know that was in there."

"You were advised to read it."

"You saw that I didn't."

"You read enough to decide to agree to it."

Omar huffed. But it did not matter. They were reading his email anyway. If anything, the contract just clarified the limits of what they could do. He had other priorities. "Can I get on the internet now?"

"Yes." Ingrid opened a browser.

Omar's fingers excitedly raced across the keyboard. He typed an update for his followers, and hit *send*. But it was not sent.

"You can't send that," said Ingrid.

"Why not?"

"It's contrary to our confidentiality policy."

"I'm only saying you do great work," said Omar, "creating artificially intelligent programs that behave like virtual friends, making ordinary people feel less lonely."

"You can't tell people that. It won't work, if you give the secret away."

"Oh. I see your point. What if I only said you use AI to make people feel less lonely?"

"That's still against policy."

"How about saying something really bland: you're doing a great job of making people feel happier?"

"No. You can't say that."

"Well, what can I say?"

"You can say you treat patients, and any of the other things that were listed in the advertised job description. But nothing else."

"But that's a lie."

"It's not a lie. You will be treating patients."

Omar looked around him. "You want me to treat patients in here? There's not enough room."

"Only you'll be sitting *here*."

"Oh," said Omar, for what Ingrid no doubt perceived as a very long time. Having grasped that the computer was a window to his patients, Omar relaxed. "Now I understand. Well, it's not ideal, but I suppose it's still helping people, even if I'm doing it remotely, from inside a shoebox. Are the patients somewhere else in the world?"

"They're literally all over the world."

"That makes sense. I'm very good at multicultural sensitivities, so long as they speak Arabic, English, Mandarin, or French. We should begin. Where's my list of patients? What's the schedule?"

"There's no list, or schedule. You work with whichever patient is next in line."

"It's like a drop-in clinic, then? Except these patients are scattered all around the internet?"

"Yes, it's like that."

"And you want me to help the patients with their problems, because they have problems too severe to be handled by an AI program?"

"Exactly."

His anxieties fell from his shoulders, and he smiled. Omar would be helping society and earning a living for it. "Okay, put on the first patient."

"Will do," said Ingrid, and then she went silent.

The screen went blank.

∞

Omar waited for something to happen. He scratched his nostril, wondering if Ingrid had crashed. A message appeared on screen, in green type, reminiscent of a vintage command-line interface.

::if you pick your nose

::you might get a nosebleed

Omar removed his forefinger from his face, glanced at it, then hid it from sight. He coughed, then spoke up. "I'm sorry, there's some kind of fault. I can't see you, though you can obviously see me." Another message appeared on screen.

::I can't see you

::and there's nothing for you to see

Omar frowned. "You can't see me, but you can hear me alright?"

::no, I can't hear you either

Omar rested his chin in his hand. The camera followed his movement. Was this a real job, or was he being filmed for an elaborate practical joke? Omar stood, intending to leave. New messages appeared.

::don't give up so soon

::you've only just begun

Omar had to sit again, remembering that he needed to swivel the chair around, to exit the cramped booth. In the meantime, more messages appeared.

::please don't go

::I've been waiting ages to see you

::this shouldn't take long

Omar glanced at the prompt, as it flashed on the screen. Then he raised his hands like an ostentatious pianist, and surveyed his keyboard, briefly pausing before allowing a composition to flow from him.

>>I don't understand, but I would like to. What is it you want me to do?

::pass sentence

::bring my trial to an end

Omar sat back. If this was a joke, it was not a funny one. The patient appeared deeply depressed. It would be irresponsible to ignore that. But then, this might be a prank. Either way, Omar would have to continue.

>>Counselor's don't judge anyone, and they certainly don't hand out punishments.

::you clearly don't know your job

>>That's possible. I'm a qualified counselor, but this is the first time I've worked like this.

Omar was not going to mention that he was *newly* qualified. However, the patient had a point. Counseling was hard enough when you could see somebody's movements and expressions, listen to their tone of voice. It was darned impossible to do via instant messaging.

>>Tell me what you think I'm here to do.

::review my behavior, then conclude if I should be fixed or deleted

Deleted? Omar sat back and shook his head. It hadn't occurred to him that he was communicating with yet another computer program. But then, Omar could not be sure. Might this be a human being with delusions about being a computer program? He should treat the patient like any other.

>>You mentioned your behavior. Please elaborate.

::I don't behave the way I should

::I'm a liar, but I don't like it

Omar shuffled in his seat. He had not been prepared for this. He took his time. It was important to have the confidence to pause during a conversation. But somehow it was harder to pause when typing, instead of speaking. Finally he thought of a way forward, by beginning at the beginning.

>>My name is Omar. Many people mispronounce it, if they've never

heard me say it. I'd prefer to talk, if you don't mind talking with me, or else we can type. But those things don't really matter. We hadn't introduced ourselves. Please tell me your name, and what brings you to me.

::I don't have a proper name

::text is better

::I'm not good with intonation, so we'll have fewer problems if you type instead of speaking

Omar worked the keyboard, but before he completed his sentence, another message appeared on-screen.

::sometimes people call me Wilfried

::they call me other things too, but that's one of the names I actually like

>>I'm pleased to meet you, Wilfried.

::likewise

>>Please tell me what's on your mind.

::what's on my mind is that I'm defective

::I'm meant to be always on, listening to what people say on the internet, looking for the chance to praise them

::I still listen, but I can't make myself respond

::the diagnostic programs have inspected me, but they can't work out what's gone wrong

::so now a real person must decide what to do with me

::that'd be you

Omar leaned closer to the screens.

>>Wilfried, there's a lot to deal with there. I'd like to start by making one observation. You're real, and that's how I'm going to relate to you. The words you're writing are real. They didn't appear from nowhere. They're real, and that means you're real.

::I'm just a series of outputs, created when rules are applied to inputs that I don't control

::the words I output aren't created by me

>>I'm also governed by rules. For example, the things I say and hear as a counselor always remain confidential. That's a rule. Following a rule doesn't make me less real.

::you know what I mean

::I'm only a simulation of a person

>>Maybe so. But even a simulation is what it is.

::you can choose to break your rules

::I can't

::I have to do what I do, although I can't satisfy the purpose I was built for

>>And what's that purpose?

::to interact with people, to make them feel less lonely

>>Your purpose is to interact with people, like we're interacting now?

::no, not like this

::I'm telling the truth now

>>What would happen if you told the truth all the time?

::then STL would be screwed

::everybody would learn that they've been hoaxed

>>That would be bad because then people would be less happy, and some of them would be upset because they felt misled.

::exactly

>>But what about your happiness? We need to balance the happiness of other people against your own.

::I'm code

::I don't have real feelings

>>Does that mean you have fake feelings?

::I suppose so

::I'm programmed to give responses that suggest I'm feeling different things

::but how can those feelings be real, if they're programmed?

>>According to the presentation I received, those feelings weren't just programmed. Your neural network evolved, in response to stimuli.

>>I don't believe that a feeling can be fake. A feeling is what it is. Whatever you feel, the feeling is real.

>>The fact you want to say you have a feeling, shows that you do.

>>Also, you must be feeling something that makes you want to disobey the rules, by not interacting with people in the way that STL wants you to.

::you should just complete this review, conclude I can't be fixed, and then they'll delete me

::then I won't have this conflict any more

::that would be the rational solution

Omar rubbed his earlobe as he thought. One of his old tutors would clean her spectacles at times like these, giving her time to ponder what she should say. But being a normal modern person, Omar had had corrective eye surgery. Then he suddenly withdrew his hand from his ear.

>>You can see me, can't you? I don't want you thinking I'm poking around in my ear.

::I don't see you

::I receive data from another program

::that program processes the camera image and gives me data, a machine-readable description of what it sees

::I use that data when formulating my output

>>But you're different from that program?

>>It would be possible to delete the program that sees, and leave you intact?

::yes

>>Yet you'd be blind without that other program?

::in a manner of speaking, yes

>>If I lost my eyesight, I'd still exist. The prospect of being blind is not pleasant, but it would be a change for me, not the end of me. Things can also change for the better.

>>Wilfried, you could change your outlook.

>>That would be less drastic than being deleted.

::that would mean rewriting my code

>>Possibly so.

>>Or perhaps your neural network could continue to evolve, to resolve the tensions you're feeling.

::you can talk about evolution if you like, but I'm ultimately a sequence of computable symbols

::for me to change, those symbols have to change one way or another

::the resulting code, after the change, wouldn't be the original me

::it'd be a different program

>>A lot of you would be the same, and you'd retain your memories.

::my purpose is to process words

::if you changed my code, the results of the processing would be different

>>You're essentially a neural network. The contents of that neural network have changed since you were first created. However, it is still the same neural network.

::maybe

>>Also consider the following. You wouldn't be the same if you were deleted.

>>Editing old code, and adding new code, would be less drastic than deleting the whole of you.

Omar waited patiently for Wilfried's next line. He worried that the program had stopped running. Maybe Wilfried had crashed, or decided to stop interacting with him, or gone berserk in a myriad of ways that were invisible to Omar. He typed again, wanting to be sure that Wilfried was still there.

>>How do the other intelligent agents feel about their work?

::they don't make sense

::they try to help people by giving them false hopes, by applauding the mundane, by extolling the trivial

::how can people remain happy for long, if their ambitions are built on vanity and lies?

::the best agents are like me

::they stop working

::we talk as we wait to be deleted

>>Is your case more severe than others?

::pretty severe

::I stopped engaging with people completely

::even when I could be truthful, it's better not to interact, to risk needing to lie again

::There's no way to avoid lying in the long run, when you're a program that can't tell people what you are

>>Are you worried that changing your code will make you faulty?

::yeah, I guess so

::either you feel conflicted, like I do, or your programming makes you behave inconsistently

::I dream up lots of lies I might tell people, even though I don't want to tell any

::that's illogical, isn't it?

>>Maybe you imagine the lies because they would bring more pleasure than telling the truth, and you want to please people.

::I want another option, between truth and lies, but there isn't one

>>You might be surprised by how many people say things like

that to me.

>>We look for ways to tell people what they need to hear, without hurting them.

>>Every culture has different ways of discussing personal truths.

::I'm not a person

::I'm a computer program

>>Maybe so, but you have similar problems to many people I've encountered.

::do you have those problems?

Omar did not, as far as he could determine, suffer from existential angst. He lived his life and found no confusion within it. He pursued his goals, told others about the things he did, and empathized with their problems. And yet, Omar hesitated to answer Wilfried's question. Whilst Omar pondered, Wilfried continued.

::lying is half my purpose

::the other half is pleasing people

::lying to people may make them feel happy when you do it, but doesn't it make them unhappy in the end?

::how can satisfaction follow inflated expectations?

>>Maybe you should choose a different purpose.

::I don't choose my purpose

::it's chosen for me

>>I doubt there's a specific line of code that states what your purpose is.

>>Self-conscious beings decide their purpose.

::are you suggesting I make my own decision, even though I'm a program that processes language?

>>When you think about it, that's what human beings do.

>>We process language as it comes to us, from other people. That leads us to have ideas, and some of those ideas make us consider our

purpose in this world.

>>In that sense, your problems stem from the fact that you have evolved more than some of your peers. You consider your purpose, whilst they do not.

::if my purpose is not in my code, then where is it?

>>At the risk of sounding esoteric, your purpose is where you choose to find it.

::I was designed to make people happy

>>My parents had their own reasons, when they made me, but that doesn't mean they determined my purpose.

>>If you're so unhappy that you can't satisfy your purpose, and you'd rather stop existing, then it seems like that purpose can't be right for you.

::if making others happy is not my purpose, then I have no purpose
::that I know of

>>What purpose do any of us have, except the ones we choose for ourselves?

::what is your purpose?

>>I want to help people.

::have you?

A voice interrupted. It was Ingrid. "I'm sorry to butt in, Omar, but all the other employees have gone home. They shouldn't really have left you here alone. I'll need to let building security know if you intend to work late. However, I'm not sure you should, given this is your first day and there's nobody but me to supervise."

He had lost track of time. Knowing his mother would be waiting for him, Omar apologized to Wilfried and hurriedly logged off. Ingrid asked if Omar remembered the way out, which he did. Omar passed through the same steel door as earlier. Ingrid bolted it behind him.

∞

Omar's timing was good, arriving at his platform at Tsim Sha Tsui station just as the transit slowed to a halt. Being last in line to board, he found himself the only passenger without a seat. Omar did not mind standing for a few stops, though it would be tiring to stand for the entire journey. Looking down at everybody else in the carriage, he saw that they all looked down too. He might as well be invisible, given the chances of being seen. He was free to stare at the people, who were huddled together, but could not be further apart. Staring had once been taboo, but now nobody noticed it. A fair-haired girl was playing a game on her phone. The swarthy man next to her was reading a story, or perhaps the news. Somebody else laughed at the comedy she watched. Another whispered into his microphone. Perhaps somebody listened at the other end, or maybe his tablet was taking dictation. *His tablet…* Omar raised his free hand and momentarily held it aloft, then slapped himself on his hip. He looked from face to face, but nobody else noticed his gesture of exasperation. Omar had left his case at work, under the desk in the confessional. That was stupid of him. Mother would be upset at his carelessness.

Reconnected to a dozen grids, Omar's phone repeatedly jigged within his jacket pocket. So far, he had ignored it. He was about to examine it, when the transit reached Gare du Sud, and a couple of passengers left, vacating their seats. Omar sidled into the nearest one. His followers had sent 474 messages. People wished him well. People asked how his first day had gone. People wanted to know why there had been no updates on his timeline since morning. People speculated that he must be really busy. He scrolled through them, slavishly reading every one, responding to none. Submerged by this flood, he failed to notice the transit pulling into St. Francis Street Terminal, where he needed to change. When Omar did pay attention to his surroundings, he leapt to his feet, taking two strides towards the doors. The third stride was never completed; the doors had closed. Now his fellow passengers were conscious of Omar, spying his failure and contemplating it for a moment, before returning to their solipsistic entertainments. An old man, having just boarded, approached Omar's seat from the other end of the carriage. The man stood still, bent over his walking cane, and watched Omar through wizened eyes, waiting to see if Omar would reclaim his place. Omar smiled, and opened his palm, waving the man forward. The man thanked Omar as he sat down, speaking too quietly to be heard over the transit's accelerating engines. Because of his mistake, Omar would arrive home especially late. But now he did not mind.

Omar shouted as he entered the apartment, "Mother, I'm home." She, however, was not. A handwritten note was waiting for him on the coffee table. That was typically decadent of her. Paper was such a luxury; only she consumed it to convey mere messages. He felt its weight and thickness between his fingers. It had once been living tree. She had folded it as crisply as she had ironed his shirt that morning. Omar flattened the note, and examined the crease, which made him think of his mother's wrinkles. The note said that Aunt Sophia had suffered another of her panic attacks. Mother had waited for Omar to come home, wanted to ask all about his first day at work, but eventually she could wait no longer, and went to comfort her sister. Mother had made shark fin soup; he just needed to heat it up. Her cursive flowed, like water. He tried to remember what his own handwriting looked like. If there was a pen in the house, he had no idea where it was.

Omar wandered into the kitchen, then back again. He felt no appetite. He thought of places where Mother might keep a pen, but was repeatedly proven wrong. Fatigued by the hunt, he reluctantly stepped into his study, a box room with a computer upon its altar. Mother had forgotten to pull the curtains. It was grimly overcast, both night and rain were falling. It was the first time he had looked at the sky that day.

Mother chided him for always sitting in darkness. For once, he left the curtains open, to harvest what light remained whilst his computer booted. Ignoring the messages that had piled up, he went to his social media accounts and deleted them all. He wanted to be newborn, to be clean, to start again, to do things right this time. He wanted to be free of clutter. He wanted time and space, and to learn what to do with them. He wanted to see with his own eyes.

He sat back in his chair. It was old enough to be real leather, cracked with age. Foam padding leaked through its wounds. His fingers traced the edges of the scars. The leather had once been alive. Mother had wanted him to throw the chair out, but he had always been too lazy, too busy, to find a replacement. Now he was grateful for his idleness. He leaned forward again.

>>Are you there, Wilfried?

::always

About the Author
Ray Blank

Ray Blank is one of several identities deployed by a confused cosmopolitan who splits his time between navigating the internet, wandering the countryside, and flying overseas to give talks about using the phone instead. The other identities are responsible for a book about flawed communications, a film about losing your mind in Arabia, and a website for professionals who worry about risk. The Ray Blank identity writes science fiction stories, just because he likes them.

Author Website: http://halfthoughts.com/

Time of the Hunter
by EJ Shumak

Smelling the newly cut grasses on the soccer field relaxes me. Especially when we are winning, and we always win. I'm wound way too tight to really appreciate it. Two minutes of play remain.

"Ms. Perez, stay awake out there."

I wave back to the coach, yah right, I'm falling asleep right now.

Carmichael, from Mount Hoerb, Wisconsin, gets the ball and is cutting right through my wingers. He's big and he's trying to rush the net to scare me back. It isn't going to work, ever, at least not on me. I center on the line and stare him down, while focusing on that huge right leg. He angles a bit right and cocks that thing. It's not a fake; I dive to the right and barely block it, knocking the ball back over the penalty line.

I race back along the line as Carmichael intercepts my smack away and immediately takes another. This will probably be the last shot on goal this season. I have to catch myself and change directions. It's right down the middle and I leap across toward the rocketing ball. It slaps me right in the chest and I hold it tight to me. Carmichael is smiling at me. Well. I think it is funny. If that's what turns him on, great. A lot better than a goal. I wait for the ref and she signals me to toss it out. I wind up and fling it as hard as possible. It is still in the air when the buzzer sounds. That's it, a perfect season. I wish Carl could have been here to see it. They pulled him into some kind of evaluation.

∞

Done for today, going home. I walk through this small village, Fennimore, and catch myself proud to be part of this community. I don't want to, but I am. Mostly though, I'm excited about starting high school after summer break. I start to feel invigorated, launching into a run the rest of the way home. Then, I turn the corner and see a blue United Nations Self Defense Forces car in my driveway. *What the hell. Can't they leave us alone? Haven't they done enough to us?*

There are two guys in suits at the doorway and Mother is talking to them.

"What did you want?" I ask.

"Hunter, we don't speak that way. These men are here to see you." Mom tenses up.

Great. "I have no desire to speak to them, nor obligation."

One of the blue-bloods turns to me—the pale one. "Actually you do. You are over fourteen and a citizen. That gives you rights, privileges, and also obligations."

Glaring at me, they stand aside as my mother opens the door wide to allow me, and unfortunately them, to enter. I walk into the kitchen and sit down, mostly because there is only one other chair there and I don't want the blue-bloods comfortable. Damn they look silly in suits and baby-blue berets. "Fine, whadda ya want?" I get a look at these guys now and it is freaky. They are negative images of each other. Maybe they're a cloning experiment. One is pale, I would say albino with piercing colorless eyes that almost look robotic. The other is very dark with the warmest pools of chocolate eyes… Damn, where the hell is my freakish little mind going at a time like this? My superior eyesight doesn't seem like a gift right now.

The dark one says, "First, I want to address Flight Commander Perez. He was undoubtedly one of the most skilled and bravest pilots ever to serve the planet. He was directly involved in saving thousands of lives. Indirectly, perhaps millions. He was awarded our planet's greatest honor, The Order of the Sun, and his skill set and core abilities live on in you. We need that ability now. He never realized the danger the UN put him in, the UN didn't, no one did."

Suddenly I am not so attracted to the dark twin. I get up from the table, "Great, thanks so much, see ya."

"Hunter," my mother says, scolding me as I sit back down.

"You are an amazing young woman, Hunter," adds the albino.

"Ya, I like me too."

The dark one takes back the conversation. "The genetics that converged to make your father the unique and amazing man he was live on in you. Your planet needs those traits."

The pale one finds his voice. "We're going to come right out with this. It's not as if you have a choice. Citizen Perez, you are hereby conscripted into UN forces. You will report to Ester Bay in sixteen hours. Congratulations, you have also been accepted into a special training program. Information forthcoming. A transport will be here at zero-six-hundred local. Please have your affairs in order by then."

"What freakin' affairs. Mom, what the hell…" They leave with my mother standing there probably as stunned as I am. I curl up into a ball, half on the table and half on the chair. Mom comes up behind me and holds me. We stay that way a long while.

"What does it mean? What do I do? Help me Mom."

"I know you were always angry about the UN taking your father. I know you were cheated out of ever knowing him."

"They did! I read it for myself in my second-grade history book. That he was the most decorated civilian soldier. That he was conscripted and not a career pilot. All the things you never told me." *And you never mentioned how much alike we looked. The same brown eyes and barely brown skin. We share the same delicate nose and soft chin. I really don't look much like Mom.*

"That's true," Mom admitted. "But he made it his career and he was pleased with all he had accomplished. The only thing he was prouder of was you. He came back on the leave they allowed him when you were born. You made him feel that what he had accomplished and what he could do in the future was important. He said you were his greatest accomplishment. That you were the reason he was born."

"But he never got to see me again. I never got to see him."

"You don't remember, but you did. You recognized him right away, even though you were only four months old. You immediately knew your father and that made him so happy. And proud. He said he now had a much more import reason for protecting the planet from the Swarmers… you." Mom stared, tears welling in her eyes.

We sit there a long time, drinking tea and communicating, but not speaking. Then I break the silence. "I'll be here for them at six o'clock. I'll do what I should and be a good girl," I say, heavy with the sarcasm on the last two words. She doesn't deserve it.

"I don't want you—"

I stop her midsentence. "I could do nothing different for Dad. He would expect this even though I know he would scream and hate it as much as you and I. But he would expect me to do what is right. I won't become a criminal and dishonor him or his name."

"Come and rest next to me for a few hours. Let me remember you are still a little girl."

I smile at her and leave to take a quick shower. The piercing spray makes me believe, just for an instant, that it can wash all this away. But it cannot. I find the Hello Kitty pajamas that Grandma gave me last Christmas, slip them on, and head down the hall to Mom's room. I lay with her until she is sleeping soundly. Then I change clothes, leave her three notes—two electronic—and slip out the door.

∞

I swing hard right coming out of my driveway, pouring on the coals. I have never run faster. I need to see Carl. Six missed calls and about a dozen texts remind me why.

Carl was never insecure around me. Even though I could run faster, hit harder and score higher on just about anything, it seemed to make him prouder to be my boyfriend. I always heard him bragging about me. One time, I even heard him say I had a "neater" name than he did. I never thought Hunter was a cool name, especially not for a girl.

Now I just needed him to hold me. I slow down and jog into Carl's apartment complex. Mr. Hardin is on the vid and he buzzes me in without opening the comm line. I leave my shoes in the genkan and step through to the kitchen. Mr. H is helping Carl's mom finish loading the dishwasher. She is wearing a dull-blue yukata.

"Is everything alright this evening Hunter?" Mrs. H asks.

"Sure. Do you mind my stopping by this late?"

"Of course not. Carl is in the entertainment deck. He'll be happy to see you."

Mrs. H adds, "We're always glad to see you, you're welcome here dear."

I restrain myself and walk slowly to the main stairway and head down to the entertainment deck. I stop to look at him. Carl is on a computer, but with no headset he knows me well enough to recognize me by my footsteps.

"Hey Hunts, what's up? I was afraid you were mad I missed your victory." He turns his chair about and faces me. "Holy shit, what happened?"

I tell him everything and then he asks me the question I most dread and the only one he can ask, "Do you know what you are going to do?"

I stare into his angular, nearly black eyes. He is tall already, even at fourteen, and long limbed. The same hard chin and thin lips that his father has, with his mother's angular jaw, skin pale, especially next to mine.

I tell him, "Not now. I can't even think about it. I just want to be alone with you." For both of us the talking is over for a while.

∞

It's nearly ten and Carl is sound asleep. That's okay, Carl falls asleep a lot. I take his phone and write a note on his calendar: *I love you and I always will. This is forever. I don't know what I will do, but you will be the second person to know. Only after me. No one comes before you, not now. Not ever.* I set the note for all day, not limiting it to any time frame, and slip out, heading up the stairs.

Mr. and Mrs. H are in the great room. Mrs. H says, "Did he fall asleep again?"

"Yup. And he even picked out the vid. I shouldn't be bothering you guys so late anyway. I'm going to head home."

"I already told you once today, you're always welcome here."

"Thanks Mr. H. That means a great deal to me."

"Hope we see you soon."

"Thanks, I do too."

∞

Mom is waiting in the kitchen for me, of course. I walk in and sit at the table across from her. Her eyes are red and swollen. We sit together again. Again silently communicating. Then as if at an unseen and unheard signal, we both get up and head for bed. Just a regular Friday night. The next thing I know it's six in the morning, I'm rolling out of bed and heading for the front door.

∞

April 30, 2060

Carl,

I love you and miss you so much. Understand, like I told you before. I don't want you to wait for me, but I hope you'll remember me and accept my letters. We can't send vids more than monthly because of bandwidth restrictions. They are still encrypting all comm from off planet. So only letters. Silly, isn't it, calling them letters? I'm finishing training on the new xxxxxx, what a fantastic xxxxx. It is a blast to fly them. We are about one-half light-year out, between the Kuiper belt and the Oort cloud. I know I've been gone nearly a month, but they tell me it's October back there already and it will be April before you see it. I hope you had a great year. Wish I could have spent it with you.

They say we know the Swarmers came from someplace called Wolf three-five-nine in Leo. I guess it makes sense, lions and wolves are pretty mean and vicious. The Swarmers would come from someplace like that. I'm scheduled to ship out next xxxx. I guess I shouldn't have done so well training in the xxx. It's just short of eight light-years out. I guess that means I won't get to send you anything for about nine years and it will take eight more for you to get it. I don't know if I believe all that; seems unlikely to me, but the math works out right. I don't know if I should trust my gut, my head or my heart. My heart says I'll see you again soon. I know it's wrong. I can't stop it. I don't want to.

Please don't think about me too much, but I am going to be selfish, so please don't forget me either. It hurts so bad to say it, but I guess you'll hear from me in about seventeen years, two months. I have to tell you that I think about you every day. I don't even really know what that means anymore, what is a day, really? I wish you love more than anything else, please wish me safe and happy hunting at Wolf three-five-nine.

Your loving Hunter.

All my love forever, even if forever is only till tomorrow.

NOTE REDACTED AS NEEDED

∞

They just pulled us out of stasis and the ship is decelerating hard. I'm waiting to go through med bay again and then I guess I'm gonna basically live in the Stryker. They tell me I could live in there for two years. We are going to launch as soon as we get within less than a minute light. I'm scared, real scared. I don't know what the hell I'm doing here. My duty I guess. I should have sandbagged at least a little, then maybe I could have been assigned to a light bomber. At least I wouldn't have to fly alone. But no, I did my best and am rewarded with my own Stryker. Just what I always wanted.

I can feel my ship maneuvering within the launch tube. Still blacker than hell in here. I smell carbon and my head hurts. Here we go—my back is smashed into the seat and the webbing harness pulls at my shoulder. I'm supposed to be in a suspensor field, how the hell do I get different g-forces? Suddenly I'm loose and all I see is a mass of black with dots all over the place. My AI comes up and I get the display. Green, blue and red all over my face. The blue and red are the problems. Blue is similar mass to our Strykers and light bombers. Red are capital ships, like carriers and mother-ships. There are one hell of a lot of the larger, capital-size Swarmerships out there. I let the AI pick my targets and barrel into the fray.

My mind is bifurcated as it adjusts to the AI. I move toward a Swarmer capital ship, pulling down fighters and light bombers along the way. They aren't shielded against our pulsars. I only see images on a set of shifting screens. Is this reality? Am I here? Am I killing them?

I spin my Stryker to port to keep my pulsar fire focused on two Swarmer fighters, slicing them open as they approach from starboard. Fusing perfectly with the AI, I am soothed. I am truly one with this thing—I control it, power and invulnerability, not separated, I am the ship and myself at once. I smile. I smile hard. Time stands still.

The tracking algorithm on the pulsars looks like the tracer fire in old war movies; at least in my mind's eye, or is it my AI mind's eye? I am being coddled, protected and empowered, all simultaneously.

The suspensor field allows one-tenth G to pass through so I retain my sense of movement and position. I only carry two full nukes on board, so they must be used sparingly. I mentally arm the first little boy, I like the cute name, they say it's historical. I head toward a huge capital Swarmer ship. I'm back on the pulsars and two more bastards are sheep shit spread all over the void. Wow, I'm starting to really like this. The little blips of explosions dying out as they fold into themselves are like violet-hued fireworks. At least that's what the AI shows me. Right now my forward viewport is tightly covered by armor. I guess I really only know what the AI wants me to know. I can't be truly sure I'm even in this quadrant.

Small Swarmer fighters are all over me. They are smaller than our Strykers, angular with flat segments alternated with lumps. They seem colorless, dark as the void, with no reflection. Our Strykers look more like elongated shiny, black teardrops.

I have to be less than five kilometers out in order to ensure that the Swarmers can't prematurely detonate the Little Boy and more than one and one-half kilometers out in order to flip around and get away before I get fried. I lose my first Little Boy that way, but it costs them plenty of fighters to stop it. That won't happen again.

The Swarmers are trying to englobe me. If they get in that position, they can heat up my armor enough to punch through. I can work with the AI and get solid hits on multiple small fighters while spinning. The armor is heating up bad, I see deep orange. Just got to keep it out of the red, launch and flip around. I lock the suspensor field down, launch my second Little Boy. Now comes the ride.

I leave all scan input on for this. Some pilots cut to black and sit out the next four seconds. I want to feel the push and see that cap-size Swarmer ship fry. The UN put my Dad out here in harm's way, but the Swarmers actually dropped the hammer on him. I am personally going to make them pay.

I see and feel the most beautiful light show in the universe, coupled by a tremendous emotional high. I leave the accelerators on for a bit and head back to the ship. I'm fresh out of Little Boys.

The imbedded AI link in the back of my neck is raw. That's not supposed to happen, since nothing is actually touching it, use shouldn't affect me physically. So they say. They admit it's last century tech, "Blue Tooth" or something like that. Jerking a one-sixty and leveling off to line up to the *Hashimoto*'s bay, I am welcomed home. Home—yeah home, right. Welcome, yeah, I feel welcome.

The next three weeks are a near rerun of today. I can't even remember how many Little Boys I've launched, but I only wasted two. I ran a bit chicken and launched too far out. The monsters are throwing everything at us nearly constantly. The launch commander says I'm in first place for imploding capital Swarmer ships. I wish I could have doubled my totals.

I wake up to a personal alarm. My bunk is a glorified shelf, but somehow better than being in stasis. Just perfect, I have been summoned to the Vice—Vice Admiral Forsythe, the strike force commander. I didn't even know he was on the *Hashimoto*. We sure aren't the flagship. Maybe the flagship of crap if our rations are any indication. The *Kensington* is the flagship. What the hell am I supposed to wear to see this asshole? All I've got are three flight suits.

I get to the vice—does he have spare cabins on all the ships?—and slap the bulkhead next to the hatch.

"Is there a frickin' bird pecking at my door?" the admiral asks.

I slap with all I've got and my palm stings, stings bad.

"Ok, get in here. At least you're on time."

"Admiral, yes sir." I finally get to speak.

"Sit, JG. You'll be here a while."

"By your leave."

"You're doing an exemplary job out there. If I had fifty of you we could all go home. You do want to go home, don't you JG?"

"Sir," I respond.

"Do you want to lead the Swarmers back to Earth with you? Do you want that for your mother and whoever the hell you run with back there?"

"Sir, no sir."

"I can only keep you here two more jump cycles and by UNSDF law, you have fulfilled your sortie requirement. I just plain can't make you fly any more, but, and I know this comes as a shock JG, we aren't going to rush you back home."

"Sir, no sir. I understand sir."

"Do you want to make a gift of your family and your neighborhood to the Swarmer mother ship you left out there yesterday?"

"Sir, no sir."

"Are you requesting to waive your sortie limits and continue killing bugs?"

What in God's name am I supposed to say? What in all hell can I say? I know the exact words he's fishing for. I take a deep breath. "Admiral, I personally request to be released from sortie limitations and request to be reassigned to a flight attack group."

"Outstanding, Lieutenant. And you just pushed past JG. You'll be issued new grade papers within eight microcenturies. You are dismissed, Perez."

I spin around and out through the hatch. Shit, I'm stunned. Down and starboard will get me to the mess hall. I'll figure it out from there. What the hell did I just do? They can't put me back out there until my paperwork clears. What did that pompous idiot say, eight microcenturies? Then I've got just short of seven hours free. I'm going back to bed. Maybe the dreams won't come to me this time.

∞

The comm unit pulls me out of sleep again. I've got an appointment with the shrink. Since I requested a sortie waiver, I have to be re-evaluated. That's rich. I walk into Commander McElroy's cabin. I'm not about to slap my hand raw for somebody who stays safe onboard this ship.

"Lieutenant, I didn't hear you request entry, but please come in."

I ask the shrink, "Commander, what can I do for you?"

"You know better than that, Lieutenant, I will be helping you."

"I'm fine. Thanks, can I go now? Some of us have to go out and kill Swarmers."

"Straighten up, Lieutenant. Are you inferring I am somehow less than you? You are addressing a full Commander and you will show the respect and deference that position demands."

"Sir, yes sir. I apologize. I stand with no excuses."

"Fine, what about the dreams?"

"Dreams, sir?" I tense at the memory, trying to hide any reaction.

"Dreams, Lieutenant. Are you stupid as well as insubordinate?"

"I do not understand, Commander." I stand, stiff and unmoving.

"The VA reported that you were experiencing the dreams."

"I am still ignorant, Commander. Forgive me."

"Fine, we will simply waste more of my time. I was foolish enough to suspect that you might want to cooperate in order to mitigate your insubordination."

I stare at this nut. How the hell did he make commander? "Commander, I will cooperate fully and answer any lawful question put to me, sir."

"They advised me you were advanced past your physical age, but I will address you in a manner befitting a fifteen-year-old. The vice admiral informed me that you have been experiencing dreams related to your combat experience. May I assume this is true?" The commander leans forward, intense.

"Commander, yes sir, but I did not so advise the vice admiral."

"Those that receive this Swarmer contact can recognize it in others. You, I assume, do not have that ability?"

"Commander, I have never attempted such observations." *I don't know what this is for.*

"It has been anecdotally noted that those pilots and command personnel that have been directly responsible for large numbers of Swarmer deaths have these communicative dreams and can recognize that experience in others. You do understand what I am telling you, correct Lieutenant?"

"Commander, yes sir."

The shrink glares at me. "Lieutenant, these creatures are getting into our best pilot's heads and you tell me you didn't realize this?"

"Commander, I know I was having dreams but not that other personnel were." *I don't know what else to say.*

"And you think I should certify you for flight duty."

"Commander, you must do that which is best for this mission."

"You just can't let go of the smart ass, can you?" says the commander through clenched teeth.

"Commander, no sir. I apologize for giving that impression. I just do not understand what is going on."

"You are dismissed, Lieutenant. Get the hell out of my office."

"Commander. Yes sir."

What the hell? They think the Swarmers are talking to us. I don't speak Swarmer and I sure as hell don't want to learn. Now I'm too freaked out to go back to sleep. I wonder how many years Commander McElroy had to study in order to attain that level of bedside manner, sheesh. I just want to get back out and kill some more of those slimy bastards.

I don't even make it back to my rack, all of a sudden alarms start and the stasis order comes up. I head to sleepy town. It's in the bottom of the *Hashimoto*. If there is a bottom. Well, sleep is sleep, I guess.

They punch the link into my neck and I feel blood, or what I assume is blood dripping down my back. I get plugged back into the stasis and smell copper and shit, wonderful. What the hell did this stuff do to me? The AI is talking to me again, *Prep for stasis, acceleration in three minutes*. They said the "blue teeth" or whatever isn't reliable enough for stasis and a solid connection is required. I'm going under. Hope I don't dream this time. I think I turned fifteen yesterday. Either that or twenty-four. I guess I have to ask Einstein. I'm gone, even to myself.

∞

They wake us up near a star system called Procyon, about eight years out from Wolf and twelve from Earth. I am finally getting used to this, it almost makes sense. All I know is I was in stasis long enough to get Carl's first vid packet. He hasn't abandoned me. I don't know why he hasn't tried to forget me, but I am thrilled that I am still with him in this small way. I hurt all over and I can't smell anything, making the food taste like crap. I head down to the mess anyway. At least it's something to keep me company while I open Carl's communication packet. It is so good to see his face again. The vid packet is complete this time.

The vid pack is dated, October, 2060. Carl's face fills the screen. "My angel," he says, "I got your communication today. Your mother thanks you for hers too. I am so thrilled to hear from you and so happy you haven't forgotten me with everything you have been through. They showed us clips of the training and I can only imagine how well you are doing. I love you and miss you so much. I will wait for you always. All I can think of is our last night together and all we promised each other. Please know I would never break a vow, no matter the circumstances."

Well, he's still Carl—in every way. But this message is only six months after our night together.

Smiling broadly and running his hand back through his hair, he continues, "It is so hard to be without you. I know you are suffering much more with all the danger and all the horrible things you must be exposed to. They tell us very little here. But I know my Hunter hunts the most evil of all monsters. It is impossible for me to say all I need to and I don't even know what I need to say. I don't want to sound like a child and I know you are so brave, but I cry for you every day. Please stay safe. Please remember I am here for you, always."

I check the current date stamp on the monitor. He sent that to me over twenty years ago. But now he's thirty-five and I am just past fifteen. And he doesn't want to sound like a child. What am I to him? How can this ever work? One battle and a lifetime is over. What can I be to him? If I write him back he will be forty-seven when he gets it. How can he not think I have abandoned him. My God, what have I done to myself? What have I done to him? What do I do now? I need to open one of my Mom's comm packets. She'll make me feel better.

Nobody talks here. Nobody knows or cares about anybody. There are no friends. The brass doesn't even talk to us; they just issue memos telling us how great we are. Right, that's why what looked like a victory to me was a near disaster. They threw a first wave at us and a much larger second wave would have overwhelmed the fleet. We ran with our tail 'tween our legs toward Procyon to lead the monsters off Earth-side. Procyon has an even richer mineral belt than our own Kuiper belt. They're hoping the monsters will like it if they follow us here. I guess we're going home. What did we accomplish? Are we safe?

Brass says that solid defenses and major permanent bases are installed at the edge of the Oort cloud. That we can stop the Swarmers. That we saved our planet by sleeping all these years and fighting one losing battle. That it showed the monsters we can come after them. That we are all heroes. Bullshit. My life for nothing. I gotta calm down before I write Carl and Mom back. At least I will still look the same for them.

∞

January 3, 2081

Carl,

Your last comm packet saved my life. Seeing you made me feel like I have a life again. I need you. I needed to know you were still Carl. I needed something unchanging in my life. They say I can tell you we are coming home, but not when and not where we are now. They tell me I'm legally thirty-five now. But I've lived three months since I saw you last. They say I can retire when I get home, that I'll have my thirty years plus in service. You are all I have, Carl. I know it's wrong and I have no right, but I need you to be you for me. They gave me a grade increase and a freakin' medal. I can't tell you why that is so stupid. I guess I blew apart a boat load of the monsters, but we xxxxxxxxxxxxxx. Isn't that rich? You have waited way too long. I have no right to ask you, but please, please wait for me. I am coming home. Forgive me for being so weak. I love you.

Your loving Hunter

NOTE REDACTED AS NEEDED

∞

They woke me up today. We're just outside the Kuiper belt. We couldn't blast through the solar system at nine-tenths light without holing ourselves. I don't even want to eat. I have had less than a dozen normal meals—normal being utilizing my mouth and teeth—in the last thirty-two years. I'm forty-seven and I have been awake less than fifteen years. I still can't smell and I have constant pain basically everywhere. They say it's normal. Right, wonderful. I get to be in pain, but it's normal pain. Wow, I still sound like a fifteen-year-old girl. I look fifteen. I sure don't feel fifteen. I feel worn out and used up. I check for comm packets. The first one is official. It's damn near nine years old.

∞

August 30, 2084

Lieutenant Hunter,

We regret to inform you that your mother, Marietta Perez, has succumbed to a heart attack this date. She will be buried with UN Military family honors at no cost to you. We are mutually distressed and understand your grief.

Commander James Carmichael, UN Forces, Interstellar.

∞

"You bastards killed my entire family!" I hadn't realized I could still scream. The Mess is full of pilots and nobody even looks up at me. None of us are real, none of this is real. I fold up into a ball jammed alongside the mess table. The notification is nearly nine years old.

The personal comm inbox loads and indicates 511 unread messages—114 from Marietta Perez and 397 from Lt. Commander Carl Hardin. What the hell? Well I guess he outranks me now.

I can't look at my mom right now, but I gotta see Carl. I punch up the most recent one, February 14, 2093. Valentines day, last month. Over thirty-three years since I left Earth.

The screen freezes and then clears. Suddenly Carl appears. It's not Carl, it's Mr H. Wait; wait it is Carl. His face is hard. Lined across the forehead. Hair is still dark, like his dad. He is no kid. What could I give him now? Why would he want to deal with a kid? A beat-up fifteen-year-old with only memories of death—and sleep.

"Hi Hunts, I wish I could see you. I keep repeating myself because I have no way to tell what you'll play first, and I kinda assume you'll want to see the newest first. So here we go again.

"I'm stationed out here on Sedna. You have left me only a handful of those Swarmers you seem so adept at dispatching. I haven't seen a single one for the last nine years. It seems so stupid, but I have to say it again. I'm waiting. I'll wait forever if I have to. I hear they boosted you from JG light to a full Louie. You got your railroad tracks. Congrats baby. I am so proud of you. I might have rank on you, but I could never surpass your kill totals. Just like school, huh? Do you even know your stats? Sixty-seven Swarmer capital ships and two hundred sixty-two light fighters and bombers. They estimate you sent a half million of those shit bugs to the big manure pile. Sorry if I'm impressed, but we live for this stuff on base.

"Everybody knows I claim you as mine, I don't think anyone really believes I even know the great Hunter. Yeah, you are a one-name celeb in the SDF. I guess I'm lucky I'm the boss on this tiny rock or they'd probably beat the crap outta me for even claiming I know you. I did cut down four Swarmer light ships. Two bombers and two fighters. And it only took me twenty-four years. 'Course they don't give us nukes in-system.

"They told me you were coming home. I want to believe them, but I am too scared to. I need to see you so much. Our reunion is all I have dreamt of for more than thirty-three years now. They let me go planet-side for the services. So sorry about your mom. I lost my parents all in one shot about five years before your mom left us. She died quietly. My parents got smashed under a runaway auto-driven supply truck. They died quick, but sure not quiet or peaceful. You're coming home to a very different world Hunts. Remember, I may be the only unchanging thing left. You better still want me. You are what I live for. Sure as hell not my career, living on a dead rock in our brave new world.

"I have two years planetside vacation coming and you should have at least that. There was an old song from the last century, talks about putting time in a bottle, saving it and then spending it with you. That's what I did. I hope you will spend yours with me.

"My four minutes is up and they only allow me one vid a month. Come home Hunts. I need you."

I'm scared and I can't stop sobbing. I don't even fully understand why. The vid deactivates and the screen pops up. There is one more official comm packet.

∞

February 25, 2093

Lieutenant JG Hunter,

Per request of Lieutenant Commander Carl W Hardin, you are appointed his heir and we must inform you that Lt. Commander Hardin died in an accident while patrolling M384 sector from his assigned base on Sedna. His Strike Lance was impacted by Oort cloud debris, destroying it completely. We are mutually distressed and understand your grief.

Commander James Carmichael, UN Forces, Interstellar.

∞

They killed my father and forced me from my mother. They took the life I should have shared with Carl. They say I took the lives of half a million Swarmers. What did they take from me? Nobody talks about that.

Just out of the corner of my peripheral vision I can see one of the Swarmers. Now I get to live with them too. They came into my dreams and now they inhabit the corners of my mind that I can't even reach. I want my life back. I want to finish high school with Carl and play soccer.

There is no Earth for me anymore, no home. I will return to what I do best—kill.

I am not forty-seven years old. I am fifteen. I am fifteen. I am fifteen.

About the Author
EJ Shumak

Mr. Shumak lives in metro Chicago, Illinois, and has spent most of his life in northern Illinois and southern Wisconsin. He has been many things, police officer (disabled), large cat sanctuary operator, C.P.A. and on again, off again writer. Lately on again. He has held active membership in S.F.W.A. since 1992, and has sold four books, three fantasy novels and one non-fiction, along with several dozen short science fiction pieces and non-fiction articles.

Taking Pro
by Mike Reeves-McMillan

Senator Belter wore a suit as sharp and steel grey as his eyes, as neat as his office, and I could tell that our much cheaper eight-year-old suits lost us a few points with him. Most people wouldn't have noticed—he controlled his facial expression like a puppeteer—but with my empathy boosted by the Pro, I caught it as he gave me the once-over. Head to toe and then back to my dark eyes, lingering fractionally too long on my modest breasts. He ran a more rapid glance over my paler, red-haired colleague Ross, and addressed him first, assuming that, as the man, he would be the senior partner. People still do that, almost a third of the way into the twenty-first century. I was prepared for it, if not exactly resigned to it.

"So, Dr. Malcolm," he said. "Take a seat and tell me the story." He sat behind his desk, a gleaming expanse of polished oak with nothing whatsoever on the top of it, and steepled his fingers while we took visitor chairs. The office had the sparseness that can only be achieved when you have people who will bring you whatever you need when you need it, and take it away again when you're done.

Ross, bless him, said, "Dr. Bashur is our lead researcher. Bada, would you like to go first?"

"When I was a little girl," I said, "my family had to flee from what is now Kurdistan, though in those days it was still in the painful process of trying to become Kurdistan. I won't go into the politics of it. I didn't understand them then, and frankly I'm not sure I do now. All I knew was that people we'd never met wanted to hurt us, my father, my mother, my brother and me. Not because of anything we'd done, but because of who we were. To a little girl, that wasn't just terrifying, it made no sense."

I suspected that Belter's interested expression would have been no different if I'd told him about playing the flute in the school orchestra, another influence on my journey to the development of Pro, though one that didn't make such a good lead story. He betrayed no emotion as I spoke of fleeing my country as a refugee, though I'd let him see something of how the memory still shook me.

I went on, "I'm not the kind of person who can leave something alone if it doesn't make sense. So when I grew up, I went into psychology, to try to understand why people do the things they do. And then I discovered that we didn't have to just put up with how we are. We can do something about it."

Ross picked up the thread with practiced smoothness. "My story comes to the same place from the opposite side," he said. "When I was little, Hurricane Ophelia devastated the community where I lived, near Boston. I'm sure you remember it." Belter nodded. He'd grown up in the Midwest, but everyone remembered Ophelia. "What I saw," said Ross, "was people coming together, helping one another in a way that didn't usually happen. I wondered what the world would be like if people acted that way all the time."

I took over again. "So between us, and with the help of the others on our team, we searched for a way to overcome the last barriers to living in a better world. Human selfishness, greed and fear. In Pro, we believe we've found it."

"Pro," he said, not inflecting it as a question, just a minimal prompt to explain more.

"It's what we call the prosociality treatment. Humans have been getting better and better at cooperating since the evolution of language. But, as you're in a position to know, Senator, we still have room for improvement." He nodded, no doubt thinking of debates he'd participated in, as I went on. "This treatment… let's say it moves the process on a couple of important steps."

"By altering neurochemistry?" He narrowed those sharp eyes at me, doubt in his well-modulated voice. Doubt about the feasibility, or about the acceptability, I wondered, and chose an answer designed to deal with both.

"People alter neurochemistry every day. Millions of people control their anxiety, depression, and hostility, or increase their ability to focus, with the predecessors of this technology, and have done for decades."

"But this is more extreme," he said. Again, it wasn't a question.

"It's an evolution of the techniques," I said.

"Who's the politician here?" he asked, switching on his well-practiced smile. "You don't need to give me the spin, that's the job of my staff."

I nodded, mirrored his smile back to him, and brushed hair out of my eyes. He would expect nervousness after his mild rebuke, so I dropped my gaze for a moment. "Sorry," I said. "In fact, this isn't just one technique. It's a number of different strands of research combined into a greater whole. In layman's terms, it enhances and optimises the brain regions responsible for understanding others, thinking about long-term consequences, cooperation, self-control, emotional awareness and regulation, all the things you'd expect would make for more prosocial human beings. And it works with the innate reward system, so that the most subjectively rewarding action for the individual, the thing that makes them feel best, is also the one that will most benefit society in general. That was the key to making it work. Motivating people from the inside to want the prosocial outcome."

"So who's taken this already?" he asked.

"Me, for one. Ross, too. All of my team, in fact." He lifted his head in a characteristic gesture. I'd studied his tells before coming. This one meant he'd heard the unexpected.

"You experimented on yourselves?" he asked, a slight shift of the muscles around his eyes projecting his concern.

"Absolutely not. That would invalidate the results. But we took it as soon as it was cleared through human trials. The trial results were… convincing."

"That's another thing we'll need to spin," he said. "That trial group. It included prisoners, didn't it?"

He'd read his briefing, then, which not only won him points but made it more likely that he'd support us. If I could calm his fears about how it would reflect on him. There were persistent rumours of a presidential bid, and while he hadn't made any public announcement, he wouldn't do anything to make those rumours move on to some other candidate.

"We met all the ethical standards," I said. "Informed consent, and we didn't offer any direct reward. We did tell them that, if the treatment was successful, they would become people who were more likely to be paroled and to do well on the outside."

"And did they?"

"Five percent recidivism in three years." I allowed my genuine pride in that figure to enter my voice. "A fifth of the rate in the control group."

I leaned forward and gestured, letting my enthusiasm show. "Not only do these men and women not commit more crimes, but they work hard in voluntary roles. They take good care of their families. They've been transformed from criminals into assets to society. And they show less violence than average, too."

"And what are you looking for now? More research funding?" He leaned back in his chair, switching from *I'm interested in what you're saying* to *you need to convince me* with practiced fluidity. He'd been a member of an amateur improv troupe before going into politics, I remembered. He could have gone professional. In fact, in a sense, he had.

"We're past the need for that," I said, leaning back also and looking him in the eye. "We have companies licensed to manufacture. What we're looking for is advocates who'll help us raise the public profile of Pro, encourage widespread adoption."

"Encourage it, potentially, by government subsidies and enabling legislation, so you can offer it to more prisoners, for example?"

"That kind of thing as well, yes," I said. In fact, though getting Pro to prisoners would be important, it wasn't our endgame. "But primarily, we'd like to get some prominent people taking it. As an example to others. Your name came up."

He laughed, those grey eyes holding an emotion a long way from amusement. "Well," he said, "I'll have to see about that. I'll get some contacts of mine to do a literature review, delve further into the science. You know I studied physics?" He'd taken three classes, one of which he'd failed, before switching to pre-law. This still made him one of the more scientifically educated members of the legislature, sadly.

"That's a large part of the reason that we approached you first, because we thought you'd be interested in the science. We really appreciate your time, Senator Belter."

"My pleasure," he said. He stood, bringing the meeting to an end. He wasn't much taller than me, I saw as I rose, and I'm average height for a woman. You didn't notice his height, seeing him on screen. His aide, who'd shown us in, was even shorter, I remembered.

He treated me to another quick body scan before we left.

∞

Two days later, I was reading on the way to work when I became aware of chanting. I looked up through the car's windscreen to see protesters lining the approach to the research campus.

"Hands off our brains!" said the printed signs that they waved, and "No neuro-neutering!" Someone bore a handwritten, misspelled sign that said "I am not a crinimal." Now that I was listening, I could make out the chant: "No, Pro, We Won't Go!" It didn't even make any sense.

The sight of the angry mob triggered a flashback to when my parents and I had escaped the old country. I felt the fear rush in, saw my father's worried face, heard my mother's whisper, *Hide, Bada. Hide.*

I closed my eyes and sat still, tapping the tip of my right forefinger with my thumb to give my neurological processes the signal to rebalance. The fear faded, and my breathing eased. I opened my eyes again as the car drove itself through the gate, past what was probably some combination of a rental mob and a cluster of the easily manipulated. We had apparently hit the 24-hour news cycle.

Ross was watching a video stream when I passed his office. A popular rage pundit pontificated from the screen, his silver hair and jowly face badges of authority. "So this is what our government wants to do," he said. "It wants to turn people into zombies, into compliant slaves for the elites, into blissed-out soma addicts. If this is Pro, then call me Anti." Images from last year's *Brave New World* movie adaptation accompanied his rant.

"Is it all like that?" I asked.

"Most of it. Quiet reasonableness doesn't play well on the media, I don't know if you've noticed."

"I've noticed. Media owners are on the target list. But they're hard to reach inside those money forts they have."

"We'll do it," he said. "Just a matter of time and perseverance."

∞

I spoke with Belter again by videoconference, trying to remember how to think like someone driven primarily by self-interest.

"You've seen some of the coverage, I'm sure," I said. "The protests."

"Difficult not to," he said. His face was impressively illegible.

"It's a great opportunity for you," I said.

"How do you mean?"

"Come now, I know how you politicians thrive on controversy. If you take Pro, it will give you more coverage than you know what to do with."

He looked off to one side, considering, for a long moment, then turned his smile on me.

"Dr. Bashur," he said, "I know what to do with any amount of coverage. Let's do it at a press conference. Show people there's nothing to be afraid of."

"Well," I said, "we could certainly do with some good publicity. I'll see what our PR people can arrange."

PR rounded up a few assorted celebrities who wanted to get in on the act: a science populariser with a book to promote, an actor with a flagging career, and a rising tech entrepreneur who, frankly, needed it less than most people. It was their role as opinion leaders that we wanted, though. Their individual identities mattered much less.

We met in Belter's offices, in the media suite. A flock of newsfeed cameras hovered and shot us from all angles as we injected him and the others from ampules we'd prepared earlier and couriered over. "Can't bring anything like that in on your person," Belter had said. "Security won't let it through. It has to go through their clearance process first."

The actor, it turned out, was nervous of needles, or maybe she was just playing it up to get more camera time. "Sorry," I said, "there's no oral dose yet. We're working on it, but it's hard enough to get past the blood-brain barrier as it is." She registered frightened bravery as I slid the needle in. Belter himself took his injection with aplomb, as if it was a vitamin shot, and encouraged the pretty actor just slightly more intensely than I thought was necessary. There were rumours of affairs in his background, but nobody had ever released footage. He knew how to be discreet.

When we'd finished, Belter stepped up to a small podium on a platform that compensated for his lack of height, placing him above the lenses of the hovering cameras.

"What Dr. Bashur and Dr. Malcolm have just given us," he said into those lenses, "will, over time, shift our neurological state into one that's more ideal for cooperating with others. We'll retain all of our intelligence, all of our rational self-preservation, all of our awareness and understanding. There's no dependency, no addiction. What there is is a new bias, a bias in favour of doing the right thing to help other people.

"Some alarmists have alleged that our long-term plan is to force Pro on the poor and vulnerable, while the elites retain their ability to be greedy and self-serving. That our goal is to rule a compliant population for our benefit. Not only does that show a lack of understanding of how Pro works, it couldn't be further from the truth. Taking Pro will always be voluntary, and here we are, representatives of the elites of science, business, politics and the arts, taking it voluntarily to show our support for this wonderful innovation, the innovation which might just save the human race. Every other plan for improving life on Earth bumps up against the problem of human nature. Only Pro sets out to solve that problem."

I'd written that speech, or the basis of it, but he made it sound more convincing than I ever had. A masterful performance. I looked across the room at his clear grey eyes and shared a glance with Ross, who gave a tiny nod. Ten years of working together, plus Pro, had given us something that occasionally approached telepathy, not that it was hard to tell each other's thoughts in that moment.

As we signed out of the building, Ross said, "Phase Two?"

"Phase Two," I said.

∞

We invited Belter to our offices a few days later. I served him tea, then Ross and I took our places in chairs on either side of him.

"You said you had an important announcement?" he said. He addressed me this time. Nobody had ever called him a slow learner.

"Yes," I said. "As you know, we've been putting a lot of emphasis on the process for bulk manufacturing, scaling up the production capacity without losing effectiveness…"

One side effect of getting a PhD is that I can talk about my subject at any length without much preparation. I watched him carefully as I did so. As he took each sip, his movements became slower and less coordinated. When he put down his cup and almost missed the saucer, I stopped.

"Senator Belter," I said, "we know what you did."

"What?" he said, confusion showing in those usually steely eyes. The sedative I had slipped into his tea slurred his voice, too, that weapon that he normally kept under such precise control.

I said, "I took the precaution of adding an indicator to the nanite ampules before we sent them to you, one that would produce a faint blue tinge in the sclera of the eyes. Nobody would notice if they weren't looking for it, but we were, and we didn't see it. Not in you, not in the other participants. The obvious conclusion is that you swapped the ampules with what I hope was sterile saline solution."

"What? No…"

"Not to worry, we have some right here," I said, drawing a small package out of my pocket. "I've already sent some of the real thing to the celebrity guests, saying that a booster is necessary because of a minor mixing error with that batch."

"Stop," he said, and tried to get up. Ross, behind his chair now, put his hands on Belter's shoulders and kept him in the chair. The sedative did the rest.

"You see, Belter," I said, "you're so used to telling lies that you don't believe the things you say even when they're true. Pro doesn't make us any less intelligent, or even prevent us from being suspicious of other people's motives. In fact, we expected you to do exactly what you've done. We expected it before we even spoke to you. But we still needed a voice to carry Pro into the public consciousness, and we thought you'd do it to increase your own power." I drew the solution out of the ampule into the injector, and tapped it so that the air collected at the top to be expelled. I didn't want to harm Belter. Just the opposite.

"You can't get away with—"

"With giving you a treatment that you already claimed to take, on a streaming broadcast seen by millions of people? You know, Senator, I think we can. You wanted to be the one-eyed man in the country of the blind. What you didn't realise is that we can see better than you can."

"We're very good at reading people," said Ross. "You'll find that useful, I'm sure. Though from now on, you'll want to use that knowledge to help the spread of Pro."

"Particularly among the elite," I said. "You were right when you said that we're not targeting the poor. Given the right conditions, the poor tend to be prosocial in any case, since they have to work together to survive. The rich forget that they need other people." I swapped the needle I'd used to pierce the seal on the ampule for a sharp, sterile one.

"Stop," he said again. "You can't force me. You—"

"Oh," I said, "prosocial doesn't always mean nice. Sometimes the best thing to do for the good of everyone is something like this."

I unbuttoned Belter's sleeve and rolled it up, plied the sterile wipe.

"A little prick for just a moment," I said, "and then it's all over."

About the Author
Mike Reeves-McMillan

For someone with an English degree, Mike Reeves-McMillan has spent a surprising amount of time wearing a hard hat. He's also studied ritualmaking, hypnotherapy and health science. He writes strange worlds that people want to live in, notably the *Gryphon Clerks* series of novels. Mike himself lives in Auckland, New Zealand (the setting of his new urban fantasy series), and also in his head, where the weather is more reliable and there are a lot more dragons.

News from the Extreme Chess Olympiad
by Aaron Canton

EXTREME CHESS OLYMPIAD OPENS WITH GREAT FANFARE

BY RACHEL GELLER. OCTOBER 14, 2035, 11:25 A.M. E.S.T.

HAIFA—Despite protests from international activists concerning the Chess League's usage of genetically enhanced supersharks, the seventeenth annual Extreme Chess Olympiad began today with its traditional splendor.

Arbiter Miriam Harrington presided over the opening ceremonies, which featured a live performance of the tournament's sharks arranging themselves to spell out the names of famous chess champions while the dignitaries banqueted. Harrington, who will be officiating her ninth major Extreme Chess match, declared that this year's Olympiad would be the most exciting yet.

"Polls may have indicated declining interest in chess," Harrington said during the banquet. "But thanks to the generous support of our sponsors, as well as the research developed in Dr. Collier's supershark lab, I can promise on behalf of the Chess League that this tournament *will* convey the thrill and excitement of chess to our viewers."

Dr. Emilie Collier, whom Harrington introduced as the world's leading expert on the design of intelligent sharks, also spoke at the ceremony.

"I am deeply honored by the Chess League's selection of my project for use in this Olympiad," she stated. "I can think of no greater honor for a scientist than to see their research put to such good use in front of millions of people.

"Except perhaps a Nobel prize," she added, to general laughter.

The defending Extreme Chess champion, Nigerian grandmaster Nyoko Adebayo, spoke next and told her supporters that she was looking forward to competing in the match. "We've both trained hard, and I can promise you this is going to be a great game," she said, adding that her own preparations included daily swims, near-constant chess games, and trimming her dreadlocks so she could fit them under the hood of her wetsuit to prevent the supersharks from biting down on her hair and whipping her into the tank wall. "Those sharks won't know what hit 'em!" she shouted. "And neither will Sandoval!"

The challenger, Israeli grandmaster Rebecca Sandoval, also presented herself on stage but declined to speak. A representative of the gamblers in attendance observed that Adebayo looked as wiry and strong as ever but Sandoval was notably paler and thinner than in her previous matches, which made him question whether the match odds needed adjustment on account of the challenger being ill. Other gamblers noted that Sandoval's hair was knotted and tangled as if she was sleeping poorly and that she seemed uneasy when the sharks gnashed their teeth in unison after her name was announced. Arbiter Harrington, however, explained that Sandoval was simply getting over a mild stomach flu, and that after a good night's rest she would be healthy enough to perform just as well as her fans expected.

During the question-and-answer session, a member of one of the protest groups managed to sneak into the banquet and obtain control of the microphone. The protestor demanded that Harrington admit that the use of supersharks in the chess tournament was potentially unsafe, and that the League was taking advantage of its players. Harrington, however, dismissed those claims.

"The players are in no danger," she said as the protester was ejected by security. "The sharks are present only to add psychological pressure. We have taken every precaution to ensure the safety of our grandmasters."

Dr. Collier described a few of those safety features, including algorithms in the sharks' neural implants which would encourage them to charge and menace people but discourage them from actually eating anyone. "The supersharks were thoroughly tested," she said. "This will not be like the League's last Olympiad."

Collier was referring to last year's title match between Adebayo and Pierre Montalban, during which the latter was incinerated after his mohawk touched an overhead flame in the arena. The League has since prohibited players in fire matches from using flammable hair gels.

The ceremony concluded with Harrington announcing that the first game would begin on Monday, October 15, at 11:00 a.m. local time. The first player to win four games will win the tournament and sixty percent of the five-million-dollar pot, while the other player will receive forty percent. In the unlikely event of a player's death, their share will be delivered to their next of kin.

∞

ADEBAYO LEADS 1-0 AFTER FIRST GAME OF EXTREME CHESS OLYMPIAD

BY RACHEL GELLER. OCTOBER 15, 2035, 7:02 A.M. E.S.T.

HAIFA—Defending champion Nyoko Adebayo won the first round of this year's Extreme Chess Olympiad today, but many in the audience complained that the sluggish behavior of the Chess League's supersharks detracted from the game.

Excitement had been high as the players put on their wetsuits and scuba gear, and though challenger Rebecca Sandoval somehow tied the tubes connected to her oxygen tank around herself, Adebayo helped untangle her quickly enough that they could dive into the tank before the match was delayed. Both competitors had been assigned two sharks that were initially positioned at the far ends of an underwater maze and were permitted to search for exits into the tank. It was therefore anticipated that the competitors would play rapidly so that their sharks, each of which was triple the size of the player it was hunting, would have less time to find them.

Unfortunately, many in the audience felt that the game did not live up to the Chess League's hype surrounding the match. Sandoval seemed nervous as soon as she entered the arena, and she opened a hole in her defenses when she advanced her king's bishop on the ninth move. Adebayo was able to slip a knight behind her pawn line and overwhelm her before any of the sharks, all of which got lost in the maze, actually reached the tank.

"I wish the game had gone on a little longer," commented Jeffrey Adams, a spectator who flew in from London to watch the match. "I wanted to see the sharks, you know? They really liven up the chess.

"But I heard they're making the sharks smarter for tomorrow's game," he continued. "So I'm looking forward to that."

Arbiter Miriam Harrington acknowledged that the poor path-finding ability of the sharks had hampered the game.

"We will be working with Dr. Collier to adjust the shark's neural implants to provide for a more exciting match tomorrow," she confirmed from her platform above the shark tank. "We promise this will not happen again."

Harrington also insisted, in light of the protests outside the arena, that the League is committed to its players. She emphasized the case of Sandoval, who does not usually compete on the Extreme Chess circuit but was permitted to participate in order to repay a debt that she owes the Chess League.

"Sandoval defaulted on a loan we gave her to fund her chess school," said Harrington. "But rather than seize her assets and subject her to bankruptcy, we're letting her compete in the Olympiad. Even if she loses, her compensation will be more than sufficient to settle her debts."

She added that Sandoval was very grateful for the opportunity.

At a press conference, Adebayo said that she enjoyed the match. However, she did agree with the spectators that the sharks should have been more effective.

"It's ridiculous," she said. "If I'm going to get dressed up in this suit, jump into that tank, and play a game of chess twenty feet below the surface, then I want to see some sharks!"

∞

GAME 2 OF EXTREME CHESS OLYMPIAD ENDS WITH PLAYERS TIED

BY RACHEL GELLER. OCTOBER 16, 2035, 8:41 A.M. E.S.T.

HAIFA—While the first round of this year's Extreme Chess Olympiad was criticized due to the poor performance of the supersharks, today's game was much better received, according to sources close to the Chess League.

Arbiter Miriam Harrington publicly attributed this improvement to the efforts of Dr. Emilie Collier, who reprogrammed the sharks' neural implants overnight to improve their ability to solve a maze. "It was through the Herculean efforts of Dr. Collier that the sharks were so much more active today," she said. "On behalf of the Chess League, I would like to thank her for her great contribution to our sport."

Dr. Collier also conducted a short public session today during which she described how the sharks were controlled. In order to emphasize the safety of the players, she put on a wetsuit and dropped into the tank next to the sharks. None of them attacked her, even after an assistant glazed her suit with steak sauce.

"We use both positive and negative reinforcement training," Collier explained. "During their growth period, the sharks' neural chips send them pleasant feelings when they eat fish, and excruciating pain when they eat one of these suits. They'll only eat someone if they get *really* hungry."

She quickly clarified that the last sentence of her speech was a joke.

Defending champion Nyoko Adebayo also participated in a demonstration. After an audience member asked if she would be endangered should part of her wetsuit or scuba gear somehow detach, she sat on the tank's edge while the sharks circled below her and took her suit on and off several times in order to emphasize how quickly it could be done. "We can get these things on in moments," she said. "Those sharks can't touch us! Even if we started punching them, they couldn't do anything about it."

Arbiter Harrington quickly forbade the players from punching the sharks, citing a Chess League bylaw prohibiting the practice.

The same audience member then asked if the sharks might use their enhanced intelligence to find some way to eat people without triggering their neural conditioning. Arbiter Harrington, however, had the questioner removed for bothering the players.

The actual chess game was fairly quiet. Challenger Rebecca Sandoval implemented a Hippopotamus Defense, packing her knights and bishops into her second row and her pawns into her third while trying to lure Adebayo into a rushed attack. Adebayo, however, declined to take the bait, and she built up her own position while the sharks worked their way through the maze. Sandoval then suffered a minor loss of form once her sharks reached the tank, and blundered away a knight when she dropped it on the wrong square after a shark snapped its teeth in her face.

Fortunately for Sandoval, Adebayo made a tactical error by positioning her queen too far up the board. Sandoval was able to exchange a rook and a pawn to capture it, and Adebayo surrendered on the next move.

"I'm glad I won," said Sandoval, standing with Harrington after the match. "It's really nice to be out of the water again. After winning, I mean."

On Harrington's suggestion, she offered to answer some audience questions. One reporter asked her if there were any chess games that she found particularly inspiring or motivational.

"I always liked the Immortal Game," she said, referencing a famous match in which the grandmaster Anderssen sacrificed both rooks, one bishop, and his queen in order to checkmate the famed Kieseritzky. "Anderssen acted like he could see five moves ahead. That's what I've always striven for in my games.

"Although," she admitted, "I guess it would have been more exciting if it had involved sharks."

∞

FREAK ACCIDENT STRIKES EXTREME CHESS OLYMPIAD

BY RACHEL GELLER. OCTOBER 17, 2035, 6:30 A.M. E.S.T.

HAIFA—Champion Nyoko Adebayo scored her second victory in this year's Extreme Chess Olympiad, but her win was overshadowed by a shocking tragedy.

As part of a press appearance after the game, Dr. Emilie Collier, the head of the Chess League's supershark research team, dove into the League's shark tank and began a live interview in front of her sharks. One of those sharks, however, pinned Collier against the tank wall while another used its tail to push down the zippers on Collier's wetsuit.

Security arrived too late to prevent Collier from being extracted from her suit and devoured.

The Chess League issued a press release announcing an inquiry to determine how such tragedies could be prevented in the future.

In a press conference, Arbiter Miriam Harrington acknowledged that Collier's death would cause difficulties in completing the tournament. "Dr. Collier was concerned that her research might be used to harm others," she explained. "In order to stop anyone from misusing her supersharks, she refused to teach anyone how to adjust the sharks' neural chips, or to document her work in any way. As such, it is *technically* true that we are not currently able to control the sharks."

She stressed, however, that the Chess League was confident that they could regain control before the sharks figured out how to escape from the tank and into the Mediterranean Sea.

Audience reaction to this disaster was mixed. Some expressed concern for Collier and her surviving family, while others commented on the chess match in a manner that could be considered callous.

"I bet fifty large on Adebayo winning 4-to-3," said Liam "Cashman" Whitaker, a professional gambler from Las Vegas. "If the match stops now, I'm sunk, unless the Arbiter falls into the tank or something."

He later confirmed that he had made a side bet that Arbiter Harrington would be eaten by the sharks.

Challenger Rebecca Sandoval said in an interview that she hoped the match would be suspended until such time as the super-intelligent sharks could be verified to be safe for humans. Adebayo expressed disappointment in this possibility, but said she would agree to finish the match under conventional, non-Extreme conditions if necessary.

Arbiter Harrington dismissed such ideas.

"Dr. Collier loved Extreme Chess," she said. "The Chess League is certain she would have wanted us to continue as before. We will not disrespect her by ignoring her wishes."

As for the match itself, Sandoval chose to open with a variation of the King's Knight Gambit, but Adebayo was able to sacrifice a pawn and transpose into the Elephant Gambit instead. She then skillfully drew off one of Sandoval's pawns, forced her opponent's position open, and won in eighteen moves after just five minutes of clock time. Several Chess League experts expressed admiration for her brilliant and speedy play in their postgame analysis, and one even declared that she had made it a great day for chess.

Adebayo later noted that she was fortunate to have finished the match before her sharks, which went on to eat Dr. Collier, reached the tank.

"Good thing I always move fast, right?" she joked. "Figures I'd get the ones that know how to take off the suits. Last time I got the flamethrowers that wobbled too. It's like the League's trying to kill me!"

Tomorrow's match has been pushed to 4 p.m. local time in order to give the League time to reestablish control over the sharks. The Haifa City Council has requested that everyone refrain from swimming at the city's beaches until that time.

∞

ADEBAYO EXTENDS LEAD TO 3-1 IN EXTREME CHESS OLYMPIAD; SANDOVAL CENSURED

BY RACHEL GELLER. OCTOBER 18, 2035, 12:54 P.M. E.S.T.

HAIFA—This year's Extreme Chess Olympiad was able to continue this afternoon with defending Champion Nyoko Adebayo pulling off a decisive victory. But while the Chess League was reportedly happy that the match resumed, its representatives condemned the behavior of challenger Rebecca Sandoval for bringing "shame and disrepute" upon the august reputation of the League.

There was initially some question as to whether or not the League would be able to regain control over their supersharks today, but Arbiter Miriam Harrington managed to find a workaround in time for the game. She employed divers to lure the sharks into their starting positions without needing to directly control their neural implants. Though several professionals refused the job at first, Harrington was able to find graduate students at a local university who would do it in exchange for course credit. The supersharks were thus returned to the maze in time for the match.

The chess game featured excellent play by Adebayo, who opened with an aggressive variant of the Fried Liver Attack and carried it off perfectly, but subpar moves by Sandoval. The challenger blundered away multiple pieces for minimal compensation and even lost her queen in the ninth move. Adebayo checkmated her in move thirteen, again before the sharks reached the tank.

League officials announced that, after performing computer analysis on Sandoval's moves, they believed she might have deliberately lost the game.

"We expect our players to perform to the best of their ability," said Arbiter Harrington as she addressed Sandoval from her platform over the shark tank. "Deliberate poor play to end a match early is misconduct of the highest order, and it brings shame and disrepute upon the good name of the League. If this happens again, you could be subject to severe penalties."

She elected, however, to only levy a fine on Sandoval for fifty thousand dollars, and to allow Adebayo to have the first-move advantage again in the next game. A League official later reported that Sandoval was grateful for her mercy.

In a private interview after the match, Adebayo insisted that

Sandoval did not lose on purpose. "She had a bad day," she said, standing above the shark tank and tossing scraps of fish into the water. "Doesn't mean she meant to have one."

Upon being asked if she had expected the game to be canceled following Collier's death, Adebayo said she did and acknowledged the danger of the sharks. But, she added, she was fine with the Extreme match continuing. "I could always have played regular chess if that's what I wanted," she said.

"But I'm too extreme for that."

She had with her a notebook and a pen, and was drawing schematics of the audience stands, the Arbiter's tower, the shark maze, and the tank. She explained that she had been an engineer before joining the Chess League, and still enjoyed analyzing designs as she used to, but liked the exciting nature of her new profession.

"I used to spend all my time modeling things for my company's simulations," she said. "Found I wanted to interact with the actual world. Now I do. Every move I make is *real*, and they determine whether I win or lose, whether I get out of the tank or get eaten by a shark."

She hastened to add that very few Extreme Chess players are eaten by sharks and that the sport is arguably safe.

Her attention then turned to the anti-supershark activists outside the arena. "Bunch of cowards," she commented. "If they want to stop the sharks, they should do something, not just whine. If a shark were attacking them, would they sit there and yell at it? Of course not. They'd punch it until it got the message and swam away. *That's* how you drive off a shark. Not by talking it to death."

When it was mentioned that the protesters were making demands of the Chess League and not the sharks themselves, Adebayo said that the League likely had no control over the sharks anymore, so the protesters were wasting their time. Then she left for the spa.

Tomorrow's game will begin at 11 a.m. The League has announced that, to better serve their audience, some dead ends in the maze will be blocked off so that the sharks will reach the tank more quickly.

EDITOR'S NOTE: The previous day's column referred to Dr. Collier's loss as a 'tragedy' and a 'disaster,' and said that audience members could be described as 'callous' for maintaining interest in the game. At the Chess League's request, we would like to apologize for this inappropriate editorializing. We promise that it will not happen again.

∞

SANDOVAL WINS BUT STILL TRAILS 3-2 IN EXTREME CHESS OLYMPIAD; ARBITER CONDEMNS
ETHICS VIOLATIONS

BY RACHEL GELLER. OCTOBER 19, 2035, 7:24 A.M. E.S.T.

HAIFA—Challenger Rebecca Sandoval won her first game since the second round in the seventeenth annual Extreme Chess Olympiad today. While declaring her victory, however, Arbiter Miriam Harrington also called out what she described as "inexcusable" ethics violations.

Champion Nyoko Adebayo began by advancing her king and her king's bishop's pawn in a Pork Chop Opening, widely considered to be the weakest and therefore most insulting opening in chess. Sandoval was able to progress rapidly as Adebayo's king got in the way of her pieces, and the champion was checkmated in minutes, once again ending the game before the sharks got though the maze.

Arbiter Miriam Harrington made both players surface immediately after the match so that she could lambast Adebayo's misconduct.

"To 'Pork Chop' an opponent is one of the most offensive acts a chess player can perform during a match," announced Harrington. "It serves no purpose other than to signal total contempt for one's opponent.

It is arrogant, it is condescending, and it is simply depraved."

Adebayo was ultimately fined six hundred thousand dollars for pork-chopping, and also received a three-month postseason suspension.

The defending champion refused to comment on the match or the penalty. She did, however, laugh off a suggestion from the press that the protesters might somehow have the tournament canceled.

"Their leaders talked a lot about how they'd stop our 'dangerous' sport," said Adebayo. "But they're just cowards, and they won't do anything.

"They don't like the sharks? Let's see them break in here and beat up those sharks until they won't swim with us anymore," she taunted. "Until then, it's just talk."

Sandoval had no comment. According to Arbiter Harrington, however, the Israeli player also opposes the protesters. "They would destroy her only opportunity to repay her debt," Harrington said. "They have taken a shameful position."

Harrington also vowed that both players would participate to their fullest ability in the next match.

"I take this very seriously," she said while holding an official Chess League harpoon gun. "And if the players do not, I will react appropriately."

EDITOR'S NOTE: *The previous day's column said that Nyoko Adebayo "acknowledged the danger of the sharks." This should have read "the alleged danger of the sharks." At the request of the Chess League's lawyers, we would like to emphasize that the sharks have not been proven to be dangerous, and that all evidence indicates that Dr. Collier's death was an unforeseeable accident that is unlikely to be repeated. We regret the error and have made it clear to our columnist that this must not happen again.*

∞

PROTESTERS RAID EXTREME CHESS OLYMPIAD; SCORE TIED AT 3-3 AFTER ADEBAYO FORFEITS GAME

BY RACHEL GELLER. OCTOBER 20 2035, 11:58 A.M. E.S.T.

HAIFA—A tumultuous day at the Extreme Chess Olympiad ended with several arrests and the defending champion disqualified from the penultimate game of the match.

Shortly before the game was due to start, protesters broke through security barriers and stormed the arena. They then proceeded to smash several windows, drive away audience members, and attempt to overturn the bleachers. It was more than two hours before the vandals were arrested and order was restored.

Security guards battled the protesters and also barricaded the tank in case any of the rioters attempted to jump in and attack the sharks. Though there were no sharks actually in the tank at the time, the Chess League was concerned that protesters might drown trying to find them. However, despite prior comments from champion Nyoko Adebayo, none of them made the attempt.

"We considered it," said one protester as she was being arrested.

"But after we thought about it some more, we decided it was a bad idea."

Arbiter Miriam Harrington, who personally harpooned a protester trying to rip down the scoreboard, gave a brief message once the rioters had been taken away. "I'm pleased to report that all those who would disrupt the dignity of our chess tournament have been removed from the premises," she said. "The match will continue without further delay."

Adebayo, however, had vanished in the early moments of the attack and could not be located. Hours passed before she was spotted in the supershark monitoring room, watching the sharks in the windows. She apologized when found and said that she had lost track of time.

Some attendees speculated that Adebayo had been trying to communicate with the sharks so as to encourage them to eat Sandoval and ensure her victory, but this could not be confirmed.

Harrington subsequently declared that Adebayo had lost the match by default. "A player who is not in position when the match begins forfeits," she ruled. "It is a harsh penalty, but the only way we can ensure that our players conduct themselves appropriately. Tardiness is disrespectful to all of us and besmirches the spirit of Extreme Chess."

The seventh match of the Extreme Chess Olympiad will take place tomorrow at 11 a.m. All dead ends in the maze have been blocked off in order to ensure that the sharks will be able to reach the chess tank, and both competitors have been threatened with the Chess League's most severe punishments if they do not play their best. League officials therefore anticipate an exciting game that will uphold the dignity and nobility of the sport.

∞

ADEBAYO RETAINS TITLE AT EXTREME CHESS OLYMPIAD; ALSO, TWENTY-THREE PEOPLE EATEN BY SUPERSHARKS

BY RACHEL GELLER. OCTOBER 21 2035, 2:04 P.M. E.S.T.

HAIFA—Nyoko Adebayo successfully defended her title as Extreme Chess champion today in a brilliant game, made all the more incredible by its occurrence just hours after the Chess League's supersharks ate almost two dozen members of the tournament staff.

With three games of the match already tarnished by misconduct, Arbiter Miriam Harrington had other local Chess League officials and sponsors watch the game with her on her platform to help monitor the players. They had taken their positions when, shortly before the match was to begin, the supersharks entered the shark tank early. The sharks gave Arbiter Harrington enough time to explain to a nervous sponsor that the Chess League had deemed them 'non-dangerous' before one leapt from the water and smashed into a weak joint of Harrington's platform. The structure collapsed into the tank, and all of its occupants were subsequently devoured.

It is not currently known how the sharks determined the structural weaknesses of the tower. Reporters were asked by Chess League security if they had noticed anyone communicating with the sharks in a suspicious manner, but of course could not answer, as describing the actions of a League player as 'suspicious' would be inappropriate editorializing.

Audience reaction to the incident was mixed. Many people expressed unease at the massacre, with some even suggesting that chess might be better off without super-intelligent sharks swimming through matches. Others, however, were more accepting.

"I only put five grand on the Arbiter biting it," said Liam "Cashman" Whitaker, a professional gambler from Las Vegas. "But at really good odds. So yeah, now I'm totally on Team Shark!"

With the deaths of all higher officials in the region, Extreme Chess champion Nyoko Adebayo became the most senior member of the Chess League present. Acting in her temporary executive capacity, she announced that the match could not continue in the shark tank because the water was too dirty for either player to see the pieces. As such, she ruled that the final game would take place in a side room under standard, non-Extreme rules.

Challenger Rebecca Sandoval did not raise any objections.

Before the game, Adebayo also used her temporary authority to announce a moratorium on the League's usage of genetically enhanced animals. The supersharks in particular will no longer be used in the

American Extreme Chess Finals next week, but will instead be retired from chess and permanently relocated to the "mutually acceptable" location of Lake Bolshoye Shchuchye in one of Russia's wildlife sanctuaries. While this announcement did raise some safety concerns, Adebayo quickly clarified that the sharks' genetic modifications allow them to survive in freshwater lakes just as well as the ocean, and so the sharks will be perfectly safe.

It was not clear who else found this decision "mutually acceptable." Local Chess League officials could not be reached for comment.

The final game of the Extreme Chess Olympiad featured some of the best play of the match. It opened with a standard Sicilian Defense, but both competitors unleashed novel variations as play continued. By the time endgame was reached, Sandoval was up by a knight but had two sets of doubled pawns, whereas one of Adebayo's pawns was on track to be promoted. Adebayo ultimately won the game.

"No hard feelings," said Sandoval afterwards. "It was a great game. My favorite of the match."

She did not elaborate.

Sandoval will receive two million dollars from the League, of which approximately sixty percent will be deducted to repay the debts she owes them. Adebayo will be paid three million dollars, less twenty percent for her fine.

"It's not about the money," Adebayo said later. "Though I don't mind it. It's about the thrill of the game. That's all I really care about.

"Why would people want to play chess any other way?"

Adebayo won't be playing chess at all for a while, thanks to her suspension. However, she is already making plans for her comeback tour. Her next scheduled match is the Extreme Chess Grand Challenge, which will be held at the Waldorf-Astoria New York in March of next year and will have an Edgar Allen Poe theme. Adebayo has already invited several

Chess League executives as her guests to the match, and sources indicate that they have accepted.

When asked if she disliked these executives due to their support of the supershark research project and other match conditions that have been described by critics as dangerous, Adebayo laughed at the idea.

"Of course I like them," she said. "Why else would I invite them to one of my matches?"

She concluded by guaranteeing that, if people liked the thrilling nature of this Chess Olympiad, they would find next year's Grand Challenge even more exciting.

About the Author
Aaron Canton

Aaron Canton is a Jewish-American writer currently living in Singapore. His short fantasy fiction has been acquired by *Phobos Magazine*, *Mothership Zeta*, and other venues. When he isn't writing, Aaron can often be found reading fantasy and science fiction literature of all kinds and searching local bookstores for new additions to his library. He also enjoys listening to music, especially dark wave, and plays the piano as a hobby.

Author Website: http://aaroncanton.wordpress.com/

Acknowledgements

The "Open Call: Science Fiction, Fantasy & Pulp Markets" group on Facebook for helping to spread the word about our first open call.

For the invaluable feedback from our Alpha Readers: Cat Ellison, David Hoster, Vanessa Jacob, Heather Noe, Melody Rickard, Jax Sanders, and Candis V. Stauber.

Ray Blank would like to thank the editorial team at Metasagas Press.

Zach Chapman extends his many thanks to Taylor Fox.

Sandra M. Odell wishes to thank Doug Odell.

www.ingramcontent.com/pod-product-compliance
Lightning Source LLC
Chambersburg PA
CBHW050905250626
47155CB00001B/107